THE INVESTIGATOR

Margarita Khemlin

2nd Edition

Translated by Melanie Moore

Glagoslav Publications

THE INVESTIGATOR

by Margarita Khemlin

2nd Edition

First published in Russian as "Дознаватель"

Translated by Melanie Moore

Book created by Max Mendor

Cover art:
© Marc Chagall, "Interior II" (DETAIL), 1911,
c/o Pictoright Amsterdam 2015

® Chagall is a registered trademark,
owned by Comité Marc Chagall

Glagoslav Publications Ltd
88-90 Hatton Garden
EC1N 8PN London
United Kingdom

www.glagoslav.com

ISBN: 978-1-78437-965-0

A catalogue record for this book is available
from the British Library.

THE INVESTIGATOR

Margarita Khemlin

2nd Edition

Let's be honest, the only thing the people I've dealt with in my line of work ever succeeded in was not being successful at all. Destiny is something you make for yourself. And that's not easy. And it's not within everyone's power.

I'm going to tell you about a single incident from my long and extensive career. It dates back to the start of the 1950s, in what we now call the twentieth century. I'm talking about the case of one Lilia Vorobeichik.

At the time, I was a police officer in the city of Chernigov in the Ukrainian SSR. A wonderful place where anyone could listen to the nightingales or the sound of the poplars in the ancient streets, admire the calendar made of flowers in the central square or stroll around landmarks from centuries gone by.

Against a background like this, the Vorobeichik case really stood out. I thought as much when it was assigned to me.

I ought to point out that back in Civvy Street after the war, a lot of people suddenly found themselves in new occupations.

I'd been in military intelligence. More than once, I was sent behind enemy lines to capture potential informers and brought or dragged them back to make them talk. I earned decorations, including the military Red Banner and the Red Star. I lived and breathed respect for the common cause.

As a demobbed intelligence officer, I joined the police. I studied and then worked as an investigator. In the event of murders or other serious crimes, a criminal investigator was immediately brought in from our Criminal Investigations Department or the Prosecutor's Office. But on this particular occasion, things didn't turn out quite like that.

Our chief, Maksim Prokopovich Sviridenko, indulged me, a touch against the book. As a result, it fell to me, a humble investigator, to look into the murder as it stood.

A woman, Vorobeichik, had been killed with a knife. A blow to the heart from below, beneath the shoulder-blade. Consequently, there was hardly any blood.

Since I was relatively junior, I wanted to take the utmost care with this case so it would be crystal clear that the assignment had been honourably performed.

I didn't keep detailed records so I'm fairly unconcerned. It's better not to go rifling through the paper work or do any cross checking. Nothing good ever comes of that in my experience.

Vorobeichik lay in her courtyard at No. 23, Clara Zetkin Street, where she lived alone, on 18 May 1952. Which is why she was lying there in a polka-dot dress that was the height of fashion. The doctor, a woman, determined that it was the work of a good dress-maker, which led me to think I should find out who the seamstress was.

A neighbour of the victim pointed me in the direction of one Polina Lvovna Laevskaya as both dressmaker and friend. Middle-aged, unattractive, with bulging eyes and lips painted into a little pointy heart. Well-known for her skill. In addition, she had a good brain.

She was a complicated woman. Alone after all the misfortunes that had befallen everyone and her, by her own reckoning, most of all. And for that she deserved attention and respect. Although that's by way of an aside.

What I knew of Laevskaya led me to one Roman Nikolayevich Moiseenko, who had been romantically involved with the victim.

In the context of that particular year, the victim's Jewish surname immediately caused me misgivings – in case national politics came into it. Although all races here are equal all the same. Especially as a result of the Great Patriotic War.

In the normal course of events, Jews were rarely murdered. They are a quiet race, What was between us, between husband . And, since nothing pointed to a robbery, it looked set to be an innocent sort of case. By which I mean a crime of passion and jealousy, for example.

Moiseenko was the prime suspect. That's generally how it goes. The lover's first in line. Unless there's a husband, of course. Furthermore, he worked as an actor at the drama theatre and, word had it, was an enthusiastic drinker of spirits. But at that time almost everybody was. The suspect's personal profile in that regard had still to be ascertained.

The day I first met Roman Nikolayevich Moiseenko, I did a commendable job.

I found him looking distracted during a rehearsal for Hulak-Artemovsky's people's opera, "Cossacks beyond the Danube". Moiseenko wasn't taking part. Instead, he was sitting in the front row, voicing the part of an actress who was off sick. I determined that he was in the auditorium rather than on stage because he was seriously unsteady on his feet and might fall through the stagehands' trapdoor which was open for some reason, or into the orchestra pit.

When I asked him nicely, Moiseenko followed me into one of the dressing-rooms for a chat. Although I did have to take him by the arm while he loudly indicated the way.

I asked him straight out whether he knew about Lilia Vorobeichik's murder and what his thoughts about it were. Particularly since the woman had not yet been buried and her corpse awaited vengeance.

I am not a great fan of statements for the record, although these always remain a strict requirement. I prefer to meet the person I'm interested in at their place of residence or work first. At the station, the atmosphere itself encourages the person being questioned to mobilize their forces. Personally, I used to think – still do indeed – that such all-out mobilization is detrimental to an investigation. What's needed is freedom and the impression that before too long this chap will be on his way and everything will go back to normal. A few days later, I issue the citizen with a summons and by then the mobilization has no effect. It can't handle that preliminary easing off. Yet that's precisely what I offer for an ulterior motive of my own.

At the time, I preferred to operate using intuition rather than book learning. I was selected by the Party to enter the police when I was demobbed from the army. And I saw myself primarily as a human being rather than a stickler for the law. I was thirty-two.

Roman Moiseenko turned out to be a handsome man, considerably younger than Lilia Vorobeichik. At the time of her sudden death, she was thirty-eight. He was twenty-seven.

Nature itself seemed to have destined Moiseenko for a career on the stage. Black brows, hazel eyes, a cascade of dark hair, his figure, his height etc. etc. He was the complete opposite of Vorobeichik. Before she died, she had bright red hair and her eyes were blue. As for her height, she was tall and just a tiny bit overweight.

Some people like to show photos taken at the scene of the incident because they bank on shocking the suspect. I didn't. After the war, no-one could be shaken by the sight of death. Moreover, things are always worse in the imagination than in reality. I know that from my own experience.

Moiseenko looked at me calmly and directly. He didn't smell too good, his breath reeked of several days' worth of stale alcohol.

"What's there to talk about?" he said. "I killed Lilka."

I wasn't happy with such a quick confession, especially taking Moiseenko's personality into account.

With the utmost severity, I said, "You are misleading the investigation."

He lowered his gaze but stuck to his guns.

You can't argue with an unforced confession. At that point, everything has to start going on the record and so on.

The main thing was that the murder weapon hadn't been found. There were two knives of the right size in the victim's house. They were identical, sharpened and almost new. There were other styles of knife too but they were very small and clearly blunt. All the knives were clean, as clean as knives can be that are in daily use.

A close neighbour testified that there had been a third knife too. One that apparently looked just like the other two apart from having, as the late Lilia used to say before she died, a blade made of special steel. She would boast about it, demonstrating its sharpness against her own finger nail. This made it possible to suppose that that very knife was the murder weapon, missing, whereabouts unknown.

There was a thorough search but without the required result. Incidentally, concealing the murder weapon attested to the perpetrator's sober state of mind. When the balance of his mind is seriously disturbed, a malefactor tends to panic and dispose of the weapon at the scene of the crime, not always out of remorse but seemingly in sheer surprise at what he has done.

It went against Moiseenko that the neighbours had seen him in the courtyard not long before Vorobeichik was found dead.

Moiseenko gave a good verbal description of just where the knife had gone in. But that didn't mean a thing since rumours about the killing had spread quickly. Before the officers of the law arrived, the local women had come running at the scream of a neighbour who had popped into Vorobeichik's for something and, quick as a flash, they had passed on a description of the corpse and so on.

At the morgue, Moiseenko conducted himself with dignity and gazed at Vorobeichik with honest, open eyes.

My quick action earned me plenty of praise from the top brass. However, the day before the court hearing, Roman Nikolayevich Moiseenko committed suicide by hanging. He didn't leave a note as he didn't have a pen or pencil about his person and, since he was neither a writer nor a revolutionary in the Tsar's torture chambers, he hadn't requested anything to write with in advance.

His personal confession outweighed any arguments for continuing the investigation. There was no shortage of other work. Those were hectic times.

The incident receded as other business came to the fore.

One July evening, I was walking along Clara Zetkin Street at dusk. Taking a stroll before bed. For some reason, I had chosen a different route – from where I lived to the River Strizhen. Perhaps I felt drawn to go and look at the military hospital, where I'd spent a long time recovering from wounds at the front after we won the war and where good fortune had brought my wife, Lyubochka, and me together. She was an auxiliary nurse on the surgical ward.

Suddenly, I caught a clear glimpse of a shadow at the gate to No. 23. The shadow reminded me of Citizen Vorobeichik. I didn't doubt for a moment that it was she who had closed the gate, looked back and given me the once over.

The gate slammed shut. The catch caught on the inside.

I continued on my way. And, of course, once I'd recovered from the surprise, I realized I'd seen a relative of some kind, there to inherit. The incident wasn't worth a fig, as they say.

But I had been so struck by the likeness that it very much piqued my interest.

The next morning I approached the house on Clara Zetkin Street. The gate was ajar, giving me legitimate access to the courtyard.

I knocked at the door. It was opened by an old woman of Jewish appearance. So Jewish that her headscarf was even tucked behind her ears in the Jewish way and only then tied under her chin the way decent people do.

There was a good smell in the house, like bread or baking. Since the kitchen was right next to the doorway, I immediately spotted some large circles of dough on the table, thin as could be and riddled with tiny holes. There was also a little wheel with a wooden handle for evenly distributing the holes. The old woman's apron was covered in flour and there was flour on the floor.

I wasn't born yesterday. I knew this was "matzo". Special food for their Passover. From my own experience and from the nature of my work, I knew that this Passover was over. Furthermore, not only was matzo making not welcomed by the Soviet law-enforcement agencies, there were examples of it leading to convictions that cost the offenders dear, including lengthy prison sentences.

Jewish nationalism is Jewish nationalism. What can you do?

I showed my ID and gave my name. The old woman mumbled something and yelled into the house, "Evka, get out here. It's you they've come for!" Making her way towards me from behind a lace curtain was, apparently, the late Citizen Lilia Vorobeichik. Clearly, however, it was the same women I had spotted yesterday in the dark and, incidentally, alive.

She was wearing just a set of camiknickers. I'd seen a lot of those in Germany in '45.

She was perfectly at ease as she came over to me although she hadn't done her hair and was barefoot.

"What do you want?" she asked.

I repeated my name and rank and presented my ID.

She read it carefully. You could still let other people take your papers in those days.

"Police Captain Mikhail Ivanovich Tsupkoy," she read out, deliberately pronouncing each individual letter.

The woman looked me up and down from head to toe and wanted to add something of her own to what she saw in the document.

But I wouldn't let her. I asked for her passport.

She fetched it. She still hadn't got dressed or smoothed down her red hair.

As she held out the passport, I noticed that her underarm hair was light too. It was. Thick and light. I felt embarrassed for her. Being like that.

Passport details: Eva Solomonovna Vorobeichik. Registered in the town of Oster, Kozelets District, Chernigov Oblast.

I asked what she was doing in the late Lilia Vorobeichik's house and how she was related to her.

She replied, saying, "We're sisters. Twins. I'm going to wait here until the inheritance is sorted out. Once I'm entitled to do so, I intend to stay on. Or I might sell the house, I haven't made my mind up yet."

There was nothing to object to. But there was the matzo.

I said, "Citizen Vorobeichik, why are you making matzo, especially when it's not Passover? That's really not on. I'm giving you a serious warning. And it's compounded by you taking on hired labour."

Eva addressed the old woman in a loud voice. "He wants you to show him your passport. Show him. And tell him we haven't hired you, you're our auntie, mine and Lilka's."

The old woman got her passport from her room. It was well-thumbed and covered in flour. She opened it and held it out on the palm of her hand.

She had a different surname – Tsvintar. Her first name, Malka, was pure Jewish, old-fashioned, as befitted one of her years.

I asked her on which side of the family they were related.

While the old lady struggled to understand the question, Eva said with a sigh, "On the Jewish side, alright?" She didn't lower her voice as people usually do even when she used these unflattering terms. Brazen bitch. "And we're just going to crumble the matzo up quickly for the chickens. It'll be a real feast. We've got hens, out there, behind the house. We'll give it to them. It was just for something to do, out of boredom and sadness. Lilechka's gone. And she loved baking. Matzo couldn't be easier to make. Just water and flour. That's all. Water and flour. What's wrong with that? No yeast, no butter, nothing, not a thing, nothing at all."

She advanced towards me as she said "nothing" and everything beneath the repellently pink camiknickers jiggled right in my face. Although height-wise she was shorter than me.

I left.

Suddenly it dawned on me that Lilia Vorobeichik hadn't kept chickens. There had been a shed full of clutter behind the house. Moreover, I had been negligent in studying the paperwork. I had failed to check whether Eva was married. At the time many women kept their maiden names when they got married. I had no idea what her job was or where her income came from.

I scheduled a follow-up for the day after tomorrow. In order to allow Eva Vorobeichik and her so-called aunt to lower their guard.

I turned up in uniform.

The gate was locked. It was quickly opened when I knocked loudly.

The dressmaker, Polina Lvovna Laevskaya, who was in the house at the time, recognized my face and said in delight:

"You see, the Soviet system stands up for people. It really does! I was just explaining to Eva. There's nothing on earth that the Soviet authorities can't find out. Isn't that so, Comrade Captain? Have you come to talk about Lilia? If it's hard to bear, tell me first and then I'll pass it on gently to Evocha. Hand it to her on a plate. Ever so carefully. I can do that. You know me."

She was talking too much and taking her time about letting me into the house. I remarked that I was on duty and didn't want to listen to anything irrelevant.

I went ahead of her and pushed the door open myself.

Order and polish reigned in the kitchen.

Laevskaya squeezed past me and through the door. As she did so, she made sure one solid leg made contact.

"I'm sorry, Comrade Captain. I've embarrassed you. Here you are on duty and you're blushing. That wasn't very nice of me. Evochka's just popped out to the shop and Malka's asleep. There, behind the curtain. Sleeping like a baby. It's true what they say – old age is a second childhood."

On the small, round table with its white, crocheted cloth stood two thimble-sized liqueur glasses and a small decanter of cherry brandy. It was immediately obvious that it was last year's liqueur because, firstly, the new fruit had still to be picked and, secondly, it was turning to syrup. The inside of the glass was virtually coated in a layer of deep red. Like blood.

Laevskaya made herself at home and got another glass.

She turned it about in front of her face and offered it to me questioningly. "You, of course, won't be having a nice little snifter of brandy but I'll put it on the table for form's sake. Just to be friendly."

I didn't want to cause a conflict over nothing and nodded my assent.

Laevskaya sat down.

So did I.

She was first to break the silence.

"So, what do you have to say about Lilechka?"

"I'm here about something else. And it would be better if you left now, Polina Lvovna. With the utmost respect, of course."

"Oh, of course, I'll go. If that's what it takes. Just tell me one little thing. What's happened to bring you here about something else?"

I behaved entirely properly and immediately gave myself due credit without bragging or vanity. Laevskaya had taken a shine to me and a little later I would be able to milk her for a good deal of useful and important information. With a view to receiving information in return, she would tell me all she knew. Whether she might make up anything extra was the real question.

I said meaningfully, "That's police business. I'd like you to leave."

She looked behind the curtain and, blinking her eyes towards it, whispered, "If it's a secret, don't mention it in front of Malka even if she is asleep or something. She pretends to be deaf as a post but there are no flies on her."

Aloud and in the direction of the curtain, she said, "I'll be guided by you. I'm going. Please, wait for Evocha. She'll be here any minute. In the meantime, try dear Lilechka's tasty little liqueur. What the eye doesn't see... It's lovely and sweet. Poor Lilechka had a sweet tooth."

When I entered the house on Clara Zetkin Street, the clock read exactly two o'clock. I left at half past three. I read the papers on the bookshelf and listened quietly to the wireless.

Malka never emerged from behind the curtain. At the same time, I noticed that she answered little calls of nature in a pot or something of the sort.

Eva never turned up.

I drank one glass. To spite myself. It was the first time I had shown such weakness. Rules are rules. But show it I did. Right before I left. And a good job too. The liqueur was bitter and I concluded that the women hadn't been drinking it at all. Just pretending in case someone looked in.

Next I walked all around the outside of the house. There really were chickens in the backyard. The shed had been cleared of its clutter and fitted out as a henhouse. I found light coloured crumbs and broken bread on the ground. Broken into big pieces as if to prove that it really was matzo.

The plot was enclosed by a fairly low but sturdy fence. It would be impossible for an adult to pass through the thin gaps between the slats. Which meant there was only one way into the house – through the all-too-familiar gate. I checked again although I had already ascertained this during the Lilia Vorobeichik case. Next, I made a grade A study of the house.

And the backyard and outside the front. But a lot had changed in the past two months. Just look at the chickens.

I observed the gate from various vantage points. No one went into the house or came out either.

At 1700 hours, I gave up and called it a day.

There was real work waiting for me and I had no right to be distracted by a personal matter. Even then my conscience told me that it was personal.

That night I dreamt about the small, round table at the Vorobeichiks' house.

They wanted to lift the body of the murdered woman onto the table in its coffin to begin the farewells. The coffin wouldn't fit. It was losing balance, threatening to fall.

They lifted the coffin down.

On the table lay another woman, the same as the one in the coffin but naked, who said, moreover, "That's not how you do it. This is."

She curled up in a foetal position. And that worked well.

They said, "Since you fit so well there, we'll say our last goodbyes to you and Lilia can continue to thrive and prosper."

It's possible I made those last words up but that was the essence of it.

I make no secret of it. I immediately took an awful lot on myself. I didn't share my impressions with my work colleagues. And, as a result, stewed it all over by myself.

To all intents and purposes, there was nothing going on. But I began to keep a very serious eye on the house in Clara Zetkin Street. When I wasn't engaged in urgent police work, of course.

In this way, I established that the dressmaker Laevskaya was constantly visiting the house (several times in forty-eight hours).

Several times, a Jewish man of very advanced years darted in and out with a bag.

There was a dog barking. Previously, in the late Lilia Vorobeichik's time, there had been no guard dog in the yard.

The Tsvintar woman didn't put her nose outside.

And, most importantly, there was no sign whatsoever of Eva Vorobeichik.

Light showed in the windows on the side of the street where the fence was lowest until late at night. Until about eleven o'clock.

Facts are stubborn things. And these facts were saying they needed to be understood. I couldn't figure them out.

Just one fact was abundantly clear and that was Eva Vorobeichik. The one and only.

Incidentally, my family life at that time consisted of a family of three: me, my wife Lyubov Gerasimovna and our four-year-old daughter Anechka.

We were renting a room from an elderly couple named Shchupak and aspired to nothing better since we had been promised our own space in a nice new barracks on Voykov Street before too long. And, if we had another baby in short order we might even hope for a flat in an official block on Kotsyubinsky Street. But we hadn't managed to produce that other baby. And particularly not to order.

And so, off my own bat, wearing ordinary trousers and a white shirt, I set off to see Polina Lvovna Laevskaya.

She wasn't surprised. Greeted me like a dear friend.

"Mikhail Ivanovich, at last! The things people are saying in town, the things people are coming up with… And about you in particular. I'm not talking about all the different gossip. You know about that from work without me. I can tell you what's being said about you, if you like. And you can take action. Because you can't let it carry on. Not nowadays, you can't."

I asked what she meant exactly.

Laevskaya made a show of being embarrassed and began her account.

This is what she said.

Rumours about the Vorobeichik case were rife in Chernigov. No-one believed that the now late actor, Moiseenko, was guilty.

I was being accused of prejudice against the Jewish people and of blocking the investigation. In a word, people were saying, it was all a shady business. And when Malka Tsvintar told her neighbours I had called in and made Eva Vorobeichik's acquaintance, Malka Tsvintar was informed in return that they expected nothing else of me since I had personally brought the investigation to an artificial conclusion and was now intent on silencing Eva Vorobeichik as Lilia's immediate heir.

At this point, I caught Laevskaya out.

I said:

"And when did the old Tsvintar woman spread all this nonsense? What day was it? Yesterday? The day before? Or when? Have a think, Polina Lvovna. Rumours take time. Rumours are not little children. It takes more than a second to produce them."

Laevskaya shot back:

"I don't know. But Malka has been talking to people. And people have been talking to her. You won't stop her mouth."

But who could Malka have been talking to any great extent? After all, she was new in town. Laevskaya was another matter.

"I hereby declare, Polina Lvovna, that you are the person behind these rumours. And that the Tsvintar woman wasn't popping in to see you, you were going to see her a hundred times a day. And then you spread all sorts of nonsense around town. Look me in the eye when I'm talking to you! There's nothing on the floor. Or on the ceiling. Look me in the eye when I ask nicely, please."

Laevskaya looked balefully in the general area of my face but not in my eye. Of course, she wasn't brazen enough for that.

"You know something, Mikhail Ivanovich… Here you are in your nice white shirt. And no gun. So I can tell you – you don't know everything and you can't bring everything to light."

"What light are you talking about, Polina Lvovna? Show me! Go on!"

I was losing patience. Not because some goggle-eyed piece of mutton dressed as lamb was pressing her fat thighs against me but because I was insulted. I was going out on a limb. But it was as if she was looking down from above and could see.

"Mikhail Ivanovich, Lilechka's case is closed, under lock and key, isn't it?"

"And?"

"And… who has the key?"

"I have no intention of trying to guess your Jewish riddles. That's not what I shed blood for. Even now, I'm taking a risk for your sake."

At this point, Polina Lvovna grabbed me by the arm and hissed right in my face and the breath of that hiss was like Red Moscow perfume only musty and rank:

"How long have you been in this town? So, five years. At most. But it's not about how long. I haven't been here all that long either. But you, Mikhail Ivanovich, only talk to people when your works means you have to. Whereas I know everything and everyone because I choose to. And you're not doing me a favour by taking my hand. I'm the one who can do you a favour - or not. It doesn't matter who's saying what. What matters is that it's about you in person. And things don't look good for you personally. It could be reported to the Party Committee. And taken even further."

I didn't understand a thing. Maybe she'd been drinking that perfume and was drunk on it. After that rancid cherry brandy of theirs, I wouldn't have put it past her. No. She was sober. If she'd been one of ours, I might still have had my doubts. I know the Jews! A man maybe but the women, they really don't drink.

There was a knock at the door.

It was a customer with some fabric.

Polina Lvovna graciously spread the fabric on the table. She waved the crepe de chine in front of my face so that it billowed out.

She said:

"And is your wife, Lyubov Gerasimovna, planning to have a nice new frock made? If she is, she should come to me. I've made a note of all her measurements. She told me you really like what I've made for her. A woollen dress for winter – terracotta. She's such a pale little thing. Terracotta puts a bit of colour in her cheeks. That was my advice. Thank you for coming to settle your account. Say hello to your wife. And little girl. Give the little one a kiss from me, precious little poppet that she is."

And she began to chat to the woman who had come for a fitting.

I didn't know my Lyuba had her clothes made by Laevskaya. I didn't keep count of her frocks. There was nothing to count in any case. There was one, terracotta, for going out and another, brown, that she wore all the time. That was for the winter. For summer, she had a pinafore dress or something like that.

No doubt that schemer Laevskaya was now discussing me with her customer. Who knew what she would concoct? And how many women went to see her in a day? Well, two for certain. And those two would talk to another two and so on and on. No need for the Tsvintar woman at all.

And all of it baseless. Absolute twaddle.

However, if I were the type to dwell on such silliness aimed at me in person, I wouldn't be working in law-enforcement. Nor would any of our officers. We wouldn't even have won the war. It's not that there shouldn't be anything personal. A person should have everything in perfect proportion: the personal and the public. But the personal should be as little and as humble as possible.

I was particularly distressed that Laevskaya had hinted that I had been negligent in the Vorobeichik case. And yet everything was done in accordance with socialist law and order. Records kept and so on. It wasn't anyone's fault that Moiseenko had tragically departed his own life.

I reproduce what he said.

"Lilka was a fool. She believed in gypsies. A gypsy once told her fortune, before the war, telling her she'd have a husband whose name began with an 'R'. Lilka used to mimic the gypsy to a T. 'You won't be able to resist that "R". You'll give in straight away. And marry him'. And she would toss the hem of her skirt and shimmy her shoulders. What didn't she do to entrance me? I struggled to free myself. I was entirely devoted to my art. I had learnt the whole of Aleksandr Tvardovsky's Vasily Terkin off by heart to perform when we visited the regions. But she knocked me off course with her love. When I was going away to Nosovka for the first performance, I had a real skinful. I was drunk when I set out. I thought I'd sober up. I didn't. I got a slap on the wrist, a kick up the backside. You might think that's why I killed her."

I tried to corner him with an innocent question.

"Because of Vasily Terkin?" I looked him steadily in the eye.

Moiseenko looked right in my pupils, just as steadily.

"Yes," he replied. "Because of Terkin too. And the fact that she had completely discombobulated me, telling me I couldn't even imagine what goes on in warfare. Or what had happened to her. I'm practising a new role, reciting it off by heart and she couldn't give a toss about my talent. And what did happen to her to make her know and understand what no-one else understands? She didn't say. Just strung me along out of spite."

"And what did happen, for example? Any suggestions?"

"You need it, you dig around for it. You can put me to bed with a shovel, I won't say a thing about the woman I used to love. Not even if it's true. I may have boozed away my conscience but not my art. And that's how it is for us artists – we don't kiss and tell!"

I quickly cut the lad down to size:

"You have nothing to do with art. You know that yourself. Let's assume you're the killer. Who else could have knifed Lilia? Apart from you?"

At this point, Moiseenko appeared to get a grip and drop his posturing. He said nothing for a moment.

Then declared in no uncertain terms,

"Apart from me, no-one. No-one."

Inwardly, I was inclined to think he was the guilty party. There was the circumstantial evidence too. I've mentioned that already. He was drunk when he arrived in Nosovka. Lilia was murdered on the day Moiseenko came back into town. But he hadn't come back right away. It was two days after the planned performance. He'd become entrenched at the house of a friend, chief librarian Ivan Nestorovich Shostak. Drowning his sorrows with him. Shostak testified that Moiseenko had said bad things about Vorobeichik and threatened to kill her. As it turned out, he had.

And then there were these rumours in town. "I might be poor but I'm honest," my mother used to say. And I would repeat it too in unfavourable circumstances. Facing various losses, for example. But I had never been threatened with the loss of my good name.

I decided to come at things from the other end.

The old Jew seemed perfectly at home going to see Vorobeichik and the Tsvintar woman. I saw that he didn't hesitate for a second at the gate, just pushed it straight open. Strangers would hesitate even if only for the tiniest moment. Whereas the old chap would leave the house slowly, looking back at the windows, casting an eye over the fence. Strangers don't leave like that. Strangers don't look back.

Chernigov isn't a big town. From Red Bridge to Trinity Hill. From the Rampart to Five Corners. That's it, all of it. It's easy to find someone. Especially a Jew. They all know one another. It's historical.

I went to see Veniamin Yakovlevich Shtadler. A well-known figure, originally from a rabbi's family, who fervently welcomed the Revolution and the Civil War. He fought in the Red Army. Earned a number of medals, joined the Bolshevik Party. Then, clearly, he was purged but not sent to jail. And the reason why not was that somehow, when he was first questioned, he had bitten off part of his tongue. He banged his chin on the investigator's desk or something like that. These things do happen.

It was concluded that he had gone crazy since he had independently embarked upon an act of self-mutilation.

He was taken to Kiev for assessment. There the final verdict was a complete absence of mental capacity.

As a result of his self-inflicted injuries, Shtadler lost the ability to speak. Most annoying was that this was when he had been called as a witness, invited for a little chat. And the investigator was a relative, a distant one. He must have asked Shtadler an indelicate question or something and the latter was so indignant that he pulled his little stunt. The relative, incidentally, soon was sent to jail.

Shtadler's mental capacity returned in 1941 precisely. His heroic past awoke in him with terrible force and he found himself in Yankel Tsegelnik's Partisan Detachment. He became something akin to a rabbi. He was said to pray, mumbling and murmuring, but eventually he was seriously wounded on several occasions and sent back to the rear for treatment.

After the war, he showed up in Chernigov again. Still not quite all there but basically intact. The police would contact him when they needed to find something out from the Jewish community. He wasn't on the staff but he never refused to help. When he was asked questions, he would write the answers on a piece of paper. His writing was ugly and slanting. I know that, by nature, Jews have to write from right to left rather than left to right like other people. That's what the language of the Jews is like, their writing in general. His handwriting had become unbalanced, what with all this relearning.

I described the old man to Shtadler and with his help established that the person in question was one Zusel Tabachnik. He was living in temporary digs in Liskovitsa. At the foot of Trinity Hill.

For the record: a sizeable Jewish population had built up at the foot of Trinity Hill. They had been there since time immemorial, according to people in the know. After the war, their numbers didn't fall as some people had hoped, they just increased. Those who had been killed were replaced by people from other areas. People who had nobody left anywhere at all.

Contrary to popular belief, man clings not to a place but to property. Without property, he has no ties. Although there may still be relatives who can provide support. Over time, however, relatives as an institution have lost all importance. But in those days the Jews still had something of the kind. And so they would come and take lodgings with even the remotest of relations. Especially from the small shtetls surrounding the town and from isolated villages. Where, during the war, they had been a thorn in the flesh and were almost all wiped out unless they were evacuated or went to the front. And who was it who went to the front? The men. As for the women, children and old men – well, that's obvious.

Comrade Stalin, when foreign journalists tried to catch him out by asking why he hadn't evacuated all the Jews, said: "My Jews have all gone."

Perhaps they had at that.

Mikhail Vasilyevich Lomonosov, the Russian genius, was right: in nature, nothing disappears. A loss in one place means an increase somewhere else. And so there was an increase in Chernigov.

There was one comrade who served with me in the police, a friend, you might say. I haven't got a bad thing to say about him. Conscience, honour – all present and correct. A veteran. A Jew. Evsey Gutin. Born and bred in Chernigov. Knew everyone in town and could read them like an open book.

I decided to ask his advice in an informal setting. And not outright but, going by the book, in a roundabout way. I bought him a bottle of vodka and turned up at his house the following Saturday.

My visit didn't come at a good time. Evsey's wife was bathing the children, of whom there were three. Aged from two to nearly eight. And, curiously, all boys. The oldest Grishka, then Vovka, then Iosif.

Evsey had been invalided out just as Ukraine was liberated and everyone was allowed to go home. And so back he went to his own home. The house was of the kind that no-one set their sights on during the war. And so he settled back in and welcomed his wife and her father back from evacuation. Evsey's own father, mother and three sisters had, naturally, been shot owing to wartime conditions.

When war broke out, Evsey had been married for about five years. To Belka. They were regarded as childless. His wife couldn't carry her pregnancies to term. But then the children began to come along.

And there was Belka, giving them a bath.

It was a joyful, irksome affair. A family affair, of course. But I really loved children just then, mainly because of my own little daughter, my Anechka-Gannusya, and I weighed in alongside Belka and Evsey. I brought over the water, took the heated pails off the stove. It was a wood stove so I chopped the wood up a bit more, just a tad.

We all dried the children off together to make sure they didn't catch cold. Belka towelled down the littlest, carefully, carefully, while Evsey and I played rough and tumble with the other two.

All the little lads had been circumcised. I took particular notice. But in a good way.

Jokingly, I said, "Why on earth did you mark them all out like that, Evsey? Honestly, not to mention you being a Communist but, as a responsible father to your sons, how could you circumcise them and make it so easy for a potential enemy to spot an undercover agent?"

At that point, Belka's father, came into the house, Dovid Srulevich. Or Sergeyevich, which he himself preferred to avoid but which Belka and Evsey used when introducing him.

I had sort of hinted to Evsey, that he, a Communist, shouldn't be embarrassed by any names at all and even less by patronymics.

According to his passport, he was Abramovich but he would introduce himself as Arkadiyevich. And his father-in-law was Srulevich but he'd turned him into Sergeyevich. That's not good. No-one who stoops to that sort of repudiation deserves to call themselves a man.

"The war's over. There's no need to hide": that's roughly what I told him.

With his usual, crooked little smile, Evsey replied:

"It's because it sounds better."

"Better, be damned. You're not to blame for the fact that your names don't really suit the Russian language. If I'm honest, they don't really suit any language. What are you supposed to do? Give yourselves aliases or dogs' names?"

Evsey wasn't even smiling now.

"Aliases and dogs' names? What have they got to do with it? I substituted a Russian name."

I wanted to change the subject. I could see I'd hit a real nerve.

"I meant that, for you, our names are only aliases anyway so you'd be better off keeping your own."

Of course, I hadn't expressed my opinion particularly well. But Evsey didn't take offence. On the contrary, he became friendlier towards me.

Now Evsey laughed and nodded towards Dovid.

"That's the one who did it. I kept an eye on each of them so that it didn't happen and Dovid sneaked each one out from under my nose. Just who did Grisha and Vovka, I don't know. Dovid won't let on. But Iosif was done by that filthy Zusel. Yoska was named after Comrade Stalin. And Dovid was well aware of it. I specifically told him not to touch the little one with his Jewish notions. But no, the bastard went and spoiled Yoska too. Belka must have been involved. She's completely under his thumb. Fine. Circumcised, uncircumcised, so what, if they're healthy? I don't think the Germans will be coming back. And I'm not afraid of anyone else. Or the Germans come to that. I gave them a real thrashing, Mishka, you know

I did. And it's in honour of that, of that thrashing, that I made my lads. And I'll make more. Belka and I have decided we won't stop. But we'll have to keep a closer eye on Dovid and tear Belka off a strip to prevent her propagating religion. Still, what's done is done."

But I could tell that Evsey himself wasn't really opposed to Dovid's superstitious procedure. It's certainly difficult to knock things out of folk, especially customs and prejudices, if they've flourished among the people for centuries. Whether it's nationalism or anything else. Educating people isn't easy or done in one fell swoop.

This tender scene took us towards dinner.

We sat at the table. The children were racing around, snatching bits of food, playing and making a din.

We ate.

I poured us all one glass, then another.

Evsey kept pace with me.

Dovid didn't touch a drop. He took charge of the children, quietly trying to rein them in.

Then, he couldn't take it any longer. Fork in the air, the food half-way to his mouth, and presumably spurred on by what he'd been thinking, he said:

"In Tsarist times, Jews didn't drink. They were Jews with a capital J. The Jews were kept under far more observation than anyone else. The only way they could stand out was if they didn't drink, were always sober. That earned them a few good marks. There were bad marks for everything else, that's for sure. Mi-i-i-nuses! Special laws were passed for the Jews. 'Don't let them in here. Don't put them there.' But in Soviet times, everyone started all over again with a small letter – Russians and Jews alike. And in Soviet times, the Jews became just like everyone else. No more restrictions. And so the Jews drink too. What's sauce for the goose… Even though there are no good marks left. Not even the teeniest-tiniest one. Just minuses, all the way."

Evsey was pouring the drinks just then and his hand shook. He stole a look at the children. They stood, frozen to the spot, straining to hear.

Evsey took the glass he'd poured, drank it down deliberately and said to his father-in-law:

"You might think about the children, Dovid Sergeyevich. Saying such things in front of them."

Belka waved her arms at them both, the old man and her husband.

"Right, you've gone too far! Now get on with your meal quietly. It's time to put the children to bed and there you are yelling." She hissed at the little boys, "Now then, geschwind schlafen, you little wretches! Mattresses out!"

It was a game for the children – rolling the mattresses out on the floor, making the beds, swapping places till they were blue in the face. She was their mother. What other explanation is required? A mother knows how to soothe her child.

Dovid Srulevich joined in as well, dragging the pillows over, moving them around. Being involved.

Belka secretly slipped us the open bottle and some of the food.

"Out," she whispered. "Go out in the yard. Drink the rest on the logs. Out in the fresh air."

In a nutshell, I got down to business.

It turned out Evsey knew the name Tabachnik. I didn't even use the name, just described the old man in passing. An accurate description. That you'd recognize if you knew him. Evsey immediately came up with the name.

"He's an odd fish, that one. Ought to be behind bars. Or better still in hospital. A dodgy character."

"What's dodgy about him? He's not quite right in the head but he's harmless."

"But that's the point. He's spreading nonsense. You get propagandists canvassing before the elections to our Supreme Soviet, don't you? Just turning up. A knock at the door and in they come. No invitation required. Everyone understands they're there on important state business. Well, he's some sort of propagandist too. Not for the unbreakable block but for who the hell knows what."

"Counter-revolution? Against Stalin and Soviet power?"

"Well no, he doesn't go that far. He only visits people of Jewish nationality. He's got lists written down. That's what our lot are saying. The Jews, I mean. He's always doing the rounds. They send him packing and he's off again. Like a clockwork toy."

"And what, no-one's dropped a line to you know where?"

"He hasn't stopped, so no, they can't have. Although they should."

"You do it then. They'll call him in, read him the riot act, give him a bollocking. What is it he's campaigning for?"

"All sorts of nonsense. You, my dear Jews, you don't exist anymore, he says. You think you do but you don't. He says that sort of stuff then goes on his way. They give him a bit of money. Old clothes. Leftovers. Buying him off, kind of."

"Ah, so he's begging. Appealing for sympathy. People are such idiots. Give to a beggar once and you're sort of in his debt. That's what your Tabachnik's up to too."

"He's not mine!" Evsey even went purple.

I pressed on, cool as a cucumber:

"A propagandist – that's too good for him. A propagandist campaigns for the future. Tabachnik isn't campaigning for anything."

Evsey nodded uncertainly.

"So, hasn't he got a home of his own? Is he living off other people?"

"He does have a house. In Oster, they say. Not so much a house as a dugout. He told someone he'll hang around in Chernigov until the winter and the bad weather. And then off to Oster. It takes all sorts…"

I changed the subject.

"Keep an eye on Dovid Sergeyevich. He talks too much."

I deliberately called him Sergeyevich so that Evsey would realize it was a genuine warning.

I needed to go to Oster. It was where both Vorobeichik and Tabachnik came from.

I had to approach matters in a roundabout way: the first law of investigation. I might not have special training but I knew the basics. The war and military intelligence had taught me.

It was the end of July, the weather hot. Young people were out for late-night strolls, dancing in Kordovka Park and all around were thick bushes, the pull of the darkness. There were misunderstandings of a particular kind.

Then people became better off. They drank too much, squabbled, got into fights. Most often in families, between relatives and friends, but that's not the point. The slightest thing and the police were called. Whereupon there would be tears so that no-one was taken away. But even law-enforcement agents have to go on leave and so forth.

Here's what happened next.

From time to time, I would go secretly to Clara Zetkin Street only to find the shutters closed day and night.

Walking around the location on a regular basis was not practical given the need for operational discretion. Questioning the neighbours was likewise inadvisable. Making inquiries at the local registration office or on the housing lists? What was there to find out when it was less than six months since Lilia Vorobeichik died and, legally, no-one could come into the inheritance? There was no-one to inquire about. Something, yes, but not someone. Technically, of course. Essentially, I would have made inquiries had it all been official and above board but this was a matter for my private honour and conscience.

Thanks to Evsey's unwitting reports, I was up to date on Tabachnik's activities.

The old simpleton dropped in to see the Gutins once as autumn approached. And not only did he drop in, he was arm-in-arm with Dovid.

They steered away from Evsey straight away. They asked Belka to follow them into the shed in the yard where they whispered away.

Evsey wanted to follow and listen in but was held back by the children's pestering.

At the end of August, Lyubochka, in view of the approaching cold, expressed the desire to have a new dress made.

By way of illustration, she tried on the old one – the one I remembered as being perfectly fine – and said:

"I bumped into Polina Lvovna Laevskaya at the market. She said this and that and basically told me she could make me one up for half price. Of course, I flatly refused but she reassured me that it was all out of respect for you. Lilechka Vorobeichik was her friend, like a sister even, she said, and since you found the killer, she'll be grateful to you till the day she dies and, to acknowledge it, she'll give me a discount. She actually had tears in her eyes. She was begging me to do her a favour. Me, do her a favour! Imagine!"

I was wary of reaching a hasty verdict.

"Oh? And then what?

"That's what I'm asking you. They say Laevskaya's too grasping, then she does something like this. Do you think she means it, Misha?" Lyuba didn't wait for me to reply. She reached her own conclusion. "Of course, she does. Death's no laughing matter."

"What's death got to do with it?" I asked.

Lyuba replied:

"It's just a comparison. When it's just any old thing, you might not tell the truth but when it comes to death, you wouldn't dare. Maybe I should accept the discount? I've haven't got anyone to make me a decent dress."

I shrugged. Though for quite a different reason. You shouldn't be going to see Laevskaya, Lyubochka. Not for dressmaking or for discounts: you shouldn't have anything to do with her.

What I said was:

"Do it. Things are working out. We don't need to act like tight-fisted Yids." The word just slipped out. Not rude, exactly, but not Soviet. Otherwise it's a word like any other but I faltered. "There's no need to count the kopecks. We've got to be able to hold our heads up in public. You're so pretty. Castoffs are good enough if you're as plain as a pikestaff. But not for you."

Lyuba was radiant. She rushed over to the chest of drawers and took a length of bottle green material from under the sheets.

She put it under my nose.

"Look. I bought it ages ago." She unfolded it, turned it this way and that, over and back. "It's wool. From the market. From before the war. Or else brought back from Germany. It's cheap. And with a discount on top, well, it's practically free."

To please her, I felt the material. I even wanted to stroke it but understood that I shouldn't. My hands were trembling.

"It's fine. Hard-wearing. Doesn't show the dirt," I said.

Lyuba went to see Laevskaya. This is what she brought back:

Polina Lvovna kept asking how things were at work. Whether I was being moved out of town. This happened quite a lot back then so that regional officers could reinforce district police units. She had also said that if I was sent off into the sticks, we'd never see that flat. We'd get bogged down where we were. But she had connections. She could put in a good word.

Lyuba asked if I was hiding something from her about work. The bosses went to Laevskaya, or rather, their wives did. She knew a lot. She wasn't given to idle talk.

I assured Lyuba that there were no changes in store for me at work. But I took mental note of the fact that Laevskaya would be working on that bottle-green, hard-wearing, dirt-concealing dress for a long time. She'd be stitching and sewing for a good while. Getting my wife all worked up.

But there was no way out. Let her. She wouldn't worm anything out of Lyubochka. Bitch.

I talked to my colleagues, analysed the situation. The bosses' attitude towards me hadn't changed. I had been in their good books. I still was.

I dangled the bait anyway.

"All my life I've dreamt of working in a small district somewhere. Getting some peace and quiet. Get the husbands out from under their wives, that's all it takes."

We were coming back from a Party meeting with the man from personnel.

He clapped me on the shoulder, teased me good-naturedly.

"There aren't too many like you around, Misha, Mikhail Ivanovich. Now's not the time to be wasting our best officers. We're not about to hand you over to some district or other. Not even the most successful one. And we will find you a flat. Just so that you know. And tell your wife to be ready."

Lyubochka and I were so overjoyed, it shut out the whole, wide world. Despite the fact that Anechka had picked up a severe cold on the Desna and, for over a month, we nursed her at home with the doctors' assistance, we were already tasting the delight of our forthcoming space and independence.

At the end of September, we were given a one-room flat with a modest kitchen. On Kotsyubinsky Street. German POWs had built a whole street there. Our house was nearer to the new market.

We moved in. We'd done it, even without another baby. We'd been lucky.

And then, who should make her way to the flat but Laevskaya.

It wasn't a secret. They knew our address at the old place. Moreover, we'd promised to tell people the new address - anything might happen.

And this was it.

I opened the door in person.

Laevskaya and her bosom bore down on me from the very first second.

"May you be very happy in your new home, Mikhail Ivanovich, my dear! I timed it deliberately for a Sunday so that I'd find you all at home. Is Lyubochka here? And your little poppet, Anechka? Is that little lass of yours here with her Mummy and Daddy?"

She gushed and she cooed as she poked her nose into everything. She opened the door into the toilet.

She nodded, as if pleased.

"Yes. I've heard about these houses. They're warm. That's the main thing. They're warm."

Lyuba heard Laevskaya's voice and came out to greet her properly.

"My dear Polina Ivanovna, how lovely that you've managed to find us! We'll have a cup of tea right away and preserves, all sorts! These days I don't know, we haven't got an allotment any more. There won't be any preserves now. But we've still got some at the moment."

Laevskaya threw her arms wide, taking in the setting with her eyes and her fingers. Of course, it was all junk. Lyubochka and I had each been putting the odd kopeck aside but we hadn't enough put by for anything decent. Now, with Laevskaya there, I felt I needed to explain.

I put my foot right in my mouth.

"Yes, we're not particularly well off. Not like you. You can save kopeck after kopeck and hide them away. We can't." I laid particular stress on that "you".

Laevskaya laughed.

"Oh, I can, can I? I eat what I like. And literally everything goes on food. Everyone loves their food as they get older. I've even given up on my figure."

She made a dismissive gesture by way of illustration. But she lifted up the frock under her sand-coloured mackintosh just enough to reveal a plump, repulsive knee.

"Ah, well, what can I say? My youth is gone and gone forever."

The knee was one step too far.

"Come now, Polina Lvovna! You'll still get married. You'll be as safe as houses for the rest of your days. If you asked me, I could even recommend a husband. Dovid Srulevich Basin. A widower. Jewish nationality. Just the one for you. People say he's got a bit put by as well. Well, your lot always do…"

Why I said it, why I put Dovid forward, I don't know. It happens sometimes. I come up with just right word out of the blue.

Of course, Laevskaya understood the hint about her nationality and customs. But she didn't let it show. It was only experience that enabled me to see she had clenched her teeth.

"Let's not talk about me. That's all in the past. I've brought that little dress over for you, Lyubochka. I ironed it first. You must be worn out from the move. If I have a pattern, and people don't say this for nothing, I need just the one fitting to do the job. So, I finished this by sight. I wanted to gladden your heart as soon as possible. And your husband to be able to feast his eyes on you. Try it on, now. Go on, try it!"

She pulled a roll of material out of her almighty rucksack and lifted out the dress, holding it in two fingers, like a precious jewel. She laid it over both arms, like the cloth that holds out bread and salt in welcome. She presented it to Lyuba. With a bow.

Lyuba took it with a bow of her own.

She ran into the kitchen.

She came back.

I felt giddy, she was so gorgeous.

Lyuba twirled around, patting the dress.

Laevskaya walked around her as if she was a statue in a museum and tutted.

"And you, poppet," she said to Anechka, "do you want me to make you something pretty?"

"What thing?" Anechka asked.

"I'll think of something. I don't skimp when it comes to fashion. I don't usually make things for children but I will for you. A special children's design. I've got various scraps around the place. I can put some together for you. It would be a pleasure."

Tears welled in her eyes.

Lyubochka asked quietly and delicately.

"And how much do I owe you?" Since the move we'd really only had money for bread.

"I lined the skirt," Laevskaya explained. "That material's mine. The threads are mine as well. And they're silk. I put these little tucks here in the sleeve. We hadn't agreed on those, Lyubochka. And I added a neat little collar. The lace is mine. Anyway, I don't want any extra for that. So it's as we agreed, half price."

And she named the price.

I haven't the foggiest idea about the cost of women's stuff but Lyubochka looked taken aback.

"Could you wait until pay day, perhaps? Misha gets paid in a couple of days."

Laevskaya appeared to have been expecting this turn of events.

"And why wouldn't I wait? You can bring it round to my place, Mikhail Ivanovich. Please! So as not to bother Lyubochka. I can give you some nice little apples as a treat for Anechka too. I've plenty dried for stewing. The little girl needs her vitamins over the winter, all sorts. And your work must really take it out of you. Some people just don't realize but I can see that. After all, we're not just chance acquaintances, now are we? I love you like my own. I don't know why but I have right from the start. Especially, Anechka, precious little poppet that she is."

Lyuba nodded.

Not because of the stewed apples. She's a modest sort and when people mount an attack she nods without thinking.

When Laevskaya left, all Lyuba said was, "Phew, Polina! You love us all of a sudden. Maybe you do but it's still, 'Cough up the cash'. And so much of it too. I wouldn't have gone to her at that price. What am I meant to do, Misha?"

"We have to give her the money. And we will. I will. Then, let her choke on her blasted treats."

From where she was listening, Anechka repeated after me: "Let her choke."

Children. They don't really understand.

I went straight from being paid to see Laevskaya.

I put the notes on the table without waiting to be asked.

I won't hide the fact that I expected to be held up there. By her tittle-tattle, to be honest. But she didn't have much to say at all. She took the money in silence and counted it.

Almost under her breath, she chirruped:

"That's right. People don't mind paying what they owe for my work. You've done it, so take it. Isn't that so, Mikhail Ivanovich? I say you always get your due. If you take my meaning?"

"I do," I replied automatically.

Laevskaya thrust a bag into my hand: the apples. I took it to avoid any unnecessary unpleasantness. I was planning to throw it away on the way home.

But I didn't.

"I've paid up," I told Lyuba. "I brought the apples. She's a fool, that Polina Ivanovna Laevskaya, of course she is, and not even a fool. It's just her nature. Her Jewish nature. Sometimes they seem to be stupid but it's their nature that makes them do it. They can't help it."

Lyuba nodded:

"I wouldn't even think of blaming her. It's their race. You just have to know that and bear it in mind."

"Exactly. And the apples. Well, they've got nothing to do with it."

Up came Anechka, took a rosy apple and bit into it. The juice ran down her small chin.

I wiped it away with my hand. Carefully, carefully. I hugged my little daughter as tenderly as possible.

We didn't have a housewarming party as such. We combined it with my taking routine leave. Evsey was one of the guests, of course.

I have to admit that people at that time had begun looking more askance at the Jews. Some colleagues even hinted that Evsey Gutin wasn't a comrade I should trust. I didn't respond.

Cases of over-zealousness occurred and Jews were sacked not fairly but as a tribute to the rootless cosmopolitan situation. But that was the Party line and that's not something to criticize. But I didn't repudiate Gutin. And he appreciated it.

The house warming was a great success. Heart-warming too.

Lyubochka did all the cooking. Anechka helped her as best she could and they laid the table together, Anechka so small she had to reach up and Lyubochka confidently putting things on the table from above. Lyubochka's pirozhki, her garlic dough balls to go in the borscht, meat in aspic, salad and so on.

The beauty of family life enfolded me and even made me catch my breath.

My colleagues and I discussed the fact that if everyone behaved properly during their leisure time, we would have less to do. We were joking, clearly.

The guests had a very good time.

In the end, only Evsey and I were left.

Lyubochka and Anechka were washing up in the kitchen.

"Dovid Sergeyevich, doesn't seem himself," Evsey said casually. "I can't understand what's going on with him. I'm convinced Tabachnik is stirring things up. Do you remember I told you about Tabachnik, a kind of wandering fool?"

"And..."

"Dovid keeps harping on about how politics have taken something of a new turn: instead of the wholesale evacuation of the Jews, now they're going to be picked off one by one. What a thing to come up with! Pretending they're criminals so as to kill them off without the capitalist world getting itself in a flap. After all, who's bothered about criminals? But if killing them's the Party line, there could be a real hoohah over there. Is it really possible to kill them off one by one? It's madness. Beyond me."

"Them? Don't you include yourself?"

Evsey spun round in place. It was as if he was looking for change in his pockets and it had fallen through a hole, into his boot or somewhere.

"Fine. Tabachnik's not involved. He's on his uppers, a beggar, he tells tall stories. Harmful ones but stories all the same. But Dovid's in his right mind and everybody knows it. You should tell him to put a sock in it. It's not for us to set the Party line. Clearly, if you're all evacuated in an organized fashion, it will be better for you. You, for example, will find a new job straight away. If you turn up one by one, all the crooks among you will stand out. As well as the killers and the hooligans. As for the others, the professors and academics, of course, it is scary. They won't have so much respect or so much money. They're in plentiful supply – professors, academics, violinists, pianists. Just imagine, you'll be taken somewhere new and you'll build yourselves a Jewish paradise. You'll be chief of police. Well, not chief, but in a senior position. Is that a bad thing? The intelligentsia will write their poems, music, films. You should be grateful."

Evsey seemed to be feeling for something in his pocket. He nodded, delighted. "And we are grateful. We are. There, found it." And he offered me a little tube of paper. "David left his address. He's gone to stay with Tabachnik in Oster."

"Why on earth do I need his address? For what?"

"Dovid told me to give it you. And not just verbally. He wrote it down. He left late last night. Today I'm passing this on. And not at work. Properly."

I looked at Evsey with new eyes.

"What business could I possible have with Dovid? I can't stand him and I make no secret of it."

"I don't interfere in other people's business. Not ever," said Evsey, scowling. "I thought that's why you respected me. What do I know? Dovid does a bit of business in bricks. I thought he'd been letting you have some on the sly. For a shed at the old flat. You wanted to do some building. That's the hint he dropped, that I was to give you the address for some personal reason. Well, now you've moved and you've nowhere to stick a shed anyway. But you never know. You'd have the bricks, right?"

My answer was categorical.

"Wrong."

I read the piece of paper. Address: The dugout behind the last house at the far end, Frunze Street, Oster.

As we were saying farewell, Evsey muttered,

"Folk are saying that you, Misha, didn't do a proper job with Moiseenko. Remember, the one who took his own life?"

"Really? I do remember. I see him hanging there every night."

"Certain people are saying things. Even in our department. That it's a shady business. Really. I do what I can to put a stop to it. Leave Misha alone, I say. He did everything necessary. That chap was a highly-strung artiste. That's all."

I cut him off.

"I know what sort of thing you're saying. You're being weaselly and what you're saying is weaselly too. Exactly who's got it in for me?"

"The typist, Svetka. She's having a fling with the chief. She pursed her lips and deliberately, with me right there, hissed, 'That Misha of yours slipped up, Evsey. He's your friend, close to you even, but he slipped up.' Svetka's a trollop, a slut. She wouldn't come up with that herself. She's just repeating it."

I turned Evsey round to face me close up and ended our little chat as follows:

"People are using you to get at me. And see, they've got what they wanted. Gutin's a dubious character because of the nationalities question. Tsupkoy and Gutin are thick as thieves so let's give Tsupkoy hell. Well, no. It's not going to work!"

Evsey's face lit up although I was squeezing his shoulder painfully.

"It's not going to work, Misha! We shed blood together. It's not."

I didn't know how else to support my comrade so all I said was "absolutely".

I got the chance to go to Oster as I had wanted and planned. At home I explained that I was going back to my village, Ryabina, between Kharkov and Sumy. A long way from Chernigov. I put the same story about at work. The thunder of war was over. My mother and father had been tortured and killed by the fascist scum as front-rank collective farmers. My father had been an activist too. I was forced to claim that I was going to pay my respects at the graves of my parents. How humiliating!

And yet at the same time it wasn't. After Oster, I really did intend to go to Ryabina. If it came off.

For those who don't know, I'll explain.

It's always easy to judge with hindsight. And in those days feelings were running hot from the flames of the recent war. Happiness was within our grasp. And, after the bloodshed of battle, any obstacle seemed insignificant in peace time. I say this not for the sake of philosophy but by way of information.

And it was that kind of obstacle that Lilia Vorobeichik had put in my way.

Yes, she had been an attractive woman before she died. From what was said of her. But she was gone and I was in trouble. Was this irritating? Definitely. But so be it. Honour is worth more than well, I don't know what.

I said nothing to Evsey. Frankness is all very well but a clear conscience is better. And my conscience dictated that no-one should be implicated. It was a rule of operations. To be in the know was to be an accessory.

Before taking the train, I wandered down Clara Zetkin Street. Not a sound from No. 23.

I circled the house from the back, climbing over the fence.

The chicken shed was deathly silent. The door was wide-open. Not a feather or a seed to be seen.

Oster was a well-known shtetl. Jews were roughly in the majority. The rest were Ukrainians. Hardly any Russians.

In places, amid the devastation, buildings were going up. Not much to look at but made of good, solid wood. Not regular houses exactly but not jerry-built shacks either. People were building for themselves. Planks were slotted together with care, then slats placed over them. Liveable enough.

Oster greeted me with a wedding. A Jewish man taking a Jewish bride. And, let's be honest, the guests were all Jews as well. For the most part, although there were some Ukrainian comrades. Jewish was being spoken, especially by the older people.

The merrymaking had already reached such a pitch that the dancing had spilled out of the house and into the street.

There was a band playing – fiddle, tambourine and accordion. I noticed right away that the accordion was loot brought back from Germany. I'd seen plenty of them there. The Germans have two instruments when it comes to a knees-up: the mouth-organ and the accordion. The Jews have the fiddle, are famous for it. Now they've added the accordion as well. But there was something off about this fiddler. He was all skew whiff. Then I realized he was left handed. He wasn't holding the fiddle like a normal person.

The music was sort of lively but melancholy. Not many people were singing along. When they moved on to the Ukrainian "You deceived me, you betrayed me", everyone belted it out. All together. It was just the ticket. For any occasion. A proper folk song.

Typically, Jewish children were present in great numbers. Little ones and slightly older ones, all shapes and sizes. Mostly they were skinny, sickly little things. But there were some well-padded ones as well. Whereas the Ukrainians were all scrawny. It's the breed. Jewish children assimilate their food better. Or else they're fed in a special way, like geese for the slaughter. The food's forced down their gullets. Whereas ours, it's off you go, out to play, whether you've eaten or not.

Being an outsider, I hurried past.

However, a member of the wedding party wearing a red arm band attached himself to me.

"Comrade, join us in a toast to the happy couple. You are most warmly welcome."

And he clung to me so tightly, pliers wouldn't have pulled him off.

He was bellowing like a mad man.

"Come and join us, come on! Everyone's invited! The whole of Oster is here for the party!"

And then it was all eyes on my good self from the rear and the flanks.

Of course, I shouldn't have. I would only need to pause for a chat and they would let go with both barrels. Where are you from? Who are you? Who are you going to see? Why? It would be easier to do their bidding but then slip away unnoticed.

In a split second, I had it all sorted out in my head: if they asked, I'd tell them I was passing through on official business.

I went into the house. A few guests were grouped round the table. Understandably, it was a scene of complete havoc: plates of leftovers, half-empty bottles. Nothing untoward.

The head and tail of a vast stuffed pike, half the length of the table. The head was stuffed too, the Jewish way, but they hadn't eaten it.

I excused myself, saying my wound meant I didn't drink spirits. I asked for plain water. What I got was a glass of uzvar, red with haws and pears. Just as it should be.

"Thank you, comrades," I said, raising my glass. "I wish you every happiness and thank you for asking me to join you."

In came the newly-weds. She was a sturdy wench of about thirty. Hair black and shaggy. But with beautiful eyes. Black eyes. The groom was a bit of a let-down in terms of height and bearing. But not bad looking, certainly not a fright.A bit older than her. About five years. Hair light, running to ginger. Eyes of different colours, one pale blue, the other light hazel. An uncommon distinguishing feature.

It would be a sheer pleasure to have to give a verbal description of either of them. You could never mistake them for anyone else even from a general outline.

The happy couple were followed by the guests. They had roared their fill and stamped their heels. Now it was time to eat.

Again, their rasping deafened me. But, looking, I could see the Ukrainians were keeping up the conversation in the same language. Laughing merrily at the jokes. Exchanging winks.

"Comrades, we have one more guest," the man who had dragged me in by the scruff of the neck announced loudly. "He will now say a few words. Shush!"

Everyone stopped talking.

I raised my glass of uzvar with the words, "Mazel tov, to the happy couple! Mazel tov for many years together!"

Next but one to me sat an old man with sidelocks. He wore a greasy peaked cap. How had he survived? He must have escaped by being evacuated, taking up room.

And there he was nodding at me and asking literally of the surrounding space, "You Jewish?"

I laughed.

"No. I've a friend who's one of yours. He taught me. So, I wish them eternal happiness."

A portly man in a good jacket got to his feet. Ukrainian in appearance. And yet there was a hint of something. Sometimes, you can't tell just like that. We have people with big noses and dark skin too.

"Thank you for your good wishes. What you see here is a wedding. A fine wedding as it's turned out, a merry one. Please join us in the festivities and eat and drink with us."

The old man, who had wondered whether or not I was a Jew, looked straight at me with his wall-eyes. That is, his eyes could see, it seemed, but at the same time they couldn't. Horrible.

I smiled as broadly as I could and went out into the yard.

Men were smoking, children darting about, women carrying clay dishes from the outside kitchen into the house. Time? Getting dark.

I was edging slowly towards the gate. The portly chap who'd answered my toast with one of his own shouted after me.

"Comrade, not so fast! We haven't finished yet! Have you had a good time?"

"Oh, come on! Very good. Good food and better vodka, as they say."

The man came up close and put a hand on my shoulder.

"That's right, Comrade. That's right. All Oster is here to celebrate this wedding."

I made a joke to lighten the mood.

"The bride and groom have left it a bit late. They ought to be taking children to school and here they are just getting married."

"They did have children," he said, nodding. "She did, and he did. She had a husband too, and he had a wife. They were killed by the Germans and the Polizei. And where do you hail from?"

"Not from round here."

"I can tell you're a soldier. Am I right?"

I shook my head noncommittally.

The man hastened to say, "No questions. I'm not asking any questions. I understand. I was in the war myself. And before that, I had a senior position. And now… But never mind. I'm not complaining. I understand. Spend the night here."

And he offered me his hand so that we were acquainted.

"Faida, Miron Shayevich. Head of cultural and educational work. Or more precisely, temporary club steward…People are in dire need of culture. After everything."

I shook his hand.

I was deciding what name to use when the gate burst open and new guests, latecomers, entered the yard with loud shouts of greeting.

More rasping, laughter everywhere. I darted past the fence and into the street.

What a race they are! Imagine, all your relatives have been killed. Including the children. And you're getting married. In front of everyone. And fine ones they all are too. Drinking, stuffing their faces. Tinkling away on the accordion. Bloodsuckers.

Let's be honest, this was anger speaking. And mentally I let rip.

One of these days, they'll be packed off to the ends of the earth, into the bare steppe and the snow. Hey, you, get your things together, bundle them up, stuff your gold away in hidey-holes. And they're getting married! And all these children running around. Laughing. Sucking lollipops. Because they're nice and sweet. Do you want things to be sweet? They will be. Definitely. Now's not the time for them not to be.

I didn't go to the dugout on Frunze Street. I turned about face.

I travelled on a succession of five or so carts and several trucks. They gave me lifts and took no money for it. My own kind, Ukrainians.

I set course for Ryabina.

Ryabina was full of life. The centre, Polotnyanovka, was empty. But there were dogs barking, geese wandering about. The people were at work, on the collective farm.

My spirits rose a little.

I had left for Kharkov at the age of 18 through strings pulled in the Young Communist League. My father had done what he could by fair means or foul.

He brought the papers home like newly dug-up treasure.

"You go off to Kharkov, son. It's no life here in any case. Nor will it be," he said.

It hadn't even been in my plans. Let's be honest: I was an average student. Hungry and cold. I used to walk the eight kilometres to school. I preferred the natural world and knew more about it. In Class One, our teacher Didenko thought highly of me because of this. I would explain to my classmates in ways they could understand that the seasons of the year were bound to change, always. You just needed to know about it and not be afraid of the cold. Or the rain. Or the hot w eather.

But my father had spoken, so off I went to study.

Then came the war. I volunteered for the front. As someone with an education, albeit an unfinished one, I was immediately made a junior officer. And that's how it all began.

When the war was won, I didn't go back to Ryabina. My heart cautioned against it. Let those who are dead and buried rest in peace. It wouldn't bring them back. Upsetting myself for nothing would be stupid, bad for my nerves. For the rest, there was nothing for me to do. A new life was unavoidable.

There was practically nowhere for me to go in this locality. There was, one, the cemetery so that people didn't gossip or cast aspersions. And, two, my teacher, Mikola Ivanovich Didenko, the only person I remembered with affection. And that was all.

I did go to the cemetery and I was ashamed. If it hadn't been for the Jews and their foolishness, if it hadn't been for my parents bringing me up to put honour and conscience above all else, I would have been on leave in Chernigov with my family. With Lyubochka and Gannusya. And that would be that.

It suddenly hit me that I couldn't find the graves on my own.

So I turned off to see Didenko. It happened to be en route.

I knocked and was assailed by doubt: was he even still alive? Given his advanced age, the trials and tribulations.

Not only did Didenko answer the door himself, however, he wrapped me in a firm embrace as well. He recognized me immediately. And yet he was at least seventy at the time.

"So then, Mikhailik, you made it. You've remembered, my lad, you have… Are you staying long?"

"No. I'll spend the night here, if I may. Then we'll see how long I stay. Let's sleep on it first. I'm not expected home immediately. I'm on leave."

"And where are you living nowadays? Kharkov, is it?"

"Chernigov. Do you know it?"

"Course, I do. I've been. Before the war, it was. Just before too. At the foot of Trinity Hill, that's where I stayed. Tikhaya Street. That's right, isn't it?"

My heart pounded. Trinity Hill again.

"And who was it you stayed with, Mikola Ivanovich?"

"What a man he was! A Jew. Something akin to a rabbi. Do you know what that is, a rabbi?"

"A Jewish priest."

"Aye, if you like. And a philosopher to boot. Zusel, they called him. Tabachnik. I used to go and see him specially, just to chat. We served together in the first war. He was a volunteer. Of his own accord. The Jews weren't called up. Undesirables. But he went in a fit of pique. Of his own volition. I was a conscript though. The two of us fetched up in the same trench. I defended him from halfwits more than from the Germans. He was a great one for prayers. It was allowed back then. Encouraged even, the same for all religions. I'd say that if he hadn't been so clever with his prayers, our lot would never have touched him but he would make all these loud exclamations and sway backwards and forwards. It nearly always got a laugh. I used to try and hush them up."

"You know, Mikola Ivanovich, that Zusel of yours is still alive. Muddying the waters. He's made himself a dugout in Oster and is up to all sorts there. And the Soviet authorities just let him."

Didenko grinned.

"That's the Jews' portion. Stirring things up. Don't you let him put you out. He sent me a letter about a month back. Right out of the blue. That same Tabachnik. I've got it somewhere. From Chernigov like you said. Tikhaya Street. Says he wants to come and see me. That it's urgent. Asks if I'm still alive. It made me laugh, that letter did. If I'm already in the cold, cold ground, how can I reply? He was daft then and he's daft now. One foot in the grave, as the saying goes, and now he wants to travel."

"Did you write back to say you're still alive?" I said, laughing.

Didenko nodded but with an air of fatalism.

"No. After all, I can't say for certain whether I'm alive or dead. The time it takes that letter to reach Zusel, I could have breathed my last. He'd be really upset. Wasting the money. Have you been to the cemetery?"

"No, I haven't. Perhaps you'd be kind enough to go with me to show me?"

"No. I'm not going. It's not far but I won't make it on my legs. You go. You can't miss it. They're under a little pyramid, both of them. There's a star. The pyramid's blue. The star's red. Right next to the way in."

There was a knock at the window.

Mikola Ivanovich looked round.

"How's that for timing?" he said delighted. "A visitor. Petro Paly. Do you remember? The year below you. He brings me my meals. Not for nothing, mind. His wife does the cooking and he brings it round. They've no children so it's as if they had me instead."

I didn't recognize Paly. Ordinarily, I would have walked right past him.

Petro turned out to be blind. A white bandage over both eyes, from his forehead to his mouth. But fine, it was a fresh bandage, neat as could be.

He threw his head back as if trying to peer through the lower edge of the cloth.

"Got someone with you, Mikola Ivanovich?"

"Aye, a pal of yours. Mishko Tsupkoy."

The hugs I'll pass over in silence.

We decided not to put off the expedition to the cemetery. The quicker it was, the easier for me. Zusel and his letter only spurred me on.

We stood by the grave.

"They gave them another burial," Petro said. "As heroes. They were forgiven, dying like that, that's for sure. And don't you worry. Nothing was said out loud but inside everyone forgave them. That's what I think. So they can lay easy."

"What do you mean, Petka, forgiven for what? They lived an honest working life. They were setting up the collective farm. For the sake of a better life."

Petro's bandage showed white. And the bandage spoke for him.

"For that. That's what they were forgiven for, for raking the last seeds of grain from under little children's pillows on an order from above. Predators – that's the only word for them."

I said nothing.

Petro was the first to head back.

"There was a meeting," he called over his shoulder.

"Good speeches. Heartfelt. May they rest in peace."

And he went his way.

I didn't try to catch up.

I went back to Didenko's.

Mikola Ivanovich was waiting.

"Well?"

"I've paid my respects."

And then I remembered that I'd meant to take a handful of earth from the grave. But I hadn't. Petro had distracted me.

Mikola Ivanovich suggested a bite to eat. I didn't want anything. I was very shaken up. But I couldn't say no to the old man.

We sat at the table.

Didenko had found some home-made vodka. He told me he kept it for his rheumatism. But I'd already realized he liked a drink. You could see it in his face.

We drank and ate what we had.

"You haven't remembered where you hid the letter, have you?" I said. "The one from Zusel. I wonder. At such a distance and yet hearing about a friend. It does happen, I suppose. Then again, I'm not surprised. Stranger things happened at the front."

"The letter? I've not even tried to remember. After all, it turns out you know him yourself. Tell him in person that I was still among the living when you were here. Let him take a chance and just turn up."

"Right. On my way here, there was this place where I came across a Jewish wedding. What a race! Half of them killed one way or another. Children and old folk, the world and his wife. In order to wipe them out completely. And there they are getting married again. Making little yidkins. As if nothing had happened. They ought to be ashamed to be alive after such horror. And yet how they cling to life."

Mikola Ivanovich tipped a tiny drop from his glass onto the palm of his hand, the very last drop; it was all gone. He rubbed at it, sniffed it and lapped it up.

This is what he had to say:

"They're a resilient race. Like any other. You were only a boy. Your Mum and Dad were going about their business. But in '33 the graves weren't even still - the famine had only just ended. People were eating again but not much. But there were weddings. The earth on the graves was still trembling but people were living it up. Stuffing their faces and living it up. Drinking too much out of sheer joy at being alive. Cuddling up to the girls and throwing up right on the graves, even bread was thrown up. Your Dad sent you away to Kharkov. He'd worked for it. He sent you away. In return for services rendered. So that you could put everything all behind you without a second thought. And then people starved to death in '47 too. One – Zasyadko, you probably don't remember him – he came back from the front after we won, a hero. He'd been chasing one of our girls even before the war. She'd up and married. In such a state he was. And off he goes to the front in that state. 'I am going off to certain death for love of the Motherland and of you, Katerina,' he says. Right. But it's Katerina's husband that's killed at the front. Zasyadko comes back. And there she is, a widow, but she won't marry him, not for anything. Then comes the famine. She's got five children. She gives it all to them. She's nothing but a skeleton. Everyone's going through the mill but, Katerina, dear God. Zasyadko gives her food. Whatever he can. Robbing himself of his last morsel. But the children gobble it up and are hungry all over again. 'Let's get married,' he says. 'I can save you and the children.' Save them with what? He's skin and bone himself. There were strict credits for labour but you couldn't eat those. Basically, he's on his last legs. He calls for Katerina. 'Let me just have a hold of your tit before I go,' he says. So she says, 'Will you give us some bread?' 'I will,' he says and points over at a box. There's a loaf there. Rock hard. She grabs it and off she goes, out of the door. And there she drops down dead. And that's how Zasyadko died, without his tit. So many years have passed and I'm forever thinking and thinking. If only she'd fallen onto Zasyadko with that damned bread, he'd have had a pleasanter passing. But no. It wasn't to be. There was this young lad, a pupil of mine, he went to get Katerina to see Zasyadko on his death bed. He told me."

"It was a drought in '47," I said, correcting him. "You mustn't confuse '47 and '33, Mikola Ivanovich. Don't exaggerate."

"There's no need to exaggerate. That's exactly what people like to do everywhere. But not me. Before long, that's exactly what you'll be hearing about me, exaggerations. So I'll tell you myself. Even under the Germans I still taught in school. I expected the Soviet authorities to arrest me for it. But they didn't. They didn't even sack me. They'd tear me off a strip for teaching while the Germans were in charge. But they left me to it. I asked a superior once what I had done to the children that was so terrible under the Germans that it merited a reprimand. He said: 'You were drumming it into the children that God exists.' And yes, I was. With what they saw around them, all they could do was put their trust in God. And I told them straight: 'Children, God exists.' That's all. Understand?"

I nodded.

"And don't you nod at me here in my own home. How long will you be staying?"

I could tell that he still wanted to talk but I wasn't in the mood. I said I'd be leaving at cockcrow.

"Right you are," he sighed.

"We're cripples you and I, Mikhailik. Out and out invalids. Crippled by the war and by our own lives."

"Personally I'm not crippled. I'm in very good health."

Didenko patted me on the head the way he used to in school.

"Oh but you are. You are a cripple, my lad, and how!"

He asked me to wake him when I was ready to depart.

I didn't sleep a wink. The vodka was buzzing in my brain. Although there hadn't been much of it. It was still buzzing. And so were Zusel and Lilia Vorobeichik and the rest. And Didenko was shaking a crumpled letter behind my sleepless lids. In my head. And Petro Paly was brandishing his white bandage too. And they all blended into one.

I got up quietly.

Didenko was asleep and snoring. When someone's pretending, they rarely snore. It doesn't sound natural. So I was sure he was asleep.

I went through the house as best I could. I didn't find the letter.

Before day break, I was gone. I left a little money on the table and departed.

On the way, I did a lot of thinking.

I was a soldier. I grew up on military orders. Like all our great, vast country. Just take Kharkov, the town that had been home to me for a few brief years. It was designated the capital and it became the capital. And wondrously tall buildings appeared. And wondrously wide squares. Then the capital was ordered back to Kiev and Kiev became the capital again.

Or take that ill-famed famine. It was designated a famine and it became a famine. And my late parents were innocent of it.

Although life in peacetime had long since come into its own, I wished someone would issue me with a specific order, to tell me to forget the Vorobeichik case, to forget the mud being slung at me by all kinds of petty persons, primarily Jews, to forget that I would have to rake over the past and peer far into the future to see what lay ahead.

Yet no-one but myself could give that order. It couldn't even occur to anyone else in the world.

And so, I returned to Chernigov. Lyubochka was pleased to see me.

Gannusya kept flinging herself at me, saying:

"Daddy, Daddy! I love you, Daddy."

Only four and a bit but she knew what family love was.

I explained my sudden arrival to Lyuba as a desire not to postpone our meeting and to experience her affection. She was very pleased.

We scheduled a joint trip to Kiev to buy items for the house and for Gannusya who was growing not by the day but by the hour.

But I was urgently recalled from leave. Evsey Gutin had shot himself with his service weapon. At home, in the shed.

Belka was a shadow of her former self. The children were fine. Kept going by bewilderment and lack of understanding.

Dovid Srulevich rose to the occasion. I offered to arrange the funeral but he took it all upon himself.

"Now is not a time for you to be organizing a Jewish funeral," he said by way of justification. "People will get the wrong idea. And Belka and I want it to be Jewish. Without a rabbi, but still. I'll say kaddish myself, quietly. Zusel will offer his own prayers too, off to one side, keeping his distance, although somebody's bound to see. If there's a problem, it'll be me the finger points at. And you'll be in the clear. Isn't that right? You're not offended?"

The deceased, Evsey, was lying on the floor. On a sheet. As Jewish law requires. He had shot himself in the heart. His face was fine.

There were candles on every windowsill.

The collar of Dovid's shirt had been ripped. Belka's frock was damaged, ever so slightly, unpicked along the seam.

I asked why. Dovid shook his head – tradition. It means they're suffering. They rend the clothes they stand up in. Fair enough.

People came in.

The women wailed. The men were silent.

Zusel was mumbling in the next room. Swaying back and forth, his head covered in a striped shawl. The mumbling was coming from beneath it. A prayer.

It reminded me of Didenko.

Quietly, I said, "Citizen Tabachnik. Didenko says hello."

Zusel appeared not to have heard but the mumbling got louder. And the swaying stronger.

I didn't insist. Now wasn't the time.

My comrades from work came over at the funeral. They said the right things but everyone was clear that what Evsey had done deserved to be condemned. With sorrow, yes, but unanimously.

Evsey had broken the first commandment: an officer, and especially a Communist, has the right to shoot himself in one situation and only one: in the face of unavoidable capture. To do the enemy as much damage as possible and, staring death right in the face, to shoot himself. That's heroism. Evsey had taken his action in peace time. How come?

There were a great many citizens of Jewish nationality. A crowd of various ages. Evsey was well-known. Dovid even more so. People were showing their respects, had rallied round.

My police colleagues stayed in a separate group. All in uniform. Dark blue. Like a clear autumn sky. It looked good. Leather holsters. Many brought back from Germany, they'd had them since the war. Boots polished, obviously. Although they'd had to walk through mud to reach the grave.

As a close friend, I was asked to bid Evsey farewell.

This is what I said:

"Dear Evsey. You leave sons behind. We will not abandon them. All sons are needed by our Motherland. Your family will be happy albeit without you. Rest in peace."

I said nothing about duty, our war time youth, Evsey's medals. I talked about what grieved him at the very moment that he pulled the trigger. As the bullet flew towards his heart.

I know some people criticized me. But I couldn't put it any other way. The truth was begging to be told. And so I set it free.

Everything was done as Dovid had promised. Once those present had thrown earth into the grave and begun to depart, he said a prayer discreetly and tactfully.

Zusel moved off behind the bushes and snivelled away in his own fashion.

That was his business.

Tabachnik, evidently, on his own initiative had stuffed a bundle under Evsey's head – some kind of striped religious thing and something else besides. At my blank expression, Dovid explained: a tallit and a kipa.

"A Jew can't go there," Dovid motioned upwards, "without them."

It was all for show. Secret but for show nonetheless.

As for Belka and the children. I'm not going to say anything. For anyone with a heart, it was impossible to describe. Anyone without one can make do with the single word: awful.

Laevskaya was at the funeral as well.

She watched me. Made eyes at me. She'd made sure to wear lipstick. I wanted to just drop in the question as to why she hadn't made any tears in that silk mackintosh of hers.

She came over to me, took my arm and whispered confidentially:

"What a good thing Evsey shot himself in the heart. If it had been the head, it would have been just dreadful. And a closed coffin would have been unbearable. Don't you think?"

I nodded automatically but remarked in measured tones, "Why closed? They'd have covered the head and left the body on view."

Polina snorted and moved away.

Indeed, having been at the front, I had been able to ascertain more than once that once someone was dead they were fine. If they had died an agonizing death, things were rather different. Basically, however, on completion of the process, there was still eternal rest. And so Evsey was fine. Especially since it had been straight to the heart.

There was a question for the living: what to do with the children? Three little boys and Belka on her own. Well, there was

Dovid, of course. But a mother's a mother and she was the one who would be primarily responsible for their food and clothing, their upbringing etc. But Belka ceded her position at lightning speed and at a single stroke.

Her work colleagues came to her assistance. They collected money. I did too. Lyubochka and I made a sizeable contribution from the little we had left. She spent every free minute with Belka and the children. She took Gannusya with her and did everything she could. In word and deed.

All in all it became clear that Belka had gone out of her mind. It was hardly surprising. But you can't explain to children why their mother has stopped speaking in words and is wailing and moaning. And that was just for starters.

The hut the children had built in the nearby woods during the summer became Belka's sanctuary. She sat there and sat there. In the cold and the rain, she sat, like a beaten dog. They took food out to her – Dovid or my Lyubochka did. They left it at the door and tried to persuade her to eat. She was having none of it. At night she came out, apparently to take a walk. Without popping into the house, to see the children. And they wept and wondered where Mummy was. And then there was the appalling neglect of sanitary regulations.

Dovid and I put our heads together and took the difficult decision to have Belka committed for a course of treatment at the hospital in Khalyavin.

The doctors said her condition might pass. There was a vague possibility of this happening.

Everyone has their own life to lead, however. For Lyubochka and me, life led us to take in the youngest boy, Iosif, aged two. Until such time as Belka was fully recovered. However long it took. As foster carers.

Dovid undertook to provide for Grigory and Vladimir. He gathered up all their clutter, sold Evsey and Belka's shack and his own little house with the good-sized vegetable garden and went off to Oster. Why Oster is unclear but to each his own. Apparently, it was under the influence of Zusel Tabachnik.

My colleagues were enthusiastic about the action Lyubochka and I had taken. They each tried to get involved, bringing produce from their vegetable gardens, home-made meals and so on. But food is only half the battle.

Shortly, a couple of months after she had gone into hospital, it became clear that Belka would not be restored to health. The doctors' verdict was harsh but honest. For which we were thankful. Too much hope was of no use to anyone. It only made things worse.

And so a son legally joined our family. For good, as Lyubochka and I promised one another and the boy himself. In Gannusya's presence.

The past receded into the distance and could only be seen as if through freezing fog.

And then, one Sunday, I set off for the market.

It was almost holiday time – New Year. With a long list from Lyubochka and in a joyful, festive frame of mind, I was walking along the lovely road that led past the former, badly bomb-damaged Pyatnitskaya Church. But white snow concealed the grievous wounds of war and it appeared not as a wasteland but as a landscape of velvet hills and dales and beneath was purity and, perhaps, the grass and flowers to come.

For some reason Didenko and his views on God came to mind. Was it really so baffling? If God existed, how he had befuddled his children's brains! Would He really have allowed such a war? He would not. Simple logic. I even stood still for a moment and inwardly and for Didenko's benefit I said firmly: 'Without logic, anything can add up. Any ends can meet. But with logic, they can't. There's no addling people's brains with logic.'

And at that point, Laevskaya descended upon me. In all her glory. A fox round her neck, a downy shawl, a good, tightly-waisted coat. White felt boots with a brown trim. And heels, too. And it was on these heels that she lost her balance, slipped and grabbed onto me.

She lifted her eyes heavenward and shrieked:

"Oy, Comrade Tsupkoy!"

"Tsupkoy, in person, yes," I said, "who else, Polina Lvovna, my dear, would hold on to you so that you don't go down with a real bang?!" I laughed heartily.

It was all high spirits.

A broad grin appeared on Laevskaya's painted mouth. I spotted a gold crown. That hadn't been there before. I would have noticed. A significant distinguishing feature.

"Mikhail Ivanovich. I've been planning to come and see you. With a little something for New Year."

And she said it as if she was offering charity.

My reply was curt.

"There's nothing we need. We've got everything. The children aren't short of food, clothes or shoes."

And I went on my way.

But Laevskaya wouldn't let go.

She pulled me back by the arm.

"It's not from me. It's from everyone. Evochka Vorobeichik wants you to have something too. Remember her? Poor Lilechka's sister? Do you?"

And, as was her custom, she stuck her bright red lips right in my face. The crown glittered. So did her beady pupils. What a fright!

I stopped.

"Right then, come on round. We're always in in the evening. It's too cold to go out. Come round. Not for long though. Yoska's not very well. And Gannusya's got a bad cough."

Laevskaya nodded understandingly and I had already gone past when she called after me in a loud whisper:

"You're quite simply a hero, Mikhail Ivanovich! Simply a hero. I tell everybody what a hero you are. An absolute hero. Absolutely. Yes, you are."

I don't know how many more times she said the word hero. My ears felt as blocked as if there had been an explosion.

Polina Lvovna arrived two days before the New Year, 1953. In the evening. At around ten, 2200 that is. Decent people do not show up at a family house at such a late hour. Not even with presents.

She cooed over the children. They were already asleep, as they should be. She melted particularly at the sight of Iosif. That's understandable – he was an orphan. The first spoonful goes to the orphan, as the saying has it. And quite right too. Obviously.

It really bothered Lyubochka that Laevskaya turned up without being asked when the children's sheets had seen better days. They were clean and warm but worn thin by prolonged use. Lyubochka herself had slept in them when she was little. She was about to change the bedding as a matter of urgency but I forbade it. They'd wake up and that was impermissible: ruining the children's lives in order to make a good impression. And it's in their sleep that they do most of their growing.

We went into the kitchen. Where I had a camp bed. I had already made it up. At least I hadn't taken my clothes off. I was in my uniform trousers and a vest. Let's be honest, I looked alright. But Lyubochka was in a housecoat. Not the finest quality, naturally. How on earth could we come by a luxury silk housecoat when we had two children? And Lyubochka had given up work because Iosif was a sickly child and Gannusya was picking up his ailments. The nursery didn't keep a proper eye on them. Not like their mother.

Laevskaya plonked herself down on a stool and cast her eye over our establishment.

Lyubochka began to offer tea and jam but Laevskaya smiled and sailed sturdily out into the corridor.

She came back with a laden bag.

She placed the gifts out on the table. Pork fat, several jars of home-made stew, about a kilo of carrots, four whole beetroot and a small bag of beans. And chocolate in a special wrapper. Not a bar but big chunks, dark and solid.

She said:

"The chocolate's for those little ones of yours. And for Lyubochka, naturally. As a mother, she needs it too. It's from Eva. Vorobeichik. She's taken up with this new young man. Something special, he is. He managed to get hold of it. Anyway, it doesn't matter now. What does matter is that it's reached you. Your table, so to speak."

Lyuba thanked her. I just hoped she wouldn't burst into tears. After all, we weren't starving. We had plenty to eat.

To Laevskaya, I said:

"Thank you, Polina Ivanovna, from the bottom of my heart. And don't you worry about the chocolate. Every single crumb will go to the children. I can give you a receipt. Lyubochka and I will sign it."

Laevskaya shook her head. Not even her whole head, just her face.

"Why do you want to insult me, Mikhail Ivanovich…? And in front of Lyubochka, too, a saint of a woman. I've no bones to pick with you. Your work's difficult and so is everything else. Things are hard for me too. If you only knew. But then, you do know."

And Polina Lvovna peeped up and into my eyes. In that way of hers. A particular way.

"I'm sorry I was late. But I've only just this minute got back. I was so shaken about in the lorry I thought it would shatter me, let alone the jars and tins. From Oster and straight here. Before the cold got to the food. It was given to me personally. By Dovid and that pal of his, Zusel Tabachnik."

And she touched my elbow. Seemingly by accident as usual. A current surged through me.

"How are our little Yosenka's brothers doing?"

Lyuba began to clear the jars and bags off the table. She was clearly trying not to hurry. But she did. I motioned with my eyes to try and make her sit down but she couldn't help herself.

Laevskaya continued:

"The children are fine, surrounded by affection. Their own grandfather – that's nothing to sneeze at. But don't you want to know about Belka?"

Lyubochka started.

"Of course, we do. Khalyavin's a long way for us to go. Especially in winter. But Misha and I were planning to visit. Weren't we, Misha?"

I answered honestly:

"Belka's not our concern just now. Even though she's ill and unhappy. We're trying to save her child. And save him we will."

Laevskaya nodded again in agreement.

"Uh-huh. You're saving him. Quite right too and that's what everyone thinks. But Belka's really poorly. She doesn't know herself. She keeps repeating one thing: 'Evsey didn't do it. Evsey didn't do it.' As to what she means by it, no-one has any idea.

"She's suffering from an obsessional delusion. That's what the doctors say. I didn't say anything at the hospital but myself I think it's as clear as day: Belka means Evsey didn't kill himself. That's what she's saying. And true enough, coming to terms with suicide, with the irresponsible action of the father of your children, is no easy task. So she's gone mad. What do you think, Mikhail Ivanovich? You're a law-enforcement agent. And I can tell you agree with me entirely. And if somebody asks – people do gossip as you know – that's exactly how I interpret Belka's words for anyone who's interested. And something else. Some good news of my own: Evochka Vorobeichik is coming to Chernigov for good. And Malka's coming with her. Evochka asked me to say a big hello and to pass on her very best wishes to you, Mikhail Ivanovich. Rest assured, you are surrounded with gratitude. On all sides. Even Zusel's praying for you. Of course, you'll find that amusing but I don't think it will do any harm. Especially when it's of his own accord. You had nothing to do with it. Let him say his prayers. And Dovid too. And they're teaching the children. So be it. They'll go to school and school will put them back on the right path. Anyway, I'll be off. I am free, not always, but you can pick a time. And the house is nice and warm. To give yourselves a break, you could always bring the little ones round to me for a while. Or I could come and collect them myself - take them out, give them something to eat and a wash. I know what to do. I had three of my own. Just a little bit older than yours. Girls, as it happens."

And she spoke with such delight about her slaughtered children that it was if she had brought them up and they had gone off to live in distant lands. And now, to replace them, she was asking to borrow one of ours.

Lyubochka couldn't take any more. Her eyes filled with tears.

"Thank you. Thank you, Polina Lvovna. Of course, we won't trouble you unless we need to but in an emergency -- of course. Thank you."

Laevskaya embraced her and nothing of my Lyubochka could be seen.

I went to see her out. I offered to accompany her all the way home but Polina Lvovna would have none of it.

I walked her through the darkest area, through the alley to the square, and she began to say her farewells.

I replied in the same spirit:

"Thank you and good-bye."

She waved right in my face. As if trying to clear away fog with her hand.

I walked off quickly. But I did look back. Laevskaya hadn't moved. She wasn't watching me. She was still standing there, just standing. Looking down at her feet. And the snow beneath.

Lyubochka couldn't sleep. She wanted to know how we could thank Polina Lvovna.

I assured her no special thanks were needed. People help other people. They had during the war. They were doing it still. Being grateful for too long on purpose puts you in a humiliating position. As if you didn't trust people to be kind. We just had to be decent people. And, if Laevskaya ever needed our help, up to and including shedding blood for her, then that's what we would do.

Lyuba was mollified by the example.

And now back to Evsey. A case was opened and immediately closed – it was obviously suicide.

But Laevskaya's chatter had set me thinking. I put together her various statements of an unsavoury bent and it emerged that she was casting aspersions on me. Over and over again. All the time. She wasn't even aware she was doing it or why.

Let's be honest. I hadn't forgotten my unsuccessful journey to Oster. Since returning from Ryabina, just in time for Evsey's funeral, I hadn't noticed any interest on Dovid's part in talking to me about anything other than the children and Belka. If something had been bothering him, it had vanished as a result of their family tragedy. Zusel didn't count. Halfwit.

When we drew up the paperwork for Iosif, Dovid signed everything on the spot. Thanks to my connections, the matter was settled in a jiffy. All in all, nothing connected Basin and me any more. Other than that Iosif's big brothers lived with him. But so what? Weren't there plenty of children farmed out to different families during the war? What were people meant to do now? Bring them all back into one big family to trundle along together?

Independently, I had thought a good deal thought about Gutin's death. As it turned out, I couldn't come up with anything that made sense. Evsey had lived an honest life. Everything above board. He loved Belka. And the children. Was well thought of at work.

I won't hide that I was glad he killed himself in my absence. As a police officer I realized that had I been in Chernigov at the time, they would have questioned me to death, plagued me with reports. I would have been the main interpreter of my best friend's actions. Who else should it be? Precisely! Who else?

On 31 December, I told Lyubochka I had work to do in an outlying district. In fact, I went to Khalyavin, to the psychiatric hospital.

The doctor in charge, Yuly Petrovich Dashevsky, was welcoming. He came to say hello himself. The smile never left his face. He said soothingly of Belka that she wasn't feeling herself. That in that state she was calm.

I wondered if she could get better.

Dashevsky assured me she couldn't.

I pressed the issue.

"Have there been cases of that happening?"

Yuly Petrovich thought for a moment then said,

"There was one case. Before the war we had a patient like that – Shtadler. He did recover his wits somewhat. Even though to begin with the doctors had thought him a hopeless case. Now, though, he's almost compos mentis. Incidentally, he's been in to see Bella. She's had lots of visitors by the way. Bearing in mind the nature of the establishment. Her father, naturally. Shtadler. Polina Lvovna Laevskaya. An attractive young woman – Eva Vorobeichik. And one other person – potentially one of our patients. I'm telling you as a doctor, we'll come across him at some time. I can find out the surname if you need it."

I asked:

"Does this future resident of yours sway as he walks? As if he's praying as he goes along, the way you do?

The doctor pricked up his ears.

"What does that mean, the way we do?"

"The Jewish way. You know."

Sheepishly, Yuly Petrovich muttered,

"Ah yes, of course."

"No need for further clarification. He's called Tabachnik. In his passport. In actual fact, who the hell knows? He's the sort that could do anything."

The doctor agreed.

"Quite so. Quite."

Belka was outside in the yard. Over a grey, flannelette gown, a jersey had been pulled on any which way. She had a warm scarf on her head, brown with a white trim. Felt boots without rubber protectors.

She didn't recognize me.

I didn't insist. I hung a string bag of goodies over her arm, over her clenched fist: a bun, some sweets with chewy centres. I stroked her shoulder.

For some reason, Belka immediately recognized the sweets in the bag.

"Chewy centres? My very favourites. Is Evsey's bed comfortable? Does he lie easy?"

I took out a sweet and popped it right into her slightly open mouth.

She chewed and, quite content, answered her own question.

"He does lie easy. He does."

There were only a few hours to go to New Year. I had to leave enough time to decorate the tree for the children.

There was no time for a proper conversation and no-one to have it with. Belka was a blank space. Blanker than Evsey in his coffin on his red calico pillow.

I was thinking. Everyone, and the investigator above all, wanted to know why Gutin shot himself. I had read the case file. It was very slim. It always is for a suicide. It set out in plain Russian: "For a number of reasons linked to his state of health." Reference materials appended.

Evsey hadn't been in the best of health. The effect of injuries and shell-shock. That's true. Headaches too.

He'd told me more than once:

"The way my poor head rattles is impossible to describe. Maybe I should shoot myself?"

I would say:

"You're your own boss. If you want to, you will."

And we would laugh about such a potential turn of events.

He would always go on to say, "No, Misha, my poorly head doesn't bother me when I'm making babies. Should I shoot myself because the rest of my life is less exciting? No, I'm going to live. And why not? I'm going to live – full stop!"

I knew the headaches didn't come into it. But I deliberately told the investigator about them. So the family would be left in peace, not tormented by formal questioning. And to put a stop to idle talk here, there and everywhere.

But there was idle talk, even so. Dovid and I agreed to stick to the most plausible version - Evsey's state of health. I drilled it into Belka too. She was still in more or less her right mind at the time.

She kept on repeating:

"Yes, of course, he was fed up with the headaches. I could see what he was going through. But still, Mishenka, tell me, just me, why did he do this to us?"

I squashed that right away.

"Get it into your head once and for all. When a man shoots himself or something, he's not doing it to those left behind, he's doing it to himself. And you keep your nose out of that last business of his. Shooting himself was his last, personal business."

Evidently, this explanation hadn't stuck in Belka's head. But another one had. Someone had drummed something into her that had confused everything in her female brain once and for all and it spilled from her mouth, like meat from a mincer: "Evsey didn't do it."

But what if we looked at this differently? What didn't Evsey do? Kill himself or someone else? In other words, perhaps someone believed Evsey had killed somebody or he really had but Belka didn't believe it: Evsey didn't do it. And he shot himself precisely because he didn't and someone had wrongly accused him of murder.

Or he really had killed someone and did away with himself in remorse. That is, he personally made certain that no-one would ever be any the wiser.

Another person might think that Evsey was the one who was murdered. That he didn't kill himself. Someone else did it.

People will imagine terrible things once they start to speculate. When there are no solid grounds, I mean.

But that what happened, in the final analysis, was a suicide had been ascertained as fact not only by the investigation but, above all, by medicine in every possible way and by the book. It was cast iron.

But now, there was Belka, her troubled mind protesting that Evsey was accused of an unknown murder. It wasn't just the fact of her husband's death that had driven her mad but the fact that he hadn't only killed himself but someone else as well.

And she had plenty of visitors. They even came a good distance, making the effort to listen to a sick woman. And people will talk.

Who were these visitors? Laevskaya. Zusel. Dovid. Shtadler who had no tongue. Evka Vorobeichik.

The assortment of names in itself told me the woman who was murdered in the spring was back on the scene. Lilia Vorobeichik.

And some of the above-mentioned comrades most probably brought up Evsey's name in connection with her murder. As if he had killed her and I, Police Captain Mikhail Ivanovich Tsupkoy, as a faithful comrade-in-arms, had stymied the case.

And along they came. At first, they had prattled about me. That didn't work. They started on Evsey.

True, Dovid was his father-in-law. But everyone knew he could be far too stubborn and principled on certain matters.

And what was especially annoying was that first it was Moiseenko, a travelling player, and now it was Evsey.

People have no staying power. They just don't. Although they should. We had the staying power to get through the war. Yet now, they can't cope with ordinary life! They don't want to. They've gone soft.

I searched back through my memory and reached one conclusion after another.

One. All of them – Belka's visitors in the loony bin – were after one thing.

Two. What was that one thing?

Three. Clearly – the late Vorobeichik was at the root of it.

That was the main thing. That was the root cause. And it was making me feel as if every tooth in my head ached. I was in pain but just which tooth was aching I couldn't say for certain.

Never mind. I'd have to take it one tooth at a time. One by one. Tap them with a hammer and I'd find the culprit. It would take some patience. But I'd been patient through worse things.

At home, Lyubochka had decorated the tree without me. To be honest, she was still adding the finishing touches. The children were helping. Bringing her simple decorations. Most of them made of paper. But pretty and brightly-coloured. Just after Gannusya was born, Lyubochka decided she would put a tree up every year. She made the baubles herself. She collected the silver paper from packets of tea – a rarity, of course, but over four years she had acquired enough baubles to make things look festive. Lyubochka had the idea of wrapping little bits of chocolate, from the chocolate Laevskaya brought, in some of the silver paper she'd collected over the past year. She told me about the chocolate in a whisper so the children didn't hear. That was the main treat and we hung it the branches, right at the bottom, when the children were in bed. For them the main event was 1st January, New Year's Day, and finding presents under the tree. For the grown-ups, it was New Year's Eve. In the morning, of course, there was nothing new for the grown-ups except the date in the calendar. And the dreams they'd had that night.

Lyubochka and I celebrated in the kitchen. Afterwards we lay so close together on my camp bed, we were like a single person.

It was then that Lyubochka confessed she was expecting a baby. It was very early days but she was. She wanted to know how I felt.

I said I welcomed it with all my heart, positively and with pleasure. Despite the impending hardships.

Lyubochka went into the other room. It was where she and Gannusya slept nowadays, sharing a bed, while Iosif had taken over Gannusya's old room. For an instant, I was sorry I wouldn't be spending the whole night alongside my wife on such a momentous family occasion. But the interests of the child, by which I mean Iosif, required that he have his comforts. I consoled myself with this thought and fell into a deep sleep.

Next morning, the children were nibbling at their chocolate. Gannusya was wearing a new frock. It had been given to Lyubochka by a friend whose daughter had outgrown it. Iosif was playing with a teddy bear: red velvet, its eyes black beads. I'd bought it in a shop. A bit pricey, to be sure, but the boy needed a treat. Something special. Something new. Although he couldn't tell the difference between a new toy and an old one. But the grown-ups could. I wanted everything Iosif had to be new.

Lyubochka and I had tacitly agreed beforehand that we wouldn't give each other presents. And yet she had given me a present! She'll put herself out, as they say, just to make me happy.

The year had started well. Confidently.

Then, just as we were thinking we would get through the winter without any major childhood illnesses, there was something the matter with Iosif. Lyubochka and I spent the whole night at his bedside. He didn't get any better.

We called an ambulance. They diagnosed a fever. Swollen glands behind the boy's ears. Mumps, in other words. Where from? How? A mystery. It always is. That's the trouble.

Iosif had to be quarantined. Even Lyubochka realized that. And not just from Gannusya either - our little girl still hadn't had that particular childhood illness yet – but from Lyubochka herself as well. She didn't know for certain whether she'd had it and there was no-one to ask. If she picked up the infection, the baby in her womb could be affected too.

However, her reply to the doctors was categorical – no, she was not letting the boy go to hospital.

The doctor departed. A woman of Jewish nationality, it seemed. That's just by the bye.

I tried to persuade Lyubochka to let Iosif go to hospital. I got nowhere. She was beset by sheer terror that doctors at the hospital would do away with the child. Plainly. The effect of the murderers in white coats.

At that point I said:

"Put the worry out of your mind. Think rationally. Let's say there are murderers there. They won't take action against one of their own."

"He's not theirs. He's ours. Our little Yosenka."

"Well, effectively, yes. But everyone in town knows we took him off Belka Gutina."

"But what if there's someone who doesn't know? Someone new or something?"

"Well, if there's a new person, he'll see the lad's been circumcised straight away. Which means he's a little Jew. They won't treat him."

Lyuba appeared to have agreed but it was mostly in words while her eyes told me a different story. "I won't hand him over" is what I read there. And from that to Belka wasn't so great a distance.

I have to say that she had always singled Iosif out among Evsey's and Belka's children. So had Gannusya. He had blue eyes, chestnut curls, was always smiling. Of course, a woman is always happy to dream of a little son like that.

When the issue of adoption came up, I never doubted Lyubochka. I was simply surprised at how attached it was possible to become to someone else's child. But attached she was. And now perhaps there was a little lad of our own in her belly and probably no worse than Yosya in appearance and everything and yet there she was, prepared to put her own child at risk for the sake, let's be honest, of a fosterling.

In desperation, I wanted to tell her how I felt but I managed to get a grip on myself.

"Fine," I said. "This is an emergency. Laevskaya offered to take the children in if something happened. And it's only one of them. True, he's poorly but that doesn't matter. I'll try and persuade her. She won't say no."

Lyuba thought rapidly and agreed.

I don't know myself why I brought Laevskaya into it. Especially with Jewish murderers in the hospital and Laevskaya too, let's be honest, was one-hundred-per-cent Jewish. I'd got her on the brain and just blurted it out. Then immediately regretted it. But there was no going back.

Lyuba brightened up. She asked me to run over to Polina Lvovna, negotiate with her, win her round.

I hurried off to Laevskaya's.

I took every short cut I could. She lived in the Five Corners area. A good way from Kotsyubinsky Street but that didn't matter.

Polina Lvovna was doing the housework. No cupid's bow painted on her lips, hair all over the place. But wearing a silk housecoat with a dragon pattern. Silk slippers too, red ones, with kitten heels even. I looked her up and down automatically although I couldn't give a damn.

I spoke from the doorstep, without so much as a "hello" or anything else.

"Lyubochka and I are in trouble."

She nearly collapsed. She felt for a wooden chair, pulled it towards her. Flopped down.

"Is it the children?"

"Yes, Polina Lvovna. Iosif. He's not well and he's simply not going into hospital. Lyuba won't hear of it. But our little chap really needs to be strictly quarantined away from Gannusya and Lyuba herself. She's pregnant. There's a risk of infection. Take him in. I'll pay you. I'll arrange with the doctors for them to come to you. To him, I mean. I'll come over and sit with him at night. If you can just provide the space."

"Alright," she replied serenely. "We'll go and get him now. I'll make arrangements with the doctors myself. One of them's a customer. She won't say no. She's a children's doctor. But why can't he go into hospital?"

I didn't know what to say. Unpardonably, I hesitated.

I forced out an answer.

"You know, Polina Ivanovna, it's the times we live in. People are frightened. And with good reason. Let's not get into that. But the facts are plain to see. You do read the papers, after all."

She raised her head and looked at me from where she sat, as though from a height I could never scale. Even though I was standing at my full height by the door. And yet she managed to scowl down at me. She scowled then paused, looking at my face. She said nothing.

Then, wheezing a little, she said:

"Ah, well, of course. Those, what do you call them, in white coats, they're there. Jews. Of course. I know. Don't worry, Mikhail Ivanovich, my dear. They're doctors. They've been trained to take lives. But I'm not a doctor and nothing like one. I've been a mother myself. A Jewish mother. You could say, I'm just a Jew without a coat. Without a white one, at least. Can you tell colours apart properly? What colour am I wearing?"

She ran a hand over the embroidered silk from her bosom down and clenched a chubby little fist against her fat thigh.

And that chubby little fist summed everything up.

"Well, will she do, this Jew lady?"

I didn't mince my words.

"She'll do. When you're saving a child, anyone will."

She turned away. So sharply, the stool creaked with the strain.

And her voice was different, not the nasty tone she usually took with me. She said:

"That's true. When you're saving children - anyone will do. Anyone at all."

Laevskaya was ready in the blink of an eye. She took the bus to go to Lyubochka. It had just pulled up at the bus stop. I flagged down a car to transport Iosif from Kotsyubinsky Street to Five Corners.

As I drove home to pick up Iosif and Laevskaya, I thought I'd been too hasty. I could have taken Iosif to the hospital and merely told Lyubochka we'd gone to Laevskaya's.

Immediately I realized that was a stupid idea. It would never work. Lyubochka would want to visit, at least once, and then what? No, I'd done the right thing. I regretted that, in the heat of the moment, I'd let slip the news about Lyuba's pregnancy, but overall, I'd done the right thing.

Laevskaya did as she had promised. And so did I.

We decided I wouldn't drop in every day and would keep my distance when I did in case I became a carrier of the infection myself.

The treatment was proceeding at a good pace as is the nature of these things.

Laevskaya took it upon herself to provide a nourishing diet, medicine and nursing care. I naturally planned to repay her down to the very last kopeck from my next pay packet.

Indeed, she'd said:

"That's fine. I've enough for now. If I haven't, I'll get it from Evochka."

Meaning Eva Vorobeichik.

I automatically inquired what Eva was doing, where her income came from now that she'd moved, whether she'd found work.

Polina Lvovna briefly explained that Eva had gone to the shoe factory where Lilya used to work and had, in fact, taken her place on the assembly line.

I nodded.

"So she's spreading the glue on the last too, is she? And is it nice and thick or are they still adding wood chips to make it go further?"

Laevskaya seized on this.

"How do you know that Lilechka used to apply the glue, Mikhail Ivanovich?"

I said nothing. Never answer loaded questions. Not ever. What did it matter how I knew? Incidentally, I knew lots of things.

"Polina Lvovna, in case you've forgotten, I would remind you that I personally conducted the investigation into Lilka's case. I went to the factory. And I spoke to the collective. And watched the whole working process. I even lifted some pieces off the assembly line. I wasn't afraid to get my hands dirty."

"Now, now, goodness me! I didn't mean to ruffle your feathers. I didn't mean anything at all. Evochka also talks to Lilechka's comrades a lot. They have a lot to tell her as the dead woman's sister. Aren't you interested? I could tell you. Or Evochka could tell you herself. Would you like that?"

To put a stop to any more unnecessary comments, I said,

"When the time comes, I'll ask myself. And she'll be as good as gold and tell me. And I'll question the work force again if I think it necessary."

Laevskaya raised her arms in a gesture of surrender. The sleeves of her housecoat rode up high. I noticed that from the elbows down her arms had become even fatter and a bit flabby. When she was talking, she would often move her hands in all kinds of ways. You couldn't fail to notice. Yes, she was no longer such a young woman. And yet she put on airs. I felt sorry for her but what can you do?

Mentally, I lost the thread for a second.

Laevskaya continued in the same vein.

"Oh, how cross you are and how rude you were about Lilechka too – Lilka's case! She's not Lilka to you, she's Lilia Solomonovna Vorobeichik, murdered by criminals in the yard of her own place of residence in broad daylight."

At first, she seemed to be joking but her tone was unpleasant by the end. Really unpleasant.

I looked at her sternly and made a suggestion.

"Polina Lvovna, while you're talking, there's a sick child to think about. Let's not be distracted by nonsense."

Immediately her face changed. She began to talk about Iosif.

We said our farewells fondly. I promised to be back the day after next but asked her to contact me immediately at work if anything happened.

Laevskaya nodded towards a scrap of paper, tucked behind a three-way mirror. My work number was written on it

"But of course, I remember," she said. "Of course, I do. Don't worry."

I had gone to see Polina Lvovna early in the morning. The telephone rang at dinner time. But it wasn't her.

It was Eva Vorobeichik.

"Mikhail Ivanovich, please, come quickly. There's no time to explain. Hurry!"

I didn't even ask where to go. I knew it was to Polina Lvovna's.

One of our lads on a motorbike dropped me off in double quick time.

I raced into the house to find a whole gathering there. Zusel Tabachnik, Dovid, Eva Vorobeichik, Malka Tsvintar. Rattling away in their own tongue.

I yelled over them.

"Shut up, the lot of you! Where's the boy?"

They fell as silent as if they'd been shot.

Eva spoke in the silence.

"The boy's fine. He's been asleep. He's probably not asleep any more. He's playing. Polina Lvovna's with him."

Dovid waded in.

"Shut up, Evka, you idiot! It's nothing to do with you. I'm the boy's legitimate grandfather. You're no-one, any of you. I'll do the talking."

I realized that nothing particularly frightening, like a death, had happened. And so I calmed down.

I had some advice for the others, too:

"Alright, talk, but take it in turns. I'm going to pop in on the little lad and then I'll listen to what you've got to say."

Polina Lvovna was sitting in the room that contained Iosif. She was working placidly on some sewing. The child was on the bed, propped up on pillows so that he didn't fall off, playing with his teddy. When he saw me, he was thrilled. He grabbed his teddy by the paw and threw it suddenly up in the air in a sign of welcome. I leapt in the right direction and caught it. I threw it back. The little boy caught it too.

Even though it was against quarantine regulations, I hugged Iosif, smothered him in kisses.

Polina Lvovna remarked gently, "I asked Eva to call you. Go back to them. I'll stay here."

I went back into the room.

I sat down at the table. I put my hands out in front of me. Firmly, palms down. For show, of course.

I said:

"Right, off you go. I'm listening. But I'm warning you. There's a sick child in this house. Bear that in mind."

Dovid stepped forward.

At that moment, I realized they had all formed a line in front of me. They looked comical.

"Why are you all standing in a line? Sit down! There are plenty of seats. Have a seat, Dovid Srulevich. You too, comrades, sit down."

No-one moved.

Dovid began.

"I am here as of right, being the nearest blood relation. I am Iosif's grandfather. You, Mikhail Ivanovich, taking advantage partly of your official position and partly of my distressed state following the tragic death of my son-in-law and the illness of my very own daughter, Bella, have appropriated my dear grandson, Iosif Gutin. And now, rather than permitting him medical treatment like any Soviet child, you have shut him up in the home of Polina Lvovna Laevskaya. I will be bringing a complaint against you and demanding the return of my grandson."

I sat there through the whole of Basin's speech. Raving nonsense. I nodded in agreement, ran a hand over the crocheted tablecloth. A couple of times I traced a pattern with my finger.

I said:

"Is there anything you would like to add, Dovid Srulevich?"

Basin said nothing.

"Next then. Who's next? You, perhaps, Citizen Tabachnik?"

Zusel said nothing. He was shifting from one foot to the other, moving his lips, speaking to himself rather than the outside world.

"Fine. Next then. Citizen Vorobeichik, what do you have to say?"

Eva said nothing. She looked me right in the eye, revealing no thoughts or expressions.

"It seems that leaves you, Citizen Tsvintar."

But Malka said nothing either, folding her arms beneath her apron, lips tightly sealed. She was swaying but said nothing.

I was livid.

"Sit down, for goodness' sake. What a circus. And real clowns too. Sit, I said. The lot of you, sit down!"

I yelled so loudly the echo bounced back off the ceiling.

Iosif began to cry. Polina leapt out, sewing in hand.

They sat where they could around the room but left an empty space around me. As if on purpose. Behind the table, I was on my own.

Evka propped her buttocks on the windowsill behind me. Zusel was right in front of me on a stool by the stove, Dovid next to him on a small bench.

Malka muttered:

"Ooh, I don't feel very well. I'm going to have a little lie-down." And she curled up on a couch.

Polina went back to the little boy. She showed no sign of surprise or anything. She simply looked to see that everyone had calmed down. Satisfied, she gave me a nod and sailed out.

"And so that no-one else feels poorly, let's not have any shouting. What's dragged you over here? If it's what Dovid was saying, then it's a load of old codswallop. Go back to where you came from. If there's anything else, let's be having it. But I don't have time to chew the fat with you. My time's not my own. I should be at work. So?"

It was Eva who spoke. I deliberately didn't turn at the sound of her voice, just pricked up my ears.

"To start with, Dovid went round to see you at home and Lyuba told him the little boy was here. So he came here. To Polina Lvovna's. She sent me to ring you."

I was already running out of patience.

"I see. So why the whole mishpocha? Dovid, fine. Nonsense aside. But Tabachnik? And you and Malka? Are you completely joined at the hip? Aren't you capable of moving around independently like normal people?"

Dovid said:

"We've come for what's ours."

I shouted, circumstances notwithstanding.

"Who is this 'we'? Give me the names of this 'we', Dovid Srulevich! Their names! Collective complaints are not accepted in this country."

Dovid complied. What's more, he counted them off on his fingers:

"Me, that's one. Zusel – two. On Belka's orders. So on her behalf. As proxies. That's three."

I turned to face Evka.

"And you, Eva, are you next on the list or what?"

"No," Eva said. "I'm against it. And I'm speaking for Malka too. She's against it as well."

I stood and walked over to Malka. She was pretending to be taking a nap. I touched her shoulder – politely.

"Malka, are you for or against?"

She unglued her eyes and burbled something.

"Dovid, translate."

"I don't have to. This isn't a formal interview."

I asked tightly:

"What on earth is going on here, folks?! Not a formal interview! If you want a formal interview, you can have a formal interview! You come along en masse to someone else's house. Where there's a sick child who has nothing to do with you. You stage a riot. Drag me away from work. You've frightened my wife to death, no doubt…"

And then it hit me like a thunderbolt: Lyubochka would be all upset and there I was chatting away to crazy people.

"What did you say to Lyuba? And make it snappy, Dovid!"

"I didn't say anything particular. I said I'd come for Iosif. She cried out and she fell down. I splashed water on her face and she got up. And came at me with her fists. I'm not faulting her. I held her tightly by the arms and asked where the boy was. Your Gannusya said he was at Auntie Polina's – poorly. Zusel and I came here. Evka and Malka were making a fuss of the little boy, helping out."

I didn't stop to hear any more. I raced back to Lyubochka. As I went, I cursed myself a hundred times over.

Lyuba was lying on the bed. As white as a sheet. Eyes closed. Gannusya was on the floor next to her. Face snuggled against her small fists, she was asleep.

I shook Gannusya first. She lifted up her face, tearstained and sleepy. Then I called Lyuba gently. She said nothing, just groaned.

And pointed to the lower part of her belly.

"You look. I'm too scared. Look. I'm wet. It must be blood."

She was right. Blood and everything.

Lyuba had to go to hospital - fast.

Carrying Gannusya, I ran full tilt to Laevskaya's. I was determined to shoot Dovid and Zusel right there and then. Or to strangle them with my bare hands. But they had vanished without trace.

Evka and Malka were fussing over Iosif.

Laevskaya had gone out. They couldn't explain where. I asked them to keep an eye on Gannusya until the evening.

Evka came out into the yard with me.

I grabbed her by the hand.

"You'll pay with your life if anything happens to my children."

Eva nodded her assent and made a face.

"Of course, Mikhail Ivanovich. Are you going to follow Dovid to Oster or what? If you do, I'll come too. Someone will have to look after the little boys if you're bringing Dovid in. But keep away from Zusel. He's crazy. But still, that's up to you."

I looked at her.

I didn't explain about Lyuba. Evka wasn't that kind of person. I'd recognized that immediately. As soon as I saw her and not Lilka by the gate, I'd realized it then.

I dashed off to the hospital and Lyubochka.

The doctor calmed me down. The sentence was only suspended though. You can't bring the baby back, the doctor said. But Lyubochka will recover.

The doctor was well on in years. He'd seen it all before. It was easy for him to say.

I said the first thing that came into my head in order to show somehow that I was holding up, rather than snivelling.

"That's good, Comrade Doctor. That's good."

He answered with a gentle little smile.

"Good-schmood, but in all probability you and your wife will never have children. Do you have other children already?"

"Yes. A daughter."

"Then go and bring up your daughter."

He turned around and went about his business.

I started inwardly. What about Yoska? Why hadn't I told the doctor about him?

And the yell I gave was as if I was going over the top unarmed.

"We've got two children. Two!"

The doctor turned and waved at me.

"Now, now, calm down. If it's two, fine. If it's one, fine. We'll keep your wife here for about a week then discharge her."

I dropped into work. I asked for a couple of days of unpaid leave. Seeing the way I looked, no-one asked any questions.

And I didn't say anything.

I went to see Lyuba three times a day. I stayed until the ward assistants drove me out.

In between, I went to Laevskaya's. Gannusya was with her round the clock. She asked to go and see mummy at the hospital but I didn't take her. I explained that mummy had a cold and was in quarantine.

The danger of catching Yoska's illness was over and Gannusya played all sorts of games with him.

I hadn't forgotten Dovid and his gang. I wasn't angry. But I hadn't forgotten, not for a single minute.

One thing I did say to Lyuba:

"Unless we decide for ourselves right now that what happened was an accidental occurrence, we'll never get over it. It would be the easiest thing in the world to shift the blame from Dovid to Yoska. But we're not going to do that. We're not going to shift the blame. Even Dovid's not to blame. After all, he didn't know you were expecting. I'd have him behind bars like a shot. I don't want that. But do you?"

"No. I want everything to stay the same. That's what I want. Dovid can't give me my baby back. Even if you sent him to jail or something."

"That's a sound argument. And, what's more, you could have fallen anyway or twisted out of the way of a car or lifted something heavy. The baby wasn't attached securely. Just by the thinnest of threads. Right? If it had been really securely attached, nothing would have happened. That's right, isn't it, Lyubochka?"

She nodded at each word.

"Yes, Mishenka, it can't have been securely attached. That's what the women advised me to think too. And I do. We'll have more babies. We're only young. There are women in here who are nearly 40. Still having babies."

I realized that I now had a secret from Lyubochka in relation to what I knew that she didn't. The doctor had told me man to man. But presumably for medical reasons, she wasn't supposed to know. About future children.

This inspired me, even. Lyuba still had hope. That would do for now.

Yosya's illness cleared up. Our family was reunited once again. I buried myself in my work. I didn't come across Laevskaya or Evka or the rest. And there was no reason why I should.

I received a letter from Didenko in Ryabina. He described his failing health and sent greetings from Blind Petro. He also asked whether I had any news about Zusel.

I was so fed up of them all that I couldn't even be bothered with the letter and its stupid question. It might be entertaining for the old man to quiz me about Zusel but it just got on my nerves.

I had no intention of answering. I don't like tittle-tattle of any kind, particularly in written form. My work has taught me: "the written word for aye lives on…"

In terms of her inner state of mind, Lyubochka was not well. She cried frequently. Not where people could see of course, but tucked away somewhere. She mentioned something about going back to work, wanting to be with her work collective where she could lose herself and her thoughts. I forbade her even to dream about working, reminded her that we had two whole children and they needed a mother at home not a shock worker on the shop-floor.

Lyubochka devoted herself entirely to the children. She turned their inevitable scratches into tragedies. I joked once that she shouldn't worry so much about it – bumps and bruises were part of growing up.

In reply she said she knew these things passed but when she put ointment on the children's cuts and bruises she felt as if she was putting it inside herself to stop an infection spreading inside.

I wondered what infection she meant and what the children had to do with it.

At which point, Lyubochka said:

"When Yosya was at Laevskaya's, they put a secret infection inside him. He's fine but we, the people close to him, can catch it. That's why I have to put the ointment on. Not to stop an infection getting in through a scratch but so that it can't come out through the blood."

I asked for more detail:

"Well, fine, let's accept that. But what have your insides got to do with it that so that you have to act as if you're putting ointment on them, cauterizing them?"

Lyuba mysteriously replied that she was indeed infected. Which was why she was trying not to come too close to me and so on, so as not to pass the infection on to me.

I had one last question.

"Has Gannusya got it?"

Lyuba assured me she hadn't. Only she, Lyuba, had. But she adored Yosenka and was prepared to suffer all her life to keep on caring for him.

At that point I had her in a corner.

"Fine, let's say it's true. But what about me? Why didn't you tell me before?"

Here Lyuba set out her main argument:

"You won't catch anything."

"Why not? How am I any better than you?"

"You're not."

And she looked at me for a long time.

And confessed:

"When Dovid came to take Yosenka away, he told me literally, 'After Lilka Vorobeichik your husband has nothing to lose. Laevskaya thinks he has but I've told her he hasn't. But you, Lyuba, you do have something to lose. You've got Gannusya. And Ioska's contaminated. Give him back to me.' So, I thought and thought all the time I was in hospital, and I'm still turning his words over and over."

All in all, this was madness if not worse. Why 'after Lilia Vorobeichik'? What had she got to do with it? It was obvious even without a doctor: going through a great tragedy is extremely difficult. Lyubochka needed to recover. To take her mind right away from real life. To look at nature, at a stream, at birds and animals. The children would manage. They'd grow of their own accord and pull Lyuba along in their wake. And pull her through. The way we did with the country after the last war. Could a brace of children really not do the same for just one woman?

Although I understood: a mother's heart is a special case. A case, so to speak, that nature handles with its own special proceedings.

The financial situation didn't stretch to resorts and sanatoriums. Although these were urgently required.

I thought for a while then took a firm decision: to send Lyubochka and the children to Ryabina. After all, it was my home. And there's nothing better for pain than going home.

I planned to put them up at Didenko's house. From spring through autumn.

I wrote. I received an answer. A delighted invitation for the rest of our lives if necessary.

I sent my family off at the beginning of May.

And at that very moment, who should appear on my horizon but Laevskaya. I don't think it was by accident. Most likely she'd found out that I was on my own.

Furthermore, she knocked at the door very gently, scratched at it even. But I opened it and pretended I was pleased to see her.

"So, Mikhail Ivanovich, were you expecting someone, you answered so quickly. I knocked quietly. I didn't expect you to be in. That bell of yours is too loud, I remember, so I tapped ever so gently. So as not to disturb the little ones or Lyubochka."

She came in uninvited, pretending to inspect the place.

"Ah… so, you're all alone. Where's the family?"

"Not here. On holiday."

"And where have they gone?"

"A long way away, Polina Lvovna. Never you mind. Let's be honest, it's none of your business. I'm sorry but it's really not. Please, have a seat. I can at least be hospitable. Offer you a cup of tea. You did us a great service. Our son got better because the doctors knew what they were doing. Thank you for that. But otherwise, you understand, I find it difficult talking to you. After what Dovid did and everything."

"I understand. I do, a thousand times over, I understand. And I'm not offended. But I had been planning to come and see Yosenka for ages. I won't talk about Lyubochka since you don't like it. But the little lad's very dear to me. You know, when you've looked after them when they're ill, other people's children become your own. As for Dovid, he's within his rights. Perhaps if there hadn't been such haste to sign Yosenko over to you legally at the time, Dovid wouldn't be letting you have him now for anything. Fine. I'm not going to get you all agitated. You're clutching the table so tightly, your knuckles have gone white. You think you're the only one suffering. I'm suffering too. The things that are happening in this country. One sorrow after another. With Comrade Stalin dead and everything. Everything's reeling. Literally everything. But people want something to hang on to. Isn't that so?"

I had to admit: Polina Lvovna was right in what she said. And she had put it gently, beautifully and kindly.

But I interrupted:

"That's enough. You don't want tea and I don't have any fruit liquor. I don't have the strength to be with or think about anyone any more. Not you, not Dovid, not Eva Vorobeichik and her minions. For the past – I'm grateful but in future, leave me alone."

A small smile spread across Laevskaya's face.

"There, there, of course. The future is the main thing, absolutely. Everything's for the sake of the future. Who could argue with that? I don't know why, Mikhail Ivanovich, but you suddenly brought up Evka Vorobeichik. And I have just stumbled upon a thought in my mind. It came into my mind, I mean. When the Strizhen flooded, it was in the middle of April, there were youngsters out playing near the hospital, under the White Bridge. Just as Evochka and I were going for a walk. So, anyway, these lads were fooling around, poking sticks near the water. And one of them found a knife. Just like that. We had a look. It was Lilka's. Lilka definitely had one just like it. Of course, it had been damaged by the water and the mud. But it was Lilka's. And they found it near Lilka's house, on the other side of the bridge. I just thought, 'What if you could do with that information?' I've got the knife. The boy let me have it if I paid him. I know him, as it happens. He lives not far from poor dead Lilya's, in a decent, working family. Incidentally, his Dad, Sergey Nikolayevich Khrobak, is a friend of Eva's. And, you know, a friend who thinks the world of her. In a neighbourly way, of course, but he really does."

I was astonished.

"Can you afford to pour money down the drain like that, Polina Lvovna? You've bought a rusty knife and you're boasting about it. And where did you get the idea that it belonged to Lilka?"

"Not to Lilka – to murder victim Citizen Vorobeichik. I've come to see you at home so as not to cause you any official difficulties at work. It's is the murder weapon, which means you didn't look for it properly. But I've found it. I've found it and I am now saying for certain that this knife belonged to murder victim Citizen Vorobeichik. Because at her house, where the sister and auntie of the late woman are now the officially registered residents, there are another two knives just like it. I know who made them too and not so very long ago. And I took the one I'd found with the help of Tarasik Khrobak, a minor, to that knife-maker and personally showed it to him without any explanation. I told him I wanted to order one like it and had brought it along as a sample, ignoring the mud. And the craftsman recognized his work. But since it's of no interest to you, I'll be off now. But, my dear Mikhail Ivanovich, don't think I have any hard feelings. Not about your behaviour towards me or anything else. It will soon have been a year without Lilya. And here's this knife. Now there's a coincidence. Goodbye. Regards to Lyubochka and the children."

I made no attempt to hold her back.

She waved farewell, her hand in a black glove. A very fine glove, covered in tiny holes. And there was a slit in the right one, near the thumb, on the back. A long slit. Indecent on a woman like Laevskaya.

Polina Lvovna glanced at the slit and said brightly,

"Oh and I ruined my glove with that knife. I was too quick to grab hold of the blade. The lace is so delicate. The gloves were brought back from Germany."

She left. And then it occurred to me: it was cold in the middle of April. People don't go wandering around in lace gloves. Especially not Laevskaya. She had a pair for every kind of weather. Perhaps she'd ruined the glove on purpose in order to drop it into the story. Or had had it for a long time but only produced it now.

If there was one thing I was pleased about that night it was that I could sleep. And sleep I did. And I didn't dream. My heart didn't ache. Nothing did. As for Laevskaya's blasted knife and her German glove, I couldn't give a damn. I just wanted to forget about them.

I worked selflessly at my post. No-one could have accused me. Then along comes Laevskaya and sticks her knife in.

Asleep, I felt nothing but in the morning it had sunk in.

It was Sunday as it happens.

I set off to see her with a single intention: to collect a potential piece of physical evidence.

Informally, without any unnecessary paperwork or records. Of course, it was an infraction. But we're only human.

And there I was, at her place.

And who should I see but Eva being fitted for a dress. No embarrassment, nothing.

Laevskaya was beetling about, busy with women's talk. To me, she just said:

"Wait in the kitchen, please, Mikhail Ivanovich. Or outside. The sun's nice and warm. Enjoy the fresh air."

I turned round to leave altogether.

Behind me, there was a loud squeal from Eva:

"Oh, for goodness sake, the tacking's come out!"

Polina began clucking. Eva laughed like a drain. In spite of myself, I looked round.

Eva stood in nothing but a slinky set of camiknickers, lifting up not her dress but her thick red hair. Hair just like that of Vorobeichik, the murder victim.

Outside I decided there was no need to be angry. Women. They hadn't meant to offend me.

Through the open door, I shouted:

"Can I come in?"

"Yes, yes."

Evka and Polina Lvovna granted permission as one.

And there they both were, looking at me and waiting. To see what I would say.

"Polina Lvovna," I said,

"I'm here on important business. Is Eva about to leave?"

Evka threw back her head.

"Why are you asking Polina Lvovna? Ask me. I'll tell you. I'm not leaving. I'll be here all day. I need that dress ready by tomorrow morning."

Polina simpered. That's right.

No need to be embarrassed. You can ask anything you like in front of Eva. You haven't come courting me, have you?"

This stupid question revealed so much nastiness in her that out of spite I answered:

"And what if I had?"

"Then I don't know. You make me blush, Mikhail Ivanovich. You can't take a joke. I noticed that ages ago. So, what does bring you here, my dear?"

I had no doubt the matter of the knife had be dealt with one to one.

It was as if Polina Lvovna had read my mind.

"It's about the knife. Yes, yes, that's it. Lilechka's knife. Don't be shy. Evochka and I were walking along the river bank together. She knows all about it."

I said nothing. I hadn't prepared properly. That was bad. My nerves weren't what they used to be.

What I said was:

"I don't give a damn about your knife. I have plenty of evidence in the Vorobeichik case without it. We know who killed her. Roman Moiseenko. That's not the point. The point is that you are allowing a gang to gather around you. A regular gang. You've brought my wife to a state of complete collapse. For instance."

Laevskaya folded her fat arms across her bosom. Like a monument. There'd be no budging her.

"Fine. Go on."

"And then there's the fact, Polina Lvovna, that I know my duty. But you don't know yours. And you're confusing everyone. Your duty is to keep your head down and your mouth shut."

Polina Lvovna's eyes widened and she pursed her lips. Daubed a bright, greasy red.

"Whoa, that's certainly loosened your tongue. So much restraint and then bang! Evochka, sweetie, go on home. I'll finish off myself."

Evochka took off like a scalded cat.

I watched her go.

Polina giggled.

"What, d'you fancy her? You're not the only one to have taken a shine to our Evochka. Anyway, fine. I'm not giving you the knife. I changed my mind yesterday. I'll keep it in loving memory of Lilechka. But what's got you in such a stew? Since Moiseenko killed her, Moiseenko has paid the price: death by suicide. You do take your work very much personally to heart. I'm the one Lilechka was close to. She was nothing to you. That's true, isn't it? Tell me."

"Nothing, to be honest," I said. "A blank space. But work is work."

Polina burst out laughing and unfolded her arms from her bosom. As if freeing herself from a boulder.

"What about a drop of liquor? Evochka and I had a glass each. A thimbleful. As for Lilya, say no more. On that score, you're undoubtedly right. And the knife I found, to hell with it. It's no use to you. Everything's clear even without it. But Gutin, now there's a murky business. I went to Oster. To see Dovid. He and I are a good fit somehow. One way and another. Life goes on. After all, you wanted to match me with him yourself once. Do you remember?"

"I do. And please, don't be angry with me either, Polina Lvovna."

I pretended to believe her. In return, Polina pretended to accept that belief.

"Goodbye. All the best."

Polina replied happily, "Yes, yes, goodbye, goodbye. Just imagine, Mikhail Ivanovich, Dovid's come up with the idea that you shot Gutin. Specifically and in person. How I laughed…"

I stood stock still.

"What? Have you gone stark, staring mad?! I wasn't in town. Or anywhere near it. What's it got to do with me?"

Polina flushed deeply. Drops of sweat even appeared above the red bow of her lips.

"Precisely. Everyone's gone a little mad. And their tongues are wagging and wagging. And I just couldn't resist. I well, erm, you know what I think about you. Something came over me, like a fog…yes, a fog. But Dovid's completely serious. He isn't just saying it, he's insisting. And Zusel's backing him up. But why have you gone so pale? You see what it means, being without your wife? Without mutual care and concern. Off you go, go on. It's the weekend. The weather's lovely. I need to finish this dress. You heard how important it is. Evochka has a crucial date tomorrow. Time and tide…"

Laevskaya didn't look at me. She scooped the scraps and bobbins up off the floor and tossed them down on the table.

And as she did so she repeated quietly like a wisewoman's whisper:

"And they cut and they cut and they tear and they tear and they tell me to sew, sew and sew again, the fools, they're never satisfied."

And I felt sorry for her that she'd taken a womanly shine to Dovid.

What I said was:

"You watch your tongue. That's my advice to you and only because we're on good terms and out of gratitude for Yoska. But even gratitude has its limits. Agreed?"

She scowled up at me. It was just as she was picking scraps up off the floor. She nodded.

But aloud she said:

"Don't depend on it. Don't depend on it at all, ever. I won't be silent. I won't because I have nothing to hide and no-one to protect."

The moment I closed the gate, I decided to go and see Evka Vorobeichik. What a hussy! And no shame. Her close friendship with Laevskaya gave me the chance to sort at least something out.

Let's be honest. I had had my fill of Polina and her gang and their stupid insinuations and jibes. I had to go on living.

Since I was no longer worried about my family, I now had the strength to take further action without pussyfooting around.

People tend to be more relaxed on Sundays. I planned to put that to good use.

My visit came as no surprise to Evka. On the contrary, she immediately turned the tables so that she was bombarding me with questions.

"Did Polina Lvovna tell you all about the knife? Who do you think threw it into the Strizhen, I wonder? Will you summon us to the station under caution? And the boy? Just so you know, he's called Taras Khrobak."

"Why all the silly questions, Eva Izrailevna?"

Evka pouted.

"My patronymic is Solomonovna. As was Lilya's incidentally."

"Fine. What difference does it make? My apologies. The criminal threw the knife into the water. Or perhaps it was someone who isn't involved at all. That's if we're even talking about the knife in question. Now, let's suppose a passer-by finds a knife in the street and there's blood. He takes fright and hurls it into the water. It does happen. What are you grinning at? If someone saw the murder being committed, the very moment that your sister was stabbed and fell to the ground, saw who killed her and that it was with that same knife, then that's another matter. So far though, well, suppose the knife is in fact the murder weapon. But it's been in the water. There are no traces on it. No fingerprints. Any blood, if there was any, has been washed away. Right?"

Eva nodded.

"And if that's so, it's not much help. Did Taras Khrobak find the knife? That's what Polina said. Perhaps she was making it up?"

Eva allowed her face to become thoughtful.

The house was quiet. But for the ticking of the clock.

To relieve the tension I said:

"Is the clock working? Does it tell the right time?"

"Yes. But I don't live by the clock. I live by my alarm clock. It rings and I come to life. First thing in the morning and that's how I go through the day."

Her expression was bitter.

"And so, Eva Solomonovna, Citizen Vorobeichik, when did you find the knife? Or should I ask the lad? I know his Dad personally. And Polina hinted that you also know Sergey Nikolayevich personally."

Eva flinched. As if the alarm clock had gone off.

"I do. What of it? He's a widower. And I have no ties at all."

"Whether or not a person is free isn't for them to decide. When did you find the knife?"

"In the middle of April. I can't remember the exact date. It was already sunny. That I do remember. The youngsters were out playing. Poking sticks into the earth on the bank of the stream. Polina Lvovna was afraid one of them would fall in. It was slippery. Mud everywhere. We went nearer. Polina warned them. They moved away from the water a bit and came towards us and the last bridge support, where they dump the rubbish. Polina went down to them, had a word, explained the danger. That's when Tarasik found the knife."

"And Polina?"

"Polina shouted up to me, 'Look, a knife like Lilechka's.'"

"She recognized it just like that? Surely it must have been covered in mud and rusty too, wasn't it?"

"I didn't look at it. It gave me the creeps. I even started feeling sick. I didn't go down there. Polina did a deal with Tarasik, gave him some money. I heard them. She said, 'There, that's for the cinema and an ice-cream soda. The older boys will take the knife off you in any case but money comes in handy.' He took the money. Gave her the knife. She put it in her handbag."

"In her handbag? All dirty and wet? Polina's bag is patent-leather. I've seen it. Dark blue. She wouldn't have gone for a walk with only a string bag."

"You're right. It is patent-leather. She wrapped it in her scarf. She wasn't bothered about the scarf. 'For Lilechka's sake,' she said."

"Good for her. So, was the scarf sodden? Did you see what it was like after she'd wrapped it round the knife?"

"I didn't look at the knife. And I didn't see her wrap it up in the scarf either. I had turned away really. I was in tears. Imagine how I was feeling right then. All I know is that one minute she was wearing a scarf, the next she wasn't. Her throat was bare. I asked where the scarf was. Polina said she'd wrapped the knife in it."

"So, you didn't see the knife itself at all? And you are unable to confirm that it matched the ones that are still safe and sound at Lilya's?"

Evka said nothing. She looked out of the window. She had a lilac tree there. The scent was strong. And a vase of lilac on the table too. White and purple.

As a distraction I said, "Why ever do you pick the flowers? They'd last for ages there outside the window but you pick them. I don't understand women. Putting them in a vase and admiring them."

Unexpectedly, Eva began to laugh.

"Oh, Mikhail Ivanovich, Polina Lvovna was right to suggest you have an effect on women. Don't take this the wrong way. You're such a nice man."

I simply asked:

"Is this thing between you and Khrobak serious?"

"Of course," Eva answered stoutly. "What do you take me for? It's very serious. Tarasik needs a mother. And in what way am I not a mother? Maybe, I'll have children of my own. Lilka didn't like children. But I do."

I asked about Malka.

Here's the explanation I received: Malka was in Oster with Dovid. Evka had given them her shack and that's where they were living: Dovid, Zusel, the boys and Malka.

I was quick off the mark.

"It seems Polina Lvovna is hoping to make a life with Dovid in future. She has rather better living conditions than him. She'll take Dovid in. It was pointless, his being in such a hurry to get rid of his and Gutin's house for a pittance. He wasn't badly off at the time. Let's be honest. And no doubt he's not short of a kopeck or two. He's a tight-fisted chap. And perhaps Malka will marry Zusel and live free as a bird in your house in Oster. You've got a house here and one in Oster now. A wealthy bride. That's nice. Isn't it?"

Eva answered in a serious tone.

"It is nice. It's worked out well."

Throughout our conversation, Evka had been sitting at the round table. Elbows propped on the edge, pushing herself back, wriggling in her seat, never still. In particular, she kept smoothing the crocheted tablecloth, pulling the edges down. I even looked, lowered my glance a little, in case someone was hiding underneath. Nothing.

The table was just like the one in my dream about Lilia Vorobeichik.

I left Eva and thought. What had I gained from this enterprise? A great deal.

Evka had not in fact seen the knife. She had recognized it from Polina's description, apparently. And what's more through tears and what have you. But it could equally well be an extraneous knife. A common way of throwing someone off the scent should the need arise. Polina could have taken any old knife, thrown it down where the lads were playing, pointed it out to them to make it seem like they'd found it themselves, personally. Then she diddled it out of young Khrobak and climbed back up to Evka, the bogus knife in her handbag. To tell the truth, she never really intended to show it to Eva. She would have invented all sorts of nonsense rather than do that. But Evka would get into her head that she'd seen it. It happens all the time. Then again, perhaps the real knife was in Polina's bag. And had been there all along.

It all came down to how quick thinking she was.

Polina hadn't known in advance that she would meet the lads down by the stream. On the other hand, where would they be when the river was in spate other than down by the Strizhen?

The murder victim's knives had been scrupulously counted and measured. That was in the records. And there was the rub. Polina was insinuating that the knife in her possession was from Vorobeichik's kitchen. What's more, the maker had confirmed it. So where had she got it? Maybe the knife concerned really had been in the stream and really had pitched up at the feet of young Master Khrobak. At the very moment Polina and Eva were strolling by arm in arm up on the White Bridge.

But it doesn't happen like that. It just doesn't.

Or maybe Polina didn't have the right knife, after all? Or she did but had taken it from the murder scene. And temporarily hidden it at home. And now she was producing the evidence. Almost exactly a year later. What a bitch!

I immediately went back to Evka's to take another look at the knives.

The gate had been locked from the inside. I hammered and yelled for Evka to let me in.

Not a sound in response.

I walked around the house from the rear. Knocked on the windows. One, giving onto the living room and wreathed in lilac, was open.

I let rip.

"Eva, open up. I'm speaking to you in my capacity as a police officer. This is an emergency."

There was no response whatsoever.

I clambered over the windowsill. In the kitchen, I took my time going through the drawers, unafraid. I remembered where the knives had been back then, incidentally. Not one there now was like the ones I remembered: big, heavy, reliable. These were new. The yellowish handles gleamed. Good wood. The steel blades no great shakes. Used in something else in a previous life. I touched one with a finger. Razor sharp. Sharpened as only a craftsman can. A housewife couldn't produce work like that in a domestic setting. These knives were new.

I took up position on a stool in the corner – waiting. With the gate barred on the inside and only the window open, she must have popped out through the back for a minute. When she came back, I would question her properly about her cutting tools.

About five minutes later, I heard the door open and someone come into the house. Laughing into the bargain.

I recognized Evka's voice. And a man's. Vaguely familiar.

Evka said:

"Just imagine. He came here to question me. Question me on and on. But I could see he was devouring me with his brazen eyes. He looked under the table too. I know why men look under a table. He was looking at my knees. What a nerve, Seryozha, really! He thinks that if I'm single and attractive, anyone can take a look at my knees."

The man laughed, each sound distinct.

"Ha, ha, ha!"

Eva gabbled on.

"The minute he made himself scarce, I came to see you. To express my indignation. And at the same time to ask you round. You're not pushy. You won't turn up without an invitation." Here Eva giggled unpleasantly. "I have a place of my own. But there's no room to swing a cat at yours. Grandma, Grandpa. They hear everything, sniff everything out. Are you pleased? We'll have something to eat now. I've got everything all nice and ready."

And so on into the kitchen. In other words towards me.

She stopped in the doorway, thunderstruck.

And the man emerged from behind her. Khrobak, Sergey Nikolayevich Khrobak.

He moved Eva aside and stepped forward.

"But he's still here. What's going on?"

Khrobak looked at me as he might at a louse. On account of his position as head of the Consumers' Union. But I couldn't give two hoots.

"I'm here on police business," I said.

Khrobak said sternly:

"On police business, people knock at the door. It's thieves, for example, who jump in through windows."

I was outraged:

"Now, wait a minute! You are insulting me in the performance of my duty. I have a question for Citizen Eva Vorobeichik. And I'm making you a witness to it."

And I turned to Eva without further ado.

"Where are the old knives left by your sister, Citizen Lilia Vorobeichik?"

Eva blushed all over. Her shoulders stuck out under the straps of her pinafore. Patches of red appeared on them too. Not to mention her face and so on.

"What knives? When Lilya was alive, she had old knives. Good ones but old. When I arrived, not one of those knives was to be found. Malka and I were particularly surprised that the police had taken all the good knives away. No, I can say for certain, there were no knives here that could be used. There were rusty ones, broken ones, small ones for peeling potatoes. I bought nice new ones. At the market. I came here and I bought them. You can ask Malka. She was boasting to herself that we'd be keeping kosher, not like that slut Lilka."

"Did Malka call the deceased victim a slut?" I inquired. "Why so rude?"

Eva shrugged:

"Malka took a real dislike to her, even when she was a child. As for calling her a slut, to Malka everyone was a slut who had, well, you know, without getting married. Especially when it was with all and sundry."

Indeed. Delightful insinuations from her own dear sister.

Khrobak came closer and took me by the shoulder.

I sat there as if nothing was happening.

"Is that it with the questions?" he said.

Slowly, I got to my feet. I removed his hand only once I had drawn myself up to my full height, taking his palm between two fingers. I was a full head taller. And, when I reached my full height, I took Khrobak's hand politely and lifted it off my shoulder.

"You, Citizen Khrobak, keep your hands to yourself. They will still come in useful. You need them. At this present moment, I have no further questions for Citizen Eva Vorobeichik. If I do, I will ask her to come to the station. By a summons. Like any Soviet citizen. See you soon."

They stood in silence as I left. Like a guard of honour.

I whistled as I walked along. I was brought up sharp on an in-breath: 'You can't take a rusty knife that has been in water, in the sludge on the bed of a stream, for nearly a year and make a neat incision in a lace glove. It can't be done. Tear it to shreds - yes – but that means holding and pulling. Cutting in a straight line – impossible!'

Greed had let Polina down. A straight cut means invisible repairs. Along the line of the cut. Something that's in shreds doesn't. No matter what you do. She'd wanted something obvious. And that's what had let her down. She'd had gone too far, that's what. Much too far.

Wasting no time at all, I headed for Polina's.

As I arrived, a woman had just come out of the gate. Stout. A customer. She guessed where I was going and told me Polina Lvovna had just left, taking a suitcase. To stay with relatives. A major expedition. To Kiev, then on to somewhere else. The customer had helped her take her bags outside. And, what's more, a taxi had picked her up right there.

'She's probably already at the station, putting her bags on the train,' I thought.

I looked at my watch. There wasn't a train to Kiev at that time. And why would a sensible person take the train anyway? They'd go by bus or take the little steamer, the Krupskaya, down the Desna. These were more frequent and more pleasant.

At this, I felt so weary at heart and everywhere inside … chasing a woman to the station, to the river port. Just to hear her come out with another load of old codswallop.

No.

I set off for my empty house. On the way I bought a bottle of vodka.

At home, I opened it but didn't drink it. I plugged it with a stopper made out of newspaper. Sat on the balcony for a long time, gazing into the distance.

Fear and love flooded me for my family, for Lyubochka, Gannusya and Yoska, for all of them.

Nevertheless, despite my fatigue and my emotional burdens, a new version of the death of Lilia Solomonovna Vorobeichik was gradually taking shape in my mind.

Moiseenko and his counterfeit love had stepped well away from the spotlight.

There had been suspicious behaviour from the following: one, Polina Lvovna Laevskaya; two, the victim's sister, Eva Solomonovna Vorobeichik.

When it came to Evka, things were quite clear. She inherited the house. And another, their parents', in Oster. She didn't have to share any more. She got the lot.

But what gesheft was there for Laevskaya in the death of her bosom pal?

No gesheft at first glance and no profit either. In terms of money and finance. But personally, emotionally? Perhaps Lilia had been an obstacle to Laevskaya in the men department? Or vice versa. Polina had snaffled some fancy man away from Lilia. There was no comparison when it came to age. Lilia was considerably younger and more attractive. But anything can happen. Not for nothing did Pushkin write in verse: all ages submit to love.

I called myself every name under the sun. I should have made a serious attempt to sound Laevskaya out ages ago. Evka too. But so much else had been going on. Evsey Gutin, Yoska, and so on. Not to mention my family. Especially when the case was closed.

But it wasn't. And it was blowing an ill wind right in my face. Poisoning the air around me.

If only Moiseenko had still been alive. I could have stuck all three of them together - Laevskaya, Evka and the luckless artiste, and they would all have started talking at the same time. Tried to outdo one another even. But Moiseenko was no more.

He wouldn't be talking now. So, as our senior comrades taught us, it was a case of investigating the ones that were still alive thoroughly. You can't bring the dead back to life.

And perhaps one slim thread would stretch as far as Evsey. I had the feeling it would. I was on tenterhooks. There was a reason Laevskaya never tired of tying Gutin in to each and every suggestion.

Next morning, early in the working day, I bumped into Khrobak at the district station.

I said hello.

He didn't reply. He was heading firmly towards a door at the end of the corridor – the chief's.

I hung back. Watched Khrobak go with an easy stare.

He threw the door open boldly. The typist's voice could be heard welcoming a familiar and respected visitor. She hurried to announce him.

Whereupon the chief's greetings made his presence known too.

The door slammed shut.

Silence. Apart from Svetka typing away with a show of speed.

It was obvious. Khrobak was there to complain. And the complaint was about me. Evka had put him up to it.

I told the lads I was going out on urgent business. A meeting with an informant.

I needed to know for certain who Laevskaya was. Beneath the exterior. Her evidence in the case was in order. But apart from her date and place of birth, where she was registered to live and her passport details, I knew nothing.

And it was with that very 'nothing' that I went to see Shtadler.

Veniamin Yakovlevich greeted me without enthusiasm. But he listened closely and attentively.

I asked one, main question. Who was Polina Lvovna Laevskaya? Over and above what she might put on a form.

He laughed, revealing gaps where teeth had been knocked out. I could see half his tongue. The half that was left, obviously. It wasn't very nice but it wasn't that bad. It was the first time I had seen it clearly. Because he'd never laughed in my presence. Whereas now he was roaring with laughter. To the point of hiccups.

In big letters on a piece of paper, he wrote: 'A terrible woman.'

And used his hands to sculpt her immense bosom.

He carried on writing and over his shoulder I read: 'Lived for a long time in Oster. Moved from there to Chernigov. Straight after the war. Sought after by widowers who were knocking on a bit. She turned them down. She was after a young one. Fool.'

Shtadler finished scribbling.

In my estimation, the information was tosh.

"Is that it?" I said.

"An ordinary woman with tits? You're having me on. What I need is information. Come on, Veniamin Yakovlevich. There's a good chap. Take it seriously. Like a Bolshevik. The way you used to. I don't know how else to get it into your head, to make you understand. I need information! Urgently!"

Shtadler held up his hands helplessly.

In fact, Shtadler had given me a whole treasure trove. Laevskaya used to live in Oster. Where Vorobeichik was from. Polina's passport gave her place of birth as Shklov. She was registered as a resident of Chernigov. There hadn't been a peep out of her about living in Oster. It hadn't been relevant. It was now.

I had long since learned from the nature of my work that anything can happen. Apart from certain coincidences that are just too outlandish. Although even they can happen in theory. They must simply be followed up with a particularly open mind.

The difficulty for me was that the Vorobeichik case, having been closed, no longer required my involvement. I couldn't ask to have it assigned to me.

So I came up with the following plan.

To take a few days' unpaid leave. A working week, even. Under the pretence of going to visit my family in Ryabina. The lads and my superiors knew about Lyubochka's health problems. And finally I would wrap up the Lilia Vorobeichik case and to hell with it. Having established complete clarity.

At work, the secretary, Svetka, was lying in wait for me.

She shouted at me as if I was a rookie.

"Where do you get to during work time? The chief wants to see you urgently."

I moved her gingerly out of the way. I knew what pressing urgency had gripped the chief. Lieutenant-Colonel Maksim Prokopovich Sviridenko was well-known for his love of urgency. Especially when it came to downing a glass.

I smiled and with that smile I pulled the office door towards me. Hitting myself right in the chest.

Svetka grumbled into the back of my neck.

Sviridenko was sitting at his desk, dialling a number. He didn't look at me.

He barked into the receiver:

"Report back every hour. You know me!"

He slammed the receiver back onto its cradle and only then did he look up at me.

"Now then, Tsupkoy, have you done skirt-chasing? I'll say you have!"

"Since you say so, Comrade Lieutenant-Colonel, then yes."

"Sit down."

I sat.

"There are reports that your conduct is not in keeping with socialist law and order. Or, to put it more simply, you're chasing after other people's women. Can't keep your hands to yourself. Upsetting respectable people. Exploiting your official position. Exceeding your authority. In short, getting on the public's nerves.

The public demands that measures be taken. Are you going to try to justify your behaviour? Or to accept this straight away and not let anything like it happen again?"

I nodded in agreement and sat up straight as if standing to attention. Although I stayed in my seat.

"Yes, sir. It won't happen again."

"Do you even know who's complained? Do you even realize just how far you've gone?"

"I do and I understand everything very clearly. Khrobak's complained. And I realize there's no cure for Khrobak. Unless you have something, Comrade Lieutenant-Colonel?"

Sviridenko sighed.

"Nope. Against criminals, I have. Against Comrade Khrobak, I haven't. So what really happened?"

"Well, I did break the rules, a touch. I entered the house of a certain woman without authorization. I was looking for material evidence. She's as slippery as a snake. It happened by accident. And Khrobak's her lover. He found me there and weighed in to defend his bit of skirt. I didn't touch him. Just the opposite. He grabbed me by the shoulder first and subjected me to humiliation."

"What's the case you're working on?"

"An old one. Been closed already. Vorobeichik. A murder. Last May. Khrobak's bit's the victim's sister."

"Ah, I see. What else are you looking for? The prime suspect is no longer of this world. No-one is in any doubt that he did it. So why are you digging around again?"

I kept my composure and promised it wouldn't happen again.

Sviridenko put the lid firmly on the conversation.

"I should think not. Go. And sin no more. Or Khrobak will have the whole town up in arms. He'll have you making confessions not even a priest could absolve."

"Yes, sir, Comrade Lieutenant Colonel. I've been stupid. Childish. I'm tired. I'd like to ask for six days off, unpaid. I'll go and see my family. You know my situation. Shall I write a report?"

"Yes. I'm making this a verbal reprimand. To shut Khrobak up. But you take note. Stay away from that woman's house. Keep well away. What are you working on now?"

"Nothing special. A week should do it. Theft. Armed robbery. Cut and dried. I'll hand it over to the courts as soon as I'm back. Full confessions from the guilty parties."

"Right then, off you go to the family."

I positively stomped past Svetka. She shook her permed hair.

"I've had enough of you, Comrade Tsupkoy," she hissed. "You're behaving like an idiot."

That hurt. More than the verbal reprimand.

I went dangerously close to her stunted little table and hissed right in her face the way she did:

"Oh, Svetka, Svetlana, I'll get my hands on you as well in the end."

She giggled in that loathsome way she had. But it kept her happy.

Of course, she had eavesdropped on my conversation with Sviridenko. Now the entire department would be discussing my advances to other people's women. Let them think that was at the root of everything. Svetka would try to blow it out of all proportion. It might even be a good thing. There was no need to find any better cover.

After dark that same day, there was a cautious ring on the door of my own home.

There, on the doorstep, was Shtadler. Behind him someone hovered by the wall. A sickly light bulb allowed me to make out Zusel.

Shtadler let Zusel go ahead, then crept in himself.

I closed the door and gestured them into the kitchen. It was my dinner time. Bachelor-style. Cold boiled potatoes, pork fat, an onion, bread from Pushkin Street, our own bread, not brought in from elsewhere. And, of course, tea.

"What's happened?" I asked them both. "Saboteurs in the synagogue?" As a joke it wasn't particularly funny but I had to begin in a way that immediately showed them where they stood.

"Out with it and look sharp. I haven't got time. I'm tired. Well?"

Zusel said nothing, turning his head as always in its dirty peaked cap. Although I immediately noticed a woman's touch about his appearance. Jacket buttons sewn on tight, trousers ironed, boots held together by a wing and a prayer but laces too. Malka evidently.

From a trouser pocket, Shtadler took a small exercise book and a tiny, sharpened copying pencil. He didn't spit on it as he usually did. He wrote dry.

'I am here as witness to Zusel Tabachnik and your conversation from this point on. It has nothing to do with me. The initiative is Zusel's. Are you going to listen or shall we leave? In my opinion, you would do better to listen.'

And for some reason, he signed it, using his full name. As if I would be adding it to the case files. He tore the paper out evenly. So he wasn't nervous. Bastard.

I deliberately read slowly although I took it all in immediately, letter and spirit.

I finished reading. I put the sheet of paper down on the table, under the plate of pork fat and onion.

Shtadler wanted to take it back but I wouldn't let him.

My opening words were addressed to Zusel.

"Citizen Tabachnik, what you have to tell me, you would be better off reporting tomorrow at my place of work and on the record. This is not a home-based cooperative. This is the police and there's one law for everyone. Is that clear?"

Zusel straightened his cap and looked at Shtadler.

Shtadler gesticulated.

I understood – I was to listen right there and then, once and for all.

That's what I'd intended in any case but I was obliged to mention the police and the law. It makes an impression.

I sat at the table. I invited my visitors to do the same. I asked whether they would like tea.

Shtadler nodded. Zusel declined with a shake of his head.

"Of course, kosher. I respect your religious feelings, Citizen Tabachnik. What matters is that you do not drag the younger generation into your superstitions. Right? Right. So, I'm listening."

Shtadler took his little book out once again and, with a gesture, offered to take notes for the record. I declined.

"If something's worth it, there's plenty of time."

Then I realized I'd slipped up. I hadn't asked what they'd come about. As if I'd already known exactly why in advance.

I immediately corrected my mistake.

"What's this about? A personal matter, perhaps? Or a public one? Or a criminal one?"

Shtadler gestured hastily as if to say he had no idea.

Zusel mumbled, "An important matter. It's all those things. A nest of vipers. Really."

What follows is Zusel's testimony:

He had taken it upon himself to come to me with the aim of making life easier for Dovid Basin. The grief and affliction brought about by the untimely death of his son-in-law Evsey Gutin and the illness of his daughter Belka had resulted in Basin's complete nervous prostration. As a result, Dovid Srulevich Basin was claiming that the blame for his son-in-law's death lay with Comrade Mikhail Ivanovich Tsupkoy. While Belka was being forcibly detained in a psychiatric hospital by that same Comrade Tsupkoy. Comrade Tsupkoy had, after all, taken his, Dovid's, very youngest grandson, one Iosif by name, into his home as a hostage under the guise of adoption. To ensure Basin kept as silent as the grave. The aim of these violations of socialist law and order and all the horrors committed by Police Captain Comrade Tsupkoy was to conceal another as yet unknown crime about which Basin had so far said nothing, while constantly dropping meaningful hints to the wider community. Oster's public was outraged by his conduct. Any popular forbearance, much less pity, towards an elderly man laid low by grief has its end. The end had come in Oster too. Several neighbours had told Zusel directly, as a long-term resident of the shtetl in question, that it was hard to turn a blind eye to Basin's malarkey. And that they would be reporting you-know-where that the old man was casting slurs on an honest police officer.

Zusel had a question. Might there some concession given Basin's age and status, a man bringing up two juvenile grandsons in his own home? It would be essential in the event that Basin, as he was threatening to do, composed and posted a detailed letter in respect of Comrade Tsupkoy to Chernigov's Communist Party agencies. And Comrade Tsupkoy ought to use his connections to secure such a concession and leniency for Basin. Because, whichever way you looked at it, Comrade Tsupkoy was bringing up Basin's grandson, Iosif. Which was the reason the grandfather had completely lost his marbles.

Zusel delivered this gobbledygook clearly and distinctly. Evidently, he had spent a long time learning his speech off by heart.

It came out well, sounding almost not Jewish even. Except that he swayed from side to side and sometimes snivelled as was his wont when he prayed.

His concluding remarks were as follows:

If, in Comrade Tsupkoy's opinion, no concession was to be granted Basin for his malicious anti-Soviet slander, then he, Zusel Tabachnik, hereby declared that first thing tomorrow morning he would hand himself in at the police station and write a statement that Basin was not the guilty party but that he, Zusel Tabachnik, was and he would face the harsh and implacable consequences up to and including execution by firing squad, for which he was prepared in advance. Because he was the one who had put Basin up to it. And the one who had forced him to spread his insinuations too.

Tabachnik finished speaking and fell to his knees. Face down. He began to pray and his arms and legs started to twitch.

I calmly poured a cup of cold tea over him.

"Let's presume," I said, "that no article and no mitigating circumstances allow of any concession. So, off you go to the station tomorrow, large as life, and dash off your statement. The first thing they'll want to know is why you needed to put poor Basin up to it, what you stand to gain. It's a serious matter. There must be something serious to gain as well. Have you thought something up, even? Hm, Citizen Tabachnik?"

Zusel raised his head. It was poorly supported on his neck and trembled slightly. He looked at me like a chicken, its throat already slit, and lowered his head sharply towards the floor. His cap flew off.

I saw that Zusel's head was completely bald, with a dent in the middle. Clearly, it had been pierced at some point and left to heal. The scar was white, knotty, tinged with blue. And the skin that covered it moved. Like a baby's soft spot.

I knew you shouldn't touch a person in that state. You had to wait until they calmed down.

I looked at Shtadler. He had frozen, mouth agape. His tongue was working, his shattered teeth rubbing against the flesh. Flecks of blood here and there. Not much. He'd managed to bite his tongue.

"And what do you think, Veniamin Yakovlevich? You're a witness after all. Happy?"

He shook his head.

"Nor am I, Veniamin Yakovlevich. Will you be tootling off to the police station with him as a witness tomorrow as well?"

Shtadler's bellow conveyed that he would not.

"Did Zusel inform you in advance of what this conversation would be about? No? So how on earth did you fall for it? You can't wriggle off the hook now. Happy about that? Me neither. Go away. And take the bit of paper you signed. I'm amazed at how unwisely you've acted. There. It's gone, forever out of mind. Put it out of your mind too. As if it never happened, you just dreamt it. That's my advice to you – you dreamt it."

Shtadler reached for the piece of paper under the plate.

At the last second, I grabbed his arm and squeezed.

"No, Citizen Shtadler. I'll keep hold of your signature all the same. I'm used to working with documents. And a document, especially with a signature, is worth its weight in gold. Isn't that so? Off you go empty-handed. And rinse your mouth out. There's blood on your lips. Next you'll be telling people I tortured you."

Shtadler gave a stiff smile and indicated with his hand that he wasn't one for gossip.

"Whether you can talk or not isn't known for certain. You could go out of here and start talking in every language in the world."

Shtadler left. As he went, he picked up the exercise book and made to scribble something down. I wouldn't let him.

Zusel was waiting for me. He was sitting by the table. Not at the table itself but sort of a little bit off to the side. He had tactfully moved the stool aside. A hint that he wasn't hankering to be fed.

I could see from experience however that he was in such a state that hot sweet tea was urgently required.

I reheated the kettle. There was just enough water for it to boil quickly. I checked specially.

I poured tea into a glass, topped it up with boiling water and added three cubes of white sugar. I placed it in his hands.

Zusel took his time about taking the cup. Evidently, he was wondering whether he ought to drink something when he was right next to pork fat, particularly in a non-kosher home.

I gave him no choice.

"When you've finished, I'll talk. I can't call you an ambulance. That would do you no good. People would talk. Agreed?"

Zusel said nothing. The glass he was holding shook.

The first words he uttered were: "A spoon. It needs stirring."

I gave him a spoon. He stirred in the sugar. He swallowed each little gulp slowly.

I didn't rush him.

I didn't take the empty glass off him either. I left it so that he would have to put it on the table himself. My intention was to watch his movement. The movement a man uses to put an empty glass on a table can reveal a great deal. Not just about his agitation but about his inner willingness to develop relations with the investigator. If he puts the glass down and stares fixedly at the floor – that's bad. He'll deny everything. If he puts it down and at the same time looks, somehow at least, at the investigator, whether directly or sidelong, you can start taking notes. He'll talk.

Zusel didn't put the glass down. He twiddled with it on his lap. Turned it around, twiddled again.

In order not to lose the initiative, I said,

"Are you going to keep your lips sealed for long? You chose to come here. And now you're choosing to stay silent."

Zusel shuddered and dropped the glass. It shattered. He dived to pick up the pieces. He cut his finger but didn't stop his ridiculous behaviour. He just carried on.

I, of course, made a show of irritation.

"Citizen Tabachnik, what is this? Did you come here to put on a performance for me?"

Taking the old man under the armpits, I jerked him up, dragged him over to the stool and plumped him down on it.

Zusel squirmed and slid back onto the floor. He seemed about to start looking for his cap. I popped it onto his head. Rammed it on then gave it a light tap.

Pushed to the limit, I said crisply:

"Right, answer my questions. For the last time, I am informing you that this isn't a circus. Are you completely off your head, dragging Shtadler here with you? Have you lost all reason, bringing in a witness to conversations of this kind?"

Zusel said nothing and looked nowhere. Not at the ground. Not at the ceiling. Not at me. He swayed on the stool, his eyes closed. The swaying was awkward because I had jammed him too close to the table when I settled him in his seat.

I pretended I wasn't bothered.

"I can see only one explanation for your stupid behaviour, so to speak: that you came here intent on a colossal act of provocation. Is that so? Answer me!"

I yelled this last out loudly, of course, and brought my fist down on the table. The plate of pork fat and onion bounced. Shtadler, trying to pull his note out from under it, had shunted it close to the very edge.

My thump made the plate bounce and slide towards Zusel's lap. The jolt made Zusel open his eyes and grasp the plate mid-flight. Halfwit or not, he had the reactions of a goalkeeper.

The time-tested strategy went disastrously wrong. Seeing the pork fat in his hands, Zusel fainted away. Or something.

And in his state of unconsciousness, he began wailing his prayers.

Loudly too, the bastard, complete with snivels. And it was already night-time. The neighbours were asleep.

I put my hand over his mouth. Now he was bleating the same sort of thing. I pressed harder. He fell silent.

I took my hand away and realized that Citizen Zusel Tabachnik was dead. And the ultimate cause had been my strong arm. I'd miscalculated. I'd stopped his mouth but covered his nose as well.

This sort of thing had happened to me at the front as well as to others who went behind enemy lines to bring back prisoners who'd talk. There had been dreadful frustration and vexation. But no feeling of distress. War is war. But here…

I was in despair.

This threatened to deal an irreparable blow not only to my own life but to my family's safe existence as well.

I'd closed Zusel Tabachnik's eyes once and for all.

Keeping irrelevant thoughts at bay, I wrapped Tabachnik tightly in my cloak-tent. A new one, only recently issued.

It created an enormous bundle but I could still lift it. Even though the dead are known to weigh more than the living. I let go of the thought that Zusel's small size and general awkwardness had always amused me and given rise to a degree of contempt. Now he brought those same qualities to my assistance. And I thanked him from the bottom of my heart. Just over fifty kilos was nothing to me.

I put on my uniform, took my gun, checked the spare magazine, and tossed some clothes, underwear and essentials into a rucksack: rope, an army entrenching tool, a sheath knife and a lantern.

A split second later and I had a plan. And I immediately got down to carrying it out.

The short May nights brooked no delay. Dawn would soon make its presence felt.

I walked calmly down the street. Like any ordinary man with a heavy weight on his shoulders. The only thing I was afraid of was coming across a police patrol, which was unlikely. Drunken hooligans were a more probable obstacle.

As always, there were collective farm lorries parked by the market. The drivers and vendors slept in them until the market opened.

I picked out a vehicle at the far end and peeped through the window.

The driver was on his own. The flatbed was empty. Clearly, everything had been sold and, to avoid travelling at night, they had hung on until morning.

I knocked on the glass.

The lorry was from a remote district. It was their first time in Chernigov. The collective farm usually sold its produce in Russia, across the river. But now the Oblast Committee had ordered them to Chernigov, a hundred kilometres away.

I persuaded the driver to drop me at Trinity Hill. My uniform and the absolute respect in which citizens held the police did their vital work.

I pointed to my lips, a warning to keep silent.

I whispered: "I'm on a mission, urgent."

The driver accelerated. And ten minutes later, with Zusel in the flatbed, the lorry drew up at the designated location.

As he drove off, the driver saluted me. And I him.

Trinity Hill by Anthony's Caves was the most desolate spot in Chernigov. There had never been any attacks here and certainly not with robbery in mind. Even drunkards and lovers throwing caution to the wind and seeking shelter for their pleasures gave the caves a wide berth. And there were impenetrable thickets too. Overgrown thistles taller than any man.

My path lay close by. To the little cemetery right next to the chapel. Burials were held there before the Revolution and, intermittently, during the Civil War. For those living immediate alongside.

I used the entrenching tool to dig a good, deep grave. Not two metres but I didn't shirk on length or breadth. The earth was yielding after the rains.

I laid Zusel out neatly. Listened to his heart, the pulse behind his ear. Nothing.

Cows were being driven from the far side of the Liskovitsa into the flood meadows nearer to the Desna.

I covered the old man's face with his peaked cap. Then changed my mind and put his headgear on properly. Over the scar. In life, the man had observed his Jewish rules, let there be order in death as well.

I make no secret of the fact that to start with I'd wanted to wrap the body in the cloak-tent. But I refrained. I knew the role of clothing when bodies were discovered.

Know it or not, I didn't go through the dead man's pockets. Something I remembered as I was going down the hill.

Back I went. I dug up the grave. Searched him. His jacket pocket held a rag and a bit of newspaper. I examined them both. Rubbish. I buried him again and replaced the turf. The impact of military savvy.

In the end, I put on my cloak-tent – to hide my muddy hands in the pockets. And in that guise I arrived at the Kiev highway.

On the way, I washed my hands at a standpipe. I quenched my thirst.

And a varied relay of vehicles took me, with a heavy heart, to Ryabina.

Some people think that police work hardens the heart. It doesn't. The face of the late Zusel was fixed, grimacing, in my mind. His death was an indisputable accident. Let's be honest, he was completely responsible for his own idiotic demise. His fanaticism, his yelping religious outpourings in the middle of the night, his provocative behaviour as a whole. So, he had seized a block of pork fat in his bare and unprotected hands. So, he had thereby violated one of his superstitious notions. So what? Was there any need to have the whole place in uproar? And the next day the neighbours would write to the police that the flat of Police Captain Such-and-Such, known, incidentally, for the fact that his family was bringing up a little Jewish boy as one of their own, was hosting an anti-Soviet synagogue, especially at night. Zusel, with his wailing and swaying, had been thinking about the opinion of his God. The opinion of his own personal God at that infernal moment had been more important to him than the opinion of Soviet power. But I am a Communist through and through. Soviet power has given me all I need.

And then Zusel was gone. His untimely death stayed with me. I had given him a decent burial and I consoled myself with the thought that perhaps the old man's pulse had ceased to function even before I gave him a bit of a fatal squeeze.

I had to draw a line under that moment. And draw it I did. At any cost, as the saying goes.

But questions remained. And I was working on them.

Shtadler knew for a fact that Tabachnik had dragged himself to Chernigov and to my house into the bargain. And Shtadler, for reasons unknown, had been called as a witness by Zusel himself.

I still had grave doubts about the fact, reported to me by Zusel, that there was any intent on Dovid Basin's part to lodge a complaint about my conduct. I know from experience that if that's what someone wants to do, they get on and do it. If someone talks about it, they won't do a thing. If Basin was even threatening to do it, it was to apply psychological pressure. He reckoned I would learn about the threats and back down.

But on what point did Dovid need me to back down? That was the question.

And to that, I didn't have a suitable answer.

I arrived in Ryabina nearly twenty-four hours later. I knocked at Didenko's house.

By the light of an oil lamp, I saw the dear, beloved faces of my wife and children.

Gannusya and Yoska were sleeping on the floor on a sheepskin coat.

Lyubochka assured me there was nothing better. A sheepskin offered complete freedom. And what's more it was thick and sent you off to sleep.

Lyubochka had made room for herself on a trunk, a stool carefully positioned so that her feet didn't dangle. Her host was still in his usual place – on the stove. Except that I immediately noticed that, whereas there wasn't a curtain before, Lyubochka had now organized a separate resting place for the old man. She'd hung up a piece of sackcloth. Full of holes, patched and darned, which was what made it so useful – it let in the fresh air.

Everything in the house breathed a woman's warmth and comfort.

The children didn't stir when I kissed them in greeting. Country sleep is the deepest and the healthiest.

Without a word, Didenko waved and muttered that he'd go out to the shed.

I approached Lyubochka gently but she shifted away.

She wanted to sleep on the floor with the children, leaving me the trunk. I preferred the stove. To indulge in remembering my childhood. Since that's how it was going to be.

In the morning, economic matters were on the agenda. The money Lyubochka had brought with her to begin with had been sufficient. They'd bought goat's milk. Lyubochka went to the market on Sundays and did a sensible shop. Nothing fancy. But they had potatoes at home, and groats and bread. They were expecting to harvest carrots, cucumbers, potatoes, beets and so on in due course. Lyubochka, under Didenko's guidance, had created a flourishing vegetable patch. Blind Petro brought the water. Lyubochka spoke well of him. Warmly even. I asked whether Petro's wife minded him putting in so much effort there.

Didenko snorted. Lyubochka blushed.

Gannusya reported that Auntie Katya helped out too.

She would come along in the evenings and say the following to Petro:

"Let's be making tracks now, my blindling, or you'll be settling in for the night. And no-one's going to kick you out, poor wretch."

I pointed out that there was no need to insult anyone and that it was very important to spend the night at home. Otherwise, the people at home would worry.

This was for Gannusya as the eldest. For future reference.

Gannusya paid close attention to the lesson then said impatiently:

"But then Auntie Katya always asks Mummy in the evening if she still needs Uncle Petro. If she does, then Auntie Katya leaves him here. She doesn't mind."

"And what does Mummy say?" I asked in jest.

Gannusya stated solemnly, "Mummy says she doesn't need anyone."

When the children had run along outside, I pursued the joke.

"Well, Lyuba, it seems you have an admirer. That's quite a worry, I must say. One up on the stove's not enough. You've let another one in. Bringing the water. Buckets of it. Buckets and buckets. So much it overflows. And now I've turned up. Perhaps I'm in the way?"

Lyuba collected the bowls from the table and ignored me. She was looking out of the wide-open window.

I looked too.

There, against the fence, was Blind Petro.

He yelled in the direction of the house. His words, like his wife's, were Ukrainian.

"Gannusya, Iosip, Uncle Petro's here. What are we going to do today? Don't tell Mummy I'm here. It'll be a secret. How's about we make a little hut?"

The children raced towards him in delight. Gannusya opened the gate while Yoska tried to climb the fence, lifting up his arms. Petro felt for him and scooped him up, planting a kiss on his cheek. He pulled him over to his side of the fence. And so carefully, he didn't scratch his small bare feet on the sharp canes.

I went outside and loudly identified myself.

"Hello, Petro. Come into the house."

Petro pricked up his ears.

"Mykhaylo? You're here? Lyuba has been waiting and waiting for you. Great!"

He came over, guided by my voice, Yoska in his arms. He offered a hand to shake but kept a firm grip on the little boy.

Firstly, I took Yoska from him and set him on the floor. Then I shook his hand.

"Thank you for helping my family."

Petro dismissed this.

"No, no, I just bring the water or a bit of wood. Anything I can do to help. Staying long?"

"We'll see. Depends on work."

I didn't answer in Ukrainian on principle to keep some distance. It's something people can always sense. Distance is of the utmost importance in relationships.

Lyubochka came out of the house. From a way off, I saw her in a new light. She was thinner. With grey in her hair. But overall looked hale and hearty.

I made a suggestion. "So, lady of the house, this evening when it's a little cooler, let's sit out under the cherry tree, have a bite to eat. The nightingale will sing and Petro, Mikola Ivanovich and I will have a glass in the Cossack tradition, hmm?"

Unwittingly, I had slipped into Ukrainian. It made me cross. As if I was cosying up to Petro and life in this place. Damn. The cherry tree, the nightingale, a bite to eat… Resolutely and ruthlessly, I put myself straight.

"There's nothing wrong with a little drink. We'll ask Katerina over too."

Lyuba nodded.

I asked Petro how much it would cost for moonshine vodka. He told me. I thrust more than that into his hand. Petro crumpled up the notes, handed back the extra.

"How can you see them? By feel?"

Petro shook his head vaguely. I noticed that the bandage over his eyes was flannel, made from a freshly-laundered footcloth. Nice and soft. Not some old rag. Stitched. With little ties. I took a deliberate look at the back of his head. For some reason, I thought: Lyuba did that.

A conversation took place with Lyuba about the children.

She voiced her pleasure at their good health and behaviour. Gannusya kept a constant eye on her brother. Warding off geese and so on with a long stick.

As for her personal well-being, I didn't ask. However, when I was attempting to embrace her with the full force of the love and respect I had for her, I whispered:

"Do you love me? Have you missed me?"

To which she replied, openly:

"I do."

I still remembered her ravings about infection but I didn't raise the matter. I had decided: slowly, slowly and everything would pass. Absolutely everything, up to and including the infection.

Petro did not put in an appearance next morning. The children asked why he wasn't there. I brought the water in person, stored up logs for a rainy day.

Later, Didenko and I lay in the shade.

"That Zusel of yours came to see me," I said. "Before I left. Not quite all there, as always. He came and hovered about a bit. Brought some pal along. What did he want? Why did he come? No idea. I was ready to go and he just sat there, saying his prayers. I practically had to push him out of the flat. Has he written to you any more?"

Mikola Ivanovich replied that he'd had no more letters.

I continued, seemingly at random.

"So there's this chap, Zusel. Living a nice cushy life. People giving him food, the odd bit of clothing. One woman said there was even a lady friend on the scene. An old girl. Living in the same house. If only he'd stayed put there in Oster. But oh, no. Off he goes, up to all sorts. And he'll get his come-uppance: drunken hooligans will bash his head in because of the way he looks. He won't come round. It's happened before. There's a scar right on the top of his head. With movement inside. Like on a baby."

Didenko said he knew about the scar. It wasn't the result of hooligans but of a deep wound and shell-shock. And if someone couldn't stay put, it wasn't a crime. He wasn't doing any harm.

I sighed and sympathized. "Of course, not. Zusel was what, a war hero? People like that don't appear in the records. They're always unsung heroes."

Almost nodding off, Didenko mumbled: "He wasn't a hero. He was always wanting to eat but there was nothing kosher. So he went without. People said he wasn't eating so he wouldn't have to fight. But that wasn't why. Anyway, they gave him a real thrashing to make him eat. That was when his skull was staved in. He survived. Started eating a bit. Took whatever they gave him. Chewed and chewed it, tucked it behind his lips and spat it out when no-one could see. I used to say, 'Why so wasteful, you bastard? I'll stick my hand out, you can spit it in there. I'll finish it myself.' And I did.

"Did you say shell-shock?"

"Well, that's what I call it. Anything from the war, it's all shell-shock. Zusel's completely barmy. He doesn't realize that once something's in your mouth it's in your body. And your blood. Even if you spit to high heaven afterwards. Dimwit."

I was brooding about Zusel as if he were still alive. I'd made the notion stick and gave myself a pat on the back. Above all, I myself had to believe that Zusel had walked away from me in good health and on his own two feet.

Once again, I told myself I'd done the right thing. Even if it was on the spur of the moment.

Didenko was asleep. His trousers were clean, his shirt freshly laundered too. His bare feet drew the eye because the nails had been trimmed by a caring female hand. 'Lyubochka,' I thought with affection, 'my wife.'

I longed so much to clasp her to my heart that I went to find her. I knew she was doing the laundry in the River Vorskla, the children busy nearby.

I saw them from a distance. Yoska was sitting, naked, on the bank. Gannusya, in just a shirt, was knee-deep in the water, helping her mother rinse the washing.

Still at a distance, I gave a shout so as not to scare them. After all, it was water, and deep.

The children were thrilled. We organized bath-time for them. Lyuba said we shouldn't waste the soap but I lathered the children's heads and the foam floated prettily with the current.

Then I gave myself a good scrub. Behind some reeds.

I called Lyuba over. She didn't come. She didn't want to leave the children. I said I could see them from there and nothing would happen if she left them and came over. I threw a temper tantrum.

We all went home together. I was dragging the buckets full of clean washing. Lyuba was carrying Yoska and holding Gannusya's hand.

Not really thinking, I said reproachfully, "I have so much love for you, so much. Is that so hard for you?"

"Yes," Lyuba answered. "You can't even imagine how hard."

Out of sheer rage, I wanted to throw the buckets down so that the washing fell out and got dirty. But I dismissed the notion as unworthy. On the contrary, I set the buckets carefully down on the grass and said:

"Have it your own way. I won't come near you till you ask me to."

Lyuba quickened her pace without answering.

Towards evening, Petro and Katerina arrived.

They sat at the table in the garden, drinking and having a bite to eat, all very right and proper.

We came to the singing. I launched into "Katyusha" in honour of Petro's wife, Katerina-Katya. Gannusya joined in.

Lyuba was constantly dashing into the house to get one thing or another, laughing loudly for no reason. Each time, Petro would turn his head at the sound, like a cockerel. It was as if she was letting him know her whereabouts at every given second.

Didenko drank a great deal right away but refused to go to bed. He kept refilling his glass then lapsed into Ukrainian when he said:

"Mishko, you bastard, come and stay with me. It's paradise here. Sheer paradise. No going to the collective farm. Not for you. What would you do there? Nothing. No power for you or terror to wield there, you madman, you. Work would be better for you here. You could wave a gun around. Like your Dad. Everyone would be afraid of you. Everyone. Lyuba and the children. And Petro. You'd be afraid of him, wouldn't you, Petro?"

"Of course, I would. I really would," Petro replied immediately, the way people do when someone's drunk.

Even I joined in. And spoke Ukrainian too.

"I'll come and stay, Mikola Ivanovich. I will, for sure. I can be a local police officer. Order would finally come to Ryabina! Everyone would be scared. But not you? Do you think I'd make an exception for you? Pah! No exceptions. None at all!"

As a joke, it didn't go down too well.

Didenko collapsed, his upper half sprawled across the table. I barely had time to snatch up the bottle. There was still a third of a litre of moonshine left.

Didenko suddenly jumped up.

He started shouting like a madman.

"Out of my house, you scum! Out! Out!" And he shook his fists as well.

The children were scared and started to cry. Petro tried to calm them down.

Lyuba looked on indifferently.

Katerina tugged at Petro's sleeve so that he'd leave the children and help take Didenko into the house. The children wouldn't let go of the blind man.

Somehow I took the drunkard into the house. Laid him down on the floor. There, where the children slept. Then I changed my mind and dragged the old man out into the yard, where he had his day-time naps, in the long grass under the cherry tree.

I looked at Didenko stretched out on the grass and was amazed that this was the second time in a short while that I had carried a man from one place to another.

Petro called me. We still had some vodka left. We had to finish it.

We put the children to bed. Lyuba turned in as well.

Katerina went home alone, stroking her husband's head in farewell.

She asked me:

"If you do drink too much, don't let this man of mine out of the yard. He'll be traipsing around the village all night long. Making a nuisance of himself. Put him to bed here. Better yet, don't let him drink. He can't handle it."

Off she went, leaving Petro behind as if he were an inanimate object she was afraid someone might not so much steal as put back in the wrong place for her to track down later.

Petro drained his glass then didn't touch another drop. I drank heartily. Petro sang. He didn't have a good voice, even in Ukrainian, it was too weak. And, well, honestly:

Oh what a moonlit night, starry and bright.

I watch you set your sewing aside.

My work-weary darling, come into the night

And spend just a moment outside.

He sang, turning his head towards the house. I thought, 'And what can you see, you miserable cripple? "I watch you set your sewing aside." What is it you're watching? Eh? Fixing your shameless blind eyes on another man's wife? I'd give you "sewing" if you could see.'

And at some point in the third verse, I said, "You're a good singer, Petro. Beautiful. Have you ever tried making any money from it? You could sing and people would give you what they could. Here at Didenko's, you're filling your face with food bought with my money, aren't you? Lyubochka makes a tasty meal. Tried her cooking, have you? Like it, do you?"

Petro dried up mid-word. Soberly and matter of factly he said, "I eat at home. I'm not interested in your food. It will make me sick. And singing for a crust of bread, yes, I've done that.

"I sang. They coughed up. Strangers. Not here. Here no-one would give anyone anything."

He stood up and went out, slightly off balance, to be fair. But his fingers found the gate straight away.

I didn't even touch Lyuba. I had a conversation planned for the next day. The bare outlines.

The items on the agenda were as follows:

One: What was between us, between husband – that was me – and wife – that was Lyuba.

Two: Had Lyuba got the infection Dovid had drummed into her out of her head?

Three: The relationship between us could no longer be tolerated without some explanation.

Lyuba replied to each of the points tabled.

She said that what was going on between us was ordinary life. Before, she had loved me blindly because of her own wonderment and my physical strength. Now her love for me was steady and she could see certain failings and shortcomings on my part in the past. For example, I had changed a great deal over the past year. I had become jittery. I was loving towards her but forceful as if she owed me something. But she didn't. Hence the confusion. And the inner turmoil nobody needed.

She remembered the conversation with Dovid and went over and over it in her mind all the time. Of course, given her condition at the time, she had mixed some of it up in her head. Some of it, she had recreated. And, ultimately, Dovid hadn't said anything particular. Apart from the fact that he wanted Yosenka back. And, Lyuba said, it was Laevskaya who had instructed Dovid about the infection. Out of womanly spite and envy. Of her age and so on.

Here I asked a leading question: Why was Lyuba bringing Laevskaya up now? Laevskaya had helped our son recover. If it hadn't been for her, who knew how well Yosenko would have fared in hospital hands? I even put Lyuba gently to shame, on purpose, so that she wouldn't say too much. So that she would rise above it.

Lyuba said that Laevskaya used to visit her in hospital. And, incidentally, had hinted that Lilia Vorobeichik, who had been murdered and whom I had investigated, was not a complete stranger to a certain person.

"Is that what she said," I asked, "'not a complete stranger?'"

Lyuba nodded.

"You didn't ask a stranger to whom? Or what 'not entirely' meant?"

"Entirely, not entirely, what difference does it make? I heard it as if I was dreaming. I was on a drip. I really thought I was dreaming. Laevskaya was feeding me words through the drip. And she sat, stroking my hand. And Dovid was there…"

I took note: Dovid had scuttled off to the hospital, not satisfied that what he had said had put Lyuba there.

"The doctor tried to get rid of him but he wouldn't let up. He pushed Laevskaya out of the way. She slid off the stool and he took her place. He began stroking my hand as well. Laevskaya told Dovid that he was too late, that earlier there had been an understanding but now it would soon be dinner time and a new doctor would come in and send him packing…"

I understood. Lyuba had got everything confused. Laevskaya and Dovid. They'd been singing from the same song sheet. Laevskaya had dragged Dovid in. Deliberately, to stand in for her, so that in Lyuba's head everything would be all mixed up: Polina's fabrications and Dovid's. Laevskaya was the stronger one. I could tell. I always can.

Laevskaya was clearly in charge. But where did her interest lie?

About the infection, Lyuba said that she had completed the picture from the available facts and the conversations of her neighbours. It amounted to nix.

That's the word she used: "Nix".

That wasn't her speaking. It was Laevskaya.

She'd hissed at it me once, oh, so very gently:

"But don't you know what happens, my good Mikhail Ivanovich? A person existed, then they're gone. And there's no remorse. None at all. Not from that person or from anyone else. Nix. Then even that's gone."

She had used the word, squirming as I questioned her about Vorobeichik. 'I don't remember, didn't see, don't know. I don't feel comfortable talking about such things out loud. My conscience will be nagging me for talking about such things on my own with a man.'

I raised my voice and said sternly that we were talking about the death of a person. Who should at least be remembered kindly. And that I wasn't a man to her. I was an investigator, an officer in the Soviet police force. Or was she unaware that justice must prevail? With or without remorse.

And she let that "nix" pass her painted lips with such relish that I remember it even now, and shudder.

The third point went effectively unanswered.

In response to a direct hint that Lyuba might have developed feelings for Petro, even though he was a cripple, blind and so on, Lyuba shrugged her shoulders and accused me of not understanding the female character. The female character needs to care for the weak. And the maimed in particular. To her, Didenko and Petro were like children to be cared for. Just like her own, Gannusya and Yosenka.

I assured Lyuba that I understood her state of mind. But she shouldn't do too much and should remember that she wasn't Didenko's hired help. Otherwise they'd sit around, dangling their feet with her there to cut their dirty toenails.

Lyuba agreed with my line of reasoning.

We decided she would stay in the village until the autumn and not let anything untoward be undertaken by any party.

Didenko woke sober. Warded off a hangover with sour milk. He asked when I was leaving.

I replied that I didn't intend to stay long. I had ascertained that the atmosphere there was healthy and I would be leaving today or tomorrow.

Not a peep from Didenko about yesterday's speech. I didn't remind him either. Instead, I asked whether he still had Zusel's letter.

Mikola Ivanovich readily put it right in my hand.

The letter began by saying that Zusel found it hard to write in Russian and that someone else was doing it for him. Zusel was making inquiries about me. Literally: wasn't I known for having done something against Soviet power or, perhaps, it was my parents who were guilty in that respect. Weren't they liquidated for being kulaks? Perhaps Didenko knew someone who knew me from Kharkov or the front? Zusel claimed the information was needed by an acquaintance who wanted to thank me about an important matter but was himself in high office and wanted to be certain there was nothing amiss in my biography. So as not to find himself in an awkward position because of a dodgy acquaintance.

Twaddle! Beyond the realms of any sober thinking. And to trust such matters to the post!

The writing in the letter seemed familiar.

It was Polina Lvovna Laevskaya's. Slanted to the left, the letters fine and precise, i's dotted, t's crossed. Not any old how, the way normal people sometimes write, but neat and deliberate.

The note on the three-way mirror in Laevskaya's house came to mind. With my telephone number at work, plus my name, patronymic and surname. And underneath, 'Comrade Investigator'. Circled several times in red.

The record of the interview with witness Polina Lvovna Laevskaya also contained her signature: 'This is an accurate account of my statement – P.L. Laevskaya'. She had then asked to read through it again and without being asked had added: 'A faithful and accurate account'. I'd reread the wretched thing shortly before leaving for Ryabina. I'd noted that even the lady's handwriting was flowery.

Didenko was smiling.

"Well, then, read enough? So, tell me, what's Zusel getting at with all this? He might as well have written that he's putting a book of honour together. That he's afraid of making a fool of himself so he's filing the information away in an exercise book.

And who does he write to, the dolt? A Fascist toady, a Polizei minion? Right, Mikhail?"

I gave the letter back to Didenko, saying,

"Right, Mikola Ivanovich. Quite right. Zusel himself is a bad lot, of course. But worse is that someone's put him up to this and I know who. And you, Mikola Ivanovich, with a letter like this in a house where there are children here, there and everywhere, you just sit on the stove and twiddle your feet. What if someone with an interest in you should find that letter? And dig out old files? How would that be? How would you like that? And ask whose little children those were, playing here in the summer? And whose wife that was, seen day and night in the vegetable patch in the summer? And who was it came to see you? A policeman from Chernigov? About whom you were being pestered for no apparent reason in a letter from the Zionist, Tabachnik? And, let's be honest, whoever it is that grabs you by the throat, won't give a shit that I'm a war hero, that my parents died as martyrs during the Fascist occupation. They'll haul us in too, me, the children and my wife. And they'll question people. And people will talk. And what they'll say, you know yourself. They said it about you without batting an eyelid. And it will be off to Karaganda like the real Polizei."

Didenko had stopped smiling. His face was livid, white. Like his shirt. Unchanged since yesterday's events. But even so.

"What should we do?"

I moved on to the next part.

"Let me have the letter for good. And the envelope. And if there's anything else from Tabachnik, hand it all over."

Didenko held out the letter. He went over to the stove, scrabbled around under some old clothes and found the envelope.

"Take it," he said breaking into Ukrainian. "And this. I grumbled about you yesterday. I don't regret it. But I am sorry it was in front of the children. I'm not afraid for myself. Do you believe me when I say that?"

"I do," I replied in kind.

Although, to be honest, I didn't believe him one little bit. Everyone says they're not afraid for themselves but for the children. It's the done thing.

I found Yoska and Gannnusya out in the meadow.

They were picking cornflowers. The flowers had only just come out. The children were picking the bigger ones. Their basket was full to the brim but they went on picking more and more.

"Stakhanovites, time to knock off! The norm's been fulfilled and over-fulfilled! Let's go home. I'm about to leave. We'll have some lunch and say our goodbyes."

I sat Yoska on my shoulders and held Gannusya's hand. We went into the house. Through the cornflowers, through the grass. I looked at us from the outside and a wave of happiness ran down my spine.

Lyuba looked at us from behind the fence, hand shielding her eyes. The way they do in nice, heart-warming films.

At lunch Lyuba said the children had been gathering cornflowers to dry them and make herbal tea. For Petro. On Mikola Ivanovich's advice.

Gannusya said the same.

"Uh-huh. If you wash your eyes in cornflowers, they see better. And if you haven't got any eyes at all, like Uncle Petro, you have to wash the place where they used to be and they'll grow again."

Gannusya spoke Ukrainian well, better than she had in Chernigov. But I answered her in Russian so that she didn't forget the language she would be taking into adult life.

"Do what Mummy and Mikola Ivanovich tell you. They want the best for you. Do it and be helpful. Help them and help anyone weak and feeble. Help them and they'll help you. And don't shout at one another. You're brother and sister. Family. And family comes first."

The children nodded and ate.

That was what children should be taught. Not about cornflowers. Eyes don't grow back once they've been put out. But the children hoped they would and how would Didenko be able to look them in the eye afterwards?

It was alright for him. He might die soon. And not see them or have to answer any of their questions.

I got ready quickly. I gave Didenko my cloak-tent. I would account for it at work somehow, for the loss of official property. I'd ask for a second-hand one in exchange.

Didenko immediately tried his new outfit on for size. It turned out to be a bit on the long side. He couldn't walk.

Lyuba volunteered to take it up.

And said in delight:

"It might not fit you but it's just right for Petro. He wanders around the village at night but, covered up like this, even rain and snow wouldn't a problem."

I said I had no objections.

"Let Petro have it."

Didenko supported Lyubochka's initiative.

I no longer felt good. Mentally, I blamed myself for a minute's outburst that meant the cloak-tent had gone to a blind man I didn't even like.

I had three days of leave left. Four, including Sunday.

My next plan was as follows:

To go to Oster and shake up Dovid in the light of Zusel's statements.

And then to tackle Laevskaya properly.

I only just made the train. I squeezed myself into a carriage, without a ticket. I climbed onto the third bunk up and listened, unthinking, to conversations about nothing.

And suddenly I remembered that I hadn't left Lyubochka any money to live on. I'd been worn out. You should always do what matters most first. Whereas my head had been spinning from the moment I set eyes on my wife. And she had, let's be honest, given me the cold shoulder rather than any affection. But that was beside the point. I'd send the money as soon as I could. It might even be a good thing. The postwoman would put it about to all and sundry how much had been sent and to whom. Let the village know the woman staying at Didenko's had money. She wasn't sponging off anyone.

Speculation would travel along a thread that led back to the postwoman.

I reached for the envelope containing Zusel's letter. To look at the return address. In my haste, I hadn't even glanced at it. It was Lilia Vorobeichik's. 23, Clara Zetkin Street. The sender's name was illegible. Especially on the move. But the postmark was clear. As if painted on. The letter had been sent on 28 June 1952.

One month after the death of Lilia Vorobeichik. Or more precisely, a month and a half.

Calmly I hid the envelope in one place and the letter in another. To be on the safe side. And once again I begrudged that cloak-tent. There was a torrential downpour; water came trickling down onto my head. It would be good to wrap myself up properly now and then sleep well, dear comrade.

Some youngsters pointed me to what used to be Evka Vorobeichik's house and was now Basin's place of residence. They even took me there.

One, who had reddish hair and looked like a Jew boy, put out feelers.

"Are you staying long?"

"Oh, do I need to register my assignment with you then? Are you the boss around here?" I replied.

He stopped talking and dropped back a little. I felt sorry for the lad. But still, he needed to know his place. He would let the others know a policeman had turned up – and a proper strict one too.

In passing, I noted to myself that the lad looked like someone I knew. I put the feeling down to his generally Jewish looks.

At the house, I was greeted by Malka.

She pretended not to recognize me.

"Nobody here, there ain't," she burbled.

I could see that for myself. And not just nobody but nothing either. They were really poor. The embroidered curtains at the windows were all that was left of Evka's womanly touch. For the rest, it was bare walls and a bare floor. As poky as Didenko's. What's more, the stove could have done with a clean.

Malka hovered around, gesticulating at my uniform.

"They's all at the river. That's where you gotta go. They's all at the river. Me, I have dinner to cook. All at the river. Go there."

I asked the lads outside where people usually went to swim. They wanted to know if I meant old or young people, women or what. I said it was a grandfather and two little ones. They showed me which way to go.

I headed for the Desna, behind the park.

The Desna sparkled, dazzlingly bright. I was greeted by a jaw-dropping picture.

Ahead of me was Dovid, a cloth on his head, in longjohns and a wraparound undershirt down to his belly button. He was thwacking a stick from side to side, hacking down the tall weeds blocking his next step. Plodding behind him in shiny black underpants were Grishka and Vovka. The elder, Grisha, was using both hands to tow along a canvas bag that was dripping water. He tried to lift the bag up to stop it catching on prickles but catch it did – the boy simply didn't have the height. Vovka lifted the bag up, just a little, whenever he remembered he should be helping his brother. Otherwise, he kept turning his head. Looking over his shoulder at someone behind and hanging back to let the dawdler fall into line.

From behind the willow trees, another individual appeared. His movements like clockwork gone haywire. Arms waving disjointedly.

Once I was no longer dazzled by the water, I understood clearly that the individual concerned was Zusel Tabachnik. He wasn't wearing his cap. He wasn't wearing anything at all. He was walking along stark naked.

To steady myself, I planted my feet wide apart. My boots were burning the soles of my feet – I could feel the heat even through the grass.

I took off my police cap and waved it in the air.

"'Lads, who's your commander,
Who leads you to the fight,
Marching although wounded
Neath our red banner bright?'
Grisha, Vovka, come here. Sing the marching song with me!"

The little lads recognized my voice and hurtled towards me. Grishka was so thrilled he tried to wave the bag but dropped it instead.

I didn't move an inch. I was rooted to the spot. I had cramp.

Grishka picked up the bag, clutched it to his stomach and yelled:

"Uncle Misha! Uncle Misha! Hooray! Grandpa, Uncle Misha's here. Uncle Misha, have you brought your gun? Can I aim it?"

Holding the bag he ran up to me and plonked the dirty, sodden thing down on my boots. My legs felt better, just a touch. The burning sensation had passed. The cramp hadn't.

The little boys clambered all over me out of old habit. They clung to my belt, my holster strap. Stood on the top of my boots in their bare feet.

I couldn't take the onslaught. I sank down on the grass.

Grishka and Vovka bellowed out the Song about Shchors.

Just as my best comrade, Evsey Gutin, used to do, I said:

"Put a sock in it!"

And they did.

I removed the children gingerly and straightened up to my full height.

Dovid was standing before me, having taken Zusel, as if he were a fine lady, by the arm.

Zusel looked as if he'd been through the mill.

"Why is this citizen naked?" I asked without a hint of harshness.

Vovka eagerly explained:

"We've been washing our clothes. Malka sent us." The boy poked around in the bag and began presenting the crumpled rags one by one. "There's Grandpa's shirt, and trousers, and Zusel's trousers. Here's his longjohns, his shirt, his cap, and his… Grandpa, his what..?

In the end it was Dovid who supplied the word:

"Tallit, yingele."

I looked curiously at the sopping bundle.

"It's called doing the laundry. What did you use to wash it?"

"Soap," Dovid replied and immediately yelled, "Where's the soap, boys? I'm asking you: where's the soap? Who's got it? Have you forgotten it? Used it all up? Grishka, Vovka!"

The soap was still by the river. The lads raced back.

Dovid, as if there was nothing out of the ordinary, asked, "Are you here on your own or with Lyuba and Yoska?"

I shook my head.

"On my own. I was just passing. So I thought I'd pop in and see you. Why are you holding on to Zusel? He's not going to fall. He was walking by himself and he'll stay up by himself."

Dovid let go of Tabachnik's elbow.

I greeted Zusel personally:

"Hello, Citizen Tabachnik. Long time, no see."

He didn't reply. He looked me in the eye and didn't reply.

Dovid stepped in.

"He's not himself. He's not recognizing anyone. What a carry-on. I'll tell you at home. Let's go. The children will come along themselves. We'll go through the vegetable patches, where no-one can see us."

Dovid scooped the washing back into the bag, stuffed it in any old how and tossed the bag over his shoulder. I suggested that for Zusel, as a decent person, it might be awkward to walk along naked, even if it was through the vegetable patches. Despite Dovid replying that he couldn't be bothered trying to persuade Zusel to cover himself, I personally took the cloth off Dovid's head and wrapped it round Tabachnik's nether regions.

Zusel gave off a clean, watery smell.

He smoothed down the cloth and walked placidly on. But I ordered Dovid to take the lead so that we'd go the right way.

The children arrived home before us. Malka had quickly put their food on the table.

When we came in she shouted at the youngsters to shoo.

They made themselves scarce. They stuffed anything they hadn't eaten into their pockets and ran outside.

Malka darted over to Zusel, began rasping away with him, asking questions. He didn't answer, smiling and holding onto the cloth as if threatening to let it drop at any minute.

Malka took him behind the curtain and continued her nurturing, her voice now raised.

Dovid sat down on a stool at the table. He invited me to eat.

I was in no hurry to do so. Even though I was hungry. There's more to be gained when someone's sitting down and another man is standing, looming over him, particularly a man in uniform.

"So tell me," I said, "what's sent Zusel completely round the bend? And keep it brief. Well?"

Dovid appeared to want to make his report in a standing position but I pressed him lightly down on the stool. He looked up at me and talked.

And here's what he said:

A few days earlier, Evka had arrived, her arms around Zusel. She'd brought him there virtually unconscious. Propping him up. He had been wandering around Liskovitsa in a state that beggared description. Covered in earth, filthy, his face black with mud, his fingernails torn to the quick. A Liskovitsa Jew who knew him took him in and gave him a wash.

Evka was informed through the Jewish grapevine. She took Zusel by the scruff of the neck and off to Oster. In addition, she told Dovid to look after Tabachnik like a child and not to let him go to anyone, not to hospital, not anywhere.

"It's not easy with someone like that. He needs to go to hospital. I can arrange it. Same place as Belka. We'll put Zusel in there too. He'd be fed and looked after. After all, Dovid, you have the children. They might see so much of him sick that they could go that way themselves. Especially when their mother has already. And everything."

Dovid began to tap his feet. He sat there, tapping. Clearly, he no longer had the strength to stand up.

"No! Evka said not to let him go to anyone. And since you've mentioned Belka, I'll tell you that I know everything about my daughter. And I know about your doctor too, how he's keeping her there. I smoked him out. All by myself."

Here Dovid stopped. He realized he'd said too much. But it's that too much that the investigator relies on. And that was what I seized hold of.

"Really, now. But do you know that Zusel fetched up at my place in Chernigov and informed on you? He brought a witness too. Some Shtadler or other. Told me what you had in mind for me. You want to smoke me out too. And apparently you've sent a letter you-know-where. Saying I've been killing people with my bare hands all over the place, taking advantage of my official position. That I'm an enemy of the people. Zusel came to me and tried to defend you. Wanted to take the blame for you stabbing me in the back. I heard him out and sent him packing. I have nothing to fear. But look how you're treating Zusel. Perhaps you'll be keeping him on a chain on Evka's orders so he doesn't get out of the yard? He needs treatment. To get him back on his feet. Superstition means you put everything upon God. You're even ruining the youngsters, turning them into enemies. Damn but you're a fool, Dovid. Evsey would have thrashed you as a relative. But I can't. I have no right. Under the law. Under our Soviet law. Do you understand?"

Dovid was silent.

When I shouted, Malka leant around the curtain.

She swept the flower-patterned rag aside with a flourish – even the cord shook a little – and squawked:

"Zusel went to see you. He took all the money we had. Where is it? Give it back."

Zusel had had no money on him. I had personally turned his pockets inside out.

Malka put her hands on her hips and began to wail:

"Give me back that money! I have children to feed!"

I couldn't stand this contemptible attitude.

I went up to her and said, quietly and confidently:

"So what, you've started speaking Russian now it's about money, have you? You're all the same. You'd be hanged for a kopeck. I know nothing about any money. I don't need your blasted money. I've got my own, honest pay. I'll never step foot in this shithole again. I treat you like decent people and you just squawk at me, right where it hurts."

Zusel, meanwhile, was lying on the couch by the window. The drawn-back curtain covering half of his face. And he was watching me out of one eye.

I gave up and shot out into the yard.

There stood the little boys, chewing on slices of black bread. I wondered how long they'd been chewing away. Dovid and I had been talking for about twenty minutes. Which meant the boys had been listening to our conversation. Had been distracted from their chewing. Heard the details. And could now spread a topsy-turvy version all over Oster.

I said nothing to them by way of goodbye.

But still I went back after I'd passed the fence. I went back and patted each one on the head in turn. They hadn't done anything wrong.

I had a lot on my mind just then.

Firstly, spending the night. And early the next day going to see Dovid again and having a quiet chat. About Yoska, about Belka, about Evsey and his totally unnecessary death. About Dovid's own intentions regarding his scandal-mongering. And taking a peek at Zusel under normal circumstances. As well as shedding light on the money he allegedly had on him at the time of his trip to Chernigov. There might be a thread there too. What, I didn't know, but a thread nonetheless. A lead is what matters most in our business.

Zusel's resurrection from the trusty grave quickly settled into my mind and found its rightful place. Alive was alive. My fault. My oversight. I hadn't checked his condition sufficiently. Had failed to tell a dead body not just from a living person but even from a pretend corpse. Hadn't tamped the earth down properly when I buried him the second time, when I pulled my cloak-tent out from under him.

A blunder like that and I'd be ashamed in front of my colleagues. That's how I catch people out and I turn out to be no cleverer myself.

One thing was certain and I hadn't kept it from Dovid: Zusel had been to see me and told me Dovid's plans and Shtadler witnessed it. Zusel took leave of me unharmed and under his own steam, as I had both casually and deliberately told Dovid and Malka behind her curtain.

I was walking through tall grass as I turned off immediately behind the vegetable patches.

All of a suddenly, I longed to take a nap. I was so tired.

I pulled off my boots, unwound my footcloths. Threw them aside, I wouldn't say in anger but certainly with force. And plonked myself face down on the ground. I wanted to undo my belt to relax. Something was clenched up inside and wouldn't relax properly. But I sank into a deep sleep. My belt done up. I always did it up really tightly. In the last hole. So that I could feel myself breathing. Now, I wasn't breathing too well. Something wasn't right.

I woke up with a sore head.

My mouth crammed with earth.

The question arose of where to spend the night. I thought of asking someone to take in a poor traveller. But shelved that idea. Oster had already been told that a policeman had been to see Dovid. If I went and foisted myself on people, there would be questions and I'd be obliged to talk. I might let something slip. Especially as I'd left my haversack at Dovid's. And good riddance. But the entrenching tool, the lantern, the knife were all there too. Not so good.

I went back. As if I had calmed down and now wanted to talk properly. Which was the truth.

Dovid was sitting on a tree stump by the house. Back to the road. Facing a man.

Dovid's arms were going in all directions, his voice conducting the movements:

"And I do know where he's got to, do I? There? There? Or maybe there? I don't answer for him. He's on duty. He answers for himself."

The man patted Dovid on the shoulder soothingly. He spoke quietly.

I gave a hearty hello as I approached.

The man turned round. I recognized Faida.

He shook my hand firmly as if he knew me well.

He inquired simply:

"Where are you going to be staying? Dovid doesn't have room. I'd like to ask you to stay with us. My son told me a policeman had come to Oster. Had gone to see Dovid Basin. I came over. Faida. Miron Shayevich Faida."

Of course I remembered him. A real pest. Now he'd tell Dovid where and when we met and under what circumstances. But no.

Faida took me a little aside and in a brisk whisper said:

"There's no holding him back. Two minutes and he'd told me your name, patronymic and surname. Told me about his grandson, who's living with you, too. The needle's stuck. But we are acquainted. Remember the wedding?"

"I do. You do cultural work."

"That's right, kind of. At least I'm on the alert. So, coming to us? My wife will give us dinner. We'll have a glass apiece. Find something to chat about."

Faida looked at me questioningly.

Dovid was drawing in the sand with a stick. Displaying his lack of interest.

"Dovid Srulevich, I'll collect my things now. I'll stay over at Comrade Faida's. So as not to be in your way. We'll have a talk come the morning."

Dovid made not a sound in reply, stood up and barked through the open window:

"Malka, get his stuff!"

Malka leant across the window sill with my haversack. She needed all her strength to hold it out.

And so I took my property from her: and not nicely. Like a thief receiving something from another thief.

Faida looked on with a crooked grin.

Behind us, Malka slammed the window. Hard enough to break the glass, it seemed. I turned round. From behind the curtain, Zusel was shaking his fist.

I stole a peek at the knot I'd used to tie the haversack. It was mine. No-one had been inside.

Faida's wife was making dinner.

Her husband and I sat out in the little garden.

He began talking about general matters.

But soon cut to the chase.

"Mikhail Ivanovich, I have to warn you that we keep our ears to the ground here. I have personally, and not just once or twice, had conversations aimed at educating Citizen Basin and Citizen Tsvintar. They take incredible liberties. Blackening your good name on every corner. Are you aware of that?"

I shook my head.

"Well, then, you won't know either that intrigues are being woven against you. The last time you were in Oster, did you call in on Basin and Zusel? No, you didn't. Dovid even complained about it to me, that you'd been to Oster and not dropped in. He saw you out of the corner of his eye. Didn't you see him? Of course, you didn't. Otherwise, why wouldn't you have dropped in? He says you were coming to see him but didn't stop by. He was put out. I explained that you were probably just passing for work. You can rely on me entirely."

It was as though Faida was making a speech rather than having a chat at the table in his own home.

"And now, in a situation where all the forces of our people are being mobilized in the light of Comrade Stalin's death, Dovid is stepping up his crazy ramblings. How do you like that? I don't like it. And no-one in Oster's Jewish community likes it either. No-one. I can tell you that for certain."

I snapped.

"What's the Jewish community got to do with it? So, Dovid's gone mad with grief. He's had every reason to. His son-in-law, his own daughter. And his grandsons scattered in all directions. Yes, he's of Jewish nationality. No disputing that. But why do you keep making the distinction: us Jews, us, the Jewish community. He's out to get me as a man not as a Jew. This thing between us is a family matter. A family matter. About Iosif. And we need to rally round our Stalin's memory. But once again you're making distinctions. That I'm in uniform at the moment doesn't mean a thing, still less anything bad. I'm here to see a relative, the grandfather of my adopted child, Iosif. And the adoption of that child, Iosif, was completely by the book. And with Dovid, it's a case of live and let live. The doctors will soon be sending him for treatment. I'm sorry for the little boys. That is true."

Perplexed, Faida said nothing. He realized he'd taken the wrong tack.

"Fine, Miron Shayevich. You've shown your concern and thank you. But tell me, who used to live in the house where Dovid hangs out these days? It's not much to look at but it is sturdy. It's a shame Dovid will let it go to rack and ruin given his current attitude to life."

I had put the man in his place and then asked a clear, practical question. As if to reduce the tension, for his own good. Now he would blurt out a lot he hadn't been planning to say. In order to ease the discomfort of what had gone before.

And so I brought Faida round to discussing Evka Vorobeichik and her family. Including Lilia too, of course. Then I intended to turn the conversation to Laevskaya as a former resident of Oster.

What came out was this:

The Vorobeichik family had lived in Oster since time immemorial. In the very same house as Dovid did now.

It was because of the house that Lilia and Eva's parents perished. They wouldn't accept evacuation although they were warned. They were afraid to leave their property. It had fine beds and a table famous throughout Oster – it was vast, as big as a whole room, made out of really good wood of some kind, had belonged to a great-great-grandfather. Women's gossip whispered that there was gold hidden in the table legs.

Anyway, the old folk stayed to guard the house for future generations. Naturally, they were killed by the Germans.

As for their daughters: Evka was evacuated, while Lilka vanished for the duration of the war. It was known for a fact that Evka came back from evacuation in 1944 alone. She didn't talk about her sister and when Lilka was brought up she would burst into tears, loudly and pointedly.

Evka lived alone in her parents' house. Malka Tsvintar stuck to her like a leech. Relative or not, she lived with Evka and took the role of auntie.

At the end of the 1940s, there was a rumour in Oster that Lilka had been seen in Chernigov. Looking good – coat, hat, boots with nice little heels and so on. Lilka had determinedly failed to acknowledge an Oster resident who said hello.

As for Evka… Somehow in 1936, Evka managed to get herself pregnant. Her belly was so huge, twins or triplets were being predicted. Whose they were, was a secret. Evka had never been known as no better than she should be. There was Evka with her belly and then suddenly the whole lot disappeared. As if she'd lost the baby. A hint that was dropped by Evka's and Lilka's Mum. If she had, that was grief enough. People left well alone.

It has to be said that in Oster Evka and Lilka were pitied rather than liked. They were both attractive to look at. But they brushed aside suitors from Oster as beneath them in intelligence and upbringing. They had no particular qualifications. They worked in a cooperative that made buttons. Their father was a supervisor there. Their Mum had always been a housewife.

And then Lilka was murdered in Chernigov. Evka went there as soon as she found out. Back and forth she went several times: from Oster to Chernigov, from Chernigov to Oster. Then she collected Malka and declared that she would be taking up residence in her late sister's house with Malka in tow.

A few months later, Malka appeared in Oster and some time after that circumstances apparently led Dovid to buy the house from Evka or something, to leave his dugout, along with Zusel and the two children, and move in as the owner.

Faida spoke uneasily, in a rush.

I didn't interrupt. An interrupted person might pause for reflection. And reflection was just what I didn't need. I needed his outpourings to snowball.

He said:

"Those young girls, Evka and Lilka, they were an odd pair. Good luck to the one who's still alive and may the one who's dead rest in peace. The house is still standing though. You were right: it is sturdy."

I asked about the table, where it had gone.

Faida grew stern, pulling down his jacket as if it were a military coat.

"What happened to the table is this: after the Germans came to Oster, the arrests started. Activists, Party members, Young Communists. As happens during occupation. And Jews, of course. They were shot on the spot. Or in a centralized manner by the Desna." He lowered his voice when he mentioned the Jews, as if ashamed to say it.

I taunted him. I still had to worm information out of him about Laevskaya.

"Surely you're not embarrassed, Miron Shayevich? Everyone knows the Jews were killed. No need to lower your voice."

Faida swiftly nodded and said it again, more loudly:

"The Jews were shot, en masse, yes."

I even touched his hand. The man was clearly suffering. But I had a job to do.

"So, they were killed. And then? You were talking about the table."

"People immediately raked through the Vorobeichiks' house. The Polizei did their best. The aim was to take the table out of the house. Someone had their eye on it. But it couldn't be done. They started chopping it into pieces out of spite. They couldn't cut through the wood. Then a high-ranking German officer moved into the house. He lived there right through the occupation. During his time, the table was taken apart and removed from the house. They took it apart like this: it turned out there were pins that had to be squeezed, just a tiny bit, and the table would come apart, in sections. The sections were thrown out on the street. People dragged them off to their own houses. But when Evka came back after being evacuated, she deliberately went from house to house, gathering them up again. One person had made a wall for a kennel, another a trap-door into the cellar. Some people wouldn't give them back. Evka won them round. She laid the pieces of wood down in her empty house and kept watch over them. Then, under her guidance, they were removed to the old Jewish cemetery. Dumped in a corner. In front of everyone, Evka said: 'That's it. Kaput. It's my property and I, personally, have buried it. I don't want to say or hear anything more about it. I've done what I had to do.' Some people said she initially wanted to put the planks in the ravine by the Desna where the Jews were shot. Her own Mum and Dad. But she was advised against it. I tell you – they were odd. Both Evka and Lilka. People here think there was some reason Lilka was murdered."

I remarked that people aren't murdered for no reason. A stray bullet, that's another matter. But when it's with a knife, there's a reason.

Faida agreed.

Then I said that a lot of people from Oster lived in Chernigov. One Laevskaya, for example. A dressmaker. And an attractive woman.

Faida's eyes reacted to the name.

At that point, his wife appeared, asking us to go to dinner.

There was a tiny sink with a mirror in the small corridor. I just wanted to rinse my hands. But when I looked, I had a black ring round my mouth. Dried-on earth. Where I'd dribbled in my sleep.

I washed my face.

With a smile I asked Faida, "Why didn't you tell me my face was dirty? It's embarrassing."

Faida dismissed this.

"I didn't even notice."

Oh, really? Didn't notice. He'd done it on purpose. He was pleased I was dirty.

I was not in a good mood as I sat down at the table.

Faida's wife – Sima Zakharovna – was a persistent hostess. She tried to speak Ukrainian. I answered her in Russian once, then again.

On she went. "Please, help yourself. Help yourself."

Jewish cooking. Which I praised. Fruit liquor, vodka.

Faida drank deep but little.

I drank several glasses of vodka. It loosened me up.

I asked the woman if she knew a Polina Lvovna Laevskaya. By the by.

She looked at her husband and stopped, a spoonful of beans held over my plate.

Faida loudly proposed a toast to my family and, especially, the children.

We drank.

I had to give up on Laevskaya.

I turned the talk to Faida's son.

Miron was proud of the lad's achievements. He was at vocational college, going to be a builder.

I asked what he was called.

"Sunya. Samuil." Faida pointed at his wife. "In honour of her grandfather, Samuil Laevsky."

Sima Zakharovna nodded in agreement.

Immediately, I said, "So your maiden name was Laevskaya? Might you be related to Polina Lvovna?"

I could barely make out the answer.

"She's my cousin."

Faida's chair practically bounced.

"Pah, some cousin! No cousin at all. Absolutely not! A bitch, not a cousin. Cousins like that should be got rid of!"

A lot gets said when people have had a bit to drink, especially when they're not used to it. It's better not to force a conversation in a state of intoxication. Let it be. In his mind, the other person will regret letting the cat out of the bag. And, at the same time, be pleased no-one realized or noticed. Then, if you raise the subject when he's sobered up, goodness only knows what will come out.

I started talking about Oster, how lovely it was, about the children growing up despite all the deaths.

By the time my hosts' son, Sunya, arrived home, the table was practically empty. But he showed no desire to join us. He grabbed a piece of bread and went into the next room.

I recognized him. The same little Jew boy who'd met me when I first set foot in Oster. And I realized who he was like. Evka Vorobeichik. Specifically Evka. Her eyes, with their particular set. And her nose. Lilia had a hawk nose while Evka's wasn't just a hawk nose but was slightly flattened at the tip as well.

I was given the master bed, despite my objections. Pillows, a feather mattress and so forth.

I tossed and turned and then I went outside.

For a long time I sat on a bench in the garden. I wasn't thinking. I was breathing in the air. Even if I'd been a smoker, I wouldn't have lit up. I was breathing so deeply. Not calmly but deeply.

I set off to see Dovid at dawn. Sima tried to hold me back with a promise of cream-cheese pancakes but I stood my ground.

There are people who believe food can hold a man back.

At Dovid's everyone was asleep. No-one answered my knock at the window.

I didn't want to wake the children, otherwise I would have banged with all my might.

Given this state of affairs, I wandered off to the Desna. Along yesterday's little path. To have a decent wash and change my clothes. It was awkward at Faida's. I undid my haversack on the bank. And discovered the knife was missing. Where my bag had been unfastened – at Dovid's or Faida's – I had no idea. It was an unusual knot, from Kalmykia. Taught me by Sergeant Damdinov at the front. It had been skilfully copied. Which meant someone had made a real effort. Had understood that the knot instantly gave away whether or not anyone had gone into the bag. But the drawing end hadn't been folded in two. I'd tried to teach Evsey once. He'd managed but got muddled up. It took him ages.

But Grisha had got it straight away even though he was only a kiddie at the time. But, even trickier knots do get tied and untied by chance. Faida, maybe, or Sunka?

The only thing to be pleased about was that the letter was in the pocket of my uniform coat. I felt the pocket. It was empty. I unbuttoned it, turned myself inside out as well as the pocket. Still empty.

Nix.

The only place I'd taken my coat off was at Faida's. I'd drawn a stool up to the bed and hung it over that. When I went out into the garden, I hadn't put it on.

That's what food does for you. A telling slip-up. I needed to work on my mistakes.

I washed my whole body in every sense of the word. My skin squeaked to touch.

I hid the coat. I put a jacket on over my shirt. Kept on my breeches and boots. I was satisfied with my outward appearance – I was in uniform and, at the same time, was dropping a hint – I was in uniform but not full uniform. I could speak not forcefully but indirectly. Kindly. That is, I could even bypass the law a touch if the need arose.

The children weren't at home.

Dovid looked at me uncertainly.

I took the stool without waiting to be asked. Was deliberately noisy as I shunted myself towards the table so that I would alert Malka behind her curtain. But there wasn't a sound from there. I decided she wasn't there.

I nodded in that direction:

"Has the missus gone to the market, then?"

Dovid replied that she had given up the ghost. She had passed away in the night. She was carrying out Zusel's chamber pot and, as she did so, she collapsed.

Dovid sat quietly. Back straight, head back, chin high.

"Is she there?" I pointed to the curtain.

Dovid nodded.

Malka lay dead on the couch. Beside her, curled up like a baby, lay Zusel. They both had their eyes closed. And neither of them was breathing.

I yelled out:

"What's going on here? Sleeping like the dead?"

Zusel opened his eyes, as if in shock, at the noise. Not the meaning.

"Zusel's alive," he said.

And again he seemed to stop breathing. Snuggled up to Malka with all his might.

I realized there was no point talking to Dovid according to the plan I'd drawn up in advance.

"Is it long since Laevskaya arrived?"

He answered in a single word:

"Yesterday."

"You need to send her a telegram. You do have a relationship after all."

Dovid dismissed this.

"As if she needs a telegram from me! It was Evsey she needed. She got to me through Evsey. Relationship. Bah!"

And he clasped his head as if he had only just realized what had happened to Malka, that she was no longer alive. That the house would now lack a woman's touch.

As it turned out, Dovid had sent the boys off to inform the neighbours.

People began to assemble.

Zusel was torn away from Malka and carried out into the room. Later it occurred to them: it would be better to bring Malka into the room for general viewing and farewells and to leave Zusel behind the curtain.

I didn't get involved. I took Grishka and Vovka and went off to the Desna.

I organized a race. In the shallow water. The children had a high old time. We sang songs.

We marched our way back home.

Faida had taken charge. I gave some money. I had a tiny bit left after the money I'd given to Lyubochka. I promised to send more. To his address. To be passed on to Dovid when he was back on his feet.

In farewell, I also said:

"Miron Shayevich, Polina Lvovna called to see you during the night. I expect I'd occupied her space. Was she upset? And where did she spend the night?"

It was a guess. A hunch.

Faida blinked and blurted out:

"She did. She was going to Chernigov for good. There was a car waiting. She dropped in for a minute. When you were sitting out the back. I wanted to bring her to you out of politeness. She was embarrassed. She'd brought books for Sunya. I can show you if need be. For college. Three of them. Not new but clean. Not written in."

I said nothing as if I was wondering whether to ask to be shown the books. I didn't say a word.

Just whispered from the doorway to Sima – she was loitering there, wringing her hands:

"I have urgent business to attend to. I won't stay for the funeral. Keep the little lads here for a couple of days until Dovid perks up."

I went back to Chernigov at the end of the working day. Popped into the department.

Svetka the typist stood on the doorstep in a smart frock, clutching a handbag and looking for someone.

I struck up a conversation, "Not waiting for me, are you, gorgeous?"

"Everyone's leaving work and here you are turning up."

"You're the one with the regular hours. I envy you. Planning on going to the pictures?"

"Yes. I'm waiting for my friend. She's late."

Svetka made an angry face but her round shaven eyebrows interfered. It made her look comical.

Not stopping to think, I made a suggestion.

"Take me instead of your friend. I'm still down as on leave."

Somehow it came out right.

I'd worked out in a flash that I could get more out of Svetka than of anyone else. She was a woman. If you asked the right way, you'd find out things a bloke would die before telling you.

There was music before the film. Some people were dancing.

We arrived with time to spare, enough time to go to the café.

Svetka asked for lemonade and cakes. I bought them. That said, I was wary as I dug into my pocket. I'd emptied all the money out in Oster for Faida.

But there was enough. If that was everything. Svetka wouldn't be getting a second helping.

For myself, I declined, saying I didn't want anything, I'd eaten at home.

Svetka smirked.

"At home? Why didn't you get changed? Your jacket's crumpled. It's got something nasty on it. Your boots are dusty. You didn't even leave that heavy bag behind. Were you in a tearing hurry?"

All the same, this girl had been with the police a long time. She'd picked things up. Her questions caught me unawares. Another needless mistake.

However, I said cheerfully, putting an arm round Svetka:

"Well, my girl! We should be awarding you a rank. Instead, you're just typing away. Aren't you bored?"

Svetka removed my arm and said sternly:

"I got the tickets under the counter. In advance, incidentally. Had to pay extra too. Don't you forget to give me the money for yours. And I can see through anything. Certain people think I'm stupid. Let them. Men prefer stupid girls anyway. Isn't that so?"

"It certainly is. I'll give you the money for the ticket tomorrow. For mine and yours. I always pay when I take a woman to the pictures. Why don't you tell me what's going on at the station instead? What's the news? I'm really not looking forward to getting back in harness. They'll saddle me with some rubbish case and that's the summer gone. I have a friend who lives in Ladinka. There are some pretty places there. And fish and everything. We could go there on Sunday. What do think? Just as friends, of course. We've worked side by side for years."

Svetka thought about it.

I looked around. I couldn't see anyone I knew. There were five minutes left until the show started. Svetka was taking her time over the lemonade. She hadn't touched the cake.

Her answer came tumbling out.

"Let's go. As friends, of course. I'm not the kind of girl who'd go otherwise. And a woman came to see you while you were away. A pretty one. Well, not that pretty, but not bad. Nicely dressed. Open-toed shoes and little socks. And a handbag. Shameless red hair. You could tell right away she was a bad lot. Kept on and on asking, over and over again: when, when, when, on and on. I answered her in riddles on purpose. Bold as brass, she was." Svetka looked at me fixedly. "She accused me of being rude to the public. But she was banging her head against a brick wall. She went to Sviridenko's office. But he wasn't there. He'd gone to a meeting in Kiev in the light of the new instructions. Went off with a real sour face. She didn't come back again. She loafed around in the corridors, asking the lads."

I realized it had been Evka. And just at the time that Zusel scrambled out.

That was the main news. Svetka also said there was speculation in town about criminals snatching people and burying them alive. One old man had been buried but had dug himself out. He wouldn't have if it hadn't been for the stray dogs. They dug him up. But no-one reported it so the general feeling was that people had gone slightly barmy and didn't know what to come up to explain a situation that was so out of kilter.

I sat unmoving in the auditorium. Through the newsreel and the film.

It hadn't been worth paying through the nose for such drivel.

Just the once, Svetka moved her forearm closer to mine as if by accident but I didn't respond. I meant what I said: we were just friends.

The programme finished and I walked Svetka home. She lived right in the centre on Valovaya Street. In farewell, I reminded her about Ladinka but didn't try to give her a hug. Although she was expecting me to.

Now my path led to Shtadler. First, though, I made a flying visit home, changed into civvies and left the haversack behind.

I was on the very point of leaving when I spotted a note on the table.

"I'm waiting," it read. "Come over. We need to talk."

It wasn't signed. But it didn't have to be. I's dotted, t's crossed – just like the letter. Laevskaya. I didn't even wonder how she'd entered the house to plant her wretched message.

I lunged for the door to rush over there but stopped.

No. I mustn't rush. Not today or tomorrow. Not if I could help it. Let her come to me. Let her come and beg to speak to me.

And I didn't need to go to Shtadler either.

Or Evka.

Or anyone.

I needed to get a good sleep. For Lyubochka's sake. For Yoska's and Gannusya's.

I undressed properly, folded my clothes, the way Lyubochka would when she was picking them up after me: jacket on a hanger in the wardrobe, trousers too, on a special hanger, with clips, shirt over the back of a chair, socks not thrown on the floor but draped over the crossbar of a stool. I put the old sandals I wore at home next to one another. Toes forward, backs towards the bed. And straightened them up. The heels against the grain of the wood. That's how I made sure they were straight.

Trying to go to sleep I was restless but had the sense of a job well done.

I dreamt Sviridenko was giving me a dressing down: 'You didn't tamp it down. You were careless.'

There wasn't a sound from Laevskaya. Or Evka.

I tried not to think about them. One thought bothered me – how Basin and the little boys were doing.

But what could I do?

And at the end of June Svetka waylaid me, eyes round:

"Do you know Shtadler?"

"Why?"

Shtadler was my secret collaborator and none of Svetka's business.

But she got right in my face.

"The chap who can't speak. Bit Jewish. Yes?"

"Not a bit Jewish but a person of Jewish nationality. And?"

"Mm-hmm. Very Jewish. He was here yesterday. And not alone. With some vamp. Thick paint on her lips. Looked revolting. At her age, all made-up. They were looking for you about urgent official business. Her with the lips, she says: 'I am Polina Lvovna Laevskaya and this is Comrade Veniamin Yakovlevich Shtadler. He suffers from ill health and is dumb so I am accompanying him. He would like to meet Comrade Investigator Tsupkoy.' And she looks at me as though I'm going to produce you from under the table. I say to her, even though I'm not obliged to, 'The Comrade Investigator is on an assignment.' And she goes: 'And when will he be in the office? He's supposed to talk to citizens not just gad around town.' So I go: 'It's so that people like you can live peaceful lives that the Comrade Investigator is gadding about. Write a statement and leave it here. I'll pass it on.' And with a little smile, she yaps out: 'I won't be writing any statements and nor will Comrade Shtadler. We need to see him in person.' And that Comrade Shtadler could hardly stay on his feet. I say, 'Comrade Shtadler, take a seat. Have a rest. We don't need anyone fainting. A lot of people have fainted here. It didn't help.' That woman, she grabs Shtadler by the arm and drags him out. And off he toddles, good as gold. I tell you the woman is definitely in charge. And he does her bidding."

Svetka was making smug little faces as she looked at me.

I complimented her.

"Quite right, Svetlana, no wasting words on these impudent folk. I've seen that Laevskaya as a witness. What she wants, I can't imagine. Shtadler I don't know. Even so, it's a shame I didn't speak to them. I'm here to help."

Svetka's face fell:

"To help… You can help me. I've got this neighbour. He's gone bonkers. At night he bangs the wall between us. It frightens my Mum. I can't sleep. At the moment, I'm all on my own. Mum's gone off to the village for a week. And what am I supposed to do with a maniac next door? We got those, you know, adobe walls. Push it with your fist and it'll collapse. And I'm there. Alone. Defenceless. So, it turns out I work for the police and much good it does me."

Towards the end of her speech, Svetka crumpled with the intention of weeping.

I couldn't let that happen.

I put a hand on her thin shoulder and said:

"I'll see what sort of chap he is. Put the wind up him. You won't be left defenceless."

"When will you be there?" Svetka was so impatient she went up on her toes.

"When does he get home?"

"He's always home. He doesn't work anywhere. He's a parasitic element. I could get off work now."

"No, I have urgent business just now. I'll drop by when I'm off shift. Don't be scared."

Svetka was a good actress but a stupid one. Her entire appearance revealed that she wasn't frightened. On the contrary, she wanted to lure me in. As just friends.

I went back into the office. Asked my colleagues in general terms whether anyone had been looking for me the day before. I roamed the corridor. Still trying to find out if there had been any visitors for me. Nothing from anyone.

I didn't have urgent business right then. But I did need to think. Really think and come to some conclusions about what was going on.

I headed for the town park behind Red Bridge. Sat on my, and Lyubochka's, favourite bench near the Stalin monument. Under a Persian lilac. It was as if I'd conjured up an image of Lyubochka. I even bought myself an ice-cream in her honour.

My conclusions were as follows:

I'd outwaited, outlasted Laevskaya. She had revealed her unease. Had set out to trap me. Had said in public that she was trying to contact me. Dragged Shtadler along to make a visual impression. Which meant Dovid had managed to let her know from what I'd told him that Shtadler had called at my house with Zusel. She'd taken Shtadler by the scruff of the neck and dragged him there. As if to say, she had Veniamin Yakovlevich, a dumb invalid, in her power as well. With all he knew about Zusel's visit.

So, she'd called in. But what if I had been there? It's hard to say what would have happened. Having her say at the police station wouldn't get her anywhere. That's not what she was banking on. How did she sniff out that I was away? I was in Kolichevka yesterday. Working on a case.

What's more, she'd gone straight to the secretary. Right next to the chief's office. But she knew perfectly well where I worked. She would have gone there. No. She hadn't been into the office. We always have someone there.

What then? Had Laevskaya been following me in all her glory? I would have noticed. You can't not notice her. Or had she sent someone else to keep an eye on me?

She must have done. But why? Wasting her advancing years on me of all people? Driving me into a frenzy, tormenting me, and my wife and children?

A frontal assault. That's what it was – on all sides. The note on my table at home. And the trip to Oster literally on my heels.

I ate my ice-cream mechanically. The scoop between the two wafers shifted about like a ball-bearing. And shot out. It fell onto my boot. The sparrows flocked down straight away. I shooed them away with my foot.

Yes. Let's be honest. Lilia Vorobeichik. It was all to do with her. It started and it ended with her.

I stood up. Ruthlessly pulverizing the remains of the ice-cream.

I wiped my boot on a clump of grass. Till it shone. I knew just where I was going – to Laevskaya's.

As it happened, the gate was open. So was the door to the house.

Polina Lvovna was lying on a couch. Dozing. But from her arms, held by her sides, I ascertained that the dozing was fake. Her hands were tense. And at an awkward angle. No doubt she had spotted me from the window at a distance or heard the gate and taken up her position for the encounter.

The room smelt of Red Moscow perfume.

I didn't bother to say hello.

"Well, now, my dear Polina Lvovna, did you enjoy going through someone else's pockets? Do you make a habit of it or was this the first time, just an accident, as thieves always say?"

Polina opened her eyes wide and half sat, like an actress.

She leant a chubby elbow on a cushion and, with a yawn in her voice, said:

"Ah, Mikhail Ivanovich! One of your buttons is hanging by a thread. Take it off, chop chop, and I'll sew it back on. Lyubochka has other things on her plate. Don't think twice about it. Off with it, come on. And the lining's split. I'll do it all."

From the couch, she stretched an arm towards me, her hand cupped.

I contained myself. I'd cracked stronger nuts than her.

"Get up this instant, Citizen Laevskaya! Stop trying to confuse me. Are you going to answer my questions here or shall we continue this at the station? I have a lot of questions. You will answer each one."

Laevskaya lowered her legs, thrust her feet in their sheer stockings into her slippers, shuffled a few times, sat up more comfortably, and adjusted her housecoat with its dragon pattern.

"Fine. That's just what I'll do, answer each one. Whether you like it or not. You'll have your answer. Especially to the question about Lilia Vorobeichik. And about who killed her. Let's begin there, shall we? Or are you going to choose which one? After all, you must have a long list."

"I haven't got a list. I keep it all in my head."

I maintained my composure and, in order to demonstrate to just what extent, went out into the kitchen, lit a gas burner and put the kettle on.

Laevskaya spoke quietly from the other room.

"Get some challah out of the cupboard. It's fresh. With poppy seeds. Bring it in, please. I'd really like something to eat."

A second later Laevskaya herself came into the kitchen, took the plaited loaf and licked the seeds off the crust.

"I have no patience. I love poppy seeds. You can get the knife out of the table drawer. Don't stand on ceremony. We're like relatives now. Or that's what I think."

I didn't move a muscle.

She opened the drawer herself. And one after the other she picked out three knives. They were the ones from Lilia Vorobeichik's house. All three of them. Which meant they had to include the one that had killed the murder victim.

Laevskaya was watching me in a friendly manner.

"Pick the one you like most. They're all identical, by the way. But one brings greetings. And you know who from."

It took all the strength I had left not to reply.

I pulled out the knives and took them into the other room.

I laid them on the table. As I was putting the last in place, the edge caught on the embroidered tablecloth. I tugged and almost ripped it.

Laevskaya jumped up. She began smoothing the pattern with the palm of her hand.

"How could you be so careless?! This is the tablecloth from my bottom drawer. I made it myself. Poltava stich. One touch from you and there'll be none of its beauty left – nix!"

In all likelihood, it was that "nix" of Polina's that was the last straw.

"I know all about your nixes! You wanted to do away with my wife with those nixes of yours. Didn't you? Answer me!"

Laevskaya carried on cutting the loaf in silence. She cut and cut. Cut and cut. One slice with one knife. One slice with the second. One slice with the third. I snatched the knife away, the last one, as it happens. Particularly well-polished and gleaming.

"Don't you have a shred of humanity? Why are you constantly subjecting me to this all-out attack? Do you think I haven't realized that Lilka was killed with this knife? You've cleaned it up and you're deliberately showing it to me from all angles. Except you didn't find that knife in the river. You had it all along. And how did it come to be here? That's what I want to know. You even tore your own glove on purpose. But were too much the stingy Jew to rip it right open the way a rusty knife that had been in the water would really have done. You slit it so that it would be easier and less noticeable to sew up later on. And the knife's here because you yourself used it in person to kill Citizen Lilia Vorobeichik."

Laevskaya threw up her hands so that the skin from her watch strap to her elbow quivered:

"Oy! Myself? In person? So why am I walking around with this knife then? Why haven't I got rid of it so that it's missing without trace? Why am I showing you over and over again but you're not paying any attention?"

"At the moment, I don't know what your aims are. I understand the main thing – you're a crafty so-and-so and not to be trusted. You're creating a mountain out of a molehill so as to shirk all responsibility and shift it onto someone else."

"Onto you, right?"

"And there we have it. From your own lips. Thank you."

Laevskaya took a piece of challah and offered it to me.

"Have some, please. I'll bring the tea through. And a bit of butter. From the market. I rushed off first thing this morning and bought it. In anticipation. Svetlana told you about Shtadler and me and you came running. Well done. I've no customers today. At least we can talk in peace."

I declined the bread but Polina Lvovna didn't care. She brought in the teapot, two cups on saucers, a dish of preserve. She took her time setting them out, moving them first to one side, then the other.

She picked up two knives and took them back into the kitchen.

And from there she shouted to me as if just dropping it in:

"And let go of that knife. Your hand's gone numb. It's all white. Put the knife on the table. Just don't tear anything."

And it was true. I still had the knife in my fist. And my fist was as white as could be.

Laevskaya went back and forth a few more times: bringing first the sugar, then the little decanter of fruit liquor, then the glasses.

"So, have a seat, Mikhail Ivanovich. Take the weight off your feet. So, what do you say? Is this the knife that killed Lilia Vorobeichik?"

I was on the point of answering sharply and even of leaving. Instead, I sat down and drew my chair up to the table. I placed my hands in my lap.

Laevskaya poured the tea, put a piece of the poppy-seed loaf on her saucer. With her teaspoon, she collected the poppy seeds that had fallen off, made a little heap and put them back on the crust. Then she took a pinch and popped it in her mouth.

"You must take me as you find me. Not terribly well mannered, you might say. Manners always get in the way. Different ceremonies, hocus-pocus. Lilechka used to tell me. You're not one for ceremony. You like to use force with a woman. If she doesn't object, of course. And Lilechka didn't. How much she used to tell me about you! You can't imagine how much I've heard her say. And all about her attraction to you. And your love for her. Surely she wasn't making it all up? Mm?"

I gave Laevskaya a look, aware that my expression at that moment was not a pleasant one. And that it would be better to lower my eyes and give myself a breather.

Laevskaya chewed her challah and drank her tea. She wasn't looking at me. She was looking somewhere off to one side. I turned my own gaze that way and there, in the wall, was a large nail. And on the nail hung a cap. I recognized it right away. It was Zusel's. I remembered it because I'd used it to cover Zusel's face in the grave on Trinity Hill.

Laevskaya stood, hiding the cap from my sight.

"So, are you and Svetochka serious? Like you were with Lilechka or more than that? Svetlana's an attractive girl but she is dense. She's hammered her brains out on that typewriter. Poor thing."

I remembered the ticket for the pictures. I hadn't given her the money. I'd forgotten. Svetka hadn't reminded me. I felt a jab of shame right in the heart. Inwardly, I promised to repay her with interest. In sweets.

Laevskaya touched the cap as if it was on display in a museum.

"I really worry about Zusel without Malka. And about Dovid. And those little lads. I was planning to go for a visit. On Sunday. Perhaps we could go together? The lads would be thrilled. You're a great man to them. In your uniform, with your gun. You've got Yosya. Their own little brother. And when's Lyubochka coming back? I miss her. And Gannusya. Why you sent her away, I don't know. She needs your attention not food and fresh air. But attention's not so big a thing for you. Lilechka used to say that as well."

Laevskaya said all this with her back to me. Like an actress on the stage. And the stage was somewhere in the region of Zusel's cap.

I said firmly:

"First, turn round to face me, Citizen Laevskaya."

She didn't. She shrugged a shoulder.

"Second, I'm not some gossiping woman you've hired to cut out pairs of drawers."

Laevskaya laughed and, laughing, turned to face me.

"Yes, Lilechka's right. You really do know how to choose your words. You're so funny."

And immediately, she hissed: "But for her, it ended in tears."

I couldn't stand that sort of thing. I really couldn't. Enough!

"I feel sorry for you now. You're not yourself. You've been through a lot in your life. More even than some. Perhaps you've dreamt something up without really knowing why. I'll leave you and your conscience in peace. Pull yourself together. Get well. Unlike you, I am a person first of all. And only then a law-enforcement officer."

I left to the sound of her laughter.

At this stage, I had suffered a defeat. My humane attitude suited Laevskaya down to the ground. She would have it her own way as long as she could. But how far was that? That was the question.

I was so deep in my own thoughts that I didn't notice where I was going.

My feet took me to Clara Zetkin Street, to Lilia Vorobeichik's house. Eva Vorobeichik's, that is.

She, with no regard for working hours, was standing at the gate, larger than life, and chatting to Khrobak. Clearly, they were saying goodbye. In full view of everyone. They saw me but deliberately turned away.

I walked the hundred or so metres to the corner. Hid behind the trees. When Khrobak had gone on his way and Evka had slammed the gate, I set off by the back way to her house.

I entered the room at the same time as Evka. I went through the open window. She went through the door.

"Eva, hello." In my haste, I went straight to informal terms of address. "How come you're not saying hello?"

Evka was frightened. But maintained her fake pride. She said defiantly:

"Not only have you received a reprimand at work, they'll throw you out altogether now!"

"Sit down, Evochka. Why aren't you at work? The assembly line's busy and you're not there. Dallying with your beau in work time."

"I've left. I'm not working for the time being. And he's not my beau, he's my fiancé. The wedding's in two weeks' time."

"Is your fiancé aware that you keep company with Zionists? Zusel Tabachnik, for example. Paying to take him to Oster. Threatening Dovid into keeping Zusel as the apple of his eye."

Evka gave up. She seemed to crumple.

"What have Zionists got to do with anything? Laevskaya asked me to take Zusel to Oster."

"Come now. And that you were pregnant by who knows who, does your fiancé know that? Or did you pretend to be a virgin?"

Evka sat on the sofa so quickly it hurt. An antimacassar on the back of the sofa slid off.

And onto her head. Evka began to brush it off and caught an earring.

She cried out:

"I've ripped my ear."

I looked – nothing. A tiny drop of blood.

"Don't panic, Evochka, it'll heal before the wedding. The veil will cover it. No-one will notice."

Evka shrank back into the corner and tucked her legs beneath her. Her knees were round.

Evka recovered and calmly said:

"I'm not of an age to pretend to be a virgin."

But I understood that her bygone pregnancy still weighed upon her like a stone. And I had to aim that stone well. If I hit the target, it would be to my advantage. If I missed, there would be nothing I could use to hook Evka. And through her Laevskaya.

Evka sat, completely at her ease. She didn't pull her dress down over her knees. She arranged her feet prettily in their red, high-heeled shoes.

"Oh, and greetings, Eva, from Oster. From the family of Miron Shayevich Faida. Sima Zakharovna gave me lunch. We talked a lot about you, reminiscing."

Eva brushed this off.

"Whatever could they tell you when they're up to their ears in shit themselves? Both Sima and Miron. I know them through and through and inside out."

"They're good people. Your mud won't stick. And their son's a good lad. Sunya."

At this point, Eva retreated. The tiniest bit. Small as the drop on her ear. Just that much.

And I pressed my advantage:

"Yes, Sunya. A first rate lad. A student at the vocational college. To be fair, he did turn out to be light-fingered. Went into my bag and stole my knife. I didn't make a fuss. Why ruin a young life for a bit of metal? I didn't even tell his Dad. But I am telling you, Eva. You need to keep an eye on him. He could get himself into trouble. For petty theft, to start with, and that's putting it nicely. In fact, it was stealing from an officer of the police in the performance of his duty. An aggravated crime – carries about ten years."

Evka said nothing and gaped at me in fright.

"Yes, Eva. I also had important documents on my person – they've gone too. Must have been Sunya. A cut and dried case. Straight-forward. His life's ruined."

Evka put a finger to her ear. Touched it, probed around – and stared at her finger. Looked and looked then touched her ear again. But her eyes were empty. And in them I could see Sunya.

I raised my voice.

"Eva, look at me! Not at your finger. Here, at me! Look me in the eye. Understand this. Your life is in your own hands. You've banked on Khrobak and all his future concern for you. Wake up to just how far you're going, Eva. Really wake up. Everything you say will be in confidence and kept secret. I want to help you. Not because I owe you anything but sincerely. One person to another. Tell me, Eva."

"Tell you what?"

I gave the answer usually given during questioning. "Everything."

And she did.

Evka really had been pregnant in 1936 at the age of 22. And the baby she was carrying just happened to be Faida's. This was no accident. It was entirely purposeful since back then Faida worked for the Party organizations of the district centre,

Kozelets. And Evka's family had become acquainted with Faida against their will in the following manner.

In 1935 Solomon Vorobeichik found himself facing an unsubstantiated accusation of sabotage at the button factory. Where both Evka and Lilka worked. They began to be drawn in. Not quickly but little by little. In order to meet the mandatory norm for exposing sabotage networks and organizations.

Polina Lvovna Laevskaya often visited the house to pick up trimmings for sewing. Solomon would filch the odd button or fastening from the artel for her for a reasonable price. Of course, Polina was aware of the disturbing allegations and, as an interested person, sought protection from potential accusations.

In 1936, Laevskaya introduced Evka and Lilka to Faida. Seemingly so that if something happened, Faida would come to the family's aid out of pity for the pretty Jewish twins.

As a leader of Kozelets District Faida had influence and, to Evka and Lilka, he was a god. What's more, he was good at reciting all kinds of poems by heart off the top of his head. Evka was wild about him since he wasn't considered a threat and her parents even egged her on in the hope of future assistance.

That Faida was married only surfaced later. He was working in Kozelets at the time and not everything about his life was plain for all to see. And Laevskaya said nothing about a wife. And so, Evka became pregnant, as is often the way.

And at precisely that critical moment who should put in an appearance but Faida's wife, who was at the very same time Polina Laevskaya's cousin, Sima Zakharovna. This wife of Faida's lay in wait for Evka on waste ground and pushed her up against a wall. Right up against the wall, Evka and her belly. And said, 'I know all about Miron. I have one condition. A simple one. You will have that baby and you will hand it over to me and it will be mine in every sense of the word. Miron and I have talked it over. He doesn't mind. And you'll tell people you miscarried. I don't care whether my husband and I have children of our own. Although I don't think we will. I'm in poor health and would be ill-advised to give birth. But that one's mine. If you don't do it my way, I'll turn Miron against you and the whole of your precious family will be sent to Siberia."

Evka agreed out of fright. And from that day forth, she didn't see Faida again.

Malka organized the birth in Kozelets in accordance with all the Jewish customs. Evka handed the little boy over to Sima. The matter was closed.

Laevskaya stopped going to see the Vorobeichiks and some time later she and all her family vanished from Oster. Many people said her husband had been sent to work in Central Asia. Her husband, incidentally, rarely showed up in Oster at all and was generally said to be an engineer or a foreman, working all over our vast country. Laevskaya was proud and never wanted for anything materially or emotionally. She only made clothes for herself – snazzy ones too. And for her children, of course. But she did best when they were for her. And she kept her maiden name, incidentally. Had no desire to take her husband's.

The truth about the birth was known only to Lilka, Laevskaya, Malka, Faida and his wife, damn her. The snake!

Their father, once he had taken fright with Laevskaya's assistance, didn't come out of that state until the beginning of the war. Nor did their mother. When war was declared, they recovered slightly since rumours were doing the rounds in Oster that it was the end of Soviet power and there might be a return to the old way of life. Their daughters didn't agree. Evka grabbed onto someone's cart and left to be evacuated, taking only the clothes she stood up in, while Lilka disappeared, whereabouts unknown.

Evka came back from evacuation to Oster. Lilka didn't. Evka lived with Malka who found a haven as her dependent and a witness to her ugly deed.

A couple of years ago, Faida arrived to take up residence in Oster. Inasmuch as he had been given his marching orders as one of the high-ups in Kozelets. He had become steward of the club based in the former synagogue. That's how he described himself. The job title embarrassed him.

So Sunya ended up where Evka couldn't help but see him. Which constantly tormented her and inwardly put her to shame. She would have done anything to escape Oster for pastures new. Evka tried to sell her house and, with the money, to buy something somewhere else. But there wasn't much available. A house might look nice enough then turn out to be falling apart.

She suggested to her sister that they could join forces in Chernigov but Lilka wouldn't have her and gave no reason.

And what reason could there be when being identical had made them a burden to one another since birth? Everyone treated them both the same, regarding them as a single whole. But they longed to be separate.

And then Lilka was murdered and the opportunity arose of leaving Oster for somewhere new.

Laevskaya put Evka in touch with Khrobak. They were on course to be married.

And I wouldn't have got a single word out of Evka if it hadn't been for Laevskaya once again.

Two weeks ago Polina Lvovna had arrived, making insinuations, stirring up the past and finally saying directly: 'Lilka's gone, Malka's gone. Now I'm the only one who knows about Sunechka. Miron and Sima don't count. Of course, I won't betray you for anything. Go ahead, sort out your personal destiny. It's a sacred thing. I'm always happy for everyone. Don't think I'll ask you for anything. It's not even a request – nix. Tell Tsupkoy, if he asks, and he will definitely ask, that you heard from Zusel's very own mouth that Tsupkoy put him in the ground.'

The request drove Evka almost out of her mind. But she didn't let it show. She'd made a promise. The next day Laevskaya brought Zusel to her and told her to take him to Oster, to Dovid. Zusel didn't make a sound. Evka was astonished as Zusel had previously been given to ceaseless praying aloud and to imposing his rules on everyone.

Laevskaya said that Zusel had lost his mind after an illness and wouldn't say boo to a goose any more. Evka asked whether Zusel could be regarded as dumb. Laevskaya put Evka's mind at rest by saying that he could. And noted particularly that Evka was to speak to Dovid and tell him that Zusel was out of bounds to all and sundry, especially and particularly to Tsupkoy.

Evka calmed down a little as she reckoned Laevskaya's lies would be on her own conscience and Zusel himself wouldn't object. What had really happened didn't matter. What did was keeping Laevskaya happy and Khrobak learning nothing for the moment at least.

Evka had long since noted and sensed Laevskaya's negative attitude towards Tsupkoy, towards me, myself, in person in other words. However, Laevskaya had dismissed her bewildered questions and laughed: 'We've had dealings.'

Evka decided to let it go.

And so she delivered Zusel to Oster.

Soon she would be marrying Khrobak. Then I showed up. Now what was she supposed to do? She had told me everything in great detail because she didn't particularly trust Laevskaya. It was always one thing one day, another the next. If Polina and I had had a disagreement, it had nothing to do with her. But as it turned out I was going after Sunya and if I did that, Sima and Miron would rush off to Laevskaya and Laevskaya was playing her stupid games with me and, no doubt, she, Evka, would end up being dragged in as well. Polina was just back from Oster. She'd told her herself. Had called in the previous day and told her she'd been to see Dovid and Faida. And that I had been there. And had been interrogating Faida and Sima about Evka. As if there was a suspicion that Evka had murdered her own sister or was an intimate accomplice. And that Faida, as her one-time lover, had remembered the past and taken up with Evka again and was also involved. And, as a result, Sunya might end up being implicated in some way and off they'd all go to you-know-where. So it was clearly necessary to bring Tsupkoy to heel. And they'd do it through Zusel.

Only Evka didn't agree. Not only had she not killed anyone, she hadn't done anything else wrong either. And so that I knew, she was not to blame. If Sunya had done something on his own – let him answer for it. But Evka was not going to answer for a lie. Let everyone answer separately, not the whole gang together. She had suffered a lot since childhood for everyone at once and she had no fear left. For everyone else, that is. For herself, personally, that was another matter. For herself, of course, she was afraid. Because of Khrobak. It would be a shame to lose this chance. Perhaps a suitable husband, a good and loving husband might come along but she wasn't as young as she was.

And would I please say outright whether I suspected Evka of killing her sister or not.

I gave her an honest answer: no, no, a thousand times no. And that I'd never expressed such thoughts to anyone. Far less Laevskaya.

Evka paused for breath.

"Well, then, of course, Laevskaya made it up. And you can deal with Sunya. He's an adult. He's been separate from me for a long time."

Evka stood up from the sofa, went over to the mirror and combed her hair.

She put on lipstick, turned to look over her shoulder and asked, her voice all innocence:

"Perhaps you really did bury Zusel? I've told you the truth, now you tell me. So that we're quits."

What kind of people are they?

She had just recounted the unsavoury details of her own life, finding them hard to spit out even. And there she was admiring herself in the mirror. What's more, in the presence of a male stranger. And being provocative into the bargain.

I couldn't help myself.

"Eva, have a heart. I'll be gone in a flash, titivate yourself up then."

It was as if I hadn't even noticed what she said about Zusel.

She smirked.

I pressed my advantage.

"Eva, aren't you surprised there's no-one left?"

"Who do you mean?" she asked distractedly.

"It's obvious. Lilka, Malka. And yet you're still here?"

Evka froze, mouth open.

I went on the offensive.

"You're still here and entirely in Laevskaya's hands. You've given me a whole pile of muck. Do you think I'll protect you from her? That I'll shut her mouth? But how? What authority do I have over her? Whether she loves me or not is up to her. But she's got you on a hook. There you sit, on that hook, all on your own-ee-o. And she can do what she likes to you. Today -it's Sunya, tomorrow it'll be - you killed your sister, the day after that – everyone off to Siberia. And she'll get the things she wants. Each more baffling than the last. If only I knew what she gets out of it. What is it, tell me? That's the question. You'll marry Khrobak. You'll be at peace. And there she'll be again. Bear in mind, the fewer fish on a hook, the harder for them to escape. And if there's only one, it's on that hook till it dies."

Evka automatically snatched up her lipstick and plastered it on. She kept smudging it.

I went up behind her, took her lightly by the waist and whispered in her ear, the one she'd scratched:

"Eva, use your brain. As long as Laevskaya has a hold on you, you'll have no peace. Your entire life is in her hands. Whether it's with Khrobak or somebody else. And she will hold on to the very end. Until death. Be it hers or yours. And when it comes to Zusel, when has Laevskaya ever told the truth? She couldn't tell the truth if she tried. And you spread what she says. Shame on you. I don't mean you any harm."

And I left. Through the door. As is right and proper.

Evka called after me:

"Hang on. There's more to tell you."

I turned round. I stood in the doorway, half turned towards her.

"Go on."

Evka hesitated.

Then she jerked her head up and ground out:

"Laevskaya said there was something between you and Lilka. Something serious."

I shrugged this off.

"Go to hell, the lot of you. Stupid women. Sit there on your hook but keep away from me. I won't let you hook me in."

And with that I really did leave. I didn't slam the door or if I did then it was more gently than I needed to.

And although I'd shown restraint, my mind was in complete uproar.

There was one thing that reassured me – both Laevskaya and Evka, their heads were a complete mess.

Why did I need quiet? Because I was almost at the end of my tether. I was worried about Lyubochka and the children. Dovid with Vovka and Grishka were always on my mind. Zusel too.

True, Zusel was a special case. A misunderstanding. But now the misunderstanding was the priority and Laevskaya was poking that misunderstanding right in my face.

And, of course, there was Lilka Vorobeichik. And what was supposed to have been between us.

I set off for home. It was nearly five o'clock and I was still expected at Svetka's.

I wanted to change into clean clothes. The undershirt beneath my service coat was soaked. The strap was so tight over my ribs, there was a stabbing pain in my heart. I deliberately tightened it another notch. I don't know why. But it was on purpose.

It was clear to me now that somehow Laevskaya had got Svetka involved in her games. But why the hell had Svetka let her? Probably in exchange for a polka dot dress. With a fitted waist and a low neck. Like the late Vorobeichik's.

Neither Evka nor Svetka had a mind of their own. You just took them by the hand and led them. And along they'd shuffle if they thought they stood to gain. And that gain could be tiny or even a loss.

Laevskaya was different. Laevskaya knew just what she was doing. She was dangerous.

Nature has made women so that no matter what happens to them, afterwards it's like water off a duck's back. Because whichever way you look at it there's a husband to attend to and children to keep an eye on, and old folk too.

But if a woman has awareness, it's goodbye to all that. Awareness is the most awful thing that can happen to a women. It means she takes leave of her own nature. And then there's no holding her back. That's what it was like with Laevskaya. Only now had I realized to what extent.

And what if she'd got Lyubochka on her side too? Hooked her in, offered her something in return?

No. It simply couldn't happen. It wasn't in Lyuba's nature at all.

In a white, open-necked shirt, a good pair of trousers with a thin civilian belt, I knocked on the door of Svetka's living space.

A hung-over fizzog poked out of next door.

"Svetka ain't in. Some woman, all dolled up, came round. Off they both went at a right pace. Svetka was just back from work, you could tell, and off out again. She was going so fast her petticoat was showing. All lacy and pink. I know all her petticoats. Dries them out in the yard, she does. And now the police! You'd think she'd have some shame!"

The fellow laughed and winked.

I shook my fist at him and said in a pleasant voice:

"One word and I'll kill you."

The man paled and put his hands up to protect himself.

He'd had enough. I'd seen the last of him. I had that little trick off pat. Never failed. And I'd tested it on better men than him too. The main thing is not to be rude.

Yes. That wouldn't work on Laevskaya. If she'd begun to advance, there was no stopping her. Any more than a tank! Which meant she didn't give two hoots for prison or for death. It wasn't the facts that came first with her but her own way of thinking. And that couldn't be changed.

I knew from experience that for people like that there was no such thing as facts. They're not afraid of facts. They'll twist them and rehash them so much it's as if they've been turned inside out. They're the same but not the same. And what's more, they have fewer cracks than reality. And this is the sum total of their reasoning.

I went to the Rampart to look out over the Desna and drink in the watery expanse. To breathe in the scent of the acacias. I felt a little calmer. In my head, I put everything in order.

And the order I established was as follows:

What was most important? Most important was my own family. Lyubochka, the children.

What came next? Next was a clear conscience.

And only then came Laevskaya and her inventions.

Evka would hold that little tongue of hers when it came to me now. She'd spilled the beans about Sunka out of fright. It was useful information. In any case, now I had as much influence over Evka as Laevskaya did. So there wouldn't be a squeak out of Evka about Zusel, ever. And she would start avoiding me like the plague.

Then there was Zusel. Completely separate. An accident with no bearing on the main matter. If necessary, I'd answer in court, serve my time.

Suddenly, I thought calmly about time in jail. After all, people came out of prison and got on with their lives. As long as it wasn't political, it wasn't so bad. The family wasn't liable in any way. It would be a bit tough in financial terms. But I wouldn't be sent down for long. They'd take Zusel's character into account. And mine too. My combat medals. And so on. The main thing was that Zusel was still alive. And it would be hard to prove whether I'd buried him or not.

But calmness descended only for a minute.

There was still one unresolved matter. And that was coming to a head.

The insinuations about Lilka Vorobeichik.

I looked round. I was alone in the emptiness. Before me lay the clear waters of the Desna, behind me a tangle of acacias and other trees and bushes, including jasmine and lilac, the scent Lyubochka so adored.

Give all this up? And to whom? Laevskaya? She'd choke on it. She wouldn't be happy even then. She still wouldn't have a family or children. Whereas I was happy already. I didn't need anything else.

And my conclusion?

I looked up at the sky. It seemed I was about to reach a conclusion.

But then Svetka called me.

"Misha. How lovely, you're here. I knew I'd find you."

And, of course, she used the informal term of address on purpose. I didn't object.

"I've been running around the whole Rampart. My wretched neighbour was lying in wait for me in the street. Afraid of missing me. I'd just come back from the shop and he practically picked me up and put me in the porch. And he said: 'Svetlana, you know yourself how much I respect you and your mother. And from this moment on, I'm going to respect you even more. A friend of yours has just been round. Tall, handsome, nice and clean, clothes ironed.

"'He's just gone. Towards the Rampart. Off you go now and catch him up. I'll keep an eye on everything here so the hooligans don't smash your windows like they did a month ago.' Can you imagine, Misha? He smashed our windows to smithereens himself when he was plastered and now he's going to keep a look out for hooligans. I realized straight away it was you who'd called. I got back from work at exactly ten to five to meet you but my neighbour dropped in – she's a terrible fashion plate – and she'd heard there was some good fabric for sale at the shop on Mendeleyev Street. And I really needed some. We both dashed over there. I was assuming you'd wait. But you didn't."

Svetka pulled a hurt face.

"What friend's this? What's her name? Where does she live? Where does she work? Out with it, double quick!"

Svetka rapped out:

"Storozhenko. Nina Vladimirovna Storozhenko. No.3, Valovaya Street. Across the road from us. She a dispatcher at the port. Single. Getting on a bit. Not at all attractive. Fat."

I smiled sweetly.

"You're were a bit too quick there, Svetka. Don't lie to me. Tell me where you sloped off to and who with."

Svetka lowered her eyes.

"What difference does it make? It was women's business. What's it matter to you?"

I insisted. Twisted Svetka's arm even.

She snatched it away and cried:

"That hurts. Is that what you call a caress, Misha? Can't you be any gentler?"

"No, I can't. Well?"

"If I tell you, will you come back to my place?" Svetka had stopped trying to hide her cunning intentions. The come-hither look was insistent.

"Let's go. Tell me."

"Let's walk first. I'll tell you at home."

I switched to another tactic:

"Svetochka, now's not the right time to go to yours. I do want to. It's just that I still have an awful lot to do today. For work.

Understand? And I was only joking. Why should I interfere with your women's stuff? I just thought maybe you'd been off somewhere with another man. I was jealous. I'm sorry."

Svetka laughed in delight.

"What other man? Fine. I'll tell you. It was Polina Lvovna Laevskaya who called. The dressmaker. But it's true that we went to buy material. She wanted to buy some extra but one person wasn't allowed that much so she asked me. We bought seven metres between us. She paid. She'll make me a nice little blouse with cap sleeves – free of charge. For services rendered."

Svetka linked her arm through mine and dragged me off.

Then suddenly came to her senses

"Oh, Misha. Did you just catch me out? You did. You swine, Misha!"

I changed the position of my arm and now it was me keeping a tight grip Svetka.

"Indeed, Svetlana. You might work for the police but you've no experience of working with real people. Let's go back to your place. We'll have a little chat and take it from there."

Svetka's neighbour noticed us from a distance and walked pointedly in the opposite direction to the barracks. Showing just how sensitive he was.

Svetka perched on the bed, lowered her head and said:

"What can I say? I haven't done anything wrong. And I certainly haven't committed a crime. I got to know Polina recently. About a month ago. She waylaid me after work as if by accident. She complimented me on my figure. We went for a walk around the Rampart. She told me that she was a dressmaker, that she only got to sew for the wives of the top brass. And they're like so many barrels. No waists or anything. Whereas she'd like to sew for the pleasure of it. We said goodbye and a few days later she bumped into me again and invited me round. To visit. I went. She told me she has one other interest apart from sewing. She's a matchmaker. She has heaps of potential husbands in Kiev and Kharkov, not to mention the local district centres. And widowers, too, young ones since the war. And she tries to find them nice girls to marry. Pretty ones too, obviously. And that I am just right on every count for one in Kiev. He's away on a long work assignment just now but will soon be back and she'll introduce us. Of course, I could tell right away just by looking at her that she's of Jewish nationality. And for that reason I asked the nationality of this bridegroom. She assured me he's Russian or, at a pinch, Ukrainian."

Svetka went droning on. She didn't raise her eyes. At that point she stopped and fell silent.

"So you were just toying with me?"

"You're married. It doesn't count."

I agreed. It didn't.

Svetka cast caution to the winds.

"I've fancied you for ages. And now everything's come together. What? Am I supposed to just while away my time waiting for some bloke to come along? I have needs. And they make themselves felt. Anyone who judges me can look to themselves."

I backed her up.

"Quite right, Svetlana. Quite right."

"Well, then."

Svetka began plumping up the pillow. A huge one in an embroidered pillow case, white thread on white cloth, with tiny eyeholes. She heaved it onto her lap and kneaded it. Like dough.

"Did you make it yourself?"

"No. My mother did. Part of her dowry. But I can do it too." Svetka pushed the pillow off, stuffed it behind her back and settled down as if she was in an armchair. "I can do lots of things. But no-one needs them." Svetka looked as though she was going to cry.

I waited.

She didn't cry. She couldn't.

"Go on, Svetlana. Have a little cry."

"I can't. You're standing over me like a sentry. You're even in my light. Sit down. Here, next to me."

I sat.

I put my arms round Svetka's shoulders and said:

"If you don't want to, don't say anything else. I'll tell you instead. Next, Laevskaya asked you to make sure a rumour reached my ears that she and Shtadler had been to the station. And she asked you to let her read the evidence in the case of Lilia Solomonovna Vorobeichik. To take it out of the archive. As if out of mere curiosity. As if she was a relative. And you did what she asked."

I wasn't even stroking Svetka's shoulder, just propping her up. I gave her no excuse for offering herself to me in the fullest sense of the word.

But of course, that's not how she understood me.

And I'm not made of stone.

When Svetlana asked me if I loved her, afterwards, I gave her the honest answer that I didn't. But that I respected her as a woman and a human being who had simply lost her way.

Svetka asked whether I thought Polina would let her down regarding the husband-to-be.

I assured her she was bound to. But beforehand Svetka would have to work on Polina a little. Svetka wasn't the first woman Polina had treated this way and she wouldn't be the last.

When Svetka asked what I'd done to Polina for her to be undermining me, I held my tongue.

I gave Svetka the following task: to break off all contact with Polina, to tell her she'd found a fiancé all by herself and didn't need her services any more, and didn't need any blouses either. As for what Svetka had already done, she'd made a clean breast of it to me personally and I had forgiven her without taking it any higher up.

I also assured Svetka that Polina would keep her mouth shut. She didn't need any scandals. She was up to her eyes in bullshit. She'd tied herself in knots and was afraid that, if there was a weak spot, the bullshit would come pouring down and crush her first of all.

At home, the first thing I did was write a letter to Lyubochka. I put all the warmth I had in it. At the end I added a special note that she shouldn't let Yoska go swimming naked because the other children would laugh at him. That's a village for you: they see something and it sets them cackling. They're not interested in the rules. Or other people's superstitions. And our little chap didn't need any extra fun being made of him. He'd have plenty to put up with as it was.

Then I had a little think.

What I thought was this: Svetka would be no trouble now. She wasn't a danger at all. I was sure of that.

But Laevskaya! A real spy with a whole network. And she seized on what hurt most – love. She'd hooked Evka. Svetka.

And the following words pounded in my head like a sledgehammer: 'And my Lyubochka, she's hooked my Lyubochka too!' But such a thought would have finished me off altogether and I kept it at bay.

I'm a human being. And I had to live. For the sake of my family.

And so, I gave myself a break from Laevskaya and everyone to do with her.

Several days passed. Eventually, I regained my usual confidence.

I had already assessed Laevskaya's actions as malicious hooliganism, nothing more. Women's foolery. Nix. If I didn't give in to her antics, she'd get fed up with hounding me.

At work, things were going well, successfully even.

I was sitting quietly at work, going through police paperwork.

It was only when I was called to take a phone call that I sensed my break was over.

It was Evka. She said to keep her wedding in mind. I'd been invited by Khrobak. Sviridenko would be there, as would a lot of the top brass. On the groom's side. Left to her own devices, she wouldn't have invited me but Khrobak had ordered her to make sure I turned up. They would be celebrating at Evka's house. That is at Lilia Vorobeichik's.

Initially, I decided not to go. Then experience in the field won the upper day: I couldn't not go.

Meanwhile Shtadler was next on my agenda. For some reason Laevskaya had given Svetka instructions to put on a performance. She had even stressed amid all her bullshit that it was Shtadler who should turn up, while she acted as the invalid's attendant.

I smiled as I walked towards Shtadler's. There I was trotting off to see a dumb man. To ask him about Zusel who couldn't speak any more either.

Shtadler greeted me sorrowfully. He immediately set about writing something down.

I read each letter as he wrote it. He was so flustered he left a lot out or put them in the wrong places.

His account said that Laevskaya had been pumping him about me for ages. But he'd said nothing. And how had she come to know that he and I were rather too well acquainted? Through the late Gutin, she'd assured Shtadler.

To my question as to where Shtadler went after I'd sent him away the evening Zusel arrived, he wrote that he'd gone home and that he'd had no other plans at the time nor could have had.

As he wrote, Shtadler frequently moistened his copying pencil and stains appeared on his face. In particular, on his lips and forehead because he kept wiping his fist over his slavering mouth, then rubbing his forehead.

I told him I'd seen Zusel very recently and he sent his greetings. And had reminded me of the money.

At the mention of the money, Shtadler became anxious, mumbling whole sentences and gesticulating with his hands to show his denial.

Directly but gently I asked why Zusel had taken the money away with him. Was he going to offer me a bribe, perhaps?

Shtadler didn't write anything. But he didn't shrug his shoulders or dismiss what I'd said. He didn't even shake his head.

From which I concluded that he was telling lies and concealing something.

So I changed my tune.

I scrunched up what he'd written, threw it on the floor and ground it under foot.

I pointed down at it for effect.

"That's what you wrote. At the moment. But it could be you lying there like that. With a boot pulverizing you. Where's the money?"

Shtadler didn't move a muscle. He pushed the pencil away. It rolled towards his elbow. I caught the pencil and aimed it right at Shtadler's eye. It wasn't a particularly sharp pencil. But Shtadler had experience with law-enforcement. He knew where it could lead.

"Well, Veniamin Yakovlevich?"

Shtadler looked at the beslobbered lead as if at a fearsome enemy. As if I were holding a gun.

He looked and looked then suddenly lowered his head, arms hanging freely down the sides of the chair. He flung himself back. Stretched out his legs. Cockily even. Grazing my boots ever so slightly.

And sat, stock still.

I yelled at him to behave like a decent person not an old lag refusing to answer questions.

Shtadler got up, stood to attention. Lifted his chin and roared with laughter. For a long time. And fixed his eyes right on me. And dribbled his blue drool.

But I'd seen worse than that.

I gathered the papers up off the floor and stuffed them in my map case. I took my time, did up all the fasteners.

And in farewell I said:

"Thank you, Citizen Shtadler. You've told the authorities, as represented by me, what they need to know. And had a jolly good spit too, right from the heart. Enough for a lifetime. But what was it you were spitting? What kind of spit? The saliva you used to soak that squealy little pencil so that I could see more clearly. It turns my stomach just to look at you."

Shtadler mumbled something in response. It was muffled. I didn't hear.

Everything I needed from him, I already had.

And what I had was as follows:

One. Shtadler hadn't been following me when I was dragging the putatively departed Zusel.

Two. Laevskaya was somehow linked to Gutin.

Three. Zusel had had the wretched money after all. And it had disappeared somewhere. And Shtadler knew where and why Zusel had taken it with him to Chernigov. And, most importantly, he knew I didn't have it. If he'd thought I had the money, he wouldn't have shown his hand like that. He would have done everything he could to prove it was none of his business to know about the money. On the contrary, however, he hadn't tried especially hard to hide that he knew. Although he wasn't giving way as a matter of principle. Even the spitting had been to make a show of his principles.

And this was the result.

The money in Zusel's possession concerned not him alone but someone else as well. In other words, to put it plainly, it was a common fund. Not of thieves but for some shared purpose. And Zusel was some kind of treasurer or collector.

I seized on the word "collector". And remembered Evsey telling me about Zusel, calling in on people, bothering them with his chatter and propaganda.

But perhaps that had been when he collected the money. Not seeking alms but specifically making a collection. In other words, he wasn't being given money to live off, it was for some cause. Some Zionist cause. After all, he visited Jews exclusively.

Some would give for the sake of the idea. Others would tell him to sling his hook.

He was perfectly at home with Evka and Malka too. And Malka wouldn't squawk a word in anything but her own language. Grr, grr. And Zusel had circumcised Evsey's boys. On Dovid's orders. He and Dovid and Malka had all come together and woven their prayers together.

It was a gang. An honest-to-goodness gang.

So what? Evsey was gone. Malka was gone. Zusel was at death's door. Dovid wasn't at all well. Belka was in hospital. Evka was scared and trotting after Khrobak like a puppy.

Only Laevskaya was fine. And she was pulling all their strings.

She thought she had me all tied up too. Let her. She could think it for now. Or it might just so happen that she wouldn't be able to think at all if she was grabbed by the throat properly and asked outright:

"What right do you have to torment me, you bitch? What do you know? What did you see?"

I realized, right then and there, that Laevskaya wouldn't tell me a thing. Not a thing. She'd die rather than tell me. She'd choke on her silk housecoat with its embroidered dragons and still not tell.

My thoughts jumped to Moiseenko and his untimely death. If only he hadn't killed himself, none of this would be happening.

He would have answered for the death of Citizen Lilia Vorobeichik as was quite right and proper. The case would have been closed and no-one would have gone rooting around in it. Stirring up riddles out of the blue. Slinging mud at me.

I set myself a goal: to tie up every loose end. Without exception.

And that meant one thing: putting things in order in Laevskaya's head. So that she shut up for good or told me the truth about her intentions and her motives once and for all.

That same day, a colleague who was said to be always parroting what the top brass had to say – Kruk, they called him, Fedka, we sat next to one another in the same corner of the station – began a conversation with me.

First he asked about my health then he switched to my appearance.

"You're changing before my very eyes, Mikhail," he said. "You've gone nearly completely grey. And you're only young. And you walk like a sailor at sea. You haven't started drinking, have you? Our work's stressful, of course. What I mean is if you are drinking, I can always keep you company. Do you go on these sprees by yourself? You should ask me along. We could have a drop or two together." And he took a long and very fixed look at me.

My reply, by the way, was firm and uncompromising.

"Have you been topping up my glass? Where did you get the idea that I'm drinking? Can you smell it on me?"

"No. I've had a little sniff just in case. But you look like you're drinking and like you're permanently hung-over. I'm not the only one wondering, mind. There are all kinds of conjectures going around. You don't come out of it well. You've had the flat, favours. And the whole collective can see. You're not concentrating. You rush around during work hours but not actually doing your job."

Fedka sprawled in his chair, enjoying feeding me this nonsense and more of the same, like a little girl at the market who'd snipped the buttons off a fine lady's coat.

"So, give me an example of the kind of favours I've had?" I said.

"You get unpaid leave when there's work to be done. The work isn't going in the right direction. You come back from leave and the work's still there. And people see you all over town, chasing after one bit of skirt, then another. It's got to the stage that you can't keep your hands to yourself at work."

"For example?"

"For example, some Polina Lvovna Laevskaya. You run after her. Then it's Eva Vorobeichik. Khrobak himself put in a complaint about you. You've got your sights on our Svetka too, so to speak."

I wasn't at all surprised.

"I see. Svetlana's been telling tales out of school, is that it?"

"I'm not saying. Do you deny it?"

"You know what? Fuck you!"

I slammed the door so that the cardboard walls shook and plaster flaked off.

I grabbed Svetka by the neck and forced her down towards the typewriter. Her forehead nearly hit the carriage.

"Got your eye on Fedka now, have you? Just type, damn you! Keep your fingers busy on your bloody machine and keep your damn tongue still! I'm warning you!"

I released my hand.

Svetka lifted her head.

"Mishenka, I never said a thing, not to anyone!"

I nodded at the door to Sviridenko's office.

"Is he in?"

Svetka nodded. She might at least have blushed or shed a tear. But no.

Maxim Prokopovich rose to meet me.

Not taking in that my superior was on his feet and in addition was heading towards me, I plopped down on the chair near his desk.

Sviridenko went white.

"How dare you take such liberties?"

"I'm taking the liberty of writing my letter of resignation in your presence. You can sack me yourself if you prefer. I don't believe I can carry on working. I've given my all. I've nothing left. Since that's not enough, sack me. But I will not have talking behind my back. You know what I'm like. Everyone does. Perfectly well."

Sviridenko sat back down at his desk.

He sat, elbows wide, and without pausing for breath, he replied:

"Stop yelling. From when? Today? Fine, leave today. The District Committee will find you a job. You could even end up running the bakery. And won't that be nice, having hot fresh bread to eat every day? Well?"

I said nothing.

Sviridenko elaborated.

"Yes, people are talking. And I tell them, 'Tsupkoy's our best officer. Everyone has temporary difficulties from time to time.' Everyone! Do you understand me, Misha?"

"I'm not everyone."

Sviridenko raised a pointing index finger up high.

"And that's your one mistake to date. You think everyone else is just everyone and you're not. And if you did think that you were just everyone, like the whole Soviet people, you would have come to me and said, 'Comrade Colonel, Maksim Prokopovich, I'm just an ordinary person. I've been through a rough time, myself, my wife, my adopted son and so on. I will do my utmost to make up for lost time.' And said the same to your colleagues. Would they have failed to give you their support? Of course not. But you want to do everything yourself. By yourself. And people are talking and will continue to talk. And they'll have something helpful to say to you, I can tell you that for certain. How long do you need to have done with all this racing around? One week? Two? I'll give you as long as you say. I'll reallocate your cases. You won't hear a peep out of anyone. We are working in law-enforcement, not just anywhere."

I told him I needed two weeks. It could be recorded as unpaid leave, leave in lieu, whatever.

I drew up a list of operational activities with the intention of strictly sticking to it. And getting on with it right away. Because I'd had enough. I'd run out of patience. Let's be honest.

Belka. I hadn't looked at things from that angle for a long time. She had seemed far removed from where I was going.

I went to the hospital to see her.

Doctor Dashevsky was welcoming and quick to assure me that Belka had had a bit of a breakthrough. How long it would last, science couldn't tell.

When I asked about visitors, he answered in a whisper.

"No-one. I can assure you. No-one. For about three weeks now."

"Isn't she bothered at all?"

"No. She says she's glad they've left her in peace. I would even advise you not to touch her at the moment. Just look from the sidelines. Talk to the nurses. As the people closest to her, they know better than the doctors. I'll make arrangements so that they're polite and don't try to avoid explanations. You'll understand, I'm sure, that our staff aren't keen on talking to relatives. People become anxious when they don't understand but sometimes no explanation is possible."

Belka was wandering among the apple trees. She was picking little green apples, not proper apples even, just fruit that was beginning to form. She was biting into them then throwing them away. Over and over again.

I called out.

"Belka! How come you're not going home?"

Belka answered me calmly.

"I don't want to yet. When I do, I will. I'm not going till I've eaten enough apples."

"I'll eat them with you. I could do with some too."

We began to race each other to pick the not-quite apples.

Belka laughed.

"You're taller. I can't reach. You pull them off and I'll hide them. Under my shirt. I've got another one on underneath. I'll tie the hem up and pop them in there. Right up to my neck. That way I'll have a belly. I like it when I have a belly. Evsey likes it too. Do you?"

"I do, Belochka, I do."

She tied the shirt underneath, hitching it up above her knees. Like a great big sack.

It was ugly and untidy.

I gave my advice:

"Let's not pick any just now. These unripe ones make an ugly belly. You need good big ones, you know."

Belka nodded and began to undo the knot. Clearly, she'd pulled it too tight and couldn't manage.

I wanted to help. I knelt down in front of her. But when I reached for the knot, Belka kicked me out of the way.

I was so surprised I fell flat on my back.

Belka stood over me, legs apart, shirt raised. It was like being hemmed in between two posts. She might well be insane but it wasn't very nice. She was still a woman. Should have some shame.

I touched her leg. I wanted her to move aside. She stood planted in place.

I used a little force. She moved a little.

Sternly, I said:

"Belka, what will Evsey think about you and about me? You mustn't stand like that with a man. Do be sensible, Belka."

Belka lifted her head up and breathed out a long "oh".

But didn't budge. She just lowered the shirt and it hung over my face like a sack.

I dealt with Belka. Landed her face down in the grass. She went quiet. Closed her eyes. I shook her by the shoulder like a little girl. She appeared to have fallen asleep.

As she slept, I asked:

"Belochka, tell me, sunbeam, are you cross with Laevskaya? After all, there was something going on between her and your Evsey. Do you know that?"

Belka didn't open her eyes. A bubble appeared between her lips.

Then, she said, forcing out each individual sound.

"I kn-o-w."

And fell into such a deep sleep that she couldn't feel me shaking her or hear me yelling at her.

Belka had given me a lead. Laevskaya again.
But it wasn't time to go to Polina yet. I had to go to Oster.

In Dovid's house in Oster I found Sima Zakharovna and Sunka.
Sima had something on the boil on the stove. Sunka was reading a book out loud. Vovka and Grishka were listening.
To defuse the tension, I asked from the doorway:
"So what's the next generation reading?"
Sunka looked round and said clearly:
"Gaidar. 'Chuk and Gek.' We've already read 'The Drummer's Fate' and 'Timur and his Team'. And loads more besides. To counter the superstitions Zusel's drummed into them."
I offered my compliments. A good writer and a military man too, who died at the front in the war.
"Enjoying it, lads?" Vovka and Grishka hurled themselves towards me, hugging me round the stomach. They lowed in welcome like calves.
I lifted one up in each arm. They were heavy. Growing up.

Dovid wasn't surprised I'd turned up.
He himself had become very thin. Otherwise, outwardly he looked well enough.
He said:
"So, shall we go and see Malka at the cemetery? Zusel's there."
"Why do we need to go straight to the cemetery? I'm just as happy with the living. Especially when everything's so clean. Is it Sima making all this effort?"
Sima turned round holding an iron pan:
"I just pop in. It's Sunka who does the bulk of it. And the girls he knows too. They've made them their social project."
"I see. Quite right too. Children are our future. And the old deserve our respect.

'Here the young will always have clear roadway
And the old are always shown respect'.
Isn't that right, Dovid Srulevich?"
Dovid made no reply.
I noticed that he didn't have his Jewish prayer book on his lap and that no such books were in my field of vision.
"How's Zusel feeling?" I asked Dovid.
"Feeling at least. He's begun to speak a bit. All sorts of rubbish. But he's using his voice."
Dovid showed no particular joy at Zusel's recovery. Clearly, something specific was on his mind and he hadn't taken my speech in properly. And I needed him to do that.
I said:
"Fine, Dovid. While Sima and Sunka are in command here, let's go to the cemetery. I'll pay my respects to Malka. She was a hard-working woman. Ignorant but a hard worker. We didn't get on, she and I. But I should pay my respects. Right? Can you hear me, Dovid? I should, shouldn't I?"
Dovid nodded.

Nature was blooming.
I inquired as to their financial resources. Whether they were sufficient.
Dovid wasn't complaining. They weren't going hungry and that was enough.
In turn, he asked about Yoska. I assured him everything was going very well. The boy was perfectly healthy, developing properly and at the present time was on holiday with Lyubochka.
Dovid stopped, stared at the ground and said:
"You won't give him back?"
"No."
"Never?"
"Never."
Dovid went smoothly on to say:

"Malka wasn't happy with you about the money. Zusel has said where it's buried. We need to go and dig it up. I'll give it to you. You work for the state. You'll use it legally."

"What money is this? Where did Zusel get it?"

Dovid brushed this aside.

Zusel was standing by Malka's grave in the cemetery. Wearing a railway worker's red peaked cap, the badge taken off, to be sure, but otherwise not worn at all. He was engaged in his usual activity. Praying. A black skullcap at an odd angle peeked from beneath the cap.

I nudged Dovid in the side.

"Well, Zusel's quite a character. And there was I thinking you'd have to take his whole head off to get that old cap off him."

Dovid pointed at Malka's permanent resting place.

"She bought it. She had a jumper left over from before the war. She swapped it. Since Evka brought him back from Chernigov, Zusel had been clutching his bare head and shouting like crazy for it to be covered. Malka brought him the hat. He fell in love with it. The first thing he said when he started speaking again was: 'Malka covered me.'"

Dovid sat down on a small bench. He began to sway like Zusel, repeating the words after him.

And what do you know? Zusel paid me no attention at all. Glanced at me quickly as if he didn't know me. Didn't even interrupt his flow.

I asked Dovid who made the bench.

"Sunka," he said without hesitation. He stroked the seat with pride.

"Smooth as a baby's bottom. He put his heart and soul into it." And he clicked his tongue in pleasure.

The old man prayed for a long time. Towards the end, Dovid stood up alongside him.

I lay down on the grass nearby between the graves. Waiting for them to stop wailing and so on.

Dovid didn't immediately notice me in the grass.

"Mikhail," he called, "where are you?"

I responded and the old men came towards my voice.

"Lie down," I said. "The grass is nice and soft. Where else can we lie quietly if not here? It's cool and shady. The birds are singing. Pure paradise."

Dovid was first to sit on the grass. Zusel followed suit.

I got down to business.

"Well, comrades, let's start at the beginning. Talk, whoever can. You first, Dovid Srulevich. We'll have a little look and a listen, and Citizen Tabachnik might put in a word or two as well. It's a good thing we're having this conversation in Malka's presence. She went to the grave with it on her mind that I'd nicked that money or something."

Dovid looked in Zusel's direction. Zusel was lying on his back. Snoozing. The peak of his cap poked up right at the top. The hat itself was as flat as a fluke, it was rammed so tightly onto his head. A bit on the small side. As if it had been grafted on.

I pointed at Zusel's head.

"Doesn't that hurt? It's tight."

Dovid's reply was confident.

"It doesn't bother him." He stopped speaking, looked around on all sides, glanced up at the sky, then down at the ground where he lay.

"Why are you looking around like that?" I asked. "Has someone put the wind up you?"

Dovid grinned and it occurred to me that he had only really awoken now, this very instant. After Evsey, after Belka, after everything. His face had become less crumpled, younger even. As much as it could. Obviously, appearances are deceptive but I was delighted. He'd be there for Vovka and Grishka for a long time to come.

To cheer him up, I said:

"Chin up, Dovid Srulevich. The state won't abandon you. Decent folk will help as well. There's Sima and Sunka and even

Faida treating you kindly. And Zusel's getting better. You'll reach your shining path as well. Not unscathed, of course. But you'll get there. And I'll be right there beside you. And Lubochka too. Agreed?"

Dovid agreed.

But he managed to say:

"It's not that I miss Yoska. I weep such bitter tears I can hardly breathe but I don't miss him. What does that make me? Tell me, Misha."

"I'll tell you and I'll tell you honestly. You don't miss him because you've thought about it and come to the right conclusion. Yoska's better off with Lyubochka and me. He's so little he's already forgotten his real parents. Or at least they've taken a back seat. We're his closest family now. And you, as an intelligent man, have registered this in your mind. The older boys – it's harder for them to forget. They're better off with you. And after all this, you are a man who thinks straight. Which means, you'll do alright."

"Perhaps… Is that really what you think? That living is possible?"

"Yes. Definitely, yes."

"I had my doubts just after Evsey and Belka. Now, I don't seem to any more. I wanted you to come to harm. Serious harm. I'd got it into my head that you were to blame. But you're not to blame, are you?"

"For what?" I could tell the thread I needed was about to appear. I would have to give it a tug. Dovid couldn't manage on his own. It was a delicate task.

"They've got you totally befuddled. Zusel on the one hand, Laevskaya on the other. Zusel's not responsible. A religious leftover. But Laevskaya had her eye on the main chance. Am I right? I know everything. Just confirm it for me. We'll pick over the tiniest bones like filleting a fish. There won't be a bone left in it. It'll be minced up thoroughly. We'll eat it and it won't choke us. It won't, Dovid! You have the boys to bring up, use your head."

Dovid was looking at my feet. My sandals were full of dust and the holes were packed with earth. My wide non-uniform trousers had ridden up high and my hairy white legs looked ugly.

I adjusted my trousers. Shook the legs down.

To change the subject, I said:

"I'm not in uniform, Dovid. It's too hot. It gives me more freedom. People aren't expecting me to set the law on them. Although if people have a clear conscience, that's music to a policeman's ear. It puts his mind at rest. What do you think, do you prefer me in uniform?"

Dovid remarked impassively:

"I can see you're not wearing boots. It's cooler without boots in the summer. And they don't make such a clatter in the house. Evsey liked clattering about. The children would ask him to and he would. Tap dance for them."

Zusel stirred. I turned towards him.

He opened his eyes, said something in Yiddish. One word. A question.

Dovid stroked the peaked cap.

"Sleep, Zusel, sleep. Schlafen."

Then I went on the attack.

"Keep going. Don't get distracted. You're going in the right direction. Towards rooting out errors. What's more, I'm not on duty now. So!"

For the sake of intimacy, I gave his shoulder a push.

This is the evidence he gave.

Laevskaya settled in Chernigov after the war. Basin knew her by sight as an attractive woman.

Once he spotted Evsey out for a walk with this lady in an inappropriate location – near Yelovshchina, where the forest begins. What's more they were walking close together, arm in arm, barely a hair's breadth between them. Whereas Basin was in the forest on business. He and some pal of his were stealing timber for firewood. They had an arrangement with the forester. Under these circumstances, Basin couldn't reveal himself and postponed any clarification until an opportunity arose in a less fraught setting.

Basin met Evsey outside work and asked him whether he had a conscience. A bewildered Evsey said that he did. Basin asked how come, if he had a conscience, he, the husband of his Belka, had been strolling arm in arm with a woman who wasn't his wife away from prying eyes in a forested area?

Evsey cottoned on, his father-in-law wanted to pick a fight. He assured him he was making a fatal error. The lady was an undercover police officer and they'd had a secret meeting in the forest. But he spoke unevenly and without much conviction. He was moving away from the police building and looking over his shoulder as if expecting to be cut down on the spot.

Basin pretended to believe him. Inside, he was worried.

Evsey used to go on various assignments in the districts of Chernigov Region. Sometimes staying away overnight. Each time Basin would take mental note, given his suspicions. He took stock of his daughter's and son-in-law's shared life with new interest. Especially when he spent the night there. He organized things so that he sat up late into the night and they made him a bed up on the floor. Dovid strained to hear any evidence of intimacy between Evsey and Belka, tactfully nodding off when the bed they were lying on began to shake.

In the end, Dovid concluded that everything between them was in order. Strict silence prevailed on the subject thereafter.

Dovid continued.

"In '48, or '49 rather, Evsey began drinking hard. On one occasion, I sat with him with various thoughts in my head. Spoke in a whisper, as you're supposed to do. So, I say, people are discussing an interesting subject. They've been going on and on about it since '48. They thought it would reach the ears of you-know-who but it didn't. Or rather it did but not in anything like the right way. That's why there's persecution now. The Jewish population is split down Party/government lines. There have been rumours among the Jews that they're going to be shipped off wholesale to the newly formed state of Israel. The world's not stable. What with imperialists and so on. If there's another war, they'll take it out on the Jews again because they haven't all been killed. And the Soviet state feels a responsibility to its citizens, even the Jews, and so it's considering whether to pack them off somewhere. If, during a new war with an as yet unknown enemy, there's a need for mass evacuation, at least there'll be no need to worry about the Jews. Then, when everything in the world has gone back to normal for good, they'll bring everyone back to their former places of residence. I got this from Zusel. He goes to Jewish houses, listening to people. People are puzzled. Everything's a muddle. Either the aim is to gather up the Jews to revive them or to reduce their numbers again. I wasn't making this up. I was repeating what Zusel had said. He also said he would send a letter to the very top.

"Evsey looked at me, in his cups, of course, and yelled: 'What do you mean the very top? Why is he pestering people? What is he trying to get out of them? He could get people prosecuted.'

"I said to Evsey: 'For what? Israel will take the path of Communism. Everyone knows that. The imperialists won't deflect Israel from its course. The Jews are always in the forefront of revolution. Everyone knows that too.'

"Evsey yelled at me again. 'You old fool, you're the one that'll be deflected. Then squeezed flat as an accordion if you so much as fart! The state's not there to feel responsibility, it's there to exist.' I understood that as meaning the Jews would be persecuted on a country-wide basis."

That was the one and only time Dovid and Evsey were at loggerheads. However, since it had no bearing on family life, Dovid didn't pay particular attention. And had told me now to reveal Evsey's attitude to the Jewish question. He'd reacted in a Soviet fashion, in a Party fashion. Properly.

Before Evsey died, before his funeral, Dovid saw Laevskaya several times. Excluding chance encounters at the market. But including the following:

She came running over to Evsey's towards nightfall. Dovid happened to be spending the night. She called Evsey out of the house into the yard and they talked, voices raised, for some time. When Evsey went back in he was all red and angry.

I asked when approximately the meeting had taken place.

Dovid answered quickly, as if reading it out:

"18th May 1952."

I jumped up in surprise. The day Lilia Vorobeichik died.

"Why do you remember it? Answer me and be quick about it!"

Frightened, Dovid mumbled:

"Why are you shouting at me? We're not at the station. You said so yourself. I remember because that day was young Yoska's birthday. He was born on 18th May 1950. I kept track of when all my grandsons were born."

"And then?"

There was no then. Something in Dovid had simply snapped. I noticed just in time that he'd started to sway and propped him up in a safe position.

What ridiculous things people believe! They don't understand our reality. Even when it's in the papers they still don't twig.

"It's alright, Dovid. Sima's got lunch ready. Or dinner. Let's eat. Wake Zusel up."

Zusel woke up of his own accord. Got up, went over to Malka's grave and stood for a moment. Then set off, going in the right direction.

He led the way. It was a large cemetery. And old. It had built up a lot over some three hundred years. However many Jews had lived during that time, it had grown to take them all in.

There was no-one in the house. On the table was a pot, covered by a towel, some bowls.

Zusel baulked right on the doorstep, shook his head and plodded off behind his curtain.

I remarked sympathetically, "Is he on hunger strike? He's skinny enough as it is."

Dovid explained that Tabachnik kept kosher. Sima didn't. She chopped everything up with the same knife. And she brought pork fat home. And didn't drain all the blood from the chicken. Malka used to make an effort. Zusel trusted her. But he followed Sima around, prodding at her. To no avail. An old Jewish woman living nearby brought him bread and rusks. He washed them down with water from his own cup.

"I had the impression that simpleton of ours had gone completely bonkers. But there he is theologizing. Amazing."

Dovid made a helpless gesture.

"And here you are eating pork fat and stuff. Adapting quickly once again. You and Zusel were running a synagogue here, after all. And teaching the lads from religious books."

"Ah, and much good it did me. Things only got worse. I read and read and and discovered I'd done everything wrong in real life. It was too much to take."

My patience lasted as long as the meal.

Then in a whisper to keep Dovid happy I said:

"Let's go. Is it far?"

"It is."

Dovid took me via the vegetable patches then through the collective farm field, then through a clump of trees, then over the railway line. I followed him, thinking.

And here's where my thoughts took me.

"Halt! Dovid, halt and freeze! About turn!"

And Dovid did freeze.

"Dovid, where are you taking me? I'm armed. Be sensible, man."

Dovid slowly turned round. He still hadn't turned right round when he yelled out, midway through a sigh: "We're here, you bastard!"

And dived at me. With a knife. I recognized my own sheath-knife. From my haversack. I'd blamed Laevskaya. I'd thought it might be Sunka. It had been Dovid all along.

He was an old man. Of course, I wrenched it off him. I tied his hands behind his back with his own shirt. Neatly enough. Out of respect for his age.

"Dovid Srulevich," I said, "do you really take me for such a blithering idiot? You said we had to dig the money up but you didn't take a spade. You went behind the curtain, supposedly to look in on Zusel before we left, and came out with your pocket bulging. You've been lying to me. What could Zusel have said to you about the money if his mind's so addled? Why would you let me in on your Jewish mysteries unless it was to pull the wool over my eyes and ears? So that I'd believe I had your complete trust. I'm the stronger one. I always have been. Why so silent, Dovid Srulevich?"

Dovid wasn't silent as such. He was howling and sobbing, howling and sobbing. And rolling around on the ground. And eating the earth. And spitting it out. And eating it again.

But at that moment I was wondering about something else, purely out of human curiosity.

"Did Evsey teach you to tie that knot?"

Dovid lay unmoving. Muddy, wet with sweat and more besides. He'd had a terrible fright, of course.

He didn't answer.

It was a simple question. On an everyday subject. A good question for moving on to serious matters.

I asked again more forcefully.

Dovid nodded.

"Liar. It takes nimble fingers. Yours are fat and twisted. Belka used to make lotions for you so that your joints wouldn't creak. Evsey got the ingredients from friends. I know who untied it and did it up again. Griskha. It was Grishka, clearly. Evsey must have taught him. Not another word! Fancy falling so low! A grandfather involving his very own grandson, a minor, in planning a crime. Why did you go into my haversack? Were you looking for the money? Even if Zusel had given it to me I'm not an idiot to be carting it around in that. Especially when I've never even set eyes on that money of yours. Look for it among yourselves. Your stories don't tally!"

Dovid said nothing.

He tried to stand. I helped him. Untied his hands. Pulled on his shirt. Asked where the stream was so that he could have a bit of a wash, clean his dirty trousers.

Dovid looked at me calmly. I understood. The deed was done. It hadn't gone they way it should. But it was done.

I twirled the knife in my hands as I spoke. While I lifted and dressed Dovid, I laid the weapon of attack on the grass some way off.

I stood the old man firmly on his feet.

I said:

"The knife's over there. If you like, I'll give it you. If you like, we'll throw it away here. Perhaps you'll have another go? I'll stay the night at yours. I've missed the boys. I'll read them a bedtime story. You'll make an attempt during the night. I will be sleeping soundly. I've had enough of moaning at you. Well?"

I didn't wait for an answer. I took the knife and stuck it in Dovid's trouser pocket. That was nasty, putting my hand in those trousers. Oh, well.

Dovid walked slowly along. He wasn't sure which way the river was but soon found it.

He had a wash in the fading light. So did I.

I wrung Dovid's trousers out to dry. By the time we reached home, they were completely dry.

The night passed, as I had expected, without incident. The little boys and I romped around till they dropped. They didn't want me to read to them so I told them a story from my time in the army with Evsey.

Zusel was snoring behind his curtain.

Dovid spent the night out in the yard.

He didn't take the knife from his pocket in my presence. I didn't watch where he put it. Its part was done.

I knew for certain: in the morning, he'd tell the truth. About everything.

The next day Faida arrived very early. We were still asleep. Zusel was the only one up. He'd been praying since before dawn. During the night, in other words. Mumbling, of course, not praying in words but as it came out in view of his situation.

I called out to him quietly behind the curtain to be more careful, he'd scare the boys.

Faida was in a cheerful mood, well and truly sounding reveille.

I lost my temper.

"Miron Shayevich, the children were fast asleep and your shouting's woken them up."

Faida was embarrassed. He started explaining that he'd brought a little something from Sima and wanted to get it to the table while it was still hot. And it was after eight and everyone was already at work in the fields or offices.

I said:

"So what about you? Haven't you got anything to do? You could've sent Sumka or his Young Communist girls.

Faida's general appearance drove me to distraction. His shirt open to the belly-button. Belt below his gut. Standing there with his briefcase, every bit the big boss. With Simka's cooking in the briefcase.

I stood up despite being virtually naked, went over and took the briefcase off Faida. Pulled out the food, wrapped in newspaper, and put it on the table. Grease proof paper, a strong smell – like potato cakes, fritters cooked in pork fat. I opened them. I was right. I took one and popped it in my mouth.

"I'll try them myself first. Just in case you've poisoned them. Or Sima has. Or Sunka. After all, you all hate me here. But the way I think is this: If I die – so what? As long as the boys are still alive. The children aren't involved. Are they?"

Faida froze. Then his small hands began to twitch. The fiddly little buttons on his shirt wouldn't go through the holes.

No matter how he tried to fasten them from his belly-button to his throat.

"Mikhail Ivanovich, what do you mean…? What poison…? There are no grounds for accusations. I was perfectly sincere. So was Sima. And Sunya. Poison…"

My joke had touched a nerve. The times had their effect too, of course.

But Faida's alarm brought something else to mind.

"Miron Shayevich, why weren't you here yesterday? Sima must have told you I was at Dovid's, surely?"

"She did." Faida had managed to fasten the fiddly buttons, every other one at least. He was still holding the neck together. There was no button there. There really wasn't.

"I set off. It was nearly evening. I saw you and Dovid heading off somewhere. At a distance. Not close up. Otherwise, I'd have come over, at least to say hello. But from a distance, why disturb you? It's not something I like doing. I don't poke my nose in. Ever. Well. And you were a long away off. Walking along, quite content. I turned round and went home again."

"Racing back and forth like a stripling. Why didn't you give us a shout?"

I stayed calm and ate standing up. Little bits of pork rind were stuck to the fritter on all sides and I licked my fingers. It wasn't polite but who needs politeness at a time like that?

Faida went red. He waved an arm – not the one holding his shirt together.

"Mikhail Ivanovich. This is all suspicion on your part. Unfounded suspicion. You're making a mountain out of a molehill. Maybe I needed the toilet and couldn't go chasing after you. And then you were out of sight. The long grass, thistles, prickles of all kinds. You and Dovid were going at a good pace."

Grishka and Vovka had been listening for some time and tittering into their fists. Especially about the toilet.

I gave them a fritter each but ordered them not to wipe themselves on the sackcloth they slept under. In extremis, they could lick their arms clean as far as their elbows.

The lads ate cheerfully. I feasted my eyes on them.

Then came Dovid's voice.

"Miron, shut your mouth. Go home or wherever you need to be. Thanks for the food."

The way he said it sent Miron bowling out of the house. He snatched up his briefcase though. He didn't forget that. Or let go of his shirt.

Dovid went into the yard.

I followed him.

He wasn't dressed. Neither was I.

I said:

"Not after the knife eh, Dovid?"

"No. I threw it down the toilet last night. You can look in the hole if you like."

"I will if I need to. And I'll find it. I've found things in worse places than that. I'm not afraid to get my hands dirty."

"What are you doing to me?" Dovid asked calmly. I wasn't surprised that he wasn't worried. He wasn't afraid. Other things I might miss but fear, no.

I replied that I didn't intend to do anything to him. All I needed was for him not to take me for a fool. That was my sole request, an order indeed. So he'd dived at me with a knife? These things happen. Evsey did the same once. With a gun. We were three sheets to the wind. Squabbled over politics.

Dovid nodded.

"But it's not politics with you and me, Dovid Srulevich. That's not what's come between us. What's come between us is Citizen Polina Lvovna Laevskaya. A clever and cunning enemy."

Dovid nodded at this too.

I continued:

"Let's get washed now and everything. Give the boys a wash. Have something to eat. And then take the children to the Desna. We'll take Zusel too. Let everyone in Oster see that we're on the same side. We can postpone our talk for now."

Vovka, Grishka and I polished off everything Faida had brought.

The old men hadn't touched Miron's food as yet. Dovid drank his tea. Zusel – I don't know how he'd staved off hunger. Not a peep could be heard from behind the curtain.

The children were thrilled to be going to the Desna.

Dovid left Zusel at home. Said something to him in Yiddish.

We stationed ourselves on the bank under a willow. I kept the children in sight and constantly called out to them to be careful and not to dive where it was deep.

Dovid threw shells from the bank into the water. Over and over again. They made ripples.

I began to do the same. Mine went further.

The little boys spotted the game and expressed the desire to hold a competition.

I was in no hurry to question Dovid closely about the matter that was of interest to me.

For about half an hour, I played with the boys in the shallows, throwing shells to the accompaniment of various children's rhymes.

Dovid wasn't watching us. He'd laid down and seemed to have nodded off.

I didn't get in the way. Sleep is the best medicine. Sleep takes people out of themselves and I needed Dovid to be taken out of himself, to be distracted from himself. If a person in that state is suddenly forced to wake up and asked questions, you can acquire much needed information.

And that's what I did.

Dovid's eyes shot open.

I didn't give him chance to come round properly.

"Why did Evsey shoot himself? Hurry up."

I was going on a hunch. And rightly so, as it turned out. Dovid hadn't been expecting that. He'd expected something about Laevskaya. I came at it from the other end. Where it hurt most.

He lay and talked straight up at the sky. His eyes were't looking at me.

After Laevskaya turned up at Evsey's on 18th May 1952 and called him outside to talk, Dovid began to suspect that something was wrong. The surrounding situation and the reports about cosmopolitans gleaned from the newspapers and the wireless kept Dovid on the alert.

Once, in the dead of night, Dovid hadn't had a wink of sleep. Evsey had gone into the yard to smoke several times. Moreover, as well as tobacco, Dovid could smell vodka. From which he concluded that Evsey wasn't so much smoking as drinking in his hidey-hole, the shed.

By morning Evsey was completely sozzled and sleeping noisily. Dovid noticed his hands. They had traces of earth and grass. Dovid couldn't help but see that the spade was missing from the narrow corridor. It was kept there rather than in the shed in case it was stolen by strangers for mercenary motives. Just that evening, Dovid had personally dug over the front garden then carefully washed the spade and set it in its usual corner near the water bucket. He did the digging before bedtime both as a constitutional and to avoid the heat.

In the morning light, Dovid wandered around the garden and discovered a hiding place. Over by the fence, half in the grass, half in the bare earth. Dovid could make out his own digging because he always turned the soil over afterwards rather than hoeing it. Here, though, not only had the soil been overturned, there had been some shallow hoeing too.

Dovid dug deeper into the soil and came across a rolled-up newspaper. Inside was a knife with traces of a dried brown substance. And streaks along the length of the blade. It was a kitchen knife. A big one.

Dovid took fright, concealed the hiding place and rolled the newspaper bundle up in his jacket. Back inside, he left his jacket in the corridor.

He woke Belka, said a cheerful goodbye and rushed home.

At home, he didn't take his underground find out of the newspaper but hid it in his turn in the vegetable patch. Once again in the ground.

For reasons of sheer terror he didn't ask Evsey a thing. Intending to keep his secret no matter what the threats. One thing tormented Dovid – that Evsey would go to get the knife, on police business or out of some other necessity, wouldn't find it and the sense of responsibility would drive him out of his mind. And yet Dovid could see no possibility of admitting that the knife had been dug up and hidden elsewhere. He intended to do so from one day to the next.

What had taken shape in his mind was this:

Laevskaya had brought the knife. Apparently, bearing traces of blood. Dovid had seen blood in all its states and could tell what it was. That was no secret for him. The secret lay in why Polina had brought a blood-stained weapon to Evsey.

Dovid decided Evsey had been drawn into something dreadful. If it had been to do with a police assignment, Polina wouldn't have been lugging stuff around in the middle of the night and Evsey, in a drunken stupor, would not have been hiding that same stuff at night either. Which meant the knife was directly linked to Evsey as an individual given that Polina had made this arrangement.

Soon, verifiable rumours began to circulate in town about the murder of Lilia Vorobeichik. There was a view among the Jewish community that this was the start of their being slaughtered one by one in connection with the cosmopolitans and others of that ilk.

In Dovid's mind, Vorobeichik was connected to Evsey. On the basis of the knife. Nothing else. He set off to see Polina and delivered an ultimatum that he would go to the police and report her visit with the knife.

Polina was astonished and assured him she had indeed dropped in to see Evsey. But hadn't brought any knife. And as for the knife, well, there could be anything at Evsey's. He worked in law-enforcement and had links with all sorts of elements through work. And it wasn't for Dovid to say what for or why.

Dovid's suspicions evaporated on the instant. But only until he saw Evsey that same evening.

His son-in-law grabbed him by the lapels, took him out in the yard and ranted that they must all disappear from the face of the earth right there and then since he, Evsey, had cooked their collective goose and there was no escape now on any side.

Evsey's general look left no room for hope of any kind.

Dovid's alarm was growing with each day that passed.

He needed advice. He told Zusel. Zusel listened, asked for the knife, was given it from underground still in its newspaper, and told Dovid it no longer existed. And never had. Dovid had had an awful dream. As for Evsey and his panicky disposition, time would tell. Zusel said: "What's in the ground doesn't exist. But you took it and brought it into being. It's your own fault."

A little while later Evsey shot himself.

I listened carefully and asked a further question:

"But where did you get the idea it had anything to do with me? I wasn't even in town that day. But you've been shouting it from the rooftops, here, there and everywhere. Planning to write letters."

"It was Laevskaya's explanation, that it was all to do with you."

Dovid shifted his gaze from the sky to me and gave me an affectionate look.

"Oh, Misha, you were so handsome. And Evsey too. Now he's in the ground. Gone, in other words. That handsome man is gone. What hurts me most is that lying there," Dovid pointed at the ground, "he isn't handsome. Anything but. And my Belka fell in love with a handsome man. I'm upset for her.

Have you seen her recently? I can't get away, what with one thing or another."

"I've seen your Belka. She'll recover."

"Is she pretty?"

"She is. Not as much as she was but not too bad at all."

Dovid stared upwards again.

I asked:

"Why did you say I was handsome? Does that mean I'm not any more?"

Dovid didn't answer.

I noticed his hand was feeling for a large shell. An open one, with sharp edges.

I tore it away from him. Forcefully but not enough to insult him.

I said: "You'll hurt yourself. The edges are like knives."

"Indeed," Dovid concurred gleefully.

I looked at Dovid, at his overall appearance. I'd get nothing more out of him.

I dressed, shouted to the lads that I was off.

They raced out of the water and stood on the bank. They didn't ask me to stay longer or if I'd be coming back to Oster.

I went over to them, kissed each one on his damp head. If I'd been able to weep, I would have done so then. The boys were covered in water droplets. As if they had just left Belka's belly. It gave me an unpleasant feeling.

The question of the money remained open.

I turned away from the water, yelled at Dovid.

"So where's this money? Dovid! The money, where is it? I want an answer!"

Dovid didn't answer. He turned over onto his stomach and buried his face in the sand.

It was Grisha who spoke.

"I know."

Dovid raised his head and immediately let it fall again. He stretched his hands out in front of him with their twisted fingers as if wanting to hang on to something. There was nothing there. He rose onto all fours then up to his full height, turned and flung himself at Grishka. Taking a good run-up. I had no time to take it in. He shoved the lad into the water, where it was shallow to be fair, but he was pushing his back down firmly with both hands. Grisha sank face forward into the sludge.

There was a dreadful shout from Dovid:

"Drown, you bastard. Drown, I tell you. Drown to death!"

Grishka's arms flailed as he kicked out. I launched myself at Dovid and dragged him off.

Basin sat in the water, there, where I'd hurled him.

Close by, Vovka seemed to be just puttering about. In fact he was stroking Dovid's arms, shoulders, back. Sniffling one minute at me, the next at his brother.

"Don't worry, my lads. Grandpa and I thought a game up specially. You didn't know. Grandpa told me about the money ages ago. I'd forgotten for a moment. And Grishka, what was it you called out? I didn't hear."

"Nothing," muttered Grishka.

"And good for you. Come on now, Grandpa, up you get! I'll give you a bit of a hand. You need to cover your head the way Zusel does. Halfwit he might be but he does take care of his head. And so should you."

To begin with, Grishka kept looking over his shoulder at me as he walked. A beaten puppy. But soon stopped.

I walked along and waited for Dovid to catch up. I looked round.

Dovid was rubbing his face, his chest, over his heart.

I went back.

I called Grishka. He ran up.

Dovid groaned.

"I need to sit down. For a minute. The lads will find their own way back. You tell them."

So I did.

I scraped some money out of my pocket, poured it into Grishka's, checked there weren't any holes, thrust his little fist in there too:

"Your mission: Buy some halva or something. You choose."

Grishka nodded loyally.

"Thank you, Uncle Misha."

Vovka, without any thanks, charged up through the thistles.

I explained to Grishka:

"Grandpa's going to get his breath back. He and I will take a stroll. You're the oldest. Don't forget. Don't be scared. I won't abandon you."

Dovid was sitting quietly. By the time I reached him, he'd got a grip on himself. Pulled a large open shell out of his trouser pocket – the one I'd only just taken off him.

"What kind of man are you, Dovid? I said throw it away."

So he did. It didn't go far but its gleam couldn't be seen through the grass.

"Great. It's forgotten. All that went before, it's forgotten. You do realize, I could have really shaken it out of Grishka then. But I don't mess with children. Especially in the presence of close relatives. You're the ones who have to live together. You have to carry on bringing him up forever and ever. He didn't want to tell me about the money. He saw his father in me. Evsey. He wanted to tell Evsey. Understand?"

Dovid's entire body nodded. His leg twitched.

"How careless you are… letting a child be in on it. That's not allowed. By the laws of humanity, you don't rope in children."

Dovid said nothing. His foot kept twitching and twitching. The right one. He grabbed it in his hands and planted it on the ground.

"I can't walk. Can't feel my leg."

Dovid attempted to stand. Fell down. Tried again.

"Oh, we've a regular invalid unit here. Money, secrets… They've one foot in the grave but still don't mend their ways."

I bundled Dovid onto my shoulders and hauled him along. He was no Zusel. He weighed a ton.

A cart greeted us on the other side of the copse. We rattled home.

There was no Grishka or Vovka. I asked the driver of the cart to find Faida so that he could sort out a village doctor or something of the kind.

It was roughly an hour before Miron showed up. With the doctor and a cart.

Dovid lay, barely lucid. The boys raced up with the halva. Dashed in to regale their grandfather. Smeared it all over him until I drove them away, explaining that Grandpa wasn't feeling too good and they had to be quiet.

Zusel peeped out from behind his curtain, making puzzled cries.

I asked him to move closer to Dovid.

Zusel stayed put. He gripped the cloth and pulled, pulled downwards until the string broke and he was completely engulfed in the sackcloth full of holes. From beneath, he kept up his inability to understand at shouting pitch. But he wasn't praying. Definitely not. Prayers I would have picked out.

Vovka and Grishka sat close together. The twist of halva was in pieces on their laps and they were dabbing their fingers in it. Then licking them.

Dovid was loaded on to the cart and taken off to hospital.

I didn't go. Nor did Faida. I began to doubt whether I should perhaps have followed.

Faida said contentedly:

"If the order's come from me, everything will be done in fine fashion. We would only be in the way. Medicine! I know. I've spent my time in military hospitals. Will you be staying the night here, Comrade Tsupkoy? If not, I'll take the lads back with me. Zusel can stay here. I'll ask a neighbour to look in on him. Not to worry."

"I'll stay. Until there's a clearer picture."

Grishka and Vovka whispered to one another for a long time before they went to sleep.

Grishka asked what would happen to them if their grandfather died.

I said Dovid was going to live until they were grown up. I had been reliably informed.

The little lads went off to sleep.

I went behind the curtain to see Zusel. He was lying down, eyes open.

I addressed him directly as I would a normal person and spoke softly.

"See what's happening, Zusel? Dovid's in hospital. It could go either way. Do you realize that?"

I spoke almost without hope that he would reciprocate.

But Zusel answered in a whisper:

"Why did you dig me up?"

I was flummoxed. Not at what he said. Which was rational, incidentally. At the significance of the question.

Zusel continued.

"You dug me up but won't let me live my life. You wouldn't let Malka. You wouldn't let Dovid. So better not let me either."

"Zusel, I don't … are you putting this on? You can talk?"

"Aye, I can that. I don't want to. Why did you dig me up?"

I said nothing. Tabachnik had a warped mental picture of what I had done. He was evaluating my actions from an underground rather than an over-ground perspective. I had been burying him. What he registered was me digging him up.

"There, now, Zusel. Sleep tight. Dovid will pull through. You and I will have a little chat in the morning. About where you've put the money Malka was harrying me about."

No reply. Zusel was breathing deeply. He was asleep.

If he'd breathed as deeply and strongly as that when I was burying him, would I really have left him in the ground? Not in a million years.

My head was spinning. I felt as sick as several dogs. I was burning up inside.

I felt no better outside. I couldn't get any air. It flowed around me. As if I was inside something tied with a hundred knots. A sack perhaps. The air moved with the wind over the sackcloth but didn't penetrate – not even to my skin. Much less my insides.

I dragged myself to the river.

There I let my mind wander – feet in the water so that it would cool me down.

It was dawn when I awoke. Remembered everything immediately. Ran back.

The door to the house was wide open. There was a real draught. Zusel's curtain swung. The couch was empty. Zusel had slipped between my fingers. Like dry earth. Or water.

When he'd left – was unknown. Perhaps after me, at night, perhaps just now.

I was crushed with tiredness. And no longer hot but cold. As cold as underground.

I dropped where I stood.

I came to at Faida's house.

Sima was rushing around me with a wet towel and vinegar. Feeding me tiny spoonfuls of homemade kogel-mogel.

Trials and tribulations do not make a man healthier. Stronger – yes. But not healthier. Something in me had snapped, where it had worn thin. The thinness had been in a place I wasn't aware of but, since I am a living person, my body had reacted.

Miron brought news from Dovid in hospital. Things weren't going well.

Miron moved Grishka and Vovka in with him.

It had taken me two days to regain consciousness, Sima explained. They hadn't called a doctor since my only request in my delirium had been to lay down the law: "No doctors!"

And at the same time to issue threats in choice words, up to and including outright obscenities.

When I was almost better and had gone outside on my own, Sunka arrived all in a rush to announce that Dovid had died from complications of the heart.

Sunka shouted this news at my back. I glanced round but didn't think to stop. I kept going – to the toilet. Only there did the message sink in that Dovid was dead.

It sank in like an insurmountable burden. I thought I would never get back on my feet.

Miron, Sima and Sunka convened a family council around my bed.

It didn't take long to discuss the details of Dovid's funeral. It was quite clear. He'd be buried in Soviet fashion, with no prayers and no shroud, wearing his jacket. Particularly since Zusel had gone and there was no-one to bewail him properly.

We got stuck on the children.

Faida gave Sima the floor as a woman and a mother.

Sima said she didn't know how to proceed. The children were now utterly orphaned. That was on the one hand. On the other, not so utterly since Belka was alive. Anything could be expected of a living, breathing mother. If they let her out of hospital, she'd come looking for the little boys. Then what?

If Belka had no longer existed, Sima, for her part, would have taken the children in. Especially since Sunya was due to go into the army at any moment and would be away for three years. There was plenty of room. And then he might fancy living in some big city for a while and using his qualifications as a builder.

Oster was gathering dust. It was just a big village. The wrong population. There was nowhere for a young man to spread his wings. Not like before.

Miron interrupted Sima's line of reasoning.

He asked:

"Mikhail Ivanovich, you adopted the boy, Iosif, legally while Belka and Dovid were still alive. Are you up to the situation now? Can you do the same for his brothers too?"

I might have appeared to be better but I couldn't make out their voices very well. Although I could grasp the essentials. I didn't want to respond to a serious question from my bed. I had a sense of responsibility after all.

I said:

"Anything's possible. Absolutely anything. Not before burying Dovid though. After that. Is he really dead? Tell me: has Dovid really passed away?"

My voice rose unforgivably to a shriek. Albeit a quiet, hoarse one.

Miron, Sima and Sunka exchanged glances. Each with each. I deliberately followed their eyes out of the usual police habit.

Miron placed a hand on my forehead, heavily, significantly even:

"Get some rest, Mikhail Ivanovich. Dovid is definitely dead. We have the papers. All in order. He's dead in law and everything. You only get a one-way ticket. Never you fear."

I struggled to take part in the funeral. Grishka and Vovka each held my hand. And I held them. So that they didn't scatter in different directions.

The proceedings went off in an orderly fashion.

Faida had arranged for an amateur band from the club. They played the funeral march, kept it in time. As the coffin was brought to the grave. And later. During the burial.

No words were said. There was no one to say them. Dovid had been new in Oster and had no close friends. He had always been with Zusel… Zusel… Even Zusel was gone.

Jewish law doesn't provide for funeral banquets so casual onlookers went their way from the cemetery while Miron, Sima, Sunka, the boys and myself went home.

The band plodded along behind us and, rather than dragging their instruments pointlessly along, played something mournful.

I remarked to Faida that there was no need.

Miron protested that it was of their own free will and there was no point being offended. Let them play.

Grishka and Vovka were each given a drum. They kept banging at the wrong time. They stretched their arms out at the same level but, when it came to it, one was much higher, the other much lower. They couldn't keep time. Kept hitting the rim. Miron and I showed them how to do it. We were not met with understanding.

Sima fed us lunch. Miron and I drank a glass apiece in Dovid's memory. Sunka went off about his own business.

Miron began preparing to go to the club. I went with him.

"So, Miron, what are we going to do?"

Miron readily set out his programme.

"Grishka and Vovka live with us. We'll have to make it official, of course. Will you help?"

"I have a plan of my own. I've got Yoska. Without Grisha and Vovka, there's a rift. It was one thing when they were with their own grandfather. It's another thing for them to go to strangers. I want to take the lads in. Lyubochka and I, we're not like you and Sima. What I say goes. Of course, I'll take Lyuba's opinion into account but I'll do things my way."

I was speaking from the heart. I'd thought it over on the way back from the cemetery as the band played. What I said was what I'd been thinking.

Miron stopped and said gamely:

"Why are we the strangers? We're no strangers. They're of Jewish nationality. So are Sima and I. We'll never reproach them for being 'yidlets'. And that's just one example. And not an insignificant one, as it happens. You will say it to Yoska. Oh, yes, you will. Don't take it the wrong way, Mikhail Ivanovich. You will."

"Perhaps I will. But I can't imagine it right now. He's my own dear son and Grishka and Vovka would be too. By law. Whereas you, Miron Shayevich, are going too far. You can be brought to book for that kind of talk."

Miron was embarrassed.

"And what's more, I don't sense any burning desire on yours and Sima's part. You want people to speak well of you. Especially those of Jewish nationality. Jews don't abandon their own. That's the qahal for you. But why are you the first to volunteer, Miron Shayevich? You were what, a friend of Dovid's? You didn't know he existed until he moved to Oster. And now you're first at every turn. What then? Did he ask you to take the lads in in his will? Instruct you to that effect before he died? Put it down on paper?"

Miron asked:

"Did he write to you? I know what he wrote to you. Dovid read it out to me in person. The kind of thing he wrote about you, Mikhail Ivanovich, it's the stuff of nightmares. If there's even the smallest droplet of truth in it, it makes your head spin. And you want to snaffle his grandsons. Will they be your protection? Or your hostages? Well, will they?"

Miron grinned but he wiped that little grin away with his sleeve and ended on a serious note.

"Of course, I have nothing against you. Me, a cosmopolitan, driven out of a senior position. Whereas you're in law enforcement. You can do anything. You've taken one and you'll take the others. Go on, take them! Take the lot. Round them up. Remake them in your own image! They'll thank you for it. Of that, I have no doubt. They'll thank you."

My patience had been uncoiling like a spring. But it reached its limits. It sprang back.

"Indeed. I'm taking the yidlets. And it puts your nose out of joint. But you ripped your own yidlet away from his mother. Sunka. Evka confessed. And you can see it in Sunka's face. The spitting image of his mother. You'd better stuff that clear conscience of yours away somewhere. Otherwise any minute now, it'll be covered in shit. If you cast your mind back in all honesty to what really happened."

Faida's eyes boggled. His mouth fell open but no words came out.

We stood facing one another in silence.

How long we stood like that – I don't know. A long time.

Miron said:

"To what really happened, you say? I remember, I remember. Come on. I'll make a report. From the rostrum. With a jug of water and a glass. That's what I'll do."

At a shop on the way, Faida bought two bottles of wine while the shop assistant sighed over the untimely demise of Dovid Srulevich. She couldn't help spluttering with laughter when she said Srulevich, but she immediately covered her mouth and nose with a corner of her headscarf and blew her nose loudly.

Then she endorsed our plan.

"But then, 'course he should be remembered. 'Course he should. Else, he'll rise up and come back. Even then there'll be no life in him. And he'll plague everyone, and scare the children. You have to, you have to drink to his memory. And pour the dregs on the grave."

We shut ourselves away in the steward's cubbyhole. In the huge building of the former synagogue, the partitions didn't go all the way up to the faraway ceiling. The shelves were heaped with jumble. Just as it should be.

The executive desk was empty. Faida placed the bottles on it, found the glasses.

He held a bottle out to me.

I have noticed on more than one occasion how people can change their outer and inner appearance in a second. Not by design. If it is by design, it's easy to spot. It creates tension. The person is all preparation, holding himself in an imagined knot, monitoring every part of himself. He can't pull it off because he has a body and a voice and gestures as well. But if it isn't by design but stems from desperate need, then it is possible not to recognize someone. He's himself and not himself.

The Faida before me wasn't Faida. Previously, he'd been a tad shorter, lived in my presence as if having to look up to me. Now it was the other way around. He was looking down from on high.

I sat on a stool. Popped the cork. Deliberately made a meal of it. Let him calm down a bit. Excess nerves serve no purpose.

When I poured the wine, I pretended my hand was shaking.

Faida noticed. But said nothing.

"Look, Miron Shayevich, my hand's shaking. And you accuse me of lacking feelings. You do. Don't deny it. You're making a show of wanting a drink but you don't drink. You're planning to get me drunk. But I don't get drunk. Especially not on wine. But you, you're going to drink. And a lot too. You need it. Don't you?"

Faida said he did.

He quickly downed half a glass.

I touched the merest drop.

"So, Miron Shayevich, let's have this report. Start from before the war. With Evka. And bear in mind. That chutzpah of yours will pass. In the middle of a word, it will just go. And you'll be ashamed to be speaking to me. You won't be able to look at me for hating me. Fine, look somewhere else. The main thing is: talk. I haven't forced you to speak. I came to you in the utmost sincerity."

Faida drank again.

Fists on the desk as if at a meeting, he leant forward. To give himself momentum.

In outline, his story coincided with Evka's.

It wasn't Sima who thought up the notion of taking Evka's baby. True, she did threaten to put pressure on Miron through the Party. Moral degeneracy and so on through the list. Miron didn't take fright immediately. He was cock-a-hoop. Responded to all his wife's threats by saying he'd leave his family for Eva and the future nipper. And the Party wouldn't judge him harshly since Sima was barren whereas Evka was carrying another Soviet person. And was of benefit to the country. While Sima was of no benefit at all. Answering her, all in all, from the same Party standpoints she herself had urged on him.

Sima fell silent.

But one fine day Lilia Vorobeichik came to visit Miron at his place of work. Of course, he could tell her and Evka apart. But for a second he was frightened not to detect a belly. That was how much Evka had got under his skin. He could think of nothing but her and her belly.

Lilka guessed why fright had turned Miron as white as a sheet. She laughed and said: "There, Miron Shayevich. See how nice it is. Just like Evka but without the belly. As if nothing had ever happened. Come along, let's take a little stroll. I popped over towards lunch time so as not to take your work time up with nonsense. I've brought pies. Home-made pies. Evka and I baked them. We'll find ourselves a nice little bench and eat them there. Come along, Miron Shayevich."

And the look she gave Miron told him that he was facing a critical moment in his life. And that that moment would be brought about by Lilia.

On the little bench in the square, Lilka set out her plan. No good would come of his abandoning his wife. He wouldn't be able to live with Evka in any case. She came from a suspect family. Lilka made a proposal: 'Would you like me to arrange it so that yours and Evka's baby can be with you and Sima?' Miron didn't really understand. Lilka explained: Evka would give birth and voluntarily hand the infant to Sima and Miron. That was it. Done and dusted. There'd been a belly. Then there wasn't. The main thing was that the belly was gone. They'd put a rumour about that Evka had miscarried. People would talk for a while then forget. And Miron and Sima would still have the baby. And Evka would be free until the next time.

Miron asked whether Evka agreed. Lilka assured him she'd sort things out with her sister. Miron asked for a couple of days to think. Lilka replied that it had to be that very minute. Before she finished the pies. And she ate a quantity of them, five, one after the other. She ate and looked Miron in the eye. She ate and breathed on him, her breath smelling of chicken giblets, onion and crisp chicken skin. When she reached into the bag for another one, Miron caved in.

Lilka gave him a pie. She wiped her hands on the grass and said. 'Don't say anything to Sima. You're not involved. And please, eat. Have some tea. Otherwise, they'll stick in your throat. Your throat's working. You might choke.'

How and what happened next, Miron didn't know.

He didn't see Evka again until he'd moved to Oster after being demoted at work. Whereas Sunka, well. He grew up with them. As their own son. Sima had confidence in him as his mother. And he as his father and he would give his life for him should the need arise, of course.

All that was new to me was that Lilia Vorobeichik had cropped up here. And I had little interest in her role at this moment and in these circumstances. Although further reflection lay ahead.

I was much more interested in something else.

Miron's run-up was over. But I could tell he still didn't hate me. His anger with me still hadn't driven him mad. He would reveal the final truth. That there was one last truth to come, I had no doubt. Without it, he wouldn't have given up the penultimate truth so easily. Sunka's story - that was merely the penultimate truth.

I said as much.

"I didn't need your story to know that. You keep drinking, a bit at a time, Miron Shayevich. But were you aware that Laevskaya had been going through policemen's pockets at your house?"

At that point it wasn't just Miron's run-up but his heart that came to a halt. At that point, he would have ground me into powder. At precisely that point. Regarding Laevskaya. And when it's not possible for someone to pulverize someone else, he pulverizes himself. Grinds himself to dust. To spite himself. To release his energy. Otherwise he'll burst. Explode.

"Ah, Polina… All her life my Sima's suffered at her hands. And I have too. She's a relative. She was the one who put the Vorobeichik girls my way. So that I'd save them. She knew Sima was barren. Sima had put all the doctors through the mill. For nothing. Polina would parade in front of her. She had three girls. Each one better than the last. Clever and beautiful. Top notch. Sima would cry for nights on end: why was Polinka rubbing those girls in her face? She'd cry and cry then start pawing me. It might just work this time. That was no life. It was torture. Every night was torture for me. First, for my nerves and then, well, you know. And for what? Nothing. I was so exhausted, I couldn't do a thing. And I told Sima: 'You're barren and now I'm impotent. Let's just kiss and be friends right here. People get by without children. And so will we.' I was still young, by the way. I would be raring to go, take one look at Simka and all my passion would die a thousand deaths. Simka went to Polina. So that she'd find me a doctor to consult or a wise woman of some sort.

"Polina told her: 'It's not a doctor you need, it's some young and tasty bit of stuff. I'll fix it.' And she did. And me in a position of authority, a strength to the needy. I had a fling with Eva. I think that's what Polina had expected. She got Lilka involved as well."

I nodded and drank nothing.

I topped up Miron's glass.

Faida took a sip, breathed in deeply, all wound up again like a Studebaker off the handle. He even moved his hands as if turning a handle. And didn't sit down once. I put a stool behind his knees. He kicked it away. And on we went.

"Miron Shayevich, that's enough about what you need below the waist. It turns my stomach. Tell me about Polina. Did you know she'd been through my pockets? And in your own home too?"

"I did. I went into the room when she was trying to undo the sack. She couldn't do it. Asked me. She looked out of the window to make sure you couldn't come in. I couldn't do it. She went into the pocket of your uniform coat. Personally. Got something out and stuffed it down her bra. Of course, I told her she shouldn't. Especially not from your uniform. The bag's not so bad but a uniform coat with shoulder straps… She tutted and scarpered. What did she take? An important document?"

"Rubbish. Nix, that's what she took. But she got you involved. You're an accomplice. You're all accomplices."

Miron perched on the edge of his stool. He didn't move it nearer to the table. He remembered it was further away, that he'd kicked it. He'd kicked it as though in a rage. But he remembered. He sat down and didn't miss.

"What do you mean? In what case am I her accomplice?"

"That's confidential to the investigation. You tell me. Leaving out your women. And the children. Why did Laevskaya come to you? What was she up to in general, shuttling back and forth?"

Miron sat in silence. Gazing, revolted, at his glass. At the nearly empty bottle.

I asked if I should open the second.

He replied in the negative that he couldn't look at that abomination any more. That I should put it under the table. It made him sick to his soul.

I left it where it was. Poured myself the dregs from the first bottle, filled the glass to the brim from the second.

I raised the glass and proposed a toast.

"Let's drink, Miron Shayevich, to you and your family being found innocent. And, at the same time, let's drink to Dovid's memory. Or better still, to Dovid first, and then, separately, to you all coming up smelling of roses. We shouldn't mix things up. We shouldn't, should we? You've got to live and Dovid's got to lie there in the ground."

I emptied my glass in a gulp. Topped it up again.

"Now, this is to you and your family. To Sunya, Sima and you yourself personally. We have to clink glasses. You didn't drink to Dovid but you will to your own living family."

I filled Miron's glass and placed it firmly in front of him.

He didn't clink glasses. He didn't look at me. He just drank.

"Fine. Let's assume you've turned yourself in, Miron Shayevich. Talk."

Miron leapt up and fled the cubbyhole. I heard him clattering over the stone flags. He didn't reach the street. He was still in the building when he threw up. Judging by the sounds.

I sat and waited. I thought he'd have a wash and come back.

I waited five minutes, ten.

I left the room when Miron groaned. He was lying practically on the door steps, on the flags. And in such a good position his head was slightly raised. Otherwise, he'd have choked.

I called out. The cleaning lady came over. Oohing and aahing. She said:

"He's suffered a loss. I'll tidy up. Let him lie there, where it's cool for a bit. He'll snap out of it. These stones are always cold as can be. They'll bring the poor soul round. Are you that policeman from Chernigov?"

"That's right. We've been marking Dovid's passing."

She nodded, muttering something in Yiddish.

It was light outside. My eyes were tired from the gloom of the cubbyhole. Now I could see things in a new light. And I made a plan.

Before nightfall, I would wheedle the truth out of Miron and Sima. Sit them down together and make them tell the truth.

Then off to Ryabina. To put things to rights with Lyuba.

Then on to Chernigov and Laevskaya.

I had decided what would happen to Grishka and Vovka. I was taking them.

I went in the direction of Dovid's house. I had the keys. I'd taken them from Miron as soon as I got over my illness. Miron hadn't been particularly keen on handing them over. No doubt, he already regarded the house as his own. If the boys stayed with him, so did the house.

When I collected the keys, I hadn't even thought of what to do with Grishka and Vovka. Now, though, they were definitely mine. And so was the house. When they grew up, they'd be given the house and could run it together with Yoska. By law.

I examined every nook and cranny of the empty house. Went through the rags on Zusel's couch. Inspected under and over it. Nothing. No leaves from religious books, no Jewish paraphernalia. If Zusel had taken it all with him, he'd have needed a pull-along cart or a very big suitcase. Whereas he could barely stand on his own two feet.

I tapped on the floorboards, on the walls of the rooms and the entry way.

I went down into the cellar. I lit a candle in the dark. I found it there on a little step along with the matches.

Nothing. I was about to leave when I tripped over a broken box. A nail ripped my trousers. In a temper, I kicked the box. The lid snapped and my leg was gripped as if in a trap. Tug as I might, I couldn't escape.

The candle went out.

I managed to lug myself over to the stairs. Where the light shone in from upstairs. I freed my leg and realized by feel that a small bag was attached to one side of the box. Or rather a pouch. Containing something hard but not all of a piece. Also a tightly rolled tube, compact, short.

I untied it upstairs. It was my knot. That's how I undid it. Otherwise, it would have taken me ages. Or, most probably, I would have cut it.

It was my knot. But with deviations. Some personal contributions. The person had evidently tried, though. Had been patient. Where the strands crossed, the broader string had been smoothed out. Like adjusting a bow of ribbon. Again, I thought of Evsey. He used this knot even to tie his bootlaces. He was always trying to improve his speed.

Inside were the following:

gold tooth crowns – four;

engagement rings – seven;

tsarist gold coins – five;

a brooch made of yellow metal, presumably gold, in the shape of a flower set with small blue stones – one;

a long pin with a rosebud button, made of a grey metal presumed to be tarnished silver – one.

Along with Soviet currency, banknotes, rolled up and held together by a rubber band.

Two thousand roubles in various small notes.

I put it all back inside. But didn't fasten it tightly. Just anyhow.

I set off for Miron's at a run.

Miron was sitting at the table.

Sima was feeding him chicken soup. She scowled at me disapprovingly.

I didn't respond. I slapped the open pouch on the table. Out tumbled its inner riches. The tsarist coins, the tooth crowns, the rings, the brooch, the pin and the rolled-up money.

Sima gasped. Dropped the ladle in the pot of soup. It went everywhere.

Miron merely shifted his gaze and even then not towards the gold but towards me.

I said:

"Citizens, you are now attesting witnesses. Let's count this up and record it officially."

Faida reached across the shining pile for the bread bin, scooped out several pieces all at once, put them next to his mug. He started crumbling the bread into the soup. On and on, crumbling and crumbling.

I said:

"As I understand it, Citizen Faida, this is not the first time you have seen the contents of this pouch. They're not even putting you off your food."

"No, they're not. I've seen those contents so many times they don't even put me off. Take the weight off your feet too, Mikhail Ivanovich. Let's eat. There's plenty of time. Everything will keep now."

I wasn't surprised by Miron's calm. It was part of my plan even. I had sensed at the synagogue that there was a final grain to come, after which he would calm down and come clean. Although what kind of a grain it would be, that I hadn't known. I'd even carried out my search without any clear goal. As it turned out – that's what led to the final grain. Dropped it right onto the table.

Miron was looking at me without anger. Anger was no longer of any use to me or to him. He was looking at me with release. And I realized I wouldn't have to use pressure.

"Simochka, give me a drop of that soup as well. I'll crumble a bit of bread in it too, like Miron Shayevich. You come and sit down with us. Otherwise, you'll have cold feet, cold hands and goodness knows what."

Her hands trembling, Sima offered me a full mug.

She didn't eat a thing.

Miron and I drank down our soup then spooned out the sodden bread – neither trying to beat the other. Rather the opposite. Each trying to be slower.

Eventually, Miron couldn't bear it.

"Sima. Go away. Somewhere not too close. Take the lads to the meadow. Play with them for a bit. Is Sunka there?"

Sima replied that he'd gone off with the boys already and she didn't know whether they were at the meadow or not.

Miron ordered her to find out and to await further instructions wherever the children were.

"I don't know where I'll find them," Sima said. "They could be at the river or at Wolf's Mountain. How can I await your instructions if you don't know where to find us all?"

"Go, Sima. Don't stay too close."

Miron stood, stroked his wife's back and pushed her towards the door. "Go on. I'll find you. You'll be noisy. You don't know how to be quiet. I'll find you by your voices."

Sima went.

Miron sat down.

"You've already counted it, Mikhail Ivanovich. Stop acting the goat. Witnesses-schmitnesses. You and I are the witnesses. No others are needed. If you want to know, I'm glad you found the pouch. It was really wearing me down. Where did you find it?"

"In Dovid's cellar. Whoever hid it, knew what he was doing. Don't tell me who it was. I know. It was Evsey. Right?"

"Right."

"Who knew the hiding place was in the cellar?"

"I did, and Evsey."

"What? And Zusel didn't? And Dovid didn't? And Malka? So what money were they harping on about?"

"Some other money, I suppose."

"Why didn't Evsey hide it at yours?"

"He didn't hide it at mine because my Sima's an intelligent woman. And she keeps her cellar in order. Stores her preserves down there. And other useful stuff. I wouldn't have that abomination in my cellar. It sickens me to think that my own cellar where my food's kept, the food eaten by my dear wife and son, myself included, could contain that, that, I don't know what."

Although Miron had raised his voice, there were no nerves. He'd rid himself of nerves earlier in the cubbyhole. Together with his drunken vomit. Which I'd seen with my own eyes. And he knew I'd seen and observed.

He was mine now.

"So, Miron Shayevich, go on with your story."

Miron's testimony can be summed up as follows:

Evsey turned up in Oster together with Laevskaya. They stayed at Faida's. Laevskaya showed Miron the pouch and gave directions for it to be hidden as if she was issuing an order. But so that it could be rapidly retrieved if the need arose. Evsey was in uniform. He presented his ID.

Evsey's advice was to make a hiding place somewhere in the house so that it was under constant supervision. Miron refused outright. By way of a choice, he suggested Evka Vorobeichik's house. At the time, the house was boarded up. Evka had moved to Chernigov. And that's what they did.

Evsey did it all himself. He went independently at night under cover of darkness. The door was almost off its hinges and Evsey entered practically without hindrance. As he would later recall with glee. He gave Miron a precise description of the place and warned him not to try and open the pouch. He'd never be able to fasten it up again the same way. If the need arose, Miron would be informed and he could deliver the pouch to the appropriate place.

In the morning he and Laevskaya left for Chernigov. Before the guests departed, Miron couldn't help but ask who might give instructions to hand over the pouch, and how he would know it wasn't a trap. Apart from Laevskaya and Evsey, obviously. Laevskaya replied that if it wasn't her or Evsey, he shouldn't give it to anyone. Specifically, she said: 'Whoever finds it can keep it.'

And so, when news of Evsey's death reached Oster, and Dovid and the boys took up residence there, Miron started to fret and immediately contacted Laevskaya over what to do next. Polina set his mind at rest by advising him not to think about it. He didn't need to.

Before long, Dovid, Zusel, Malka and the boys moved into the house. This was once Evka had moved to Chernigov for good. Dovid was thought to have bought the house. Miron became a frequent visitor. On the one hand out of kindness, on the other out of constant concern for the valuables in the cellar. With a view to the inevitable winter, he suggested to Dovid that it would be good to lay in a store of potatoes and other vegetables. Sadly, the Vorobeichiks' cellar had always been known as leaky and damp. He volunteered to help on that score.

Dovid and Malka declined to go down and investigate as the stairs looked to be rotten. Which was true. Moreover, Evsey had broken several treads as a distraction.

Miron made a show of fussing about in the cellar and when he emerged concluded that they should write it off. The entire house was barely standing and the cellar was the main threat. One riser after another and all of it rotten. Better to nail the door down. To keep the boys out. Dovid himself had battened it down with a huge nail. They decided to store the vegetables in a pit in the yard. Miron also promised them unlimited access to his own premises.

Incidentally, I hadn't found any such nail. I'd just opened the door and gone in.

And so I inquired:

"Who pulled the nail out? Not you? I was lying here unconscious, Dovid was in hospital. Who else could it be?"

Miron assured me it wasn't him. That not only had he not looked at the nail but he hadn't looked at the cellar even in his worst nightmare.

"Do you believe me?"

I replied that I did.

"Now, here's what I'm going to say once and for all. I can see your role clearly. It's not a good one. You're scared of Laevskaya. Your behaviour towards Evka is unbecoming. Yes, Laevskaya pushed you at the girl. But the rest, that's on your own personal conscience. I'm not going to try and frighten you that I'll tell Sunka. Sunka's an adult. He understands: your mother's the person who brought you up not the one who gave birth to you. Even if he is the spitting image of Evka. I think the lad will guess of his own accord. Or someone will just happen to tell him. But it's your behaviour Sunka won't forgive. And I will tell him about that. Should the need arise. A mother's a mother, behaviour's behaviour. You realize what will happen to Vovka and Grishka. I'm taking them. Say hello and thanks to Sima from me. I'm leaving right this minute. I'm not going to hang about to say goodbye. Tell the boys I'll be back for them soon. You've got the pouch for now. Stuff it under your pillow or something. I'll hold you responsible."

Miron listened to my verdict resignedly. But I knew he was thinking about something else. In his mind, he was right. And I hadn't persuaded him otherwise.

Now, his mind was full of joy. And that joy was because he hadn't told me everything. Not all the details. But I had to leave him with at least something. So that he didn't hate me enough to want me dead. Not that much.

I wasn't taken in by all the guff about Dovid not being in the know. Of course, Dovid knew about the pouch. A householder like Basin letting somebody else into his cellar and trusting him to rule on whether or not it was suitable for keeping potatoes?

No. Dovid knew. But why was Miron shielding a dead man? On the contrary, he could have dumped the pouch and everything on Dovid.

An answer took shape in my head.

When Dovid moved into Evka's house, Laevskaya had given him instructions to take the valuables into his keeping and hide them. But that he would hide them without looking at what was inside and how much was out of the question. He'd looked. Without letting Laevskaya know. But who had retied the knot for him? One of the boys? Grishka? If it was Grishka, then the pouch could have ended up at Dovid's when Evsey died. And Miron's tales about Evsey and Laevskaya arriving together weren't worth the breath used to tell them.

But that meant nothing was left of Faida's story. And that just doesn't happen. If someone gives false evidence, they always use some kind of truth. It's always based on something. So that they don't get totally confused.

I started thinking it through from the beginning.

For safety's sake, I sat on the grass at the side of the Kiev highway – waiting for a lift was time well spent.

What difference did it make to me how Dovid literally came by the gold?

The difference lay precisely in whether or not Laevskaya was involved.

Miron claimed she was.

Most importantly, unreservedly and categorically – the knot was tied first by Evsey. Which meant Evsey also brought along the pouch. Miron was a stranger to him but not to Laevskaya. Evsey wouldn't have delivered such a burden to a stranger. Whereas Laevskaya had gone to a relative, and what's more one who was dependent in every sense, with the confidence that everything she ordered done would be done. Miron didn't know Evsey. Conjuring him up from what Laevskaya had said – why complicate things so much?

No.

Here was the little grain of truth that Miron had been clinging to with all his might.

Laevskaya and Evsey had brought the pouch. Then Miron had given it to Dovid.

What evidence did this give me?

Evidence that Evsey and Laevskaya had been deeply involved in something together. And so deeply that he went on to shoot himself and abandon his three children and his beloved wife to their fate.

The money Zusel took to Chernigov and lost somewhere or whatever – that was a separate story. Perhaps it wasn't even from the pouch. Unconnected money.

And perhaps it was precisely this money that Grishka had had in mind.

I wasn't even thinking so much as crawling in my mind around and around the pouch of gold and paper in the form of money - about which, incidentally, Miron had said nothing specific, as if he hadn't particularly noticed it – until my whole body was spinning from head to toe and back again so that I twirled into the ground, taking root. And a mountain rose and rose above me. Up and up. Heights that had to be taken. No matter what the human cost. To spite the enemy.

I arrived in Ryabina at night.

The dogs barked after me. To myself, it seemed I was a dog.

I was running and running as if chasing my own tail. And my sense of smell was blocked: I'd been given something very hot to eat or had filched it myself.

I had made a plan so many times. And each time the plan had gone wrong or been thrown off course. And doing the throwing were Laevskaya's chubby hands. Over and over again. And not in a specific direction but any old how, like a plate of unappetising food.

Because she, Polina Lvovna Laevskaya, was sated. She wasn't in a hurry.

But I was hungry. And I couldn't wait.

And not once during the journey did I remember Zusel, who had vanished. The money he allegedly had on him, I remembered a hundred times. The man himself, not once.

I didn't knock at Didenko's house.

I lay down to sleep in the garden under the cherry tree. There was a piece of sackcloth there. And dry grass for a pillow. It must be where the old man had his afternoon naps. I settled down in his spot.

What luck! I thought delightedly. No need to explain anything I said. I hadn't had to wake anyone up.

I was up before cockcrow. I tapped gently on the window.

Lyubochka looked out. She opened the door. We hugged as hard as we could.

I whispered to her to follow me.

As we went, Lyuba asked:

"What's happened? Have you come for long?"

I turned to face her fully.

"Nothing's happened. We're leaving with the children today. Sit down. I've something important to tell you. And pack our stuff. Sit down, sit down."

Lyubochka sank down on the bench, on the very edge.

I said:

"Dovid Basin is dead. Grishka and Vovka are coming to us. Might as well be hanged for a sheep as a lamb. Isn't that right, Lyubochka?"

Lyuba burst into tears.

But pronounced a firm "yes".

Didenko was not put out by my appearance. He showed no pleasure but nor did he grumble. He said:

"You're taking your people away, then. An emergency evacuation."

I said nothing.

The children were pleased to see me, of course. I hugged them, clasped them to my heart, for a long time.

Gannusya took my hand and in her secrets voice she whispered:

"Come into the shed. I've got something to show you."

Yoska scampered after us. I took his hand so he didn't trip.

We went into the shed. As though she was in a museum, Gannusya pointed a small finger at something by the wall. Wood, tools.

"Daddy, Grandpa's making himself a coffin to lie in underground. We're helping him."

Yoska's face nestled into my neck and he repeated every one of Gannusya's words in a baby language no one could understand.

Gannusya took me up close. And sure enough, there was a coffin on two wooden stumps. Not quite finished. The planks had been planed smooth.

Gannusya ran a hand over them proudly.

"Nothing should stick out. Yoska and I test it ourselves. We love Grandpa and want it to be nice for him. The lid's still to do and then Grandpa will die."

I listened and I watched. But at some point, I lost the thread. I seemed to be dreaming. Only Yoska's weight stopped me closing my eyes altogether and sliding down on to the hard earth, although I longed to.

Yoska asked to be put down.

He went over to the open door and called:

"Grandpa, we're here! Show Daddy how you're going to lie in it."

Didenko came in. He laughed.

"Shoo, then, little sillies!" The children cheerfully begged him to lie down. I looked on in silence.

But when Didenko started to test out how best to fit into the coffin, I couldn't take any more. I wrapped an arm round his belly from behind and pushed him aside.

The old man fell flat on his face.

The children stopped laughing. Yoska started shouting. Gannusya burst into tears.

Didenko rolled onto his back, fidgeting, unable to get up. The children rushed to help.

I shot out of the shed into the sun. Lyubochka was heading towards us. In a pinafore dress. Her legs could be seen through the material, a long way up.

I said:

"I feel rough. Really rough."

The faint smile left Lyubochka's face.

I went on to say:

"Let's go down to the river, right now. Just the two of us. Shall we?"

Lyuba nodded.

She wasn't tender with me but nor did she keep me at arm's length. Of course, as a man, I didn't hold my horses at that particular moment but even so.

We lay in the grass and didn't look at one another. As if it wasn't love between man and wife that had just taken place but a misunderstanding between two strangers.

"Lyuba, what are you thinking about?"

I spoke in order to hear my own voice. So that she would remember it was me. So that she realized I was there and that it had been me there with her a moment before.

"It's time to get ready. There's no time to think, Misha. Really, there isn't."

Lyuba began to cry. Not as she sometimes did, on the sly, but out loud, right in my face.

"How are we going to get by, Misha? How are we going to feed the children?"

I understood: the woman was in hysterics. I struck her, just a touch, across the cheek, not a slap, a ... I don't know what. In any case, it didn't hurt much. How else are you supposed to stop them?

She fell silent. Her look wasn't right. It came from somewhere inside her, from the depths.

"Lyubochka, we'll bring up the children. What matters is that we're meant to be together. And to love one another. You don't mind?"

Lyubocha stood silently, straightening her dress. She tried to smooth down a strap that was torn at the front but ripped it off altogether and threw it away, far off to the side.

"Whatever you say, Misha. If you say, we'll bring them up, we will. If you say, I'll love you, I will. As best I can."

And she quickly ran back. She didn't step into the river for a quick wash.

When I went back, Lyuba was sitting on our bundled-up belongings.

Didenko was fussing about, retying a suitcase. The lid wouldn't shut. It was bent out of shape with the effort.

"What have you packed in there?" I threw the top open. Pork fat wrapped in a cloth, an enormous towel, a piece of sackcloth, the one that had been under the cherry tree, a linen shirt, longjohns, a man's drawstring underwear, a pair of nearly worn out boots, a pair of felt boots. Some nondescript bits of clothing, ancient, homespun.

I took it all out bar the pork fat and bread.

"Mikola Ivanovich, thank you, obviously, for putting a pack of presents together for me. Depriving yourself. But Lyubochka and I have everything. And you'll be needing them yourself. Where are you going to buy new ones?"

Didenko raked the jumble on the floor into a heap and began to cram it all back into the suitcase.

Lyubochka waved an arm.

"Misha, we have to take it. It makes it easier for him. I asked him to keep it. He wasn't having it."

And gently she said to Didenko:

"Mikola Ivanovich, Misha didn't mean any harm. He's really very grateful. We'll take it. We will, definitely. And Misha will wear it. You will, won't you, dear?"

She gave me such a look, that new inner look of hers, that I nodded.

Didenko's efforts had left him sprawled over the suitcase lid but he didn't have the strength to tie the rope around it. A lock didn't even enter into it. The lid gaped by about ten centimetres.

I tied the rope.

Automatically. With that same blasted knot.

We sat for a couple of minutes before the journey. The children made no noise. The silence was dreadful.

And in the silence, Petro's voice rang out:

"Hey, now, out you come! Gannusya, Iosip, let's be off to the Vorksla. The sun's in the sky, the river running high."

The children ran outside. Lyuba followed.

Gannusya was shouting, Yoska joining in.

"Petro, Petro, Sweetie-Pie-O, we're going home to Chernigov! Daddy's come to get us! We're going right now! On the train! And we'll be eating on the train and everything! On the move! Even going to bed!"

Petro stood still as a statue in his cloak-tent. He was hot. Sweat ran down his face. Round the bandage over his eyes and on down to his chin and from there dripped onto the canvas cloak.

Petro said nothing. His entire head was turned towards Lyuba. She didn't speak. But he could sense her.

Lyuba stroked his arm.

She said:

"Goodbye, Petro. Look after Mikola Ivanovich. Let me take that cloak off. You can't move for it. It is hot, you know."

Petro answered cheerily:

"But I've been up all night. It's not hot at night. At night, it's cool. All night long, I've been roaming around. Down by the Vorskla and such, along the highway. And I can take it off myself. I'm not an invalid. I do have hands."

He pushed Lyubochka's hands away and threw off the cloak himself. Underneath, he was wearing just his trousers.

His feet were bare, black with soil and grass.

But the rag over his eyes was whiter than white.

Lyubochka touched the rag. As if stroking it.

The children didn't even look back at Didenko's house. Or at Petro.

Somehow we reached Chernigov.

On the way, Lyuba's behaviour put me on my guard. She said nothing. Nothing at all. Not a word to the children or to me.

At home Lyuba inspected everything straight away and her first words were as follows:

"We need to buy another camp bed. You and the boys can sleep in one room and Gannusya and I in the kitchen. We'll have to take the table out of the kitchen into the other room so they can do their homework. You can attach a plank to the kitchen windowsill, give us a surface. That's where we'll eat."

I asked how she was feeling, whether she needed to see a doctor. Judging from her expression. Just in case.

She said she felt perfectly fine.

I hugged her and she hugged me. But not together, not as one, we didn't. It didn't work.

I had allocated a day for my trip to Oster. So off I went promptly. In full police uniform.

At Miron's, the house was empty. Everyone was at work. Dovid's house was empty too. The door wide open.

That's where I settled in. Sat for a while, relaxing after the journey.

I went to the Desna to see Grishka and Vovka. I had no doubt that's where they'd be.

The lads were cavorting about in the water with young friends of various ages.

At the sight of me, someone yelled:

"Grishka, Vovka, scram!"

Grishka and Vovka hopped out of the water and fled in an unknown direction.

I didn't try to stop them.

Calmly but loudly I said:

"Whoever told the lads to scram, come here to me this instant. Otherwise, it will go badly for the lot of you. Unless you're a coward, of course. If you're a coward, stay where you are. The others can come out instead. They will prove they're not cowards but honest, Soviet citizens."

Five youths came out of the water. There was one left, not in very deep, trying to hide his head.

I asked one standing nearby.

"What's his name?" and nodded scornfully at the water.

"Vaska."

"He can sit there till he turns blue. Find Grishka and Vovka and take them home. I'll be there. Tell them not to be scared. That there's nothing to be scared of now. In front of you all, I'm declaring them my very own children. Understand?"

I turned round and at an even pace I strode back the way I had come.

I'd calculated to some extent on making an impression and children are particularly good at understanding impressions. They think if everything's routine, it's not true.

Grisha and Vovka caught me up as I walked. They didn't shout, just trudged along behind. Whispering to one another.

I didn't let on. I turned around sharply and roared with laughter, which they always used to like.

The lads stood stock still.

Grishka said:

"You're not putting us under arrest?"

"For what?"

I was surprised and all my surprise showed in my voice and gestures.

Grishka mumbled:

"Well… I thought… Abandoned children get taken to the police. Then to a children's home, where they're really strict. Vovka and me, we've discussed it and we're against it. Grandpa's dead, that's true, but Zusel isn't, is he? He's still alive. He's gone off somewhere and he'll be back. We'll live with him. Won't we, Vovka?"

Vovka nodded.

I asked:

"Did the lads tell you what I said? You're mine. Your father was my best comrade before he died. Your brother Yoska's with me. And you'll be with me too. We'll live together. In Chernigov. I'm your father now. By law."

Grishka shook his head.

"No. The lads told us you were acting the goat, like something at the pictures. They didn't believe you. And we don't either."

I saw red.

Grabbed Vovka and Grishka by the hand and dragged them after me.

"Home! I'll give you the pictures! If you can't understand it properly, you'll just have to lump it!"

I didn't look at them. I didn't look to the side. Vovka was snivelling. Grishka clenched his teeth. I could hear him clenching and grinding. Evsey used to do the same.

At home I explained what was what properly. During this explanatory conversation, it emerged that Sunka had negatively disposed the juveniles towards me. He'd assured them I intended to put them in a children's home whereas Miron and Sima wanted to keep them with them. That is, at liberty, as they understood it. And that they shouldn't agree to go with me for anything, no matter what promises or gifts I might offer.

I didn't have any gifts. Vovka was especially put out.

He asked:

"Can you buy a whole bike?"

I said I didn't have the money for a bike.

Vovka said to Grishka:

"There, see!"

I didn't understand what that 'there, see' meant. But what I did understand was this: I had to sit Miron, Sima and Sunka down together for one final communal conversation. With the children present.

Outside, I apprehended some youngster and ordered him to run to the club and tell Miron to go to Basin's house along with Sima and Sunka. Mikhail Ivanovich from Chernigov had arrived.

While I waited for Faida I examined the door to the cellar closely and purposefully. What's more, in the presence of the children. I deliberately asked whether they had seen the big nail that had battened down the door. Whether they'd been playing soldiers or scouts or anything else under the house. Behind the backs of their Grandpa, Malka and Zusel, or indeed with them.

Grishka went ferreting all over and around the door, seeking a trace of the nail or the nail itself.

He would thrust a burnt match at me one minute, then a sliver of wood, roaring:

"The nail, the nail! Here it is!

He wanted to find it so much.

But I could see there had never been any special fastening on that door. It simply lay flat against the floorboards. There was a ring to lift it, nothing more or extra.

I stopped the searches and said to Grishka:

"Grisha, you're the eldest of all the brothers. Vova and Iosya come after you. Would you like it if people said they told lies? That all you Gutin brothers did."

"Why all of us?"

"Because if one brother tells lies, they'll say the same about all of you. That's how it is. Would you like it if for no reason at all people pointed you out in person as a liar because of Vovka or Yoska?"

Grishka said nothing.

Vovka spoke.

"Grisha isn't telling lies. He doesn't know. I saw Grandpa carrying a hammer and a whopping great nail. He wanted to nail down the cellar so we couldn't go in. And then he says to himself, 'Shame to spoil it,' and he never nailed it down. And he put the nail on the windowsill with the hammer. I took the nail. And the hammer. Without asking. We lost them down at the river. Later on. Grandpa looked for the hammer and didn't think about us straight away. But he didn't ask about the nail. Now you're asking. We don't know what happened to that nail ourselves. The hammer was a big one and we don't know where that went. Let alone a nail."

"Good. I understand. But have you been inside?"

"Yes. Loads of times." Vovka had taken the initiative. "But then Grandpa said Dad was living in the cellar. That he was dead and so he was living there. And that we shouldn't go in there and bother him. And we didn't any more."

Grishka was close to tears. He hissed at Vovka.

"So, is what you're telling me that you didn't go into the cellar after Grandpa told you not to?"

Grishka answered for them both.

"Without Vovka, there was nothing for me to do in there and he was scared. So scared he even wet himself. So why would I make him do it? There's nothing interesting down there in the cellar. No food, nothing. Just rubbish. And we don't know where the nail is. Why do you want the nail, Uncle Misha?"

It was the first time that day that he'd called me Uncle Misha the way he used to.

"I just do. I collect nails. Some people collect stamps. With me it's nails. Miron Shayevich told me Grandpa Dovid had shut the cellar up with an interesting nail. So I thought to myself, I'll find it and ask to keep it. Would you have given it to me?"

"Of course," Grisha replied seriously. Vovka repeated it after him. Like an oath.

And they had said nothing about the pouch. If they'd seen it in the cellar even once, they'd have reported it. Which means they hadn't seen it. If they had, a thread would have appeared given the way things were going: Grisha would have blurted it out – how he'd cleverly untied and retied the knot and so on. Down the list.

In that case, what money had Grishka been talking about? Any pressure now might be too much. Could ruin everything. I put it off for the moment.

Miron, Sima and Sunka arrived: the full set. They sat at the table.

So did the children.

I said:

"We are gathered here together in a grand council with respect to the future fate of our children, Grigory and Vladimir. They have been orphaned. That we know. You go first, Samuil. Do you admit to scaring them with the children's home?"

Sunka muttered that he hadn't been scaring them merely sketching the situation at their own request.

I asked Grishka to repeat what Sunka had said about the children's home.

Grishka said nothing.

"In order to close this matter, I hereby conclude: there can be no children's home or reception centre. Grigory and Vladimir are coming to live with me, to be reunited with their very own younger brother Iosif. They will have a comfortable home in Chernigov and everything necessary for continuing their education and their journey into adulthood. My wife Lyuba is waiting for them and already loves them as her own dear children. Does anyone have any questions? Grigory?"

Grisha said nothing and ground his teeth.

"Vladimir?" Vovka was sniffing but I didn't see any snot or any tears.

"Miron Shayevich?" Faida wanted to say something but didn't.

"Sima?" Sima sat, head and eyes lowered. She shrugged her shoulders but clearly whispered her agreement.

"Samuil?"

Sunka stood, moved his stool out of the way, adjusted his trouser belt and said:

"I'm in favour of things being alright for everyone. But there's something else to be considered. I'm going off into the Soviet Army. My parents will be all alone. They'd like to take in Grisha and Vova. And what's more, the Oster Young Communist organization is fully informed and has worked out a series of measures. For example…"

I went over to Sunka, put a hand on his shoulder and said warmly:

"Sunya, you're a Young Communist but I'm in the Party. Your initiative's a good one. And you've mobilized people in a good cause. But you're wrong. You're thinking just now about what's good for your parents who would like there to be children's laughter, fun and so on in a house that will be empty without you. But Oster is Oster. And Chernigov is Chernigov. What's more I am within my rights, in all fairness. Evsey Gutin is my friend.

And how would I look him in the eye, wherever he might be, if I left his children without my influence?"

Sunka blushed beyond all recognition.

"Well, Samuil, answer me." I understood that I had to bring things to a halt there.

Sunka said clearly:

"If it's a case of looking him in the eye, I agree. But it's not what I really think."

And went out into the yard.

Grishka and Vovka looked at me. So did Miron and Sima.

I said:

"This isn't a court. It's a meeting. So we're voting. Sunya's a no. Anyone else?"

There were no 'no's'. Or abstentions. Grisha and Vovka voted in favour too.

I declared the meeting over and dispatched the lads into the yard on condition that they played nearby. We'd be off soon.

Miron had brought the pouch with him. Tied any which way. He gave it to me without a word.

I took it without a word.

Sima sat quietly, swaying slightly. Otherwise, she was fine.

I asked whether Zusel had turned up. Perhaps someone in Oster had seen or heard of him. Miron assured me no one had seen him. Oster was abuzz over his disappearance but at the same time not too surprised. The general opinion was that Zusel might have gone to Chernigov as he had in the past.

I asked Miron why he claimed he'd battened down the cellar. The answer was vague.

I asked Sima to help me pack. I told her I wasn't taking any of the household goods, only the children's clothes. It came to a single bundle.

They promised to keep an eye on the house and not let it fall down altogether. If Zusel turned up, they'd send a telegram.

I asked Sunka to accompany me and the lads to the highway.

He was thrilled, especially when Grishka and Vovka fervently supported my request.

Grishka and Vovka walked ahead. They seemed to be in fine fettle. I was letting them feel grown up, as if they had a say in things. And they could tell.

Sunka pretended nothing special was going on – just the children going home. He chattered about his future military service, his hopes for leaving Oster and, after the army, most probably working on a big construction project in Kiev.

I asked:

"Sunka, what's this story about Grishka and the money? He hasn't taken to thieving on the side, has he? It happens with children. They don't mean any harm. They don't know the value of money. To them, it's like bits of paper they can swap for sweets, for example. Dovid mentioned something but didn't really say."

Sunka stopped. He took the bundle off his shoulders.

I stuck to my tactic.

"Well? I'm not going to tell him off. It's in the past now in any case. But I do need to know for the future. For bringing him up. You see."

Sunka told me that Griskha had once asked his advice as an older comrade. He'd been serious, grown-up, saying he and

Vovka had decided to leave Dovid and Malka and Zusel and strike out on their own. That lot were always drilling them in all sorts of Talmuds and, worse still, had told them they mustn't take food from their friends in the street because it might contain pork fat and not be kosher.

Grishka's spirit of protest had been coming to a head under the influence of Sunka's tales of Young Pioneers and Young Communists for a long time. And so Grishka and Vovka had decided to run away. They were going to go to Chernigov, to Mikhail Ivanovich, to where Yoska was.

Since the conversation had been before Sunka met me, he had suspected they were lying. However, so as not to find himself in Griskha's bad books straight away, he'd observed that there was no point making a run for it without any money. Without money, they'd be classed as abandoned children and would be rounded up into a children's home before they'd even got to Chernigov. Or be sent back to Dovid.

Griskha had gone off, upset. After some time, he announced that he and Vovka had the money and he showed Sunka banknotes worth a total of eighty roubles.

Sunka sternly asked whether Griskha had stolen them.

Grishka said he hadn't. He'd taken the money from Zusel. And would give it back. Once he and Vovka were settled at Mikhail Ivanovich's in Chernigov. Since they had no intention of being silly and wasting the money on the way but would present it if they were arrested.

Sunka ordered him to give the money back to Zusel straight away however he liked. Even just slipping it back where he'd got it from, if he had taken it without asking. He himself had no doubt Grishka had pinched it.

To calm the lad down, Sunka told him he'd have a chat to Dovid about his upbringing. And assured him he would have the unnecessary lessons cancelled.

The next day Grishka said that Zusel had gone off somewhere and he, Grishka, had been unable to put the money back again.

However, when Zusel returned, he would be sure to give it back on the sly.

But that was precisely when Zusel went missing for the first time and returned from Chernigov unable to speak and barking mad. Malka went around the whole of Oster bewailing the fact that a lot of money had disappeared.

In this situation, Grishka was out of his depth. On Sunka's advice, he handed the money over for temporary safekeeping to yes, Sunka.

I asked where it was now.

Sunka said it was in his pocket.

He took out a rolled-up tube of notes. Offered it to me.

"I was going to give it back without saying anything. At the last minute, as they say."

I laughed.

"Oh, Sunka... Who knows which minute's the last?"

The money, of course, I took - for the future.

I asked with one leg already in the cab, deliberately so I had my back to Sunka:

"If Laevskaya comes to visit, say hello. I like her."

Through my uniform coat and undershirt I could feel the cold from Sunka burning my skin. I jumped back onto the ground.

Sunka stood pale and as if frozen, one hand gripping a wheel. As if he wanted to stop the vehicle if it moved before I reached him.

"What is it, Sunka? Tell me, now. Afterwards will be too late."

Sunka blurted it out, not from his throat but from deep inside his belly.

"Polina was talking to Father, saying she had everything ready to make mincemeat out of you – nix. Father shouted, under his breath, not to get him involved, he didn't agree. But she insisted in these words: 'Miron, no one's asking you if you agree. But you're with me when it comes to Tsupkoy. You have been already.' I didn't understand all the details. What I want to know, Mikhail Ivanovich is: Is Laevskaya a spy?"

I gave a serious answer: it had still to be ascertained.

"When was the last time she was here?"

"When you and I first met. She popped in for a minute. You were sitting out in the garden or somewhere. She patted the bed down. Mum made some comment but Polina waved it away. Bold as brass, she is. She felt your uniform jacket, said she needed to study the cut. Father told her to go and see you in the garden if she needed something. No, she said, and took off, slinked away like a cat. Makes me think she's a spy. She shows all the signs."

"How do you know what spies are like?"

"Who doesn't?"

I promised to involve Sunka at the required stage. For now it was mum's the word.

In the lorry, I didn't think about Laevskaya or the money.

How to sum up?

As follows:

Zusel was planning to take the money to Chernigov when he came to me to speak in Dovid's defence. Either Malka had given it to him or he'd scraped it together from somewhere himself. Or Dovid had given it to him. And that was the very money young Grishka stole from him. Zusel left believing he had the money on him. But he didn't. Assuming Grishka had taken the lot. But what if he hadn't?

"Grisha, did you take all Zusel's money or was there some left?" I asked casually, by the bye, as we bounced over yet another pothole.

"All of it," Grishka answered quickly and cheerfully. He realized what he'd said. But kept a faint smile defiantly in place.

"I'm not asking what for or why, nor will I. But how? How did you take it without anyone finding out?"

"Dead easy. Malka thought I'd gone outside. But I hadn't. She'd wrapped the money in a newspaper then a rag and stuck it in Zusel's pocket. She stuck it in, took it out and put it back, over and over again. Like she was testing to see if it fitted. Zusel was planning to go to Chernigov early in the morning. Malka was forever telling folk to leave Zusel alone, that really he wasn't all there at all. She tried to do everything for him. She'd even lift the spoon to his mouth. He used to get so cross. Anyway, she stuck that money in his jacket, hung the jacket on a nail in the entrance way and went to call Zusel to come and eat up and be off on his travels. While she was gone, I took the package out of Zusel's pocket. I took the money and put the folded newspaper back. Folded it the way it was before, wrapped the rag round it. Copied it. I can do that, copy things. It's something I can do. Zusel arrived, had a bite to eat, pulled on his jacket and scarpered. He patted his pocket. My heart stopped. But all he did was pat, that was it.

"Malka squawks away at him, points at his pocket. Zusel jerks his head, gripping his pocket. Then he's gone. When he came back, I wanted to give it back. But who to? There was Malka yelling. Grandpa yelling. Zusel not saying anything at all. So I think what if they think he's lost the money? Or spent it? Let them, I think. And all the time, I've got it safe, me, Sunka. Eighty rubles. Crikey! A whole eighty!"

"And this little bag, have you seen that before?" I took the pouch out of my haversack.

"Yes," said Grishka reluctantly. "Grandpa asked me to undo it then do it up again the same way. And I did. You taught Dad. I learnt too. Better than him."

"And do you know what's inside?"

"Course, I do. It's Evka's dowry. When she gets married, they'll hand it over so the bridegroom will have her. She's afraid she'd spend it so she gave it to Grandpa to look after. She came along herself once and said, 'Let's open it up and take a bit out, just a little bit.' But Grandpa shooed her away."

"And when was this?"

"When she brought Zusel back and he couldn't speak. I heard them."

"And you didn't peek inside when you were doing it up again?"

"I wanted to. Grandpa wouldn't let me. He said anyone who looks at someone else's dowry will never have children. And what's it to me? It's women's stuff anyhow. If it had been a knife or a gun..."

"A knife? Like the one in my haversack? Right, Grisha?"

Grisha hung his head.

"Why did you go into my haversack, sonny? Who put you up to it?"

"No one. It was my idea. I thought your gun was in there or something. But it was a knife. I wanted the torch too. But I only took the knife. I fastened it up the way it was. I hid the knife. Grandpa found it. He gave me a good hiding. Took the knife for himself. Aren't you going to take me now?"

"I'm taking you. Just as you are, warts and all. You've done really well to tell me. Just bear in mind - if you're honest and admit something, you can put it behind you. Not completely, you keep a tiny bit hidden away inside. But it's deep down. A reminder not to do it again. I promise not to tell you off. And you promise me you'll remember and won't do it again. You're no thief. You just went off the rails. But now you're back on track. Understand?"

Grusha nodded and slid up close to me. He closed his eyes and fell asleep. Vovka had been snuffling away on my other side for ages.

And I closed my own eyes to draw yet another line.

I wanted to cross it but it wasn't a line any more, it was a ramp, higher than a lorry. And I couldn't raise my leg high enough. I nodded off.

But I did manage to give myself a pat on the back. My hunch had been right – Dovid and Grishka had been talking about different things. Dovid had his own concerns, Grishka his.

Everyone does.

Our own home welcomed us with a tasty meal. Borscht, dough balls, other Ukrainian dishes. Uzvar, for example. Dried fruit, most probably from Didenko's. There wasn't anywhere else they could be from. Last year's harvest. This year's wasn't ready yet.

Lyubochka said nothing, pretty much, just kept giving the little lads a cuddle and telling them to eat up. Gannusya helped her and was affectionate towards Grishka and Vovka too. Yoska was a little pickle, a bit anyway. He'd forgotten his brothers. After a while, he began to play with them.

When everyone was quiet, I asked, for the sake of conversation, what Lyubochka had been doing all day.

She said:

"Sitting."

In answer to the question as to who made the dough balls and everything, she said:

"Laevskaya."

I asked on what pretext she'd been round.

Lyuba replied that she had rung Laevskaya from a neighbour's.

Lyubochka cut through my surprise.

"Laevskaya took Yoska out. I don't have any other friends. I had to have someone to talk to, woman to woman. I would have gone mad without talking."

"You couldn't just hang on a bit and talk to me? I know you the way a woman would, every possible way, off by heart, with my eyes closed."

Lyuba said firmly that she had no intention of talking to me any more. Living with me, fine. She'd do that. Be my wife and everything. But talking to me, chatting with me, oh no.

We whispered back and forth over the children's heads. I was afraid they'd wake up and I asked Lyuba to go into the kitchen.

She stood up and went. I followed her.

And then she told me.

Didenko had told her about the letter purported to be from Zusel. About what it said. He suggested I'd broken the law in some way because higher law-enforcement agencies than the police, in the guise of Zusel, were gathering material about me. And Lyubochka should take care. Of herself and of the children.

Mikola Ivanovich had let the letter go unanswered. But when I went to see him, he linked my arrival to this epistle. Which was why he hadn't been.

Didenko was certain the letter was not the written-down version of what Tabachnik said. And now it turned out I was dragging him into my affairs as well.

Didenko was untroubled when I turned the conversation to Zusel. It confirmed his fears that a trap was being set. Either by me or by goodness knows who.

He breathed freely when I'd gone. But after receiving my written request to look after Lyubochka and the children for the summer, he was completely at a loss. It was then that he decided for himself that it was time to settle his accounts with life in a friendly fashion, in other words, to die of old age. Thereby escaping involvement in the whole story. He made himself a coffin and gave his stuff to my family so that it wouldn't go to waste. As a country dweller, he couldn't bear to think his property would fall into unknown strangers' hands.

Lyuba concluded her tale by saying:

"Petro will look after him to his last breath. He and I talked about it. And, Misha, tell me, in all honesty, what have you done? Why is it that all around you people are dying of natural causes and, especially, of not natural causes? You criticize me for wanting Laevskaya's advice rather than yours. Well, now I do want yours. What have you got to say?"

I asked Lyubochka to tell me first what advice Polina had given her.

"Polina hasn't given me any advice. She's kneaded dough and done the grocery shopping. You farmed us out then off you went, racing around again. Polina didn't say a thing. She was scared you'd find her here. She couldn't wait to leave."

"And here's my answer to you, Lyuba. I haven't done anything wrong. You trust an old man who isn't even a relative, you trust Laevskaya, you trust everyone. Just not me. What about Laevskaya plaguing you with all sorts of gobbledygook in the hospital – have you forgotten that? Forgotten that she used Lilka Vorobeichik to get at you?" I'd said too much.

Lyubochka replied readily, however.

"Ah, Lilka… Now Polina did happen to mention Lilka. She's ashamed now, says she shouldn't have spoken to me in hospital about that Lilechka of yours. That's what she said, twice, on two occasions: 'Misha's Lilechka'. I wanted more details but Polina's lips were sealed. So tightly she practically swallowed her own teeth. But I understood. You were quite ready to accuse me over Blind Petro. I thought – I'll wait till you bring it up. Then I'll have my say but I'm not going to do that now. I did want something to happen between Petro and me. And so did he. It didn't. There was no second time. You're the one who always pulls it off. You cherished me. Even when we slept together, you cherished me. But I wanted you to screw me, the way the other women talk about it, to make me scream. You've used me all up but oh, so very carefully. Left nothing but bones. You've overdone the cherishing. Now the children can have what's left of me."

I asked, if she didn't want to adopt the children, why she hadn't said so before. If she could see in advance what I was going to do. I ignored the bit about our private life. So as not to make things worse.

Lyuba shrugged.

"Why is it me who doesn't want the children? You're the one who wants or doesn't want. I don't even get to use those words. You wanted Evsey's children – all of them - and along they came. And I'll love them and I'll bring them up. But not because that's what you decided but because it doesn't matter to me who I love, who feeds off me. As long as it's not you. I won't do it for you."

Lyuba was standing by the windowsill, the one she'd previously suggested needed an extra plank – by way of a dining table. I tried to work out how wide the plank would need to be. At least 40 centimetres.

Essentially, I wasn't listening.

I asked if she'd given Laevskaya the key to our flat before.

Lyuba said she had. Before she went to Ryabina. So that Polina, if need be, wouldn't bother me about the housekeeping but would go to the flat herself, by arrangement with me.

"But where did you get the idea that I might make arrangements about the housekeeping or anything with her? You know I can't stand her."

Lyuba answered easily that she had her reasons for giving the keys to a woman she trusted. Without me knowing. She was registered to live there just as much as I was.

"So why did you give Polina the keys? So she could check up on me or so she could rustle me up some borscht?"

Lyuba didn't answer.

I stroked her bare shoulder and went back into the other room. I snuggled in on the edge alongside Grishka and Vovka.

In the morning, before six, I measured the windowsill and took my leave. I snatched up the pouch as I went - to keep it away from Griskha.

I still had a little time before I had to be in work.

I took my time as I went to Laevskaya's.

Lyuba had stabbed me in the back. And, although she wasn't using her own voice or her own words and expressions but you know whose – Polina's – I felt bitterly sad.

I went over in my mind the time we'd spent together. Apart from her inner beauty and modesty, nothing leapt out. She had cared for me diligently in hospital, had displayed selflessness. So what if she had got the habit during the war and had set hundreds and hundreds of men, maimed in battle, back on their feet? It was me she fell in love with. She said so of her own accord. Not because I asked. It was touch and go whether a piece of shrapnel would enter my heart. There was no guarantee the operation would be a success. Before they took me into surgery, Lyuba confessed her love.

Regarding her not being satisfied as a woman, she might have told me, as a comrade, as the person closest to her, rather than making a tragedy out of it now after so many years of life as a couple.

I had merely done her bidding and done what she let me do.

What's more I was convinced: Laevskaya had put her oar in here too. Spun tales about it, about you know what. What people get up to and don't get up to. Lyubochka would never have come up with it by herself. She didn't even need that kind of thing. If she had, I'd have sensed it. Guessed. There had been trust between us. And Laevskaya had destroyed it. Destroyed it during one of her fittings. She'd gulped down that wretched liquor and, like a worldly-wise friend, had put some sort of obscenity into Lyubochka's head. And Lyuba believed it. So she trusted Laevskaya. She was wide open to trust. And her trust in Laevskaya had grown greater than her trust in me. Which meant a little worm had been niggling away at her. That worm came down on Laevskaya's side and outweighed all our years as man and wife. And she hadn't let me see any of this. That's what was most insulting.

And how much I had done for her sake. Well, fine, not for her personal sake. For the sake of our love.

For a long time, I haven't wanted to blacken Lilia Vorobeichik's name. To expose what no one should touch. The time has come.

Yes, Lilka and I were involved with one another when she was alive. And for a long time too. I thought no-one knew. And she'd assured me no one had any idea. If I had imagined even for a minute that our involvement had gone beyond the bounds of secrecy, I would have broken it off with Lilka. But I didn't know. I didn't know and it never occurred to me that she and Laevskaya talked about me.

I'm not blaming her. She was a woman. She needed to share her impressions with someone. She couldn't keep them to herself. And to give Polina her due, she didn't spread them far.

Only now she was releasing them droplet by droplet. As if pressing out a splinter and blood with it. And mixing her blood with mine.

I met Lilia Vorobeichik in January 1947.

I was wandering around town on my day off. I was in a jaunty frame of mind since once again I had my whole life ahead of me. A few weeks before, the last piece of shrapnel had been successfully removed from my chest. As I mentioned, a certain Nurse Lyubochka had taken particular care of me in the hospital. I had fallen in love with her and we had agreed to marry in the near future.

Our rendezvous was for that evening in the municipal park near the monument to Iosif Vissarionovich Stalin.

I walked along with the purest and best hopes for the future. I looked up at the sky and imagined the sparse evening stars being lit and Lyubochka and me strolling along snowy paths beneath those stars.

I turned into the market with the aim of purchasing a gift. Sweets would be best of all. You can eat them on the go. What's more, sweetness inclines people towards kind-heartedness and calm.

I didn't want to buy home-made boiled sweets but the ones in special wrappers. I would unwrap them and give them to Lyubochka straight from my hand. Feed her like a little bird.

But I couldn't find any.

So then I bought some pretty cookies cut into circles. I tried one and it was just the job. I stuck the twist of paper in the pocket of my padded jacket so that I could continue along my planned route.

At this point, a woman's hand, wearing no mittens, ever so gently touched my sleeve.

"You've dropped your biscuits! You missed your pocket!"

My cookies were scattered in the snow and, moreover, in crumbs. They'd come apart on impact. In other words, they were a shoddy piece of work. I didn't attempt to gather up the crumbs.

I gave the woman selling them a damning stare.

She began to wail that I'd trodden on them and it was my own fault. I knew I hadn't though. I'd just dropped them.

The woman who had tugged my sleeve said to the one on the stall:

"I'm going to gather them all up right now and stuff them in your blasted mouth. Snow included. Give the comrade his money back. Go on!"

She spoke in such a tone that the woman immediately sprinkled the coins into my hand and hastily scooped the crumbs up from the snow and tossed them over her shoulder. Sparrows swooped down and pecked them up. Leaving no trace.

I wasn't used to a woman's voice speaking out on my behalf.

I said:

"Alright. She should be grateful, I don't want to get involved. If it happens again, I'll take her to the station."

The stallholder looked right through me, as they do when their wheeling and dealing is exposed.

I took out and presented my ID card.

She immediately changed her tune.

"Oh, I'm sorry, Comrade Officer. But the cold does damage the goods."

My champion laughed. And laughed in a way that made ever such a tiny bit of her red tongue poke out between her white teeth. She threw her arms out too and doubled up, laughing. And the frosty air made her cough.

I automatically thumped her on the back, not too much.

Her coat was thick and soft. Fluffy to touch.

She said:

"Ah, so you're a policeman? And there's me standing up for you! Oh well. Next time you can tick someone off for me. Will you?"

I promised, of course I did.

She walked away and it occurred to me that I wouldn't even recognize her if I saw her again. Apart from the red hair under her scarf. But that's a feature not a portrait.

I didn't want to but I bought some boiled sweets.

Just before I was due to meet Lyubochka, I dashed into the hostel and changed into my uniform. Put on my greatcoat. Changed my old hare-fur hat for a round kubanka. It looked better, of course, but it wasn't so warm.

Lyubochka met me but only for a second, to let me know the hospital was really busy and they couldn't give her the evening off.

We arranged to meet the next day.

Since, by way of a present, I had the boiled sweets on me, I gave the twist of paper to Lyubochka. She didn't even look, just held it tightly.

She tried to feel what was inside.

"Boiled sweets?"

"That's right."

Lyubochka pulled one out quickly and crunched it up.

I asked anxiously if it was sweet at least.

"Oh, yes!"

And off she went with the sweet in her cheek. I watched her go and imagined that sweet swirling beneath her tongue, bumping up against her teeth, the grains of sugar melting in her mouth.

I ought to have waited till the next day.

I ought to have gone straight home. But I didn't.

I walked around Comrade Stalin's monument, in the lamplight, round and round in circles. I couldn't even think straight. Seeing my police uniform, some of those out for a stroll thought I was on duty and asked me various questions. Where's the skating rink? What time does it close? Can you hire skates? Does the park shut at night? I answered, glad to be of service.

And then that same woman came up to me. From the market. The redhead. I could make out her face in the lamplight.

She said disapprovingly:

"Comrade Officer! I've been keeping an eye on you for some time. What are you doing going round in circles? You should go further in where there's no light. Otherwise, you're out here wandering around while people are frightened in there, in the dark."

I was about to answer in a jokey manner.

But at that point she recognized me.

"Is it you?"

"Yes. I'm not on any kind of duty here, just out for a stroll. But if it's dangerous for you to walk off into the darkness, I can escort you as a sign of my gratitude."

Once again, she laughed.

"I'm not afraid for myself. You don't need to escort me. And if you're going for a walk, you shouldn't be going round in circles. It looks funny from the outside."

"And are you going for a walk or just passing?"

"Just passing. From a friend's. I'm going home. I live on Clara Zetkin Street. Now that is dark. Really dark. Not even the teeniest weeniest street light. It's hair-raising. Positively hair-raising!"

"May I escort you?"

"Yes, if you like. It will give you some exercise. Are you frozen in those boots?"

I admitted that it was chilly. Even my coat was feeling the cold.

Clara Zetkin Street was a stone's throw away.

Not a word as we covered the distance.

Not a word as we went into the house.

Not a word during all that happened next.

To this day, I don't understand how Lilya Vorobeichik had the nerve to kiss me and everything. What could I do? I'm a man. But she was a woman after all. She should have been modest, proud.

Lilya wasn't proud. She immediately acted as if there was something special between us. Without talking about love. I'd never met anyone like her. Although I'd been with my fair share of girls.

Of course, I'd had occasion to hear that some woman are wildly passionate. But I hadn't come across them in my own experience.

And now there was Lilya.

She took me every little bit of me. And, like a fool, I kept on giving and giving to the very last drop as if I would have no need of anything in the future.

In the beginning, we saw an awful lot of each other. And every time, I told myself and her too: 'Never again'.

What grieved me particularly was that Lilya's house was only three minutes' walk from the hospital. The risk of meeting Lyubochka hung over me all the time.

Let's be honest, I could always think up a reason for being in the area. Once or twice. But what if it was three or four times? And the expression on my face and my overall state? I'm not good at telling lies. I have a conscience and everything.

If Lilya had taken to accompanying me as women often do: to the corner, to the next lamppost etc. I wouldn't have been able to say no.

But Lilya didn't even try.

I would get up and leave.

She would lie there as if I'd never been there. Hadn't arrived. Hadn't left.

But not once during all that time did I run into Lyubochka.

She and I registered our marriage as originally planned. Before Lilya. I couldn't break a promise. Lyuba was all on her own in Chernigov. As a result of the war, she didn't have a single relative left. She was renting a small space in a wooden shack near the market. The owner was a drunkard and his wife backed him up in everything and even took downright advantage of Lyubochka. Lyuba did their washing and the cooking.

I'd given her everything she had, not to mention the flat where we now lived. In this way, I had literally saved Lyubochka. With her health, she wouldn't have lasted long as their skivvy.

I treated Lyubochka with care. She meant the world to me.

Once, she said:

"You and I, we're orphans. That's why we'll never abandon one another. Our love is real, till death do us part."

I wanted to object immediately that she was the orphan not me. But I said nothing because I understood that she was much younger than me and still remembered her parents as if they were alive. Whereas I had come to terms with mine being dead. Because at my age I had digested their all too recent demise. Not because of my character. Because of my age.

I didn't try to explain the difference to Lyuba. So that my thoughts didn't distress her.

With Lilka, it was another matter.

She was older than me. I wasn't interested in how much.

She asked once:

"How old would you say I am to look at?"

I wasn't sure.

I said honestly:

"I don't know. I can't tell with women."

Lilya caressed her neck, along her throat, and laughed:

"My neck's beautiful. So are my hands. They're young hands. Even I'm surprised. Have I come to a standstill when it comes to age, I wonder? Maybe I've gone already and just think I'm still here?"

And she grasped her neck with both hands as if she was about to strangle herself.

It frightened me this joke.

But I managed to keep the mood going:

"Being strangled leaves an ugly mark. A ligature mark. If it's with a rope or a wire. Bare hands leave blood-red contusions. A print of every finger. I've seen plenty of them."

Lilka laughed even more.

"Don't frighten me! In that case, beauty's the last thing that matters. I've seen enough myself. So, how old?"

"I couldn't say. Not to look at, I couldn't. You're just you. You've always been like that and always will be."

Lilka agreed.

But she didn't spare me.

"Whereas you will soon get old."

"Why?"

"Because inside you, there's a real ruckus going on but on the outside you're so quiet. You cry out when we're in bed together but you don't notice. You're louder than me. I can't not make a noise. I scream out at the height of pleasure. It's all part of the same thing. You don't understand. With you, even on the inside, there's a secret, a mystery. I'm tired of secrets. Perhaps it's only when you're inside me that some sort of catch is released and I can let everything out. Absolutely everything."

I took this most amiss. True, Lilka did make a lot of noise. But me? I hadn't noticed. And this was a criticism. A bloke shouldn't cry out. Absolutely not.

I knew nothing about Lilka's life. Who her parents were or where she used to live. About her twin sister.

I didn't even look at her passport. On purpose. I knew where it was. But I hadn't sneaked a peek.

If I checked her passport, it would mean I was aware of what I was doing. I couldn't allow that. I couldn't have justified it to myself or to Lyubochka.

I found out by accident that Lilka worked at the shoe factory.

I arrived as she was bandaging up a finger.

"I did it on the assembly line. I put my finger just under the chain so that I didn't fall asleep and miss anything arriving. There'd been a breakdown. It was being repaired. One thing and another. I thought I'd have a bit of a snooze but I fell asleep. And off it went at full pelt. I nearly lost the finger!"

I asked where she worked.

She told me at the shoe factory.

Otherwise, I wouldn't have known.

I had my uniform. It spoke for itself. Lilka never tried to find out more about the job.

From then on, I would imagine her in her headscarf at work – picking up a half-finished product, smearing the sole with glue, the foreman yelling at her or saying well done. Imagined her wanting to sleep after being with me, closing her eyes for just a second to remember better and missing the pot of glue. Or sticking her finger under the conveyor belt and being woken by the pain.

I didn't make comparisons between my Lyubochka and Lilka. Love is love. And family is family. And duty is duty.

But when Lilka cried out, I was afraid they'd hear her even at the hospital. That Lyubochka would hear. Or course she wouldn't twig to what it was or why. But someone might explain.

That's where my foolishness got me.

There were times when I forced myself to break off with Lilka. It didn't work.

Lately, in the run-up to her untimely death, Lilka had given ground. Sometimes she wouldn't go into work. Just lay there on the sofa. Fully-dressed, sometimes in her snow boots.

She would say:

"I was going to go in to work but I didn't."

When she was asked why, she gave no reply.

Once I asked outright – could she be pregnant?

She flew off the handle and cut me to the quick when she said:

"If only you knew where I'd stick any future children. But you don't. No one does. Even I don't know."

Idiot.

After an insult like that, I held out for a week. And then I saw her, dead in the yard, on 18th May 1952.

Who gave her medical dispensations for her days off work, I didn't know. Now I guessed it was Laevskaya through friends.

All the rest was Laevskaya's fabrications, nasty insinuations and the attacks of a jealous woman.

There were pressing matters to deal with.

First on the agenda was Evka.

I didn't bulldoze my way in. I approached the house stealthily, by the back way. Walked around it on every side. The windows were wide open. You could hear a pin drop it was so quiet. I didn't imagine Khrobak would have spent the night at Evka's and could still be around. He was a senior official, even if a widowed one, and spent his nights at home, with his family, alongside his father, mother and child. After the wedding, yes. But just like that, no. Only every now and then. People don't miss a thing, after all.

At that late hour, half past six in the morning, Evka, who hadn't gone in to work, was asleep. Because of the heat, she was on the sofa in the main room.

I slipped in cautiously from the windowsill but the metal tips of my boots clanged.

Evka rolled onto her other side and pulled the sheet over her head. A second later she grabbed it, opened her eyes and, not making a sound, stared at my shape against the light. She couldn't make out my face.

I flung myself towards her, saying:

"Hush, Evka! It's me, Tsupkoy. With greetings from Oster. So, what now, is Khrobak taking you without a dowry? Naked as the day you were born?"

I spoke clearly. Kept my hands still.

Evka pulled herself together quickly.

"What's 'naked' got to do with it?"

"It's a saying. Don't bother to get up. Recognize this?" I waved the pouch in front of her eyes. Something inside it rustled and there was the softest of jingles.

Evka half rose in surprise.

I brought the pouch right up to her face.

"You begged Dovid to give you this. Dovid, meanwhile, has died a natural death. Now your request is being granted. Take it."

Evka licked her lips. As it was they were full and red - moistened they were utterly shameful.

"I'll turn round. Throw something on. It's uncomfortable talking like this."

I turned round, put the pouch on the table, in the middle, where the crocheted pattern came together. I put it down and kept a hand on it. As for me, I stood straight so that she could see my bearing. When there's a man in uniform standing before you, even with his back to you, it's quite another matter. He might as well be facing you. Eyeball to eyeball.

Evka fussed about, puffing and panting, and finally, clearing her throat, she said:

"Dovid's dead?"

I turned round.

Then I took a stool, sat carefully on the edge, and said:

"Come here. This is a conversation not an interrogation. Sit at the table."

Evka sat down. She tripped over the leg of the chair. I came to her assistance. She could hardly keep her balance.

"What are you so worried about? It was Dovid's heart. He died in hospital. What does it matter to you? You've only known him a short while. Or are you going to cry about it? Take the pouch. I trust you. You won't take more than your due or is it all yours? If it is, take the lot."

Evka took it, fiddled with it, weighed it. Then, as if she'd remembered something nasty, she tossed it towards me.

"I don't need anything out of it. None of it's mine. Dovid was making it up."

"Dovid might well have made it up. Except that he wasn't the one who told me about this blessed pouch. I was told by someone I trust, who couldn't have made it up. When you delivered Zusel to Oster practically unconscious you asked Dovid for your share. He didn't give it to you. Fact. This fact doesn't speak badly of you. It doesn't say anything really apart from that you wanted something out of the pouch and Dovid didn't agree. That's not a crime. You're not digging yourself into a hole. Dovid's dead. May he rest in peace in the hereafter. The pouch is no use to him. But you're still alive. And I'm telling you, if it's yours, take it. What don't you understand?"

Evka drew the pouch towards her again. She didn't even try to undo it.

"There should be five gold tsarist coins. They're mine. Not the rest."

"So you know what else is in there apart from the coins? In other words what's yours and what isn't? So what is there that isn't yours?"

Evka shifted uncomfortably.

She said, "You open it and look. I'm not."

"You do it."

"No, I won't. You brought it here, you can open it."

"Well, if you can't be bothered taking what's yours, why on earth would I look inside? Nothing in it's mine. I'll hand it in, we'll record it as state revenue. As the law requires."

Evka snatched up the pouch and began to untie it.

She couldn't do it. She was pulling the wrong end. In the wrong direction.

I waited.

When Evka had had enough, I yanked the pouch out of her hands. I undid it. The contents tumbled out in her immediate vicinity. The edges of some things caught in the holes of the tablecloth's pattern – the tooth crowns. While the gold coins lay neatly next to one another on the top, and the rings and the brooch on top of them. The money lay separately in a delicate little roll.

"Well, Eva, look. Count it. And I'll count along with you to be sure you get it right."

Evka looked at the tablecloth, at the holes. Cast an eye over each one of them, her gaze scooping up the gold coins. She made a forward movement but stopped.

"What, Eva, does it revolt you?"

Eva nodded.

"Talk, Eva. You're getting married soon. You need to live. There are cracks in your house. Your little fence, so that people can't peep through the gaps, and the window frames, they all need replacing. And the bed linen, to be nice for your husband, and the sofa and the bed. And the crockery and the pots and pans. And you need a new oil cloth on the table. A stylish one. And clothes and so on. Tell me, Eva. Surely I don't have to call Khrobak so he can pick over your dowry. All because you're being honest. You could have said it was all yours. You and your husband could have sorted it out somehow. When the revulsion had gone down."

Here is what Evka had to say.

When she and Lilka were sixteen, their father showed them the cache in the table. The five gold coins. He declared it their dowries so that they'd remember they weren't paupers when it came to sizing up future husbands.

Lilka remarked cattily that two into five didn't go. Were they supposed to saw one coin in half?

Their father interrupted her objections. He said: "You and Evochka are a single whole. I don't ever want to hear anything like that again."

It went without saying that they were meant to keep it a secret and not blabber about it all around Oster. But either Lilka or Solomon Vorobeichik himself dropped a hint to someone about the gold in the table – Evka could vouch that it wasn't her – or it was just idle speculation – but rumours started going around Oster about the Vorobeichiks' tsarist coins.

Under Soviet power the talk soon dried up but people remembered just before they were evacuated. There were even cruel jokes that Vorobeichik would use the coins to do a roaring trade under the Germans and deluge the whole place with buttons. It was probably assumed that there was an entire bank's worth of coins. In the people's way of thinking, money can do that – grow inasmuch as it's kept hidden.

Solomon brushed it off and didn't join in the jokes. The Germans were already just around the corner.

Evka was evacuated, Lilka disappeared. Their father and mother stayed at home. And so did the money. Or so it seemed.

After the war, Evka came back and discovered the dreadful truth about the deaths of her father and mother. She did the rounds of Polizei houses. Nice people told her who on that accursed day had taken the table in the Vorobeichik's house to bits. Evka didn't do the rounds on her own, she went with Faida. As a representative of the authorities. He had just come back from the front, with medals and a decoration. It was 1945. Victory had just been declared.

They went to six homes. Three of the Polizei were no longer present. They'd been given ten years in Karaganda after a public trial in the former synagogue. Another three, who were hardly vicious, attested that they had indeed scoured the table for the money. But found nothing. Evka flew at them with her fists. Faida held her back.

It became clear that no one could tell her anything she needed to know. Moreover, Evka was subjected to reproach because she was looking for the money instead of mourning her parents first and foremost. Evka replied that she had the rest of her life to mourn her parents and that it was her personal business and that whoever had destroyed her house was just getting on with their lives and not mourning anyone, only the fact they hadn't managed to snaffle anything at the Vorobeichiks.

Faida put some distance between himself and Evka. In response to her demands to help her restore justice, he said:

"The Soviet courts and the people will restore justice. But I have to work for the future."

Evka realised she had no influence over Faida. Even though he had Sunka as well as all her past.

Evka went around Oster. She knocked at every house, shouting out that she needed to have a look and take what was hers. Since, when Jews had been killed, their property had been scattered around the shtetl and there had been a lot of scandals on these grounds, Evka was allowed in. She found things here and there. In this way, she gathered together nearly all the table. The pieces. She put them on a pull-along cart and dragged them home. The general feeling was that she'd gone mad.

But she did find the coins. There, where Solomon had put them. Underneath the table top there was a large space – as if for holding household articles. But that space had a false bottom. It couldn't be discovered by looking at the table or shaking it. But if a tiny peg was removed from underneath, a little panel, fitted to leave no gaps, came away. As Solomon Vorobeichik had shown his daughters on that solemn occasion long ago.

Evka took the coins. The drawers and panels she spread around the Jewish cemetery as everyone looked on, holding a funeral for the table.

Evka now believed she really hadn't been quite right in the head back then. Even without the tsarist coins, she would have survived by hard work and her own efforts. What really hurt was the injustice of it. And her behaviour was intended purely to stand up for justice. What's more, she wanted to attend to a meeting somewhere to show everyone her coins and let them know what bastards, what idiots, they all were.

It was just at that time that Malka Tsvintar established herself as Evka's dependent once and for all. Evka had no secrets from her. Malka learnt about the coins too.

The Tsvintar woman began introducing special practices into the house to do with kosher. She baked matzo and secretly distributed it around Oster. Evka tried to make her see there would be trouble. But Malka assured her that no such trouble was possible after the war. She curbed her activities after Faida bawled at her. "We didn't fight shoulder to shoulder together with the whole people just to revert to old Jewish prejudices in the present day. Certain people think the Jewish people have earned that through their vast and unearned losses. But they haven't. The losses are one thing. Matzo's another." And he threatened to go after Malka on every count if he heard of Malka's homemade matzo circulating in Oster. What's more the innocent would suffer too. And so that all the educational and cultural work for which Faida was responsible in two districts didn't go to rack and ruin, it behoved Malka to stay put and have done with her escapades.

Miron also advised Eva not to be scared of the Tsvintar woman when it came to Sunka either. Malka would keep her mouth shut. On that subject, she had been reliably brought to heel even without Faida. He put it like this: "When it comes to Sunka, it's Polina that matters most. I take responsibility for everything else. And there will be no matzo there either. Even if it means making Malka face a fair trial, as is being discussed right now in the appropriate quarters."

Evka was again frightened that through Malka she might find herself in anti-Soviet ranks. She said that, should anything happen, she had the five gold coins. If anyone had to be paid off. Faida laughed in her face. "Have you ever heard of anyone paying off Soviet power? If they come for you through a letter or whatever, there'll be no paying them off. They'll take what they like. You included. And you'll sign everything. There's no paying off Soviet power and its agencies. And if they find tsarist gold during a search, so much the worse for you." Evka persuaded Miron to take the coins into safekeeping. Faida declined and declined then took it nonetheless. Solely because of his erstwhile love.

In this way, Evka lived relatively peacefully and steadfastly in one place. Malka didn't bake any matzo. But she did stop speaking Russian and Ukrainian. Although Evka pleaded with her not to wail her Yiddish in public.

Evka hoped that Lilka wouldn't show up too. Some people claimed she had fought in Fedorov's partisan detachment, some said it was with Jewish commander Yankel Tsegelnik. Evka didn't ask anyone anything, as if on purpose. Among themselves, people insinuated that Evka was rather pleased there was no sign of her sister. The property was hers and hers alone.

Since Evka was constantly in the process of selling the house and dreaming of a new place of residence, she lost touch with reality. She did bits and bobs of casual work where she could, here and there.

Once, in around 1948, she went to Chernigov to look around the market and find out the cost of accommodation. She didn't like the prices but she did bump into Laevskaya. Polina dragged Evka off home with her and, in particular, formally opened her eyes to the fact that Lilka had been living in Chernigov since 1946. In a house of her own. The house had been left her by an old lady Lilya used to keep an eye on. She had just registered the paperwork and was now the rightful owner.

Evka was delighted. And decided that since Lilka had her own house, she could turn that to her advantage.

Off she and Laevskaya went to Clara Zetkin Street. Lilka was at home after the early shift. A reunion took place between the two sisters. There were some tears. Evka took Lilka to task for not having gone to Oster. Lilka replied that had Evka not turned up, their paths would never have crossed again.

Evka took her sister to task for not making herself known. Whereas she, she said, had thought about her own flesh and blood every single second and had acquired their parents' gold coins at great personal cost. And now she was prepared to divide them up fairly even although everyone could see that

Lilechka didn't need a thing and was in a position, should she so desire, of course, to help her sister.

Lilka replied that Evka could quite happily choke on the coins and could rest assured that Lilka would not show up in Oster. That she was trying to forget such a place even existed, that wild horses wouldn't drag her there and that Evka was welcome to live there if she could stomach it.

Evka asked, if she couldn't stomach it, whether she might move in with Lilka. Get rid of their father's house somehow and move in. Lilka hastily set her sister straight: never and not for anything. She had her life, Evka had hers. It was enough that she had sorted out Evka's life once before, had rid her of an unwanted baby. It was then that Evka found out how and by whom the adoption arrangement had been dreamt up.

Laevskaya watched them both at once, her eyes darting from one side to the other. Approving of one then the other. At the mention of Sunka, Evka burst into tears and chided Lilka for deciding for her.

Lilka made no attempt to console her. "Perhaps that was a mistake on my part. You can't put it right. If you'd gone ahead and had the baby, I would have had to stay at home with it too. I would have had no life and neither would you. I wanted you to be free and not to ruin my own life. But you were a fool then and you're a fool now. And I'm not going to lug your stupidity around the way I did my whole life before the war. You keep your own counsel, such as it is, and I'll keep mine."

Evka left in tears, not understanding how her own sister could behave like that. Laevskaya gave her a hug and promised to find her a good husband in Chernigov. Out of curiosity, Evka asked about Lilya's private life. Laevskaya told her, between themselves, that Lilia's private life was tickety-boo. She didn't answer any further questions such as what or who.

She asked about the gold coins and laughed at Evka for attaching so much importance to them. In themselves, they weren't much for a lifetime, and for luring in a potential husband – they were a joke. Not to mention saving for a rainy day. Evka took umbrage on her parents' behalf. They'd saved everything they could and it was horrid of Laevskaya to criticise them.

Laevskaya said, "That's not what I meant. In themselves, those coins are nothing - nix. Especially when the gold still has to be sold. Who to? Just try. You'll be sorry you bothered. However, if you sold them to me, I'd buy them. You give me the gold coins. I'll give you a husband. Is that a fair price? If you trust me. You ask Faida if you can trust Polina. He'll tell you. No pressure. Have a think, let me know. Or Faida even. I go to see him. You're only a stone's throw away."

Faida did indeed describe Laevskaya as an honest woman, fair and square. Out of pride, Eva failed to say that she wanted not to make a sale but an exchange: gold for a husband. She didn't say it but she decided it was quite clear anyway. And that's how the gold coins came to be in Polina's hands.

Evka didn't meet Laevskaya again once she'd handed over the money. She wrote letters asking about the husband but they went unanswered. When Faida was sent packing from his senior post in Kozelets and settled in Oster, Evka sounded him out somehow. Miron gave her a stern dressing down, saying she mustn't embroil him in her affairs. Despite Sunka in the past. In her head, Evka kissed the coins goodbye.

Evka's house simply wouldn't sell. Time in female terms was running out. Which wasn't part of Evka's far-reaching plans.

And then a couple of months or so before Lilka died, Laevskaya turned up in Oster. Stepping out along smartly, arm in arm with some policeman. A captain. At the time, it went dark early. Evka spotted them but escaped their notice as she was wearing a padded jacket and was generally dishevelled after work.

Evka thought Polina was planning to organize a viewing of the bride. The policeman wasn't so young but then Evka wasn't eighteen either. He was just the thing. A respectable chap.

She'd liked him straight away even in the dark and she hoped Laevskaya would bring him to see her in the morning.

From early morning, Evka was all dolled up and staring out of the widow for Polina and the police officer husband-to-be. But no, no one turned up.

Evka was furious. She went off to Chernigov herself and demanded that Polina return the gold coins.

Polina refused and convinced Evka the task was in hand and a husband would be found. Moreover, Laevskaya no longer had the coins. If Evka wanted to know what had become of them, she should go to her sister. Although Laevskaya expressed disbelief that Evka wasn't aware of that. That Evochka was deliberately pretending and asking a second time for money she already had in her possession was something Polina didn't even want to think about. It was a family matter, after all.

Evka asked whether it had been a potential bridegroom with Polina in Oster, the policeman. Perhaps he hadn't taken a shine to Evka and Polina didn't want to upset her? Polina replied that it wasn't a husband for Evka but Lilka's fancy man. He and Polina had been going to see Faida. Evka wanted to know if it was the same fancy man as before or a new one. Laevskaya answered vaguely that she got Lilka's beaux all mixed up.

Evka was already in a rage and this did not go down well either.

She made a beeline for Lilka's.

The gate stood ajar because of the melting snow. Evka passed through unhindered and knocked at the door.

The same policeman opened it. Barely had he glanced at her than he rushed to struggle into his great coat and after his coat his boots. Most uncivilized.

In an undertone, he said: "Lilka, I've got to dash. No one's been round. You can wait yourself now."

Evka blurted out: "I'm not Lilka."

The policeman raised his head and gasped: "You had me fooled!"

"I'm her sister. Eva. Please, if you need to, go about your business. I'll wait for Lilechka. Are you her fiancé?"

"Her fiancé now is it? What rot. Tell Lilya to ring me at work as soon as she comes home. Her shift finished ages ago. She's gadding around somewhere."

And he tore out of the house.

Eva kept her word and waited for Lilya. She didn't go through her things.

Lilya arrived an hour later. She saw Evka and lost her temper.

She said: "What do you want from me? Consider that you don't have a sister. It'll be better for you in the end. I just go round and round in circles but it doesn't get me anywhere."

And burst into tears the like of which Evka had never even imagined a person could weep in peace time. Of course, inwardly she immediately felt sorry that her lies had affected her sister so much. But Lilka's appearance, her lovely coat with the silver-fox collar, the boots with heels and the red lipstick reassured Evka that she'd done the right thing. Let her think about her behaviour.

At this point, Evka remembered she was there for the sake of justice, for the sake of the money. Why had Lilka taken the coins from Laevskaya? Either she should give them all back or they should share them out evenly right now. To put the matter to rest.

Aloud Evka said: "Lilka, where are the gold coins? You were the one who didn't want them. And now you're the one who's taken them off Laevskaya. Supposedly, on my behalf and on my instructions. You ought to be ashamed! If it's true, of course."

Lilka paused in her sobbing and waved her arms in her sister's face: "Go away, go away, Evochka! It was just a passing thing. I'll give them back."

Evka acknowledged her victory and left. But before she went, she said a humble goodbye. She set her sister no deadline. And two months later Lilka was murdered.

Evka took a breather. She was no longer looking at the table. More at the floor. She muttered and mumbled then stopped.

I brought her some water.

Clearly, Laevskaya had gone to Oster with Evsey. And now it was at least clear that they had been in Oster together on more than one occasion. Both before the death of Lilka and afterwards when they took the pouch there. And Evsey had been to Lilka's house. And so it turned out that they were up to something the three of them – Lilka, Laevskaya and Evsey.

And Evka, fool that she was, had muddled their cards a tad.

Since, however, she claimed she hadn't asked Laevskaya to return the gold coins before the beginning to the middle of March 1952 and Polina and Evsey had taken the pouch to Faida at precisely that time, how could Evka have found out what and how much it contained? That it contained things that were hers as well as things that weren't?

"Eva, it turns out you're not telling the whole truth. How do you know what's in the pouch? Laevskaya told you conclusively that she had squirrelled away those little coins at her own discretion and yet you see that pouch and declare there's something of yours in it. Well? Not to mention that you also pleaded with Dovid when he had the pouch."

Eva raised her head. Her eyes were on stalks.

"I'm not saying," she muttered. Only her lips moved.

I didn't argue with her. She knew and what she knew would come out.

I started gathering up the valuables, making a show of it. Putting them away one at a time. I moved the gold coins with particular care. Didn't just toss them in but thrust them deep down inside.

Evka wasn't looking. She was pulling her scarf tight over her chest. Tighter and tighter until one end split. Was torn in other words. It was an old scarf. Evka gasped in embarrassment. She ripped off what was left and waved it in the air.

I saw her shoulders and noted that she'd put on weight.

"Evochka, the crucial thing is to watch your figure. Don't eat so much. You eat a lot because of your nerves. I expect your wedding dress is ready. Does it still fit? Never mind, Polina can let it out a bit at the sides."

Evka felt her sides - automatically. Women!

I continued abruptly:

"Who showed you the contents of the pouch and where?"

"No one showed me. Dovid told me in his own words. Here, he said, are the funds for a most important matter. And your share's here too, Evka. Lilia made arrangements on your behalf – five gold coins from the tsarist mint. That's what he said 'the mint'. That would never have entered my head. Believe me, Mikhail Ivanovich. I flew right off the handle. I'd already kissed them goodbye. Lilka didn't give me them before she died. I let them go with her beyond the grave. I wasn't even bothered. I'd forgiven my dear departed sister her debt. How could I not? And now once again I was hearing 'on my behalf' as if it went without saying. In other words, she took them off Laevskaya and stuffed them in the pouch on my behalf. And do you know what's in there? The crowns of Jewish teeth. Dead teeth. From people shot by the Polizei. And rings too. And they put my money in there as well, the bastards. Lilka did it to spite me. Really, she did. She was able to think up worse than that. It's exactly the kind of thing Lilka would do! I believed Dovid immediately and demanded my share back. He refused. I dragged Zusel there on my back, you could say, doing Laevskaya a favour. And it turns out my precious money is in there with all that foulness and the dead to boot so that if I put my hands in there I'd never be able to wash them clean."

Evka's back and shoulders were quivering. She didn't cry. She quivered like a gypsy. I'd seen it in Hungary. Several old gypsy women came doddering out of their camp. We gave them food. One started dancing for us. She collapsed. And her shoulders were shaking and quivering.

"No need for that, Eva. You would have washed your lovely hands clean. You would. Worse things than that can be washed off. And you've landed yourself a husband. A good one. You think you snared him yourself but maybe Laevskaya put him your way and was too modest to explain he came from her. Mmm?"

Evka trembled and hiccupped.

I was almost out of the door when I shouted from the threshold:

"Zusel's missing. Has he turned up here?"

Evka didn't reply.

I stood for about five minutes around the nearest corner. Evka hopped out of the gate and off she went somewhere at a trot. A rolled-up bundle under her arm. The newspaper bundle was torn in places and white material shone through. Silk or something. And she wasn't heading just anywhere. I had no doubt she was going to Laevskaya's.

I walked along the lane that led to the municipal gardens in long, easy strides.

There was nothing particular I needed to do in town. I wasn't going to Laevskaya's. I wanted some peace and quiet to think.

On my favourite bench, I took Eva Vorobeichik as the subject of my contemplation.

That she'd borne Sunka out of wedlock and placed him in the arms of strangers, she'd said straight off.

That her sister had virtually stolen her gold coins in criminal fashion, she'd said, despite the fact that it's wrong to speak ill of the dead.

That in her foolishness she'd entrusted herself to Laevskaya in the matter of a husband, she'd admitted.

That the pouch contained the crowns of Jewish teeth from graves, she'd babbled that. It fairly tripped off her tongue.

No shame or remorse. She'd sobbed so much she'd given herself hiccups. And then rushed off to Laevskaya's for a wedding dress fitting. To let it out at the sides.

Of the whole of our conversation, all that had stayed in her pea-sized brain was her fat sides.

I also thought about the fact that Malka, as soon as she and Evka had moved into Lilka's house, had fallen back into her old ways – happily baking matzo.

The first time I dropped by, I'd caught them red-handed. Evka had been rattled and promptly took herself off back to Oster. Without taking the matzo she'd made with her. She'd broken it into large pieces and scattered them in the back yard – for me to see. And I did. But I'd failed to realize it was just ordinary fear.

What had they done with the chickens? They couldn't have taken them alive. They make a lot of noise. Evka would scarcely have chopped off their heads herself. Malka even less so. The Jews have a special man. To let the blood and so on, according to their law. Abandoning such an asset for the neighbours to tear in all directions wasn't Evka's cup of tea. There had been eight of them clucking about. At least. Perhaps Zusel had slit their throats. Summoned by Malka – he was hanging around in Chernigov at the time. He slit their throats, Malka stuffed them in a sack and sold them to Jews.

The very people for whom she'd baked the matzo. Now she was selling them kosher chickens too. That's where her money came from. That's the other money that was talked about. And the money that she stuffed into Zusel's jacket. The money that Grishka nicked. And gave to Sunka and Sunka gave to me.

Malka had clearly yelled at me:

"Give me back that money. I have children to feed!"

So these were Malka's fabled riches. And it was because of these missing riches that she went to her grave. From the worry. But why she gave them to Zusel was a mystery. And would be now forever.

Sometimes, I pay too much attention to looking inside and the surface is left without due operational oversight. I look for complications where there are none. Older and more experienced comrades have pointed it out to me, that I complicate matters. Evsey included. Sometimes, I took it into account. And sometimes I let slip the opportunity for simplicity.

And everything was wound, as if on a bobbin, around the ordinary word "money" as understood by different people, who each had their own version: Malka, Dovid and I. I was the most comical. I'd thought of a bribe. But what had Shtadler meant when he spat at me in his last act of daring? Which money was that about?

Only because of the pouch could he have spat in my face. Dovid too – he'd gone for the shell. Purely because of the pouch. With its crowns of Jewish teeth and its grave rings and tchotchkes. Evsey's and Lilka's gold coins were an extra. Not what mattered most.

I had no desire to see Shtadler. But there's such a thing as having to. And it was there that my path lay.

Shtadler looked well.

He responded to my greeting with a clear nod of the head.

In silence I put the pouch on the table. I untied it, tipped out the contents.

"Well, Veniamin Yakovlevich, was this the reason you spat in my face?"

Shtadler abruptly hid his hands behind his back. But he didn't look me in the eye. He looked at the table. Not at any specific point, sort of moving his eyes and his whole head to and fro.

I seized his arm and pulled it towards the gold. I made only a slight effort and his arm didn't budge. Shtadler didn't want it to. I applied pressure. When the palm of his hand touched the pile, I felt a shudder run through him.

"What? Is it scary? Why is it? You've seen scarier things. You weren't even afraid to swallow and bite off your tongue. And you've been beaten within an inch of your life. Had your bones broken. And you take fright at some trinkets?"

And I kept on pressing his hand to the gold, squeezing it till the bones crunched.

He pleaded so fervently that I let go. I'm not a brute.

"Where did you get it? I'm not going to torture you. Whose is it? I want their full name and whereabouts. I'll go away and never bother you again. I promise. Everyone knows, I do what I say."

I put the little notebook right under Shtadler's hand. And placed a pencil in his fingers.

He wrote, 'Lilya Vorobeichik.'

I ripped out the page he'd written on. Folded it into quarters. Thrust it into the breast pocket of my uniform coat. Fastened the button. It was hanging by a thread. Never mind. It would last a little while yet.

I gathered up the pouch, tied it carefully and neatly.

"Farewell, Veniamin Yakovlevich. I won't ever come back. If I bump into you, I don't know you. You forget me too. Thank you. Do you know about Dovid Basin?"

Shtadler nodded.

"Did you also know that Zusel has gone missing?"

He shook his head.

"What? He hasn't? Is he alive at least?"

Shtadler confirmed that he was.

"Where did you get that information? From Laevskaya? Don't answer. Otherwise, you'll have really said too much. And we've already said our goodbyes. There's no need."

Shtadler waved a hand. Either at himself or as a token of farewell.

Of course, Shtadler had got the news from Laevskaya. Who else? But who told her? Faida. It couldn't be anyone else. The rest couldn't care less about Laevskaya or Dovid. Or Zusel. It made no difference to them whether he was dead or alive.

My two weeks' unpaid leave came to end on Monday. I still had Friday, Saturday and Sunday at my disposal. Evka's wedding was on Sunday as well.

This meant I had two days, two and a half, at most. That's what I gave myself.

At home, Lyuba and Gannusya were spring cleaning. Yoska was racing around yelling and laughing. Grishka and Vovka were out in the yard, beating the floor runners.

I asked for something to do but Lyuba said the best thing I could do would be not to get in the way. There were enough people to help without me.

I asked if I should maybe take Yoska and the boys out for a walk.

Lyuba agreed. She said she would have lunch on the table for three o'clock.

I added that Gannusya could come with us to make up a full set if Lyuba could release her chief assistant.

Lyuba didn't mind that either.

I needed to cheer myself up. So I made it happen. For three hours, we wandered around Chernigov and I noted, warmly, that Grishka and Vovka felt at home. They kept trying to walk close beside me. When Yoska was tired, they took turns to carry him and when Gannusya said she wanted to carry him too they told her it was a man's job and her special job was helping Mummy Lyuba. Vovka and Grishka offered Gannusya the last of their ice creams. Grishka first when he saw Gannusya had finished and after him Vovka as well. It was already dripping heavily onto his hands but he waited until Gannusya had licked up the last of Grishka's then offered his own.

Yoska reached out for seconds but I said no.

With only a little way to go before we were home, Grishka said:

"Mikhail Ivanovich, did Grandpa sell Dad's house? And his own as well?"

"He did."

"But the one where we lived in Oster is ours, isn't it?"

"That's right. Yours, Vovka's and Yoska's. Your grandpa bought it."

"But Auntie Eva said we were there because she let us. If she stopped letting us, we'd stop living there. It would be back to the dugout and Zusel. She's a liar!"

I stopped.

"When did she say that?"

"When she brought Zusel along, when he was poorly. When she asked Grandpa for her dowry and he wouldn't give it to her. He wouldn't let me look either."

Now there was a thing! Well, Evka, you bitch! One load of bollocks after another. She would squeeze out the truth a drop at a time and then smear it around so you couldn't put it back together. There was no point talking to her in the end.

I calmly told Grishka not to fill his head with other people's nonsense. Auntie Eva had been cross with Grandpa and so she hadn't told the truth.

I didn't stay for lunch. I whispered to Lyuba that I had to be at work urgently. Possibly, probably even, having to be out of town overnight. And she shouldn't worry.

Lyuba put together some of the food for the road. She said nothing.

Then she made a suggestion.

"Misha, the money you sent us in Ryabina. I've hardly spent any. Take it."

She took some crumpled notes out of her purse. Held them away from herself in the air.

I didn't take them. I still had some left. All our children were here, not just anywhere. Which meant the money was more needed here as well.

I left for Oster. And this time, I told myself, I was rallying for the last fight, striking while the iron was hot.

In my haversack, I had food, a change of clothes and the blasted pouch. I was tethered to it.

The driver of a lorry that was going my way turned out to be from Oster. He took me right to my destination. He was getting on a bit. I asked whether he knew anyone in Oster called Melnik or Tsegelnik.

He replied straight off that he did and that everyone respected them. Although Yankel Tsegelnik, formerly the well-known commander of a Jewish partisan detachment, had gone missing a couple of years ago. He was said to have drowned in a swamp. But Gilya Melnik, second only to him in terms of partisan glory, was alive and kicking.

I asked him to drop me off near Melnik's house.

Its owner was home alone.

Without any preliminaries, I said that I had complete trust in him as a former partisan and asked him to answer a number of questions.

I was interested in two individuals: Lilia Vorobeichik and Polina Laevskaya. To avoid confusion and excessive holding back, I mentioned straight off that Citizen Vorobeichik had passed away. But Polina was alive. Although it was better to tell only the truth about her as well and not embellish it. The law-enforcement agencies were not formally pursuing a case against her but there was interest.

"What do you want to know?"

"Everything's of interest. I'll draw my own conclusions. Start with Vorobeichik. That there were twin sisters, I know. That the father and mother died during the occupation is also clear. Eva, I know about. About Lilya, nothing. Start with her. With the war."

"Was Lilka murdered?"

"And if she was? What difference does it make?"

"The difference is it was bound to happen. I always knew she wouldn't die a natural death." Melnik smiled, tenderly, you could say. I was surprised that the smile accompanied such strange words.

He said:

"I'm smiling because she told me once when we were in the detachment, 'I won't take a bullet. And yet I don't want to live and I can't. What am I supposed to do?' I told her we'd settle accounts with the Fascists and then she'd find her place and start wanting to live. I was speaking because of my position. It wasn't what I thought. My general opinion is that people must make up their own minds as to whether they want to live. At some point she had decided once and for all that she didn't. And I realized that when the war was won she wouldn't go on. She'd win and stop living. I was only surprised she lasted so long after the war. There's nothing special to say. She fought like we all did.

"She began to despair after one incident. You asked about Laevskaya as well. And this is to do with Laevskaya too. Polina left Oster before the war. Her husband was redeployed somewhere in Central Asia. He was a good foreman. Or engineer. He worked on the big construction projects all over Ukraine. She followed him on each assignment. Took the children too. To be fair, she wasn't well liked. Then again, who is? She tried to dress well. The money came from her husband. The children stood out. They were pretty. Grade A students. All girls. In '41, the eldest was about 14. I can't remember exactly how old the little one or the middle one was. But they were in school as well. Anyway, Polina sent them here for the summer from their latest posting. For a visit. Her husband brought them and intended to have a holiday with them. It seemed he'd developed malaria or smallpox in Central Asia. Something like that.

"They stayed with Faida in Kozelets. Sima, his wife, is Polina's cousin. Faida went off to the front right away. Sima and their son were evacuated. Transport was allocated for senior officials. There was no room for Polina's children and husband. They went from pillar to post and stayed behind. The Germans shot her husband dead in the street. Someone hid the girls. In a nutshell, they ended up in Yanov with an elderly local couple. They hid them and hid them. Hid them in their house until the winter of '41.

"Then someone reported them. The usual story. The Germans turned up with the Polizei. The Germans just stood there while the Polizei set fire to the house. The children tried to climb out of the windows. They pushed them back inside. The old man and woman were shot dead in front of everyone beforehand, as an example."

"How do you know? Who saw this for certain, with their own eyes?"

"Lilia Vorobeichik. She was on a mission at the time. In Yanov. She'd been sent to find food. Or anything they'd give her. We were going hungry. We'd eaten the last hay and boiled leather. She took a sack and went off to Yanov. And with her own eyes Lilia saw them burning Polina's children. It was after that that she told me she couldn't go on living."

"That's war. Hadn't she seen any fascist brutality before that?"

"She'd seen worse things. But to be right there and unable to save children she knew… Well, what could she do? Go out and toss a grenade? She wouldn't even have had time. When strangers are dying, especially in agony, you're really sorry for them but when it's people close to you, it's unbearable. You're burnt along with them, your skin's flayed off as well as theirs, you're buried alive. I know from experience. And she was a young woman, who could go on to have children of her own. But the place inside her where children ought to be had been scorched. That's what she told me.

"Then Lilya disappeared. We buried her in absentia with military honours. Then, after the war, someone ran into her in Chernigov. Then Evka went to visit her. I heard it all by chance. She was alive, that's all I needed to know. It wasn't Laevskaya who killed Lilya was it?"

"What makes you think that?"

"I don't know. You made the connection. I thought Polina had killed her. Faida said she went crazy over her children. Have you seen her? Is she alright?"

"She's fine. A fine figure of a woman. Wears lipstick, perms her hair. Don't worry. She's fine. Can stand up for herself. Where did she find out about the children?"

"Someone told her in general terms. One of ours. That kind of thing travels by word of mouth. It got passed on."

"And so did everyone know that Lilia had watched the children die?"

"I shouldn't think so. That's the point. No one in the detachment knew where I'd sent her. Especially as I hadn't sent her to Yanov. Lilka was meant to go to a different village. But she went to Yanov. She came back, hadn't accomplished her mission essentially.

"Instead she reported what had happened to the little girls. That kind of thing goes down badly in war time, even in the army, even with the partisans. She made me promise, to be fair, that I wouldn't tell anyone what she'd seen. I promised. I kept my promise. She said something along the lines of being prepared to face the appropriate punishment. But I made something up for our commander, Yankel Tsegelnik. Shielded the girl. Could she have spoken to someone else about it? I doubt it. About a month later she disappeared. Went off on a routine mission and vanished without a trace. So who killed her? Have you found them?"

"Yes."

"And what for?"

"Comrade Melnik, you're curious but I don't have time to tell you. And anyway, it has nothing to do with this conversation. Please don't take this badly."

"I understand."

Melnik asked me by the by:

"You know Faida, don't you? There are no secrets in Oster. You can't hide anything. Ask him. He may have more to tell you. He knows a lot. It's just that he's fearful these days. Laevskaya keeps descending on him. She's scurrying about, can't seem to settle. Not often but she does come. Personally, I haven't seen her once since the war. People talk. And, bear in mind, there's no one opinion as to whether she's in her right mind or not. Of course, she's fine with Faida and Sima. They're scared but she's in the slough of despond. So, there you go."

"But you're not scared?"

Gilya shook his head uncertainly. And asked:

"What about you, Comrade Captain?"

I took a roundabout route to Faida's. To spin it out.

I sat down for a bite to eat in a spinney. There was a fine clearing with very tall grass. I couldn't be seen from anywhere.

It hadn't yet started to go dark. But I needed night to come so that every single one of Miron's little family was gathered together. Tucked up in their beds. All unawares.

I ate Lyubochka's food and thought about nothing. And such emptiness sliced through me that I could feel the wind in my bones and in my blood.

I dozed. My head on my haversack. To begin with I was very aware of the pouch through the canvas. Then, as I finally sank into sleep, I felt no particular discomfort. I slept like the dead.

There were no lights in any of the windows in Faida's house.

I knocked with gusto.

Miron opened the door. If he hadn't been wearing underpants and a vest, I'd have concluded he'd been keeping watch by the door.

"Hello, Miron Shayevich. Sound reveille. For everyone. No shilly-shallying. Is everyone home?"

Miron answered quickly and clearly that they were, all of them.

They took their seats around the table.

Sima in a nice frock. Clearly, she hadn't just grabbed the first one that came to hand when she was half asleep. Sunka was wearing trousers and a sleeveless pullover. The trouser belt done up in the last hole. Not the usual one, where the buckle had left a mark. In other words, the way he'd done his belt up was meant to convey something. Firmness and resolve. Miron was in trousers and his jacket. Every single shirt button fastened, even the one at his throat.

They weren't sitting like people in their own home. Their hands were folded in their laps.

I began:

"Well, now, expecting someone were you? Was it me?"

Miron spoke for them all.

"It was indeed, Mikhail Ivanovich."

"Good. So then, you know yourselves why you've been waiting. Talk to me, Miron Shayevich. About Laevskaya and so on. About what she had to do with Lilka Vorobeichik, Dovid, Evsey. I expect your family's in the know. You wouldn't be all togged up like that otherwise."

I glared at them all intently and looked each one in the eye.

Sima lowered her head. Sunka leaned against the back of the chair and crossed his legs. In his haste, he hadn't had time to put on his sandals. His slipper fell off. The lad was embarrassed then sat back quietly again.

I said to him personally:

"That's how it goes, Sunka. It's the little things that let us down. You were thoroughly prepared to greet me with the utmost bravery, then bang goes your slipper and all that's left of you is a damp stain. Don't be frightened. Or you, Sima. I'm just here to visit. I need to know the truth in detail. The honest truth. To know so that I can have done with it once and for all. To have it out with Laevskaya. She's been looking for trouble. I didn't make the first move."

They all exchanged glances. Sima began to cry softly. Sunka stroked her shoulder.

Miron spoke for them all:

"There's no need for play-acting. We're ready. Sima's got our things together. You'd do better telling her what we can and can't take with. So as not to drag too much along. Thank you for coming at night. Less interest from the neighbours that way. Will you seal up the house? If you need attesting witnesses, it would be best to go to the third house along, Number 18. They're good people."

Only then did I notice that there, by the window, behind a bookcase, were a suitcase, a bundle and a briefcase. They'd got their things together, expecting to be arrested. All the jumble needed by three persons.

I went over, moved the bookcase aside. It was wickerwork, not very strong. It overbalanced. I picked it up. I didn't gather up the books.

I gestured with my hand.

"How long have you been waiting?"

Miron replied:

"Ever since you left with the children. Not long. You're not a torturer. And look, twenty-four hours and here you are, back again."

I roared with laughter.

"Miron Shayevich, Sima, Sunka! What on earth are you playing at? What arrest? What for? It never even entered my head. Although of course I'm suspicious now. Talk about giving yourselves away! Suitcases ready and all! Needing attesting witnesses. I told you in plain Russian: tell me everything, up to and including I don't know what, and I'll listen carefully and be on my way. Well, you can give me breakfast if you're going to be talking for a long time. And that's it! I don't need you three at all. I promise you now and in future. Do you want me to sign somewhere? I need to know about Laevskaya and what she was up to with Dovid, Evsey and Lilia Vorobeichik. If she was up to something with anyone else, tell me about them as well. Your role's on the side-lines. It won't be taken into account in future. Is that clear?"

I flung myself at the suitcase, opened it and started tossing stuff out onto the floor. Women's underwear, a dress, a warm cardigan, boots. That done, I gutted the bundle and the briefcase. Inside were Sunka's things and Miron's.

Their rags flew through the air and landed all over the place. None of them tried to catch them. No one gave a shout.

Except for me.

"Answer me, all three of you: have you got brains or not?! Well, have you? I'm asking you as decent people?"

I shouted and shouted and then I ran out of steam.

I sat on the windowsill, feet planted on the floor, elbows tucked back, hands in the pockets of my breeches. I couldn't tell how long I was silent.

Sima was the first to speak.

"Let Samuil go. He doesn't need to hear what we have to say. He doesn't know anything in any case. And he'll be all upset for nothing. And he's been through such a lot already. We thought you'd want to take him as a family member. But since it's different, it's different. Let him go. What do you say, Mikhail Ivanovich?"

"Go, Sunka. Take a walk. When else would your Mum send you off to paint the town red at night like this? Go."

Sunka stayed put. I gave him a direct order: "Go on, Samuil. I don't need you. I have no questions for you. Don't just sit there. Well?"

Sunka stood cautiously. Then sat back down on the edge of his chair.

"I won't abandon my parents."

"Won't abandon! I'll throw you through a window pane right now if you don't get lost! I appreciate your behaviour. Well done. Now go. Don't worry about your parents. Well?"

In a voice I'd never heard him use before, Miron said:

"Go on, Samuil. Spend the night with whichever friends let you in. Tell them you've been out on the razzle, you're scared to show your face at home. You don't need me to give you instructions."

When Sunka had gone, Miron unfastened the little button on his collar and twisted the kinks out of his neck. He stood up, picked up the things I'd tossed around. Down to the very last one. In turn. Dumped them in a pile on the sofa.

He turned to Sima.

"Simochka, tidy up in here. Mikhail Ivanovich and I will have a little chat. You sort out some tea."

To me, he said, in his familiar voice, with a hint of sweetness: "We'll go to Sunka's room. I'll speak for everyone. And answer for everyone if necessary."

Miron waited for my encouragement. It wasn't forthcoming.

This is his evidence.

Polina made her way to Kozelets in '44. Immediately after liberation. Evacuees were still not allowed to return without special permission but she was there already, moving heaven and earth to find her children and her husband. In other words, to begin with, she hoped they'd survived, gone missing in the rear, been evacuated and so on. But she was told how Sima and Sunka had been bundled onto a cart and hadn't taken Polina's little girls and husband, Zinovy. There was no room.

During the war, he, Faida, that is, didn't write to Laevskaya since he'd received a letter from Sima clearly suggesting that she and their son had made it as far as the city of Ufa but, as for everyone else, she didn't know, and was constantly in tears. Which was why Miron didn't write to Laevskaya. He did, however, advise Sima to inform Polina about her family's unknown fate. But either that letter went astray or Sima ignored his advice out of shame and remorse but all through the war Polina knew nothing and went on hoping in vain.

And then she was told her husband had been killed and the little girls, Raya, Sonya and Mila had escaped. Since they'd escaped, Polina began to look further afield. People in Oster had seen a certain amount but most of what they said was hearsay. She was sent hither and thither. Then the rumours multiplied. In one location, Ukrainians had hidden as many as ten Jewish children. In another, children had survived for several years in the forest. Legends in a word.

That people hid children was true. Polina came across one small boy and girl. Then another child who'd been hidden. But not her own. In the end, at someone's prompting, she went to Yanov. There she was told that three little Jewish girls had been hidden by a Ukrainian family. But had perished. The children and their rescuers alike. Polina questioned the whole of Yanov and as one they told her the children had definitely been burnt to death. Asked to describe the girls' outward appearances, witnesses were vague. They'd only seen them when the house was already on fire amid the soot and smoke. What kind of outward appearance could there be? Their hair burnt fiercely. Meaning they had a lot of it. Which was why they were sure they were girls. If anyone had seen them when they were still alive, they didn't admit it to Polina now to avoid the conclusion: whoever saw them, betrayed them.

There weren't even any bones left. Nothing but pure ash. Pure as can be. The flames reached the sky.

All Polina could grasp in her grief was that no one had seen their appearance for certain and no bones had been found. Which meant first: they might not be her children. And if they were, there was a possibility they had been saved. No bones had been found.

Polina spent several months in Oster, always on the go, travelling around the villages. She found no traces that satisfied her in the slightest.

She met Tsegelnik. He couldn't offer any consolation whatsoever.

People who had been evacuated started to return. Polina asked those who had lived in Kozelets, in Faida's house, during the war to get word to her in Oster if the owners showed up.

And then Sima and her son did return to Kozelets. All in all, there was a meeting. Sima attempted to explain herself as best she could. She couldn't. She stressed that she had thought that, if push came to shove, Polina's girls and her husband would simply stay behind under German rule and somehow her husband would find work with the Germans rather than knocking around in the cramped space of strangers in an unknown, far flung area. Especially when Kozelets was emptying right in front of their eyes. Many houses were abandoned on trust. Sima's husband was a Communist and a senior official. She absolutely had to leave. Polina merely said that her Zinovy was a Communist too. And there was nothing to say to that. He'd died for nothing but it was still too soon to consign her girls to the afterlife. Polina would find them. But she wouldn't forgive Sima. And with that, she left.

When Miron was demobbed at the end of '45, Sima told him about Polina, about her children and so forth. Miron wanted to go to Polina's old address in Central Asia and beg forgiveness on his knees. But life put paid to that. So much sorrow was revealed all around, you couldn't draw breath.

To top it all, Evka began to use him for her own ends. She was looking for her property. He accompanied her not just because she was Evka. He accompanied a lot of people. Houses had been looted – the ones owned by people who had been evacuated. Some people had stayed behind. They had been slaughtered. Husbands and sons would return from the front – their homes were occupied. Or had gone altogether. Or were still standing but stripped bare. People had to be helped to recover. Had to be soothed. Some way of dealing with the situation found. But what way? Polizei and partisans lived on the same street, their houses very close together. You couldn't put them all in jail. Or raise the dead.

About a year later, Polina arrived in Kozelets. She went to see Miron at work. She said calmly that she wouldn't set foot in his house, where Sima was, but that she didn't blame him at all. She asked him to go for walk in the park. There she set out her request. From her manner, Miron understood: he had to do it at whatever cost, otherwise it would go badly for his family. Sunka would find out about his origins just when they had started having problems with the lad in respect of his keeping bad company.

This is the story Polina told him. The Party and the government had entrusted her with finding places in families for Jewish orphans from children's homes. Specifically, in Jewish families. In the light of the great reduction in the

Jewish population as a result of fascist zealotry. Of course, the children were fine in the children's homes. They didn't want for anything. But the Party and the government had decided that after the war very little was left of the Jewish race as such, and in children's homes Jewish children might no longer be registered as Jews. Not out of ill intent but because there was no difference: all nationalities were equal. Nevertheless, there had to be records, to prove the numbers were sufficient. A matter of politics to be displayed to the whole world.

Miron, of course, was uncomfortable. He didn't let it show, however. He asked what she expected of him.

Polina charged him with discovering and providing her with the addresses of all the children's homes in Chernigov Oblast. All of them, right down to the very smallest village home. All of them, temporary or permanent, not a single one left out. And with writing a letter on headed paper of some kind, the District Executive Committee's, for instance, where Faida worked, requesting that the recipient assist Citizen Polina Lvovna Laevskaya in her task.

Miron worked out that he could steal headed paper whereas writing a letter and signing it was going far too far. Of course, he didn't believe Polina's story of a Party and government assignment. Had there been any such thing, there would have been no need to ask for a letter from Kozelets. Moreover, how did it look? Jews adopting Jews, Tatars adopting Tatars, at a time when we were moving towards internationalism. To meet her half way, to protect her from her own enthusiasm, he suggested giving her a blank sheet of headed paper for Polina to write what she liked on. To append any signature at her own risk.

Polina agreed. Faida handed the paper over an hour later, in a secluded spot. Polina departed. She left her new address: No. 7, Five Corners, Chernigov.

From that moment on, Miron had no peace. Although everything remained quiet. For one year, then another. Faida decided Polina had flared up and died down. Her dark times were over. Life had provided her with something else.

After Faida was expelled from the District Executive Committee and the Party itself in keeping with the Party line on Jewish nationality, his anxiety arose with renewed force. He believed the danger had increased and he didn't know where the paper he had stolen had got to. Nor did he know where it might be brandished by Polina, whose mental state he also didn't know.

Miron and his family made their way to Oster. There he was informed by Evka Vorobeichik that Lilka was alive and well and living in Chernigov. She was a big friend of Laevskaya's. Polina was well off, taking in sewing, Lilka was working in the shoe factory and wasn't short of anything.

There was a lull before the news of Lilka's death.

Polina became a frequent visitor although she didn't stay in Faida's house in Oster. She just popped in. Said nothing about the task assigned by the Party. Miron didn't remind her.

Once she arrived with a police officer and the pouch. Then dropped by for literally a minute, when Comrade Tsupkoy was spending the night at Miron's. Not so very long ago. And since then – nothing.

Sima hadn't brought us any tea.

I reminded Miron.

He called for his wife to provide something to eat.

Sima replied from behind the closed door.

I quickly jerked the door towards me – Sima had one ear pressed against it.

To her, I said:

"What have you to add, Sima Zakharovna?"

"Nothing." She wasn't speaking to me but to her husband.

I had a bite to eat, lay down on Sunka's bed, on top of the cover, and said I would have a nap.

Sima suggested I got undressed and that if I had any doubts I could be sure that Sunka's bed was clean. Sima had changed the sheets only that evening but her son's head hadn't so much as touched the pillow.

She said:

"Like you are now, he lay on the top. I thought, quite right, it'll be clean if there's a search. It's awkward otherwise."

I pulled back the bedding and got in, as if I was in my own home.

It was Miron who woke me in the morning.

The first thing I asked before I even got out of bed was:

"Did Evka not sell the house to Dovid? Was he living there to keep an eye on the place?"

Miron frowned and mumbled:

"She didn't sell it. They had a verbal agreement. For him to live there and keep an eye on things. He gave her a bit of cash. It wasn't enough. She didn't take it. She said when she found a better buyer she'd just let him know. And till then, they could live there."

"So where's Dovid's money for his house in Chernigov and for Evsey's house?"

"What do you mean where is it? He put it in the pouch. The money that was rolled up. When you tipped it out on the table, there was a little roll of notes. I thought you knew. Two thousand. I was there when he put it into Evka's hands. He broke the rubber band. Then did it up again. In my presence. That's why I recognized it. When I had the pouch, there was no Soviet money in it. But when you brought it along, there was. Dovid's money. Definitely. Mind you, Dovid's no longer with us. Which means the money belongs to the little lads. Or whatever you decide."

"It's as if you were Dovid's guardian, Miron Shayevich. Was that on Evka's instructions as well?"

Miron took offence.

"Laevskaya. She was always coming around to see Dovid. And she asked me to keep an eye on him and Zusel."

"On what grounds?"

"On human grounds. That's all, on human grounds!"

Miron flew right off the handle. He'd endured and endured but he flew off all the same. Good chap!

Now it was time to drag the last details out of him.

"So what's Laevskaya been doing all these years? Apart from earning a pretty packet from her sewing? Tell me, Miron Shayevich. Tell me this one last thing. You can't not know. You're a man of experience. You wouldn't have distressed yourself over nothing. You've explained why you were upset. Why your family might suffer. You've explained that but you're holding something back. Hoping to buy me off for a pittance. You didn't just sit twiddling your thumbs, expecting to be grabbed by the scruff of the neck at any moment. You went to see Laevskaya yourself. And wormed it out of her why you needed to be prepared to suffer. Look: Malka's gone, so has Dovid, and Evsey Gutin. Zusel's goodness only knows where and Lilka Vorobeichik, Polina's friend, is no more either. Who will telling me hurt? You've got it all tangled up in your head. Let's untangle it together. It will be a relief for you and for me. Let's do it as comrades."

Miron thought. He stood there, thinking.

I didn't urge him on. He would either tell me himself now or deny everything. Then, later on, should he want to make a clean breast of it all, something in his mind would shut down and he wouldn't be able to. He would freeze up, so to speak. As if he were frozen.

Suddenly, he yelled out of the window – I'd thrown it wide open before I went to bed to let the air in.

"Sunka. Get out of here! Run!"

I grabbed Miron round the belly, pulled him down onto me and onto the bed, then crushed him with my full bodyweight.

Powerless, he lay stretched out beneath me. Like Zusel. I rolled over to one side.

A few seconds later, Miron opened his eyes. He didn't look at me. Although he could sense, of course, that I was there, flush up against him, between him and the wall.

I clambered over him as if he was a pile of logs and perched on the edge of the bed.

Sima's and Sunka's voices could be heard outside. Sunka wanted to come into the house. Sima wouldn't let him.

Miron lay and talked. Slowly, as if retelling a film in his own words.

He'd held out for a week after giving Polina the headed paper. Then he turned up at her home in Chernigov, firmly persuaded that he had to take it back again. She could do what she liked after that. Sunka and the errors of his, Miron's, youth were one thing. An official piece of paper for dubious ends was quite another. As for Sima's irredeemable guilt before Polina – well it was, indeed, irredeemable. So what? Did that mean he had to be guilty for her for the rest of his life? Irredeemable guilt, you either forgive or forget without forgiveness. But living with it is impossible. Polina too must either forgive or let bygones be bygones.

Laevskaya opened the door, said hello quietly, gladly even, asked him to wait a moment. She was making a child's frock. Adding bows, little ribbons and frills. There were plenty on the frock already. But she kept on attaching trimmings in various places. She'd fit one, give the frock a shake, then rip off a bow and sew it back on. In another spot.

Miron watched and watched and said, "Polina, you've got a rushed job on. Perhaps I'm here at a bad time. I still need to go to the Oblast Executive Committee. When should I call by?"

Polina hastily folded up her sewing and said, "No, no, never mind. It's not urgent. Once I start putting bows on, I can't stop. It's good that you stopped me, even. I've no sense of proportion. I just want to make it pretty. But if there are too many, it's not pretty anymore. I don't like too much, myself. But when it's for a child, well, you understand. It's so teeny. It's hard to tell if it's really too much or just seems it."

Polina crumpled up the material, the ribbons, the lace. She dragged a great big bundle from under the table, untied it and started stuffing the little frock inside. The slippery silk unfolded and slithered away. Polina kept on pushing it inside. So much so she rumpled the whole lot. Miron spotted that there wasn't just one frock but at least ten. And all of them little. Children's frocks. Finished, from what he could tell. Just very crushed. Which was understandable – they were all scrunched up.

He said: "Why are you crumpling them up? I told you not to rush. All your work will go to waste. The Mum will come to collect it and she won't pay."

It was a joke but Laevskaya replied: "Don't worry, Miron. I'm the Mum. I won't do myself any harm."

She stuffed the dresses into the bundle once and for all and put it away under the table. She gave Miron a triumphant look.

Faida had rehearsed his speech. He'd rehearsed it but now realized he couldn't say a thing to contradict her. He asked how her mission to the children's homes was going.

Polina replied that she hadn't embarked on it fully as yet. It called for thorough preparation. She could access Chernigov Oblast thanks to Miron's headed paper but it didn't apply to the rest of the country. Although she hoped to be able to fulfil the plan from Chernigov Oblast alone.

Miron listened to Polina and it finally dawned on him that there was no special assignment. Polina was simply unhinged when it came to her prematurely departed little girls. And she'd thought up the story of the children's homes for Miron in person in order to worm the piece of paper out of him. She really did intend to search every children's home in the Soviet Union to find her children. And not only the children's homes. She intended to scour the entire country and was establishing connections to that end.

Miron decided to put her to the test. He asked if he could help in any way. Apart from the paper. Because he believed they'd given Polina an assignment but weren't prepared to help with it. They hadn't even given her a lousy little letter on a reputable sheet of paper. Polina had been forced to turn to him. An astonishing dereliction of duty. Handing out assignments then leaving you to your own devices. It turned out Polina would be travelling on money she'd made herself whereas these were business trips. And should, therefore, involve travel expenses and a daily allowance. Not to mention that the children would have to be taken from the children's institutions to their new parents or the parents be taken to them. It was a vast expense. All in all, Miron talked nineteen to the dozen as if he was at a meeting. He waved his arms and stamped his foot, saying that no matter what Polina thought, it was essential that she asked the authorizing agencies to support her financially and with special permits and, it was odd that, given her business acumen, Polina hadn't done so and was now obliged to fend for herself. And it was a question of children! Not only had they had nationality and politics forced upon them, they'd also been entrusted to a defenceless woman. And towards the end, Miron blurted out 'and that would have been fine if she'd been only defenceless, but she herself was a casualty, who had lost her family'.

He realized what he'd said and bit his tongue. But it was too late.

Polina said: "Shut up, Miron. Do you think I'm off my rocker? There's some truth to it. Just a little. About this much." Polina indicated the nail of her little finger. "There, where my girls live inside me, yes, I've gone mad. The rest of me is fine. And there's a lot of it. Look at me. Compared to me, you're just a tiddler. And you're not carrying anyone dead in your head. Yours are all still alive. Sima and Sunka."

Polina stood up on tiptoe, stretched, put her arms out to the sides then back again, hollowed her back and tipped up her chin. She'd sat too long over her sewing. She was doing her exercises.

"As little as a week ago, I had hope. I really did think I would find my girls. But that hope ended yesterday. Do you remember

Lilka? Evka's sister? Course, you do. She was the one who dreamt up the idea of foisting Sunka on to you. Well, listen. Lilka's alive. She looks a fright, skinny as a rake, haunted but alive. Red hair sticking out. And not even hair, matted clumps. I ran into her at the market yesterday. Who knows what she's living off? Renting cubbyholes. Not working. On her uppers. I wouldn't have recognized her. She came up to me first. I brought her here, washed and fed her. And listened. All night long, I listened. I didn't make her talk...."

Polina drew breath and Miron saw how big and tall she was. He hadn't noticed before. He cast a furtive glance at her feet to see if she was wearing heels. She wasn't.

Polina said, "Listen, Miron. There's no point looking me over. My children, Raya, Sonya, and Mila died in flames. Lilka saw it in person, with her own eyes. There, you see. And now you can stick my Party assignment up your arse. I made it up and I'm calling it off. And you, Miron, are free. I'll keep hold of the paper. Don't worry too much about it. There are plenty of ways it might have come my way. Although if it comes to fingerprints, I don't know. You'll lie your way out of it somehow, go to Sima for advice and jabber your way out of it."

Polina had come to her senses during the conversation and ended it in her ordinary voice. So ordinary indeed that Miron couldn't be certain she'd told him the truth.

Miron was befuddled when he left. He was unsteady on his feet. He bumped a woman walking towards him with his elbow. Cardigan unbuttoned, men's boots with no laces, headscarf pushed back onto her neck. Matted red locks sticking out in all directions. She had gone past when Miron realized it was Lilka Vorobeichik.

'Off to Laevskaya's,' Miron thought. 'Hobbling along as if she's going to her execution.' He wanted to call out to her but didn't.

Miron didn't tell anyone he'd seen Lilka. When Evka reported meeting her sister in Chernigov, however, and said she was perfectly content, he couldn't help himself. There was only one shoe factory in Chernigov. It wasn't hard to find.

Faida recognized at first sight the Lilia Vorobeichik he used to know. Moreover, she was even lovelier and more attractive. Fashionably dressed, wearing lipstick. In heels. Miron went over and pretended it was a chance encounter. Lilya was unabashed. She responded to his greeting without a hint of pleasure and hurried on her way.

Miron stopped her. "We need to talk. About Laevskaya. I know pretty much everything. She dragged me in against my will. As I understand it, she's bound you to her as well. Talk to me. It's in your own interest."

Lilya's whole expression changed. Through the powder, Miron could even glimpse the face of the woman he had seen before and not forgotten. "Let's go," she said gruffly.

She took Miron to Maryina Roshcha not far from the factory. They sat on a fallen tree. There was poplar fluff in the air. Miron sneezed. He didn't know where to start to steer the conversation in the right direction.

He asked, "Lilya, did you see Polina's daughters die?"

To which she said, "None of your business."

"Polina told me you'd confessed. Is that not true?"

"It's true."

"So?"

"So, nothing. How could I not confess? I'm guilty. So I confessed. It's fine for you. But I can't live. Polina has brought me back to life somehow. I'll go on living. You can pass that on to everyone."

Miron said he didn't intend to pass on or spread anything to anyone. That wasn't why he wanted plain speaking.

"Lilya, I mean, Laevskaya's a good woman. But she can draw you in. You're sorry for her now because you're guilty towards her. But she'll draw you in. I fell for it too." That's what he said.

"So what, are you guilty too?" Lilya asked coolly, with an unexpected smirk.

Miron paused but answered: "Yes, I am."

Lilya gave an unpleasant laugh. An ugly laugh. Poplar fluff filled her mouth but she roared with laughter. Through the laughter, she said, "It turns out that we're all guilty on all counts. And if that's so, maybe it's possible to make no bones about it? Is that what you think?"

Miron said it wasn't but even so.

Lilka paused for breath. She was about to start speaking but didn't. As if she'd stuttered badly and swallowed the first letter, which didn't get said. In the end she said, "Fine. Don't worry. Polina isn't doing anything wrong. She's a kind of travelling matchmaker. That's not illegal, is it?"

"No. As far as the tax inspector goes, she takes in sewing. Pays her tax. Why are you all in a dither? I don't understand."

Lilka attempted to smile. It didn't work. Miron hit her where it hurt.

"So, you told her you'd seen her children die. What did she say?" Lilya shook her head so that her hair slipped out of the clips at the side and covered her face. It was through her hair that she replied, "I had a hand grenade on me. I couldn't have done anything. But Polina blamed me, saying 'What do you mean you couldn't? You could have thrown it through a window so the children didn't suffer.'

"She invited me home. I couldn't not go. I'm like a guilty dog where she's concerned. And always will be. I told her a hundred times that night how her children burned while I fingered the grenade in my pocket. She showed me the frocks she makes for her little girls. Says she would surely have found them if they'd still been alive. And made me go through the whole thing again. She just didn't believe me. Polina's insane. To look at, she's in good health. Really good health. The way she talks and walks, the way she approaches people. But in actual fact, she's not. I realize that now. I didn't understand it at the time. I wasn't far off the same myself."

"And now?"

"Now, I'm not. Now I tell Polina the whole story and my heart is at peace."

"You're still telling her?"

"She asks. How can I refuse?"

Miron moved on to the main topic. He said, "She once gave me some tale of having a plan to go around all the children's homes and find her girls. Has she called that off?"

"No, why? She goes. She's always travelling."

"What's she looking for? They're not there."

"So, they're not. But she still goes. Asks whether anyone of their description has been seen. Maybe, someone has already adopted them. All together or separately. And she takes the pouch with her. It's got gold crowns and rings inside. If she does suddenly find they've been taken in somewhere, she'll swap the gold for them."

Shivers ran down Miron's spine. "What crowns? What gold?"

"I gave them to her. We were executing the Politzei in a village. One of them had a reputation. He would personally bury Jews alive. He removed their valuables beforehand. Even pulled the crowns off their teeth. He was always on the move. Was seen in Kiev, Romny and Sumy. Then he moved westwards with the Germans. We captured him in a village near Khmelnik. He shoved that pouch at us. Asked us not to shoot him. A comrade and I had been sent. I wasn't with Tsegelnik any more, I was in Medvedev's detachment. We liquidated him. My comrade was killed on the way back. Not a single bullet hit me, damn it. I went on living."

There was anger in Lilka's words. Not at the bullets but at herself for not being hit. "I still had the pouch. I thought any minute now and I'll get caught with Politzei gold on me. He used to boast to all and sundry about that pouch too. I didn't even need it but I couldn't get rid of it. It was proof we'd liquidated him. Had accomplished our mission. The gold would be sent back behind the lines. They'd find a use for it there. We were in need of weapons and so on. My movements were aimless. It was horribly cold. I thought it would be nice to freeze to death. Painless too. I lay down and awaited deliverance. I thought, 'The children were burnt. They were hot. But me, let me die a cold, cold death.' And for myself I said a prayer: 'O, precious death, please gather me up. I am ready for anything. Even for Hell itself. Just take me away from here, from this wretched earth.' And I had already fallen, down somewhere, or perhaps up, I couldn't tell. I'd plunged upwards. That's it. Upwards. Definitely.

"I came to in a village house. A woman was smearing me with moonshine then goose fat. I was sick for a long time. They must have written me off as missing in action. The old woman, of course, found the pouch on me. And handed it to me when I was back on my feet.

"'Keep it,' I say. 'To cover your own needs.' 'No,' says she. 'It's not mine. I don't need anything that belongs to someone else.'

"I wanted to give her a ring from the pouch. And I did. I put it on the windowsill so she'd see it when I'd gone. I buried the pouch in the vegetable plot. Then I had to track down the partisans.

"Just there the front came close to the area I was roaming around in. Our army scouts found me. I spent the rest of the war in the regular army. Where could I go after we won the war? Where didn't I go? I reached Chernigov at the beginning of '46. As if someone had driven me there. I ran into Polina. I told her about the pouch too. We set off together. The old woman wasn't living in the house. Everything was neglected. The village had gone. Burnt to the ground. But I dug the pouch up. And, Miron, my dear, the damn thing could come in handy."

To which Miron said, "Lilka, as long as you don't go off your head. What good would it do? The children are gone, quite gone! No more play-acting! Not around Polina. Pull yourself together this instant or things will go completely to pot."

But Lilka smiled. "The children are gone. But they're not what Polina's looking for. She's looking for children who look like them. As like her little girls as peas in a pod. They say Hitler had doubles, and Stalin. And with actors, sometimes they can be so like the person they need to be for a performance just by changing their clothes a touch, or their hair."

Lilka was full of enthusiasm. Which was what finally filled Miron with terror. He said goodbye and promised to keep everything Lilka had told him a secret. Then came her mysterious death and Laevskaya appearing with a policeman and the pouch.

Miron stopped talking and caught his breath.

As if from memory, he said:

"I hereby confirm what I said yesterday together with the addendum here present."

I asked what his crime was, in his opinion.

Faida replied readily:

"Apart from the sheet of paper, I don't know."

"And yet you were preparing to go to jail? And had the family ready too?"

"The paper – that's a fact. You're after Polina. You'll make up whatever else you like."

"I won't make anything up, Miron Shayevich. Stand up. Let's say our farewells."

Miron stood up slowly. Stretched his legs.

I held out my hand.

He shook it.

Just before I left, I took the pouch and removed Dovid's money.

I offered it to Miron, saying:

"If anything happens to me, give it to Lyuba. Tell her it's Dovid's. For the children."

Miron nodded. Sima pretended not to see me leave.

I hadn't breathed a word about Zusel. As if he'd never existed. If he was alive, so be it. If not, what could I do? Miron hadn't brought it up. I didn't need to.

I washed in the Desna, put on clean clothes. It began to rain a little. Then came down in torrents. With thunder and lightning.

It was Saturday. The day I had appointed for my meeting with Laevskaya.

I got soaked to the skin on the way to Chernigov. I changed lifts three times. Each one got bogged down in the mud. I set aside any notion of getting changed.

I turned up at Polina's just as I was.

Laevskaya opened the door, smiled and invited me in.

"You're soaked. Right when I'm heating the stove as well. I can't bear the damp. I always keep my wood dry. Out in the shed. Take a seat. No, better stand. Or I'll give you something dry to put on. No need to be shy around me."

There was barely any light. Just a lamp on the table. It was gloomy even though it was the afternoon.

"Why would I, Polina Lvovna? A dressmaker, like a doctor, sees the man beneath the clothes."

Polina giggled.

"At least give me a sheet. I can wrap myself up, like at the banya. I'll be here a while. I'll have time to dry off and warm up. You don't mind?"

From the next room, where she evidently kept all her clutter, Polina replied that she was always happy to see me.

She came back with a sheet. Didn't leave when I began to remove my uniform. I deliberately handed her my gun belt. Heavy with rain. The leather was thick. Especially when it was soaked. I'd stuffed the pouch into the holster back at the river.

I said:

"I didn't bring my gun. Don't be frightened. The only thing there's your pouch. Have a look."

Polina unbuttoned the holster, looked inside. She couldn't fail to see the pouch. But she said nothing. Looked around the room for where to put it. Threw it on the floor.

I wasn't embarrassed as I got changed. She really did watch me like a doctor. As if I wasn't a living man but a patient and she was looking for where a particularly life-threatening spot might be. She watched till I reached my waist and turned away.

I wrapped myself in the sheet.

I took my wet things over to the shove, pulled up a couple of stools, hung the clothes out to dry. Arranged my boots and foot wraps, stood by the stove.

The smoke from the stove wasn't very nice. Not wood smoke, something else.

I opened the door, had a look.

"What do you heat it with? You've thrown a load of old clothes in there. But you were bragging about the good wood."

Polina replied from behind me.

"I'll put wood in in a minute. The clothes will get a blaze going. Fabric burns quickly but it does catch the back of your throat."

Polina was holding several dresses up at the level of her chest, examining them. Then she hurriedly scrunched them up, moved me out of the way and began poking and prodding the whole lot deep into the fire.

"You get warm and dry, Mikhail Ivanovich. This will soon burn and the smell will go. Then I'll put some wood on too. It's so that I don't mix them up. To keep them apart. To know for certain what's been burnt."

Sparks shot out of the stove. The flames flickered. Polina was scorching her hands but ignored it.

"There we go. Now I'll add the firewood. It's in the shed. I'll go and get it. You stay there. Don't get up. You've nothing on your feet. I've nothing that would fit you. Lilka had big feet. She was tall. Of course, they'd be small for you but I can't give you mine. I've only got little feet. But Lilechka's were big. For a woman. I'll bring you hers. She used to put them on when she came to see me. But you murdered Lilechka, Mikhail Ivanovich. She doesn't need slippers now. Does she?"

I stood stock still.

So did Polina.

Only her painted lips moved.

She went burbling on and on. I couldn't make out the words. Because they didn't go with their meaning. I tried to match them up but couldn't do it. Not at all. Even though I'd repeated them to myself a million times over ever since 18th May 1952.

So Laevskaya knew. She knew and had been hunting me down as if I were a wolf. Pursuing me hither and thither. I could tell she knew with absolute certainty. But I kept on hoping.

Laevskaya perched on the edge of the chair that had my uniform coat hung on the back. The shoulder straps could be seen behind her. There was soot on the dragon-patterned housecoat. Ash on her reddened, purpled arms.

"Someone has to get the wood. I'd do it but it's awkward in nothing but a sheet. Will you go?"

Polina went.

She came back with an armful of logs. She threw them down as if shedding unnecessary weight.

Sat down again.

"Well, then, Polina Lvovna, why have you said nothing all this time, played silly buggers? Why didn't you just tell me straight? Or send a letter you-know-where? You could have blown my cover and brought me to book. That would have made you happy."

Polina leant back in her seat but immediately shifted to the side: it was wet. She shrugged her shoulders. "I don't need to blow your cover. I need what's happening now. You've come here of your own accord, Mikhail Ivanovich. It's not the first time but it will be the last. The final time. I'm a woman. Each time, I've been able to tell in my bones that it wasn't the last. You would still be running around. Still going through the mill. But now I know it's the last. And so do you."

"I do."

"Well, then, Comrade Investigator, are you warm enough now?"

"No. Put some more wood on, please."

Polina did. The fire was still burning but feebly. She didn't stir it to produce a blaze. It caught of its own accord. She watched and watched.

"Sit down, Polina Lvovna. Let's tie up the loose ends since this is the last time."

"What's to tie up? I found Lilka in that state near the midden. It's revolting, just remembering it. I took her home with me. D'you know about my little girls? By my reckoning, you should by now. You'll have wormed it out bit by bit. Right?"

I nodded.

"Did you go to see Gilya Melnik even?"

"Yes."

"Well, then. Lilka told me – only Gilya knows everything. She told me the story, Lilka did, and I let her live here. Brought her back to life. Urged her to follow my example. It's impossible otherwise. I told her: they killed my three children, not to mention my husband. I should be angry, out of my mind. But I'm bearing up. And so must you, Lilka. I made her get dressed, tidy her hair, rather than wandering around looking like a trollop. Well, I had to keep her spirits up. I kept telling her: you have to help me live. I'll be lost without you. You were the last person to see my children alive. You're here to replace them. One in exchange for three. Of course, I made more of her role to spur her on. Then I bought her that shack with my own money. Chickenfeed, it was. But bit by bit we knocked it into shape, rebuilt it, stopped the roof leaking. It was nice. Later, Lilka perked up. My advice was to say she'd been left the house by an old lady she used to look after. People would have started asking all sorts of questions. 'Why's Laevskaya spending her own dosh on a house for Vorobeichik?' But the money was nothing to me. I get paid as much for a single dress as you get in a month, Mikhail Ivanovich. A woman might go hungry but she'll have a dress made. I really did need Lilka close at hand. When she wasn't at work, she always went with me to the children's homes. We'd watch the children together. She'd say: 'That one over there's like Milochka.' I'd look and no, she wasn't a bit like her. Somehow, we found a girl who was very like Raya, my eldest. Talked to her even. Lilka even pinched my arm – the spitting image. But I could tell from her voice, it wasn't her. The next day we went back after we'd slept on it. And Lilka agreed, they weren't alike. As for Sonechka, the middle one, we never came across even one child that looked the slightest, tiniest bit like her. Just imagine, Mikhail Ivanovich. So many years. Lilka was born in 1914. When you met her in '47, she was 33. Perfectly capable of having children. I told her – after all, I did understand even if I was pretending not to – I'm not going to find any little girls like mine. I told her: 'Have a baby, Lilka. It can be half whoever's you like. It'll still be half yours. And my girls will be reflected in you. We'll bring the baby up together. It'll be lovely if it's another girl. But if it's a boy, so what? What's more, twins often have twins of their own.' That was my hope. Lilka chose you. You, Mikhail Ivanovich, are not only a good looking man in your own right but you look like my Zinovy as well. You Ukrainians can sometimes be the spitting image of Jews. No offence intended. I took a peek at you once. It was Lilka's suggestion when she was waiting for you. One look and I made up my mind once and for all. You were just right. Lilka, as a woman, used to come to me for advice about everything. So bear in mind that I was right there with you, a third person in the room. Keeping an eye on things. But it just didn't happen, it just didn't. And then you fell for her. And it was that passion of yours that Lilka couldn't stand. She used to complain: 'Tsupkoy looks at me as if he wants to kill me. I'm ruining his whole life. He's working out how best to get rid of me.' You damaged her beyond repair with your attitude, Mikhail Ivanovich."

"I damaged her? And you didn't? You bound the girl to you, goodness know how. Kept her on a chain, you might say. Drove her out of her mind. But didn't Lilya herself realize what she was doing, that I'm only human too? You act like she was the Virgin Mary. So why was Moiseenko hanging around? The world and his wife knew he was her lover. The only one who didn't was me."

Laevskaya shrieked with laughter as she had before:

"Moiseenko. He was an ac – tor. He used to foist himself on her in the street, recite poems, accompany her to her gate. Then he would come and bellow songs beneath her windows. Lilka let him in to take her mind off things. Fed him, let him wet his whistle. And, I'll have you know, for your sake, she thought: Roman can come and go openly as a smoke screen to give people something to talk about. In case you got her pregnant. There would be a daddy all ready to go. Roma! Roma could recite a poem for three hours. He couldn't think of anything else. He got pie-eyed once and started running through the whole of 'Vasily Terkin'. The drink never hurt his memory. He rattled it off by heart. He got to a particular line and Lilka jumped up as if she'd been stung. 'Again,' she shouts. He refuses outright. Out of spite. 'I,' says he, 'am not going to recite the chapter about the hero's momentary lapse in front of an audience. And I don't intend to repeat it for you.' Thwack! She slaps him round the face. He hits her back. 'Read!' says she. 'I won't!' says he. Goodness only knows what a mess they'd have got themselves into if I hadn't turned up just then. Lilka was covered in bruises. So was he. I thought he might kill her. Or she might kill him. She did need to let off steam sometimes. She was seething inside. So I say: 'What's going on that you need to grab each other by the hair over mere words, even if they do rhyme?' And Lilka says: 'He didn't want to recite the bit on stage about the death of the hero. Where the hero just has to give his consent and it will all be over, he'll be at peace. But Romka's declared a boycott. "Maybe that is what the book says. I respect what someone personally made up but I'm not going to say something like that on stage. If all that was needed for the peace of the grave was personal consent, there'd be lot of people giving their consent. And that's not allowed. It's against the oath to our Soviet Motherland." Romka's a halfwit. If he only understood what death was, especially during a war.' And so Lilka flew off the handle, into a real rage…

"She had a short fuse, of course she did. Only on occasion but still. Like a woman possessed, to be honest. And you talk about Moiseenko! Moiseenko was worth his weight in gold to you. You dumped the whole thing on him and that was that. If he hadn't gone and hanged himself, of course I'd have shown you up in your true colours. For the sake of justice. But was it really suicide? Was it, Mikhail Ivanovich? Be honest, now."

"It was."

"That's good."

Then silence.

Laevskaya went out for more wood. I flung off the sheet, pulled on my still baking clothes. Didn't bother with the coat.

A damp patch had formed under my holster. I moved closer to the stove.

Polina came in.

"So you're dressed? You should have left them to dry a bit longer. Still, up to you. I look at you, Mikhail Ivanovich, I see a lucky man. If you weren't so lucky, I can't imagine how life would have worked out for you. You'd have been in prison. You buried Zusel. He dug himself out. Then Moiseenko goes and hangs himself."

"What's Zusel got to do with it? What makes you think I buried him?"

"He said so himself. Said you dragged him off and buried him. But he rose again. He spent several days with me, convalescing. Day and night I drummed it into that scatter-brained noddle of his that you didn't bury him, you dug him up. He'd forgotten everything. Well, not everything, just that he'd been to see you, had tried to protect Dovid.

"Shtadler told me in writing. I put in Zusel's head what I needed to put in. That criminals had buried him but it was you who dug him out with your bare hands and in person. Of course, you can say I behaved badly but it was for his own good. To avoid a scandal. The whole of Liskovitsa was all agog as it was. I wanted to be the only one with a case against you, no one else. I didn't want anyone else getting their teeth into you. Goodness only knows what harm you've done other people. You were to answer to me and to me alone."

I gritted my teeth and let her finish.

Then asked quietly:

"Malka used to give Zusel money. What was it for? He had it on him when he set off to see me. It never arrived. Malka went off wailing around the whole of Oster."

That Grishka had effectively stolen the money and left only the package in Zusel's pocket, I didn't add. Children must not be involved. Not ever.

Laevskaya laughed:

"Ah-ha, so the money really did exist? When he came round, Zusel told me a tale about ransoming himself from death. He said: 'I paid a bribe. I was released from beyond the grave.' Was it Malka's money he frittered away? And how did she come by it? Earn it from the matzo, did she? Sacred-schmacred but it brings in the money. People will pay for anything in order to feel good, no kvetching either, by the way. She was saving up for a copy of the Torah. In Russian. She used to bellyache about the lads, Grishka and Vovka, saying they were lazy and wouldn't learn the language, wouldn't be able to read the Torah properly. The way Jews are supposed to. So what if it's in Russian, she said, it might do. She wasn't sure, to be fair. She'd seen one in Russian before the Revolution. I promised I'd get her one. I never even came across one. Or much of that kind of thing at all after the war. They'd vanished without trace. So, Malka thought up the bright of idea of giving the task to Zusel. Collecting for the Torah, I mean. Not for anything else."

"How's that, not for anything else? What about feeding the children, buying them clothes and so on and so forth?"

Laevskaya brushed this off.

"Oh, Malka didn't think about that kind of thing. Especially not if she had any money. She ought to have given it to me. I'd have kept it safe. As for food, she just went on about the Torah teaching Grishka and Vovka. The Torah, she said, would fill them. She cut Yoska off. It was a wrench but she did it."

"Right, Polina Lvovna. Thank you for Tabachnik. Let's assume that's what happened. But Evsey? What did you expect to get out of that?"

Polina pressed her lips together. Not into the usual little heart but in a thick straight line.

"Am I getting warmer, Polina Lvovna? Really warm? Like Lilka? Where you got the knife that killed her, I can guess. But why did you take it to Evsey?"

"Did Dovid tell you? Who else? It had to be Dovid. If it had been Evsey himself, we'd be having a different conversation. I took it so that I'd have something on you, Mikhail Ivanovich. I took it with Lilya's blood on it and your fingerprints because I needed you. You'd taken Lilka from me. Stolen her away. You left me nothing of her. You left me nothing of my children. I might not be so young but I'm not so old either. When did Abraham's wife Sara give birth? When she'd hit nearly ninety. And I still bleed once a month. That's what I wanted. That's why I took the knife to Evsey.

"Take that look off your face, Mikhail Ivanovich. You'd have slept with me and everything. But Dovid ruined that little plan. He tracked down the knife and gave it to Zusel. Zusel gave it back to me. Clean as a new pin. He took away the power I had over you. Just by cleaning the knife. I had nothing on you. All I could do was keep hounding you on and on and on. To be honest, I've wept tears over that wretched knife. And Zusel! Back he came with it, the fool, with his insults, saying I was scaring people and should just hold on to the knife for future reference. To do to what with in the future? Only the grave lies ahead, whatever. Not to mention Evsey doing so much damage, killing himself outright. Dead as a door nail! Who would have thought he'd go that far?!

"But there's something else we need to talk about. I'm not arguing with the dead over who's most to blame. But I was surprised you and Lilka didn't produce a baby. I began to wonder if maybe your Lyubochka's Gannusya was a by-blow. Now, now, sit down. These things happen. I made friends with Lyubochka, chatted to her about it. Woman to woman. No. She's yours is Gannusya. I told Lyubochka about Lilka out of spite. I admit it. But, understand my situation. You've got both Lyubochka and Gannusya. And you took Yoska too. I have nothing. Nix! Can you imagine?"

And here Laevskaya smiled. And pursed her lips into the little heart.

I asked:

"Why did you go to Evsey? Dovid told me you and Evsey were up to something. And Belka confirmed it. I won't forgive you for Evsey, Polina Lvovna. Whatever you do. Evsey's a case apart."

Laevskaya crossed her arms over her bosom. Pressed her wide-spread fingers down as if she wanted to squeeze something up from under her housecoat.

"Don't change the subject, Mikhail Ivanovich. We're having an honest final conversation. Evsey knew you and Lilka were having a fling. Evsey was such a help to me. When I was going to the children's homes, I could see there were Jewish children. I read it in the paperwork too – they let me have it, I know how to make people trust me. Some knew their surnames. Some didn't. But if a boy's been circumcised, you've got your answer. Even if he's been given a different surname and a different first name.

"I got to know Evsey thanks to his father-in-law, Dovid. I had a customer, I made all her clothes. Evsey's neighbour. Getting on a bit, the perfect match for Dovid. A widow too. Jewish. Well-bred. She asked me to make her a match with Dovid. I always took these situations seriously. A person's family happiness is at stake. I got to know Evsey first, asked him about Dovid, how he felt about women. Evsey was understanding. I repeated it all back to the customer. I told her to make up her mind and I'd sound out Dovid straight away. She backtracked. Said she'd been thinking: Why on earth would she want to be looking after someone in her old age? Dovid fell by the wayside but I kept up my friendship with Evsey. Told him about the Jewish children. Without any ulterior motive. Sincerely. He said, 'Right. How many Jews were killed in the war for no reason, for the sheer hell of it?' 'What do you mean?' I said. 'For no reason? The reason was they were Jews. Fathers came back from the front and their wives and children were gone. Or the mothers, say, were alive but the Fascist scum and their henchmen had wiped out the children. The situation needs to be put to rights.'

"Evsey expressed the thought that if our government issued an appeal to the Jewish people there would be no getting away from the vast numbers wanting to adopt Jewish boys and girls. Jews for Jews. To right a historical wrong. And other peoples would fall into line as well. And would take all the children, leaving not a single one behind. One in the eye for the Fascists. Although they'd been defeated even without that. He was all worked up but I knew what he was trying to say and brought him into my searches. A man in police uniform is a big deal. He stupidly told Dovid. Dovid told Zusel. Zusel jumped up as if he'd been stabbed and went off to Jewish homes offering them children. Gather them up from the children's homes, and so on and so forth, he says. The people of Israel must live. What's the people of Israel got to do with it? Right away, it took on a religious tone. And in '49, they were rooting out Zionists. So then Zusel's nonsense wasn't welcome anywhere. Evsey dried up. Dovid too. But there's no stopping Zusel. He's got Israel and only Israel on the brain.

"I think that when I brought Evsey the knife and said that you, Mikhail Ivanovich, had killed Lilya, my assistant, who had travelled to the children's homes with him on more than one occasion, he thought you'd uncovered our organization to place Jewish children in Jewish families. And had killed Lilka on those grounds. Trying to arrest her, for example. That you'd known about it since the very beginning and had set your cap at her for operational reasons. And sooner or later you'd get round to him and because he was your friend, you'd suggest: 'Better shoot yourself and preserve your good name and your family's property. Otherwise, there'll be a scandal, a case with consequences for your friends and family.' He really respected you, loved you. Which is why he shot himself. He tried to overcome his doubts but he failed. Couldn't do it any more. That's what I think."

Laevskaya's reasoning was sound. Thought through in advance. Everything on separate shelves like bedding in the airing cupboard of a good housewife.

"And how many children did you remove like that?"

Laevskaya answered reluctantly.

"Not a single one."

"And the gold was no help?"

"We didn't get even that far."

"Well, Dovid didn't spill the beans. Never told me what you were really up to. He produced some drivel. He loved reading the papers. Would put something together in his head and pass it on to me. But the actual truth, no. And Shtadler didn't either. Does he know?"

Laevskaya said firmly that he didn't.

Seeing she was so insistent, however, only confirmed my guess that he did.

"Polina Lvovna, why have you told me all this? I would have got there myself. Already had. Not everything fitted together. It does now. As for the unfounded accusations you've levelled at me, they can be pulled apart." I clicked my fingers. "Quick as a flash and nix, as you put it. You found out from Zusel that he had a pal in Ryabina. You picked Ryabina out of my work file. Which means Svetka must have brought it to you quite a few times. You made her acquaintance some time ago. Stored up information just in case. Why did you send Didenko a letter in your own handwriting? It was deliberate, so that I'd realize it was your doing. I worked that one out straight away. A show to let me know you were after me, on my tail. You made Dovid write his little note to summon me to Oster. I fell for it. I went. The only time you fooled me. But I was lucky. I didn't go to Dovid's. I went to Ryabina. And once again I nearly fell into your trap. You'd done your research, worked out that I'd go back home if I messed up here. Where else is a man to go? The old familiar places and everything. Thank God, I didn't find your letter at Didenko's then. Otherwise I'd have gone off the deep end, turned up at yours with it and choked you to death into the bargain. I was calmer later. Especially when I had the letter in my pocket. So what if you stole it? I don't give a damn. The ball was unravelling. The threads were appearing. So there you go.

"Now, listen. I go to Miron and he says that, at your request, he stole a sheet of paper. You took that letter to the children's homes along with the late lamented Evsey Gutin, with the aim of finding Jewish children and gathering them up. But in practice, they could be non-Jewish as much as Jewish. So as to register as many as possible as Jews by means of their adoption by Jewish parents. I'll go through the list of children's homes. They'll remember your visits. With Evsey and with Lilka. Your criminal group also included the dear departed Malka Tsvintar, Dovid Basin, Veniamin Shtadler, still among the living, and it goes without saying Miron and Sima and we'll tie in Sunka too. And Evka Vorobeichik as well, bringing up the rear. Especially since, in Lilka's photographs, you can never tell if it's her or Evka. Plus the well-known die-hard Zionist Zusel Tabachnik. Lots of people will remember how he used to come and try to persuade them to take children in. Belka isn't off the hook either. And what do you have on me? That knife of yours you're always going on about, that I supposedly used to kill Lilka? You've wasted that, Polina Lvovna. As if it was a bit of soap. So did Dovid and Zusel for that matter. If there ever was anything on it – if, let's say, there was, even though there wasn't – there isn't now. You lugged it all over the place. It's been rubbed to a shine. All nice and clean. You understand. What have you got to say?"

Laevskaya looked at me, not understanding. Took me all in from head to foot. Her gaze swept over me. And her eyes widened and narrowed alternately.

She looked at me and, keeping her eyes on me, stretched a hand out for the holster, opened it, felt for the pouch, took it out, opened the metal clasp and threw the pouch into the flames.

She stared into the fire. And uttered not one word.

I wanted to bring her down to Earth and tell her, no matter, gold doesn't burn. But I said nothing. Why did I care?

I walked along in the rain and assessed the state of play. I tried to find where I'd slipped up.

One: I had never gone to see Lilka in uniform. Apart from that first time and that was deep on a winter's evening.

Two: I'd dressed differently every time even if only slightly.

Three: I'd never used the front gate. I took the long way round the back and knocked on the window on the side with the vegetable patch.

As I was making my way to Lilka's for what was to be the last time along Kulichik Street, which leads straight into Zetkin, coming towards me on the other side was Moiseenko in a state of great intoxication. He was chewing on an enormous heel of bread. Tearing off the crust like a kid. Plainly, he was coming back from Lilka's.

I had seen him at the theatre in "Shelmenko the Orderly" and knew from Lilya's scornful tales that she kept him as a close acquaintance because he was an actor.

Lilya was lolling on the sofa. She said Roman had just cleared off. He'd been feeling really peckish. Had asked for something to eat. Lilka had refused to get up on principle. He'd grabbed half a loaf and cleared off.

I looked at the table: half a loaf of rye bread and on the top a knife covered in crumbs.

A stray thought entered my head. I had never imagined or dreamt of its existence before.

To clarify, I asked:

"Did he hack the bread off himself? A drunkard with a knife. Goodness knows what he might have done. What if hadn't cut the bread but something else instead? Aren't you afraid?"

Lilka replied coolly that she wasn't.

"As if I'm going to cut slices of bread for any old drunks. If he'd slashed me, well, thank God. So long as it killed me."

In that second I realized, it was now or never.

Lilka propped herself up on an elbow and asked,

"What do I need to do for you to stop coming here? Die, maybe? I'm putting myself through hell and you as well."

I said what I thought.

"Die, Lilka. I can't. I have a wife and daughter. Whereas you've only got yourself. You don't need to live in any case. You say it yourself, over and over till you're blue in the face."

She got up, threw off her nightie, put on her crepe-de-chine polka-dot dress, did her hair.

Then she remembered she hadn't had a wash. She splashed her face at the sink in the little corridor.

She said:

"Let's go. Let's not do it in the house. People have to live here."

I wrapped the knife handle in paper. I'd torn off a bit of newspaper.

Lilka couldn't see.

She had her back to me.

She said:

"And you've silenced the guards so there won't be a peep out of them."

Lilka presented her neck. The neck sprays a lot of blood. I could have been spattered.

I struck from behind, from below, beneath the shoulder blade. The way it should be.

I threw the murder weapon down beside the body since it still had traces of Moiseenko's fingerprints.

I stole secretly away. I could have sworn no-one saw me.

But, as it turned out, someone did. Laevskaya. Maybe she spotted me stealing away from Lilka's house, maybe she'd been sitting in the next room. I wouldn't have put it past her to have come along and lain in wait for me to show up and go to bed with Lilka.

But that I deliberately left the knife with Moiseenko's prints, Polina didn't have enough operational intelligence to know. She thought I'd left my own precious prints on the handle. She snatched up the knife as soon as I'd gone but didn't report it to the police. That evening she took the knife to Evsey for safekeeping.

What happened next is as follows:

I waited at work for Citizen Vorobeichik's body to be reported. As a mere investigator, I wouldn't have been sent to the scene. That was for the criminal investigator. But the minute I arrived, I caused a commotion in Sviridenko's office about being overlooked when in fact I wanted to go on studying and achieve the rank of crime investigator. But what the hell was going on here? There was no shortage of criminal investigators who, like me, didn't have the training but were already on the job and there I was at their beck and call.

Sviridenko himself roared out:

"My criminal investigators are up to their ears in work, two have been arrested, the rest are being worked over. They've got me up against the wall and are trying to frame me for conspiracy right here in my own work place. What on earth do they need? Well? Do they need Hitler in order to calm down and find themselves some work to do? Enough! If something comes in, it's yours. Take it and let's see what you're made of. Solve it and we'll send you off to study in Kharkov. Remember. I value my staff."

Four hours later the report came in.

And off I went to investigate.

I was the detective, the junior investigator, the criminal investigator. I didn't delegate. I raced around all over the place doing the detective work myself.

Then Moiseenko killed himself. The case was closed.

After that, everything happened as I've said.

Evsey, poor chap, could see that I was conducting an investigation and, what's more, was pretending it was routine work; that the case wasn't being passed on to the Ministry of State Security; that I was here, there and everywhere, not enlisting anyone else, keeping things secret, not sharing with him. Especially when essentially I was only a humble investigator. That in itself was odd and led to rumours and suspicion. Evsey looked more deeply into the case, not just at the surface like everyone else. On the surface, it was a crime of passion, not worth a damn. But Evsey knew love had nothing to do with it. He would have sworn blind it hadn't. He'd seen Lilka in her true colours, what with the children and so on, binding her to Laevskaya. Not as she was with me. Gutin hardened to the idea that he had no other way out apart from shooting himself with his service weapon. Rather than waiting for them to come for him.

It was the first time in a long time that I wasn't thinking about Laevskaya and Lilka.

I was thinking about Evsey.

If only he'd shared his doubts with me. If only he hadn't betrayed our friendship by not trusting me.

I never saw hide nor hair of Laevskaya again as they say at this point and in such circumstances.

For many years, I've had a hunch that I would tell this story – either writing it down or telling it aloud. I've never told it out loud. I've never come across a trustworthy listener. In my own words, face to face, of course, it would have been better and more vivid. Moreover, it's not impossible that a listener's question might prompt the storyteller to change his tune or remember something he'd forgotten.

I set out to describe this case as an example of my work. Not to cover up my part in the events of that long-ago year of 1952. But to avoid any prejudice against me from the very first word. For the sake of objectivity. Which, after all, is the main goal of justice.

An example breaks down solely into established facts. That's what I sought to set out. Gradually, however, it became apparent that even the facts can be deceptive if examined closely from all angles. In this instance, certain facts purport to be against me. But, even if that's so, I'm not guilty.

Life is not determined here. I used to think it was. But then I changed my mind despite the fact that in 1959 I graduated with good grades from the Kharkov Institute of Law, a correspondence course, and worked as a criminal investigator for many years.

After all this, life simply resumed its course.

Gnedich

by Maria Rybakova

The poetic language of *Gnedich* is refined: it combines the clarity of Rybakova's syllabic verses and the sophistication of her metaphors with distinct, novelistic depictions of certain landscapes, people, and their interactions.

The novel is spectacularly designed: Rybakova's style resembles a movie projection with stop-cards at the key moments in Gnedich's life, his long conversations with his friend, and particular striking sceneries. It creates a novelistic effect on the tale about Gnedich's life, spanning over twenty years. The narrative is often interrupted by streams of consciousness and reminiscence by its main heroes. At the same time, it continues the traditions of Russian classic literature with its attention to detail and the psychology of the characters.

Buy it > www.glagoslav.com

Leo Tolstoy – Flight from Paradise

by Pavel Basinsky

Over a hundred years ago, something truly outrageous occurred at Yasnaya Polyana. Count Leo Tolstoy, a famous author aged eighty-two at the time, took off, destination unknown. Since then, the circumstances surrounding the writer's whereabouts during his final days and his eventual death have given rise to many myths and legends. In this book, popular Russian writer and reporter Pavel Basinsky delves into the archives and presents his interpretation of the situation prior to Leo Tolstoy's mysterious disappearance. Basinsky follows Leo Tolstoy throughout his life, right up to his final moments. Reconstructing the story from historical documents, he creates a visionary account of the events that led to the Tolstoys' family drama.

Flight from Paradise will be of particular interest to international researchers studying Leo Tolstoy's life and works, and is highly recommended to a broader audience worldwide.

Buy it > www.glagoslav.com

The Tale of Aypi

by Ak Welsapar

The Tale of Aypi follows the fate of a group of Turkmen fishermen dwelling on the coast of the Caspian Sea. The fear of losing their ancestral home looms over the entire village. This injustice is being made to look like a voluntary initiative on the part of the fishermen themselves, whilst the ruling powers cynically attempt to confiscate their land. One brave fisherman from the village rises up to confront them and fights for his native shore, as a response to an act of cruelty inflicted on a defenceless young woman centuries ago. This unjustly executed soul returns as a ghost during this troubled time to exact a terrible revenge on the men of the village.

The relationships among the characters mirror the eternal opposition between the forces of nature, with the intervention of mystical forces ratcheting up the tension.

Buy it > www.glagoslav.com

Marina Tsvetaeva - The Essential Poetry

by Marina Tsvetaeva

Marina Tsvetaeva: The Essential Poetry includes translations by Michael M. Naydan and Slava I. Yastremski of lyric poetry from all of the great Modernist Russian poet Marina Tsvetaeva's published collections and from all periods of her life. It also includes a translation of two of Tsvetaeva's masterpieces in the genre of the long poem, "Poem of the End" and "Poem of the Mountain." The collection strives to present the best of Tsvetaeva's poetry in a single small volume and to provide a representative overview of Tsvetaeva's high art and the development of different poetic styles over the course of her creative lifetime. Also included in this volume are a guest introduction by eminent American poet Tess Gallagher, a translator's introduction and extensive endnotes.

Buy it > www.glagoslav.com

DEAR READER,

Thank you for purchasing this book.

We at Glagoslav Publications are glad to welcome you, and hope that you find our books to be a source of knowledge and inspiration.

We want to show the beauty and depth of the Slavic region to everyone looking to expand their horizon and learn something new about different cultures, different people, and we believe that with this book we have managed to do just that.

Now that you've got to know us, we want to get to know you. We value communication with our readers and want to hear from you! We offer several options:

- Join our Book Club on Goodreads, Library Thing and Shelfari, and receive special offers and information about our giveaways;

- Share your opinion about our books on Amazon, Barnes & Noble, Waterstones and other bookstores;

- Join us on Facebook and Twitter for updates on our publications and news about our authors;

- Visit our site www.glagoslav.com to check out our Catalogue and subscribe to our Newsletter.

Glagoslav Publications is getting ready to release a new collection and planning some interesting surprises — stay with us to find out!

Glagoslav Publications
Office 36, 88-90 Hatton Garden
EC1N 8PN London, UK
Tel: + 44 (0) 20 32 86 99 82
Email: contact@glagoslav.com

Glagoslav Publications Catalogue

- *The Time of Women* by Elena Chizhova
- *Sin* by Zakhar Prilepin
- *Hardly Ever Otherwise* by Maria Matios
- *The Lost Button* by Irene Rozdobudko
- *Khatyn* by Ales Adamovich
- *Christened with Crosses* by Eduard Kochergin
- *The Vital Needs of the Dead* by Igor Sakhnovsky
- *A Poet and Bin Laden* by Hamid Ismailov
- *Kobzar* by Taras Shevchenko
- *White Shanghai* by Elvira Baryakina
- *The Stone Bridge* by Alexander Terekhov
- *King Stakh's Wild Hunt* by Uladzimir Karatkevich
- *Depeche Mode* by Serhii Zhadan
- *Saraband Sarah's Band* by Larysa Denysenko
- *Herstories*, An Anthology of New Ukrainian Women
  Prose Writers
- *The Hawks of Peace* by Dmitry Rogozin
  by Leonid Andreev
- *The Battle of the Sexes Russian Style* by Nadezhda Ptushkina
- *A Book Without Photographs* by Sergey Shargunov
- *Sankya* by Zakhar Prilepin
- *Wolf Messing - The True Story of Russia`s Greatest Psychic*
  by Tatiana Lungin
- *Good Stalin* by Victor Erofeyev
- *Solar Plexus* by Rustam Ibragimbekov
- *Don't Call me a Victim!* by Dina Yafasova
- *A History of Belarus* by Lubov Bazan
- *Children's Fashion of the Russian Empire* by Alexander Vasiliev
- *Empire of Corruption - The Russian National Pastime*
  by Vladimir Soloviev
- *Heroes of the 90s - People and Money.*
  The Modern History of Russian Capitalism
- *Boris Yeltsin - The Decade that Shook the World* by Boris Minaev
- *A Man Of Change - A study of the political life of Boris Yeltsin*
- *Gnedich* by Maria Rybakova
- *Marina Tsvetaeva - The Essential Poetry*
- *Multiple Personalities* by Tatyana Shcherbina

More coming soon...